The Leap Year Boy

BY MARC SIMON

The Leap Year Boy

Copyright © 2013 Marc Simon
The author is hereby established as the sole holder of the copyright.

Front cover image by Ginny Glass and Untreed Reads Publishing
Interior and back cover design by Leslie Logemann, Logemann Design

This is a work of fiction. Any resemblance to the living or dead is entirely coincidental.

Acknowledgments

I thank the members of the Hanover Street Writers Group for their tough literary love in helping me to shape this novel and see it through: Stace Budzko, Steve MacKinnon, Dave Demerjian, Mike Schiavone, and especially Sue Williams, who never let me get away with anything.

I thank my agent Joelle Delbourgo, who believed in this novel and me.

I thank Grub Street for being a constant source of inspiration.

For my wife Linda and Grandpa Abe

Chapter 1

Alex Miller was born on February 29, 1908, at 12:01 a.m., precisely nine months and a day after he was conceived. He weighed a mere two pounds, one ounce and measured just nine inches long, yet despite his size, his breathing was relaxed, his heart beat like a metronome and his blue eyes were active and alert.

Alex entered the world headfirst in the home of Abe and Irene Miller at 707 Mellon Street, Pittsburgh, less than 20 minutes after Irene had gone into labor. Ida Murphy, Irene's mother, was in attendance, not so much out of concern for her daughter or the welfare of her nascent grandchild, whom she hoped would be her first female grandchild; rather, Ida wanted to see firsthand why her daughter had engaged the services of a medical doctor, since she herself had delivered without an attending physician during the births of her own three children, the third stillborn, each more agonizing than the one before it.

Ida felt a pang of jealousy when her daughter delivered so quickly and relatively pain free. Not that she didn't love her daughter, in her own guarded way, or wish her well, but still, she thought, suffering builds character. If she'd had to go through it, why should her daughter get off so easy?

When she saw the tiny baby, she remarked to the doctor, "That's it?"

Irene's physician, Dr. Malkin, shrugged and assured her that it was indeed "it."

Malkin was a hairy, bear-like Russian/Jewish immigrant with filmy pince-nez glasses he wore on the tip of his pointy nose. The veracity of his medical credentials was somewhat suspect, had anyone cared to investigate, since his professional certificates were printed in Cyrillic type and framed in clouded glass on the walls of his so-called surgery, which happened to be on the second floor of a cold-water walkup. He served the Miller family as general practitioner, pediatrician and dentist.

"But it's so small. Are you sure there aren't more babies in there somewhere?" Irene admonished him to keep looking, that there had to be one or two more, look at the size of the thing, it was no bigger than the runt in a litter of pigs. It was all she could do to keep from looking herself. But when

Malkin shook his head no, that's it, Ida put her hands on her wide hips and said, "Well, in that case, *doctor*, there's no use me dilly-dallying around here anymore, is there?" She washed her hands with rough soap in the basin on the dresser next to the bed, put on her gloves, quickly kissed her daughter on her damp forehead, harrumphed at the tiny baby boy and went downstairs. As she put on her coat, she told Abe Miller, who was waiting with a cigar in one hand and a beer in the other, that his wife had given him another boy, and that she was fine, and he should go on upstairs but be ready for a surprise—and no thank you, she didn't care to spend the night at their house, she was perfectly capable of walking home by herself or catching a trolley.

Abe bent down to look at the baby. His cigar fell out of his mouth. The baby blanket quickly smoldered until he tamped it out.

Malkin came by the next morning, expecting to find the teensy baby dead in its crib, but there it was, alive and kicking, nursing and crying and eliminating like any other newborn, albeit in miniscule quantities. He asked after Irene as well, who happily reported that she felt so good, she was ready to go down to Rooney's for a ham sandwich and a bottle of lager.

Irene had gained twenty-three pounds during her pregnancy and carried Alex full term. She'd had only a minimum of discomfort, the one exception being a bruise on her cheek from a nasty slapping fight she'd had with Abe around her fourth month. The encounter had been precipitated by his infidelity—vehemently denied, yet certainly verifiable, had they been asked by his cohorts at The Squeaky Wheel. Several of them had observed with envy his dalliances with Delia Novak, the bookkeeper at Gross Hardware, located three doors down from The Wheel. Delia often stopped by for a quick schnapps on her way home to her boarding house, and to signal Abe to come on by.

Ida arrived as Malkin was leaving. She carried a box full of baby clothes and toys that she'd purchased on sale some weeks earlier. The clothes were several sizes too large, but she had no intention of returning them; she couldn't be troubled, she told her daughter, they didn't make them that small anyway, had she known she would have purchased doll's clothes, and besides, the squirt might grow into them some day, that is, if he lived out the year, let's be honest about this. And besides, what did Irene expect? She had told her no good would come from marrying out of the faith, especially to a Jew. She was damn lucky that the first two half-breeds weren't born with horns sprouting out of their heads, or tails coming out of their arses, and now Irene's poor choice in men had finally caught up with her.

Irene said, "Shut up, Ma."

After two hours and two cups of tea laced with Old Bushmills from her silver flask, and some cakes from Lieberman's Bakery—you had to hand it to those German Jews, they knew how to make a tea cake—Ida left for her Bible study group, run by "that nincompoop priest Kiernan." She promised she would return every other day, one of many promises she had made to Irene over years but neglected to keep.

Even with his remarkable size—"this is yet mine hand to God the teensiest baby what I ever did in America deliver," Malkin liked to say—Alex remained in excellent health, perfectly if diminutively formed: lungs no larger than lemons, inhaling and exhaling without much discernable effort; ten pink fingers, perfectly formed right down to the tiny cuticles; ten toes the size of nubbins; a head just eight inches around, topped with fine strands of reddish blond hair, full enough to part; torso and legs in proportions even an ancient Greek would appreciate. His cries of hunger and consternation were high-pitched and as clear as the yips of a prairie dog. And when he suckled at Irene's sprawling breasts—she was careful not to smother him with her milky fullness—he made soft sucking sounds and his wee lips puckered like a guppy.

Malkin returned to the Millers' house a month later, to see if the boy had begun to catch up to normal in length and weight. To his naked eye, that didn't seem to be the case, but if the doctor had been better acquainted with the developmental patterns of newborns, his cursory measurements would have indicated this: Alex's 212 bones, 22 internal organs, 680 muscles, 230 joints and miles of vessels were growing at a rate one-fourth that of a normal child's. However, unlike his body, Alex's mind was maturing much, much faster.

As Malkin examined his son, Abe sat on his red brick stoop, a stoop not unlike so many others that protruded like buckteeth from the row of stolid houses on Mellon Street. He tried to understand why God had given him such a tiny son. Perhaps God was testing him, although he had no idea why God would have singled him out. He scratched his stubbly beard. His faith in the Almighty was a combination of hazy Judaism tinged with a shade of pantheism. "There must be a God, else how do you explain all this?" he had said to Irene on their wedding day, waxing metaphysical as he pointed to the Pittsburgh sunset, the colors made even more vivid by the sulfuric soot wafting up from the mills.

In the early days following Alex's birth, Abe had been loath to hold the boy, fearing his jackhammer grip might squish the little thing. But, feeling reassured after Malkin's one-month visit and his all-clear report, Abe decided that, since it had lived so far, the little thing probably wasn't going to die any time soon. He began to treat Alex with far less indifference and far more indulgence than he showed to his other sons, Arthur and Benjamin, ages ten and seven—sullen, chunky red-haired boys with large appetites for meat and potatoes and for throwing rocks at girls and at each other.

On Saturdays in the spring of that first year, Abe took Alex around the neighborhood to show him off. The neighbors, always ready for the circus to come to town, welcomed Abe and the boy warmly, toasting his health with a glass or two of spirits, which Abe never turned down. They often had a little something for Alex: an eyedropper of milk, a thimble of applesauce, and presents, too, like the red-knit doll sweater given by Mrs. Klemmer. Alex usually behaved well, which is to say he behaved like a baby his age, sleeping angelically or crying daintily, his little hands curled into fists. The women were eager to hold him and change him, to touch his tiny digits and to see his "down-there" parts. He became the neighborhood celebrity/mascot, much as if he were a two-tailed dog. Mrs. Klemmer even wrote to the *Pittsburgh Gazette Times*, suggesting they do a feature on Alex, but her letter went unanswered, so she suspended her subscription.

Inevitably, Abe and Alex would end up at The Squeaky Wheel, even though Delia had moved to Youngstown, Ohio, weeks before to be near her dying mother. The Wheel had pinewood walls, glass block windows, a yellow linoleum floor, square tables with oilcloth tablecloths, a 30-foot maple bar with a brass rail attached near its base so that the patrons could put a boot up to relieve the pressure on their backs, and a rusty tractor wheel mounted over a huge glass mirror behind the bar. On the wall opposite the snooker table were framed portraits—reprints, actually—of George Washington, Thomas Jefferson, Abraham Lincoln and, for reasons known only to John Kravic, owner and bartender, a portrait of Santa Claus. John kept a Bible, a tire iron, a revolver and a shotgun on the shelf beneath the cash register. He gladly gave advances to his regulars on their paychecks in return for 3% vigorish. If a man complained about the terms, John directed them to drink elsewhere.

Abe was accepted as just another guy at the bar at The Wheel—the begrudging consensus of opinion among the regulars was, he's all right for a Jew as long as he don't get out of line—but after he arrived the first time with Alex, their fascination with the boy moved him way up on the likeability scale.

Abe would place Alex on the bar in his lunch pail, lined with clean dishtowels. The afternoon and early evening regulars and rummies would stare glazed and red-eyed at him. Some were spooked by the boy, saying to each other that a child that size just wasn't natural, and was perhaps evil even; but most of the men would punch each other in the arms with delight at such a marvelous little thing, beg Abe to let them hold the little bugger or bastard or whatever drunken assignation they might come up in their soupy states to describe the boy. But Abe, uncharacteristically displaying the wisdom of a much earlier Abraham, had the good sense to refuse their entreaties, lest one of them accidentally drop his son into a tankard of ale or a tureen of John's stew.

And so Abe turned away all petitioners—save one, Davy O'Brien, a burly ironworker permanently disabled with a mangled hip. Davy had been leveled sideways during the collapse of a 12-foot section of The Hot Metal Bridge, a span J&L was building to connect the blast furnaces on the South Side to the rolling mills across the Monongahela. Davy' singing voice was sweet, especially when he was well into his cups, but he hadn't sung much since his accident. The first time he saw Alex, however, his voice rose anew, and he cooed to him a lullaby his grandmother had sung to him when he was boy in Ulster:

> Blow, blow, breath and blow, wind of the Western Sea,
> Blow, blow, breath and blow, wind of the Western Sea
> Over the rolling waters blow, down from the dying moon and glow
> Blow him again to me
> While my little one, while my pretty one sleeps.

As Davy sang, the rough men fell silent. Even the smoke from their pipes and cigars seemed to hang still in the air as Davy's sweet tenor filled the room. Alex curled up in the crook of Davy's thick forearm and slept like a kitten sated with cream. The boys at the bar kept their faces downcast toward their drinks, fearful that another man might see the tears in their eyes.

Abe looked at the men and looked at his son, and as Davy's notes floated over the hushed drinkers, he wondered how such a wondrous little creature had sprung from a tough, surly Jew like himself. He touched the baby's forehead with a callused finger. With his eyes still closed, Alex smiled.

*

After four months, Alex had gained but four ounces. Dr. Malkin scratched his balding crown. He examined him for signs of all the afflictions he knew—jaundice, diphtheria, smallpox, shingles, the gout, cholera, hoof and mouth, whooping cough, palsy, neuritis, neuralgia, phlebitis, canker, the fits—yet the child, in Malkin's pseudo-professional opinion, had "no-think" wrong with him, and sure enough, according to Irene, Alex smiled, cried, ate, burped, peed and shat as regularly as the shifts changed at the steel mills.

At first, other mothers from the neighborhood came by often, out of curiosity or neighborly obligation, but as April, May and June went by, their visits grew less frequent, and for them at least there wasn't all that much to see. The pace of the boy's growth was so snail-like as to be virtually unrecognizable.

In quiet late afternoons while Alex slept, while Abe was at work lathing tubes at Shields Metals, while Arthur and Benjamin were still in school, Irene would snatch a moment of peace for herself as rocked her littlest boy. She would wonder, what will become of you, what was the good Lord thinking when He cooked you up so small? Not to question the Lord's blessings, but on these afternoons by the kitchen window, fading sunlight highlighting the dust and dead insects on the windowsills, she couldn't help but ask herself where in the divine scheme of things this small gift or strange burden fit in. But then the Lord doesn't mete out to us more than we can handle, as Father Kiernan, a man given to answering in clichés when confronted with an issue temporal or of the faith beyond his ability to fathom might say. And so, in these moments of uncertainty, with an iron gray headache in her forehead and rusty bile rising in her throat, the Big Picture and her purpose in it became increasingly oblique. She wanted to believe that living in her six-room brick house on Mellon Street, with its elms and oak trees and small backyard, with enough sun so that she could grow tomatoes and green beans and some pumpkins for the boys, and a grocery store just two blocks away, where the Jew grocer let her run a weekly tab until Abe got paid on Fridays was just fine, that this life was at least a decent life. Her girlhood dreams of ponies and petticoats and princes and husbands that wore shined shoes and bow ties and worked with their minds and brought her perfume and pecans and wrote poetry were silly after all, weren't they? The truth was, instead of a fairy tale, she'd ended up with hairy, cheating Abe. And in those moments, as the flowers on the wallpaper blurred with tears of regret, well, what if she were to quash little Alex with her milk-heavy breasts and snuff out the little gnat, what would it matter, really? Two boys had been enough. This one was nothing more than the issue of an unwanted midnight coupling by her cheating pig of a husband, wasn't he? At least she could have been given a normal-sized child, a girl, for her troubles. It would serve Abe right if she squished the little imp he so doted on. But just when her thoughts were at their most infanticidal, Alex would squeak or burp or reach toward her with his tiny paws or nestle his head against her heart and Irene would flush with hot remorse and cover him with gentle kisses.

*

July 4th, 1908, broke hot and steamy, 80° at 8 a.m. Irene woke in sheets clammy from troubling dreams of screaming skeletal horses to the snap of firecrackers on the street. Abraham slept on, unaffected by the racket, his blocky chest rising and falling, his snores deep and resonant from four bottles of ale the night before, his genitals exposed from beneath the twisted sheet. For several fleeting moments, Irene considered how easy it would be to kill him as he slept, with the stroke of an iron skillet across his head, and when they asked her why, she would say she was sickened by the sight of his yellowed big toe toenail, and wasn't that reason enough? But instead she slid out of bed, pulled on her graying nightgown and went to check on Alex, only to find his miniature bed empty, his cigar-singed blanket strewn on the floor next to Abraham's pants and suspenders.

"Alex!"

She dropped to her knees, digging through the flotsam, swiping under the bed with outstretched arms.

The grandfather clock in the hallway, a wedding gift from her mother, read 8:13. Irene rushed into Arthur and Benjamin's bedroom, screaming for her older sons, but there was no sound, save her desperate breathing against the backdrop of firecrackers. She staggered back into the bedroom, pounded on Abe's back. "Abe, for the love of God get up, the baby, the baby," her fists puny against his broad buffalo flesh.

"What? By God let a man sleep in for one stinking holiday morning. Have you lost your mind?"

"Abe! Get up, Abe, the boys. The boys, they're all gone. All of them."

"What, what are you saying, what, where?"

"The boys, listen to me. Alex and Arthur and Benjamin, they're not in their beds. They've been taken, oh my God, get up, please help me."

Abe the Hung Over Avenger rushed down the steps in his nightshirt and bare feet, trouser cuffs flapping against the threadbare runners, yelling for his sons through the beer and cigar aftermath in his mouth, rage and fear frothing his saliva.

He flung the door wide open. Up and down Mellon Street front porches were festooned with American flags and red, white and blue bunting. Hanging from a second-floor window on the house across the street was a hand-lettered banner that read *Remember the Maine*! Even at the early hour, people were up and about—boys throwing and catching baseballs, with visions of Honus Wagner, The Flying Dutchman, dancing in their heads; little girls with red, white and blue ribbons in their hair playing Red Rover Red Rover; wives sweeping their porches as their husbands slept in on their one day off from the mill or the sanitation department or the artificial limb factory, a booming local industry and a natural for Pittsburgh, thanks to the plethora of appendage-consuming accidents in the mills. Arms and legs for the world, that was the motto.

Abe burst into the street. He stepped directly onto a glass-specked cinder but barely felt it. Mrs. Angela Sanflippo, who'd lost her husband in an explosion at the J&L #4 Open Hearth some three years earlier and still dressed in widow's black, sat on her stoop with her only child, 14-year-old Phillip. The boy had a mustache many a grown man would have been proud to wear, as did his mother, although she kept hers well-trimmed so as to be nothing more than a hint of a shadow on her upper lip. Mrs. Sanflippo waved at Abe and pointed to the left, toward Jackson Avenue.

Abe ran down Mellon Street, shirttails flying behind him. When he got to the corner of Jackson Avenue, two blocks away, he found Arthur and Benjamin, standing next to their wagon, shouting like carnival barkers. On the wood fence behind them hung a hand-painted sign: "See Tiny Alex, 1¢.

Inside the wagon was their baby brother.

Their marketing effort had attracted quite a crowd, even at this early hour, with several children and a few adults lined up behind the wagon. At the front of the line were two boys in shorts and baseball caps, the Walsh brothers, classmates and sometimes mortal enemies of Benjamin and Arthur. Behind them stood their two younger Walsh sisters, born eleven months apart, known as the Irish twins. Next in line was the mildly mentally impaired August Daly, age 36, from nearby Portland Street, holding the hand of his mother Gertrude. August, nearly six and a half feet tall, gawked over the children in from of him, eager to see the show, and he might have pushed ahead had Gertrude not tethered his hand tightly. Behind the Daly family was Giuseppe Traficante, ice and coal deliveryman and self-proclaimed mayor of Mellon Street, smoking his ever-present Perodi and wiping his brow with a dingy white handkerchief. He waved a politician's hello to Abe.

Although Abe grudgingly admired his sons' P.T. Barnum-ish display of all-American entrepreneurship, his rage had reached the boiling point. He snatched Benjamin and Arthur by their necks like two chickens. It took all of his willpower not to knock their heads together. He announced his intention to lock the boys in the coal cellar for the remainder of the holiday, maybe longer.

Irene, who'd managed to throw on a robe and catch up with the family, intervened on the boys' behalf, arguing that the baby was none the worse for wear, and though they'd had given her the shock of her life and should have known better, they meant Alex no harm. In her heart she wanted to strangle both of them, and in due time they would pay for their misguided effort at free enterprise. But at least the baby was unharmed. She lifted Alex from the wagon and kissed his forehead.

The Walsh brood yelled for their money back. August Daly bounced up and down, yanking his mother so hard her hat fell off.

As the Millers turned up the walkway to their house, in a voice as high and crisp as the cracking of a bird's egg, Alex said, "Momma. Dadda. Arthur. Benjamin. Alex. Home."

"Alex?" What in God's name was going on here, Abe thought, a child this young shouldn't know how to talk, this wasn't normal, but not a damn thing about this boy *was* normal. He pulled Irene against his chest and, as if to check his own sanity, he said, "You heard him, too, didn't you?"

Irene gawked at the boy, too. "By God, I did."

Alex didn't speak again for nearly a year. Neither his brothers nor his parents could get him to talk, despite a variety of inducements—Alex want a cookie, Alex want a candy, show Momma what a smart boy you are, come on, sonny boy, I bet a quarter with that bastard Walsh from across the street that you could talk. Day after day, until they grew tired of asking, Alex gave them nothing but smiles and silence.

Chapter 2

On March 1, 1909, a year to the day after Alex Miller was born, Delia Novak's mother died in her sleep from complications due to a variety of maladies, the final manifestation of which was congestive heart failure. One month later, a mildly bereaved, mostly relieved Delia sold her mother's house for $1,850, cash, to Reverend Jeremiah Johnston, the new pastor at The Church of the Holy Shepherd in Youngstown, Ohio. Since there was no will and she was the only living member of the immediate family, all of the house money went to her, as did the $255.45 in her mother's passbook account at Youngstown Dollar Bank. For the first time in her life, Delia was flush.

With nothing to keep her in Youngstown—not her 71-year-old Aunt Tilda; not her sometimes friend Dolores Wozniak, who at 24 was married with three sons and a boozehound for a husband; and certainly not the hawk-nosed, sooty-fingered coal and ice man, Richard Stutz, who had on several occasions tried to convince her to go for a Sunday drive in his delivery wagon—Delia took a series of trains from Youngstown to the most exciting destination she could imagine: New York City. She was determined to live high for once in her life.

Feeling free as an orphan—her father had abandoned the family when she was six, so technically she *was* an orphan——Delia rode in first-class births all the way to Manhattan. She booked a room at the Waldorf Hotel, which she'd read about on the train and which offered electricity throughout and, to her amazement and delight, a private bathroom. She ordered room service breakfast the first morning. Her waiter called her "My Lady Delia." Flattery got him everywhere, and the newly titled Lady Delia tipped copiously.

Without any particular agenda in mind, other than to see how the other half lived, Delia started to explore the Old Town. On her third day, during a leisurely springtime stroll along Fifth Avenue, she saw a hat exactly like the one she'd admired in the *Harper's Bazaar* she'd thumbed through in the hotel lobby. She absolutely had to have it. It featured two longish feathers plucked from a snowy egret, a Florida bird close to extinction. The hat cost more than her weekly salary at Gross Hardware, but, she reasoned, who cared?

In her first two weeks on the town, she took in several Broadway plays and heard Sophie Tucker sing "Some of These Days" at the American Music Hall. She marveled that she and Sophie were almost the same age, but there was Sophie and here she was, somewhat well off but now pretty much at a loss as to how to fill her hours. At night, as she lay in her feathered bed, she had to admit she was lonely. She missed her friends from Gross Hardware and the risqué camaraderie of the rooming house girls. She also missed Abe Miller and his husky laugh and rough hands and the "big boy in his pants," as she called it, and she was curious about what happened to that cute, tiny bump of a child he brought with him Saturday afternoons to The Squeaky Wheel. She couldn't imagine the boy was still alive, but then, she never could have imagined herself here in New York.

The next evening, as she was pondering the menu in the Waldorf's dining room and trying to figure out what kind of a duck confit was, a thin young man in a tuxedo and slick-backed blond hair asked if he might join her for dinner. Delia liked what she saw; he even smelled good.

He introduced himself. "Devon Jenkins, London and New York, at your service."

"Delia Novak, uh, Youngstown and Pittsburgh, I'm sure."

He kissed her hand. No one had ever kissed her there before. She thought it was a bit twitty—Abe never kissed her like that, he would grab her around the shoulders and press his big mush into hers until she was out of breath—but it was all right with her, sort of.

Devon used a lot of what she would call fifty-cent words, and although she didn't understand half of them, she pretended she did and hoped he wasn't catching on. He ordered a bottle of champagne. "Delia, how do you feel about oysters? I must confess I have a rather obsessive affinity for them. Shall I order a dozen?"

"Yes, you shall."

By the time the second bottle of champagne was uncorked and dinner was served, Delia's shoes were off under the table.

"So, dear Delia, what do you think of the Waldorf?"

She paused. "I got my own bathroom."

Devon smiled an even-toothed smile. "Remarkable." He shifted a bit closer, his knees touching hers. "So, dearest Delia, if I may ask, what fortuitous happenstance brings you to New York and into my life?"

She thought for a moment. "Oh, this and that."

"I see."

"It's just that I've come into a bit of, you know, money."

"You don't say. However, I would be most careful not to allow your good fortune to become general knowledge." His eyes surveyed the room. "There are some, how shall I say it, charlatans with less than honorable intentions in this city."

"Really."

When the bill came, Devon snatched it up before Delia could see it, which disappointed her, since she was dying to know how expensive dinner was, just so she could tell someone sometime, like the gals at Gross Hardware, not that she was planning on seeing them any time soon, but still.

As he bid her good night at the elevators, he pressed a card into her hand, and then kissed her lightly on the cheek. "Until tomorrow?"

"Until tomorrow."

It was her first business card. Under the reading light on her night table, she read, *Devon Jenkins. Rare gems, rare opportunities. New York. London.* Her head spun. Rare opportunities. She was up for anything. Especially with a man that smelled that good.

The next night they met again, for lobster and more champagne. Devon toasted Delia's beauty with a glass of 20-year-old port. "I cannot believe a woman as radiant as you has yet to be wed."

"Oh, you know," she said, the port swimming in her head. "I'm still kind of playing field."

"Of course you are." He took her hand. "You know, dearest, I'm certain a woman with your means wouldn't have the slightest interest in matters of commerce, but, forgive me, I would feel a bit derelict if I neglected to tell you about a rare opportunity."

"Like it says on your card."

He looked confused for a second. "Oh, yes, of course." He paused again. "But no. Forget what I just said. Whatever was I thinking, bringing up something like this to a woman like you? I'm sure you wouldn't have the slightest interest."

"No, go ahead, Devon." She hiccupped. "Dearest."

"Well, if you insist." He glanced around the room. "Not here." He snapped his fingers. "Waiter."

They took a handsome carriage. Devon told her about a diamond mine in South Africa that was literally bursting at the seams with the precious stones, and that some "important" people, whose names he was not at liberty to divulge but who, suffice it to say, were "people of title," had already taken a large quantity of shares. There were still a few shares to be had, and of course he realized that Delia was "quite comfortable," and no doubt let professionals manager her wealth, but nonetheless, he felt he should tell her about the mine because, if on the off chance she *were* interested, she could in fact triple her investment, conservatively speaking, in four weeks.

What Delia knew about diamonds would have fit on the nail of her pinky finger, which was where she wore her mother's engagement ring. Nonetheless, she agreed to give Devon seven hundred dollars, in cash.

They had dinner at the Algonquin the next evening, even though Delia was somewhat embarrassed that she had to wear the same dress as the night they met. The champagne soon made her forget all about it. Once again, Devon picked up the check. Delia invited him to her room, but Devon begged off, explaining that he had to meet with one of the other investors, a cranky exiled member of the Russian royal court that needed to have his hand held, but he promised he would see her the next day, no ifs, ands or buts. She thought it was odd he'd turned down her invitation, since she'd already undone the top three buttons of her dress and leaned in against him, but, she guessed, Russian royalty came first. She went to bed and dreamed about soaking in a bathtub full of diamonds.

Delia waited for Devon in the dining room until nine o'clock the next night. She went to bed without eating. Two days went by. She thought she saw him hurrying out of the lobby on the third, and she was about yell, "Hey, Devon!" but that seemed inappropriate for a woman of her supposed station. The next morning she went to the front desk to ask about him. The clerk told her Mr. Jenkins had checked out the previous day.

It rained the next day, and Delia decided not to get up. Around two p.m., the bill for the month slid under her door. After her initial panic, she dressed and asked the concierge for the train schedule for Pittsburgh.

Her old job at Gross Hardware was long gone, her slot in the rooming house was gone, and so was ninety percent of her bank balance. She took an efficiency apartment in Mt. Washington and began waitressing at The Hometown Inn and Tavern on Forbes Avenue, two weeks before they opened the new baseball stadium, Forbes Field. New York had taught her one thing. There were the takers, and there were the taken.

Chapter 3

June 30, 1909, was a day generations of Pittsburghers would always remember. It was opening day for America's first true baseball stadium, Forbes Field, fabricated, appropriately enough, almost entirely from poured concrete and Pittsburgh steel.

Forbes Field was one of many firsts for "Hell with the Lid Off," as Boston writer James Parton had characterized the city some 40 years earlier. Pittsburgh could also legitimately boast of having the country's first museum of modern art, its first motion picture theater and its first banana split. What's more, if there had been an accurate means of compiling the statistics, Pittsburgh surely would have been America's first city for pulmonary fibrosis, silicosis and a host of other occupational and airborne maladies, thanks to the incessant appetite of its steel industry.

Abe Miller was not about to let Forbes Field's maiden voyage set sail without him. He rose early that morning, as excited as a schoolboy on the first day of summer vacation, roused Arthur and Benjamin and made them a big breakfast for this big event—generous portions of fried salami and eggs, oatmeal with molasses and butter, toast with raspberry jam and glasses of buttermilk. "Eat up, boys, this could be the best day of your lives. Like the newspaper says, we're going to be part of history." He intoned the word as if intoxicated by its significance. "Let's get it a move on, boys—like the ballplayers say, we have to hustle. We don't want to miss out."

The boys had almost finished wiping their plates with their fingers when Irene dragged herself to the kitchen with Alex slung on her hip. She'd slept restlessly, shifting as far away from Abe as their four-poster queen-sized bed would allow her without falling over the edge, like her marriage. She stared at the burned remains of salami and egg in the massive wrought iron skillet her mother had given her the prior Christmas, with instructions to either cook with it or use it to brain her husband. A wave of nausea passed over her, then a panic-like chill—she couldn't be pregnant again, please God—until she remembered that she'd just finished her period. It must have been the oily fumes of meat and eggs that hung over the frying pan that caused her to feel so queasy. She put Alex in his highchair, next to Abe at the head of the table.

Abe had the morning paper open to the sports section, reading as best as he could, skipping over the longer words. "Boys, who can tell me who the Pirates' shortstop is?"

As if he were in Mrs. Farrell's reading class, Benjamin threw up his hand. "That's easy."

Before he could continue, Alex said, "Honus Wagner, shortstop. Dots Miller, second base. George Gibson, catcher. Jap Barbeau, third base. Fred Clarke, left field. Tommy Leach, center field. Chief Wilson, right field. Bill Abstein, first base. Babe Adams, pitcher."

Abe dropped the newspaper.

Arthur said, "God damn."

"Watch your mouth, mister." Irene twisted his ear perhaps harder than he deserved, jealous that Alex had spoken to him first and rather than his own mother. "Wait—did you two know he was talking? Has he been talking to you? When did you teach him that?"

"But, Ma, I didn't."

Abe said, "Christ, it's a miracle. The miracle of opening day."

"Alex, honey, can you talk to me? Momma wants to hear you talk."

"Come on, Alex. Say it again." Benjamin tickled Alex's bare toes. "Say Honus Wagner." Both boys entreated their tiny brother in rapid-fire succession to repeat the lineup. Alex was all grins but no words.

"Let me have the boy." Abe hoisted Alex to his lap. He began in his best avuncular voice. "Now little Alex, your old man—Daddy—we think it's very good that you can talk. Very good. You're a very good boy." He winked confidentially at Irene, as if to say, you see, don't worry, Irene, a superior mind here is at work, I'll entice the boy to open up, he'll be talking like a jaybird in two shakes of a lamb's tail, you just watch and learn.

If Irene was informed, interested or impressed with Abe's gesture, she gave no indication. She poured a cup of coffee for herself and absentmindedly chewed on a crust of wheat toast.

After two minutes of begging, cajoling and yelling at Alex, all to no avail, Abe tried another tack. "All right, Alex, you don't have to talk if you don't want to," certain his clever gambit of reverse psychology would result in a torrent of words.

Alex rubbed a piece of scrambled egg in his hair.

"Leave him be, Abe. Maybe he's done talking for now. He'll talk when he wants to talk."

For once, Abe had to agree with his wife, even though it was against his basic nature to give her the satisfaction of acknowledging it to her face. "Your mother's right, boys. Now let's get our lunches and get down to the ballpark. The dedication ceremonies are at one and the trolley will be as crowded as a cattle car. Christ, look at the time, it's already 9:30. Let's go, let's go."

Alex said, "Alex go, too."

Abe said, "I'll be damned. Alex? What did he say, Irene?"

Alex repeated, "Alex go, too."

"He wants to go to the baseball game, Dad. Can we take him, can we, huh, come on?"

Abe shifted in his seat. "It's ridiculous. I can't be taking him along."

Alex screamed so loudly that the cat, which had been furtively licking the remains of the fried salami, leaped onto the curtains over the kitchen window and hung there like a sailor clinging to the mast in a hurricane.

Irene said, "Alex, sweetheart, I know you want to go, but you can't go with Daddy today. Daddy will take you to a baseball game when you get bigger, all right?" The word bigger echoed in her head. When, dear Lord, will that be? Two months, two years, twenty years from now—at the rate he's growing, I'll be long in the grave. "Isn't that right, Abraham?"

"Sure, sure," Abe said, willing to agree with anything that would get him and the boys out of the house and up to the trolley stop before the cars became too damned crowded, like they were every morning when he rode the 74 to town before he transferred to the South Side. "When you're bigger, Alex."

Alex sucked in his breath between his lips with a high-pitched whistle. After ten seconds his cheeks, the size of silver dollars turned bright red, then began to fade.

"Alex? Abe, do you see what he's doing?"

"He can't kill himself by holding his breath, Ma," Arthur said. "Stanley Filiposki tried it in school because Angelo DelGrosso bet him a nickel he couldn't hold his breath for two minutes, but Stanley then just passed out and then he started breathing. He wasn't dead."

Alex began to shiver and turn pale.

"Abraham!"

"All right, all right. Alex, listen, son, you can go with us, all right? Breathe, damn it."

Alex turned from his brothers to his mother to his father with a wide smile. He let his breath out and said, "Alex go, too."

*

There was simply no way that Irene was going to let Abe take the baby to see the new stadium without her. He wasn't responsible enough to care for the three of them by himself for ten minutes. She would go along with them to Forbes Field, and once the opening ceremonies were over, they could all go home. She packed applesauce and stewed carrots, along with two diapers, into the large burlap bag she used to keep her sewing.

Mellon Street was just two blocks from the trolley that ran from East End to Oakland. Abe muscled his way to an empty seat midway to the back and stood guard over it until Irene and the boys made it through the tangle of arms, legs and picnic baskets. He installed Irene and Alex next to the window so that she and the baby would have some air.

As people got off and on, they'd pause by the Millers' seat to gawk at Alex, who was sitting in Irene's lap, playing with his toes. Arthur stuck his tongue out at the people waiting at the stops, while Benjamin studied the lineups in the newspaper he found on the floor of the trolley.

Virtually everyone on the trolley wore some sort of Pittsburgh Pirates identification: baseball caps, ribbons, shirts and shifts hand-embroidered with a red "P" for the home team. Arthur clutched his Honus Wagner trading card. Little did he know that only 291 of these cards had been issued; the few that survived would become some of the most valuable baseball trading cards ever printed, eventually worth $250,000 at auction. However, neither Arthur nor his family would ever see a penny from his card, since it was lost along with various parts of his body during a prolonged artillery barrage during the Battle of the Argonne Forest.

It took close to 90 minutes to reach the corner of Fifth Avenue and Bouquet Street in the center of Oakland, just a few blocks from the new stadium. The weather was sunny and glorious, the air remarkably smoke free, as if the steel mills had taken the day off, too. Brass bands played, street vendors hawked popcorn and peanuts, hot dogs and bratwurst, cotton candy and snow cones with thick syrup. Abe panted when he saw trays of cold Bohemian, but Irene convinced him not to indulge for one day, for the boys' sake. Rebuffed, he took Arthur and Benjamin by the wrists and joined the thousands milling around the entrances, gawking at the new edifice. Irene followed along with the baby as best she could, working her way through the throng, her steps heavy with a premonition of impending disaster.

All the gates were shuttered and padlocked. Clusters of fans, who'd begun to gather as early as eight that morning, tromped across the new grass, crushing the neat rows of daffodils and crocuses planted along the walkways, eager to touch the great structure, the new wonder of the world, to let some of its grandeur rub off on them. Proud Pittsburghers they were, residents of the city whose muscle pumped out steel for the world and now had spawned this unmatched stadium.

Irene fed Alex some mashed carrots. He burped. He waved his tiny hands at her, as if to say all done. She sat on a wooden bench, out of the sun, and put him over her shoulder, waiting for a burp. Gradually, a small crowd of women and girls began to form around her. The questions began: How old is he, or is it a she? Is it a dwarf? Does it talk? Can I hold it? At first, Irene was proud to answer that Alex had just had his one-year, four-month birthday. No one believed her—no way could he be one year old, why, he was as little as a breadbox, small even for a premature baby. As the crush of bodies pressed up against them, Irene feared that Alex would be terrified by all the attention, but if he were, he didn't show it. His blue eyes were as clear and calm as the sky above. A woman with large yellow teeth and a broad-brimmed red hat kept touching Irene's hip, reaching her chubby arms toward Alex, and Irene worried that at any moment this woman would snatch Alex from her grasp and pass him around the crowed like a talisman of good fortune for the new stadium and the baseball team. This might well have happened except that, as the horde pressed tighter, Alex shouted, "Honus Wagner!"

Heads turned this way and that, hoping to catch a glimpse of the great Pirates shortstop. "Where, where?" they cried.

Alex pointed toward Gate B.

Immediately, the mob turned as one organism, much as a flight of starlings dips and veers and changes direction in mid-flight, and stormed toward the gate.

Irene allowed herself to breathe, now that the crowd in its hero-worshipping frenzy had forgotten about Alex. Had he really seen Honus

Wagner? And how in the world would he know it was him?

"Irene?"

It was Abe, sweat rolling down the sides of his sunburned neck. "My God, Abe, where were you? The baby and I were about to be attacked by a mob."

"We were looking around, taking it all in, right boys?" Abe looked around. "I don't see no crowd."

"But then Alex...never mind. Are we ready to leave?"

"Leave? Now?"

"But I thought we were going to see the place and go home."

"Go home now? Look." Abe held up his hand to show off his great and wonderful prize—three bleachers tickets. "Do you see this, Irene? Do you know what this means? The boys and I, we're going to be part of history. Didn't I tell you this morning, boys? History! Didn't I tell you?" In response, Arthur and Benjamin jumped and pulled at his sides like nervous boxer dogs.

"How in God's name did you get them?"

Yes, Abe explained, as sure as the day is long every seat has been sold, all 20,000, maybe 30,000, can you believe it, 30,000 people in one place to watch a baseball game, and every blessed seat has been sold, but, he ranted, no sold-out game was going to stop Abe Miller, not this remarkable day, when this fellow approaches me, and says buddy, could you use three tickets, well, you're damn right I could, I said., "Ain't that what I said, boys?", and with that he patted Benjamin and Arthur on their heads.

Irene transferred Alex to her left hip. "How much?"

"Never let it be said," said Abraham the Munificent, "that I would deny my sons this opportunity to witness history in the making."

"How much, Abe?"

He paused to wipe his mustachioed lip with the back of his cuff, "These boys are worth the six dollars I paid."

"Six dollars? Six, you say? That's a butcher's bill for two weeks! But wait a minute. How long does a baseball game take?"

"Well, it depends."

"And what about the baby and me? What are we supposed to do, wait here for you in the heat?"

Before Abe could come up with a plausible or even an implausible answer as to how his wife and Alex were going to spend the rest of the hot afternoon and early evening, while he and the bigger boys and Pirates president Barney Dreyfuss and two musical bands and United States congressmen from three states and Pittsburgh mayor William A. "Willie" Magee enjoyed the game, a familiar, annoying voice intervened. "Aha, is it not the Miller family from Mellon Street that I am seeing?" Dr. Malkin bowed. "At your service."

Irene pulled Alex tightly to her chest, as if she were afraid Malkin might snatch him away. "What are you doing here?"

"Yes, it is the logical question, no? Of course it is true that I am not understanding of it this American baseball, of men running around in pajamas in the hot sun, they could get heat stroke. However, with so many of the people gathered around here, it is a good opportunity I am thinking to pass it out to them my business address, is it not?" He held up one of his handbills: *Dr. Sergei Malkin, General Doctor and Dentist also.* "Is it not the good idea, no? I have passed it out to many of the people this vital information, for you see, America, the land of opportunity, it is for all of us, no?" He wiped his forehead with a checkered handkerchief.

Arthur said, "Dad, he talks like a greenhorn."

"Arthur!"

"It is of no matter, I have heard it this phrase more than once." Malkin pointed to the tickets in Abe's fist. "You are taking it the family to the game of baseball, I see."

Irene said, "Not all of us. Just the three of them." She folded her arms across her chest.

The sun glinted on Malkin's glasses as he stared at Alex. Such an opportunity, he thought, and he sidled his way between husband and wife. "A moment, if I may. Perhaps I can be it of the assistance to you and yours, Mr. Miller. I could see the lady to home, her and the little one, of which I must say I am quite curious as to the little fellow, for his welfare of course, as well as from it the medical point of view, naturally, as any doctor would be, you can understand it."

Benjamin said, "Alex can talk now. I think he can read, too."

"Yes? Talking and reading? But this is a remarkable sign of the developmental process, so we shall see it perhaps soon the physical development, it won't be to lagging behind, God willing."

Abe handed Malkin a dollar. "Do me a favor, Malkin. Get them home for me."

"But, Abe—"

"It would be it my pleasure to escort Mrs. Miller and the little one for nothing, but since you have offered." Malkin plucked the coin from Abe and slid it into his vest pocket. "You and your boys, enjoy it the playing of baseball."

Irene wanted to explode, to dress Abe down in front of Malkin and her sons, but this wasn't the time or place, and so she said, "Abraham, this ain't the last of this."

With his boys in tow, Abe slunk off, wondering if he had done the right thing. However, his pangs of guilt diminished as the distance grew between Irene and him and the stadium grew closer, and then he and the boys were one with the crowd, stoked by beer and the band music and the sun.

Malkin, Irene and Alex drifted against the flow. Malkin offered to buy Irene a cold drink with Abe's money, and they settled into a booth at the Home Town Inn & Tavern, not three blocks from the stadium. Malkin order a fried fish sandwich with all the trimmings and one for Irene as well, along with a plate of pickles, brown bread and beans, and two bottles of ginger beer. He urged Irene to drink. "It will be good for the baby, as it is you are nursing yet, I take it," to which Irene replied that of course she was, and what did that have to do with anything.

They ate in relative silence, broken only by Malkin's slurping and occasional belch. Irene watched him shovel in the food with his stubby, long-nailed fingers and it dawned on her that he'd put those fingers inside her to deliver Alex. She wondered if he'd washed them first. The fish rose halfway up her throat.

Malkin wiped his mouth with a flourish, but several bits of brown bread remained embedded in his goatee. He reached into his medical bag and held up a tongue depressor. "Perhaps now that I am seeing the boy here, it is the good time I shall give it to him the quick medical check."

"I'm not paying you for an examination. Besides, he doesn't need one. Especially not here in the middle of a restaurant."

"Oh, you have it the misunderstanding of me. This medical check, it is purely for the scientific interest I have in such an unusual boy. There would be no charge. He is in it the good health, no, since the last time I have seen him?"

"He's fine."

"Yes, well, such a boy as this one we cannot be it too careful, what with his tiny size which as I say it is most unusual. How are his movements? Might I examine it a used diaper, just for the precaution against parasites, to rule it out any infestation which may be sapping his growth?"

Loud enough for the man seated two tables away to hear, Irene said, "You're telling me you want to look at a dirty diaper here in the restaurant?"

The man stood and moved away.

Malkin said, "I meant no, of course, not at this time, I could take it with me, or I some time you could bring him to my surgery." He buried his embarrassment in his beans.

The waitress laid the bill on the table and lingered a bit, explaining that there was no hurry, it would be slow until the game let out, she was sure, but then all hell would break loose, especially if they won. She stooped over to admire Alex, who grabbed her finger. She asked if she could hold the little thing, he was so precious, but Irene, whose mood hadn't brightened even after a second ginger beer, told her no offense, but I just can't have every Tom, Dick and Mary grabbing at the boy, you can see how tiny he is even for a one-year-old. The waitress nodded.

Malkin watched her as she walked away, a faint look of recognition on his face, as if he'd seen her somewhere before. Perhaps at The Squeaky Wheel, when delivering his tonic to Davy O'Brien.

The waitress's nametag read *Delia*.

Chapter 4

In the fall of 1909, in one of his more popular edicts, America's heaviest president, William Howard Taft issued a proclamation that appointed November 25 as a day of general thanksgiving, perhaps in part because of his love for a big spread. In any event, the Thanksgiving holiday was born, as was the four-day weekend.

It was on a cold Saturday after the first Thanksgiving that Abe, as was his Sabbath custom, went to The Squeaky Wheel with Alex. Before he could get out the door, however, Irene made him hand over his wallet, from which she extracted all the bills, leaving Abe with just ninety cents in pocket change.

Abe was wondering how to make it last, and so he started out with beer when what he really had his eyes on a shot of Old Overholt. Davy O'Brien waved Abe and Alex over to his table. As he tickled the boy under the chin, he said, "I know something you don't know."

Abe looked at the three empty shot glasses on the table in front of him. "What?"

"Buy me a drink and I'll tell you."

Abe fingered his last seventy-five cents. The way Davy had enticed him, he had to know more. He motioned to the barmaid. "So?"

Davy threw down the shot. "She's back." He winked confidentially. He didn't have to say whom.

Abe flushed. "How do you know?"

"Malkin." Dr. Malkin had been treating Davy's injured hip with a combination of hot salts and a homemade tonic consisting of chicory, celery seeds, white vinegar, honey, cider and grain alcohol. He charged Davy a dollar for a 12-ounce bottle, half the price of Davy's beloved Irish whiskey and just as potent. "He told me yesterday."

"So Delia's back, is she? Well it's nothing to me, Davy," Abe professed, declaring that it was long over between them, he was a family man, everyone could see that. Why, didn't he take little Alex everywhere? And as if to prove his point, he sat Alex up on his shoulders. Bouncing in the smoky Wheel air, Alex laughed and waved his stubby, chubby arms, and when he said

"Davy," his voice was as clear as the plink of an ice cube in a dry tumbler.

"So you're not interested?"

Abe said, "Not in the least, but just out of curiosity, what did Malkin say about her—you know, what does she look like, does she have her old job back, is she married now or seeing someone, not that I care, you understand."

The front door rattled as Horshushky the butcher entered, sat on a stool, wiped his nose with the back of his bloody work glove and told the bartender it was colder than a dead whore's twat out there. Davy rocked Alex lightly on his bad hip, as if physical contact with the child would act as an elixir to ease his pain. He fed him bits of beer pretzel, which Alex sucked greedily in his baby-toothed mouth, and sang him a song about a happy whale with a tiny, briny eye. Alex stretched his hands toward Davy's mouth, trying to touch his lips as the words came out.

Finally, Davy said, "She come to him for a bad tooth."

"Yeah? What else did he say?"

"You know how Malkin talks, once he gets started, it's like a sick dog shitting, you can't get him to stop. You can't understand half of what the fool is saying, anyway, on account of that accent of his."

"But what did he say, Davy?"

"She got some job as a waitress somewhere. Near the stadium, I think he said. Anyways, he yanks the tooth, and she tells him she don't get paid till the end of the week, send me a bill, which of course don't go down too good with Malkin—no offense, Abe, but you members of the tribe, you got to have your gelt."

"But what else did he say?"

"For a guy that ain't interested you sure are interested."

"Come on, Davy. Did he say where she lives?"

Davy swallowed and closed his eyes. "I told you enough. Go ask Malkin."

*

That night, Abe was all over the bed, arms and legs flailing even after Irene had reluctantly "serviced" him, as she sometimes described the act to her mother. She acquiesced to his groping out of some nagging sense of marital obligation. She even moved against him a little, as if she were enjoying it. Not that she was. All she got out of it anymore was a momentary feeling of achievement once his business was done, and a wave of relief that at least it was over.

Abe's arm flopped against her nose. "Abe, wake up. Why don't you take yourself downstairs and have a pipe or a glass of warmed milk to settle yourself down? You're moving around enough to spook the Devil."

He went to the kitchen. In the icebox was a pan of leftover meatloaf and part of a chocolate fudge cake his mother-in-law had brought for the boys. He was surprised they hadn't finished it. He cut a large wedge and opened a bottle of beer, his fourth of the day. Ever since he'd left The Wheel he hadn't been able to shake an image of Delia Novak, the white of her skin against the black of her stocking tops in the candlelight of her room. It was all he'd been thinking of as he made primitive love to Irene.

Seeing Delia again was wrong, dead wrong, he knew it, but then, there were many wrongs in this world, weren't there, and if a man had to live his life always worrying if what he was doing was right or wrong, well, that was no life at all, sometimes you just had to do what you wanted to. You had to be tough and be a man in this world, especially if you were a working-class Jew, and the crap he put up with at work—the word "kike" written on his locker after an argument with Sweeney, the time Grenosovich put his work gloves in a bucket of grease—it would fill a book. Maybe he was going to Hell for his sins, and maybe he wasn't, he'd let God be the judge of that, but if he were bound for eternal damnation, he wouldn't be the only fornicator down there.

He chewed his cake. Pain shot through his left incisor. Even if he could reach Delia through Malkin, what made him think she'd even see him? He'd made no promises to her, never led her on to think that he'd be willing to leave Irene and the boys for her. Where would they go, what would they do, live on love? It wasn't love between them, but it sure was something, something that was making his groin tingle.

The stairs creaked as he went up. Irene had been on him for weeks to shim the steps, as if he didn't have enough to do. He paused outside the door to the boys' bedroom. He'd promised them new baseball gloves for their birthdays; well, he wasn't about to buy them cheap ones, he'd have to put in some overtime at the shop, which wasn't so bad, it would keep him out of the house, and with some of the extra money he could buy something for Delia, too, like some more of those stockings, just in case he did see her.

The light was on in his bedroom. To his surprise, Irene was propped up against the headboard. Her hair was down on her bare shoulders and the top sheet clung tight around her breasts, and in that moment Abe remembered the pretty, busty, teasing auburn-haired 18-year-old girl that could drive him wild with just a touch, and he felt himself stir under his nightshirt. What was it about women, he thought. Here a moment ago he was pining for Delia and now his wife, without saying a word, had him hard as poker twenty minutes after he'd finished with her. He slid into bed and brushed her thigh with his.

"Before you get too comfortable, Abe, would you please get up and get me a cold wet cloth from the bathroom, my head is pounding something fierce, and while you're up bring the baby here. I don't like that cough of his."

"But right now?" He pushed his hardness against her, hoping she'd get the hint.

"Abe, stop. He may be coming down with something, the croup maybe, or maybe it's because you insist on bringing him to that smokehouse you call a tavern. It's unhealthy. I don't know why in God's name I let you take him."

With the moment gone limp, Abe plodded to the bathroom, thinking how Delia's voice was musical compared to Irene's. He ran cold water over a thin washcloth. He turned his head sideways and raised his upper lip so he could press his finger to his incisor. It throbbed to the touch and spurted a trickle of blood and pus. Just another damn thing to worry about in a world of sorrows.

Back in bed, he sat Alex up between them. Alex sneezed three times, the sound like water droplets hitting a hotplate.

"Does my little snoogy-woogy has him da sniffles?"

"Irene, you'll make a sissy out of the boy with that kind of talk."

"Will you stop, Abe, he's a baby, and besides, it's better than the gutter language he hears from those rummy pals of yours at that Squeaky Wheel, which in my opinion ought to be burned down to the ground."

"Now, Irene, if you'd ever been there you'd see it's a damn good saloon where a working man can get a decent bowl of beef stew and a hunk of good bread for a quarter. And the boys love our little lad here, you should see their eyes light up when I bring him around, and Davy."

"Don't tell me again about the great Davy O'Brien who could have been the world's next great Irish tenor. He's just another broken-down drunk."

"Here you go again on your high horse."

Alex coughed a phlegm-filled cough. Irene held her hand in front of the boy's mouth. "Spit, spit it out, baby. Maybe I'd better take him to Malkin although my mother says the man ought to be deported, and by the way, did you ask Shields for that overtime, we need the extra." She rubbed Alex's back. "Arthur is sprouting like weeds in the backyard and Benjamin can't wear his raggedy hand-me-downs forever. Did you notice he's started to stutter?"

"What's wrong with him?"

"I wish I knew. Come on, Alex, spit it out."

"Look, Shields gives overtime when he has it, but you think he's going to give it to a Jew first?"

"Well, that's your problem, my problem is how to keep three growing boys fed and clothed. I can't have them going around looking like beggars, and you know I won't ask my mother for another penny."

Alex coughed again.

"I'll take the boy to see Malkin tomorrow, I have to go myself for this damn tooth."

Alex said, "Damn tooth."

"Hear that? See how you've taught him?"

"Aw, come on, Irene, ain't it the cutest thing, the way he speaks. You know, we're lucky to have this boy, he is going to be something special, I can just feel it. I have a nose for these things."

Her voice softened. "He is a little pistol. You know what he did the other day? He counted to twelve. I swear to God. Then he counted backward. I wish someone else was there to hear it, just to make sure I heard what I heard. I asked him how he knew it and he pointed to the clock."

Abe scratched his crotch under the sheets. "You ever notice that look in his eyes, like he understands everything around him, more than we think he does? You're a wily little bugger, aren't you?"

Alex laughed and coughed, and a thumbnail of phlegm plopped into Irene's hand.

"That's my good boy, get it all out of your system, my goodness you're a good boy. He adores his brothers but sometimes they're as mean as a witch to him. Yesterday I caught them bouncing him back and forth on the sofa, like he was a rubber ball. You need to speak to them about that."

Abe clenched his fist. "I'll bust their heads open."

"Don't hit them. Just talk to them."

"All right, I'll talk. You see, Irene, how we're having a conversation we're not yelling at each other."

She pressed a bit closer to his shoulder and thought about how big and strong and dangerous he looked when she first saw him in East Liberty at the movies, so unlike the boys her mother had wished upon her, the proper Catholic prep school boys with their neatly combed hair and clean shirts and ties. Abe was all angles and guff and trouble, and she was looking for trouble. He had courted her with daffodils and whiskey, and one mild night, as they walked along Highland Avenue toward the park, he told her his story.

Abe's father, Jacob, had come to America in 1880, when he was 18, from a village in the hills of western Austria-Hungary. He had $22.13 in his pocket, an unpronounceable last name and his Uncle Morris's address on a scrap of paper. Morris, who had changed his own unpronounceable last name to Miller, changed Jacob's, too. He put him to work in his pushcart business, selling soup, sandwiches, coffee, plug tobacco, cigarettes, candy, headache powders and such to the men coming off or going on shifts at National Tube Works in McKeesport, twenty miles south down the Monongahela from Pittsburgh. Uncle Morris also found Jacob a nice Jewish girl to marry, his 16-year-old niece Helen Rottenstein, who died from excessive bleeding 10 days after Abe was born.

Before long, Jacob realized he despised McKeesport in general and the pushcart business in particular. His passion was sketching, and he fancied himself an artist, and so he decided to follow his dream; after all, there was nothing to keep him in McKeesport except a miserable job and a bawling baby boy, and besides, wasn't America the land of opportunity? Wasn't the pursuit of happiness a fundamental part of the American credo? He took off for New York two months after Helen died, leaving Abe to his Uncle Morris. After several months, he found work as a window dresser at Macy's Department Store. He died from consumption 13 years later. With no money in the bank and no relatives to claim his body, he was buried alongside other indigents at Potter's Field Cemetery on Hart Island.

When Uncle Morris, a confirmed bachelor, died 20 years later, Abe inherited his house and fleet of pushcarts. He sold the lot and moved to

Pittsburgh. Following Morris's advice that real estate was the best investment in America you could ever make, they called it real estate because it was *real*, he bought the house on Mellon Street.

Irene was head over heels for Abe, but her mother hated him right off, which made Irene like him all the more. He had a steady, good-paying job and owned his own house—not a fancy house, but decent, with six rooms and a yard that she could pretty up. She was determined to show her mother that she wasn't the only woman that knew how to manage a household and raise a family, and as for his religion, she didn't give a hoot about her own Catholicism that seemed so damn important to her mother, so what did it matter whether he were a Jew or a Hindu?

Abe said, "Irene, you remember the dances at Renziehausen Park when we'd sneak away from the bandstand? That perfume you wore, I wanted to haul your dress off right there."

"Oh shush." She pulled his hand to her breast and stroked each finger against her nipple. She thought about how he used to be fun, how *they* used to be fun before two boys and a miscarriage and now this little one sitting between them.

Alex pointed a tiny finger at Abe and said, "Delia."

Abe turned crimson.

"What's he saying, Abe? What's that, sweetheart?"

"Delia and Daddy."

"What's he saying, Abe?"

"Christ, I don't know. It's just baby talk."

"You know damn well what he said." She pushed Abe's hand away. "Delia. It's that whore Delia Novak, you're seeing her again, aren't you?"

"By God, I swear I haven't seen the woman, she isn't even in town."

"Isn't in town? How the hell do you know where she is or where she isn't?"

Alex said, "Davy said Delia."

"Shush, boy."

"Don't you yell at him, don't you ever raise your voice to him."

"I'm not yelling."

"You're always yelling. Lower your voice, you want to wake the other boys, too?"

Abe hissed, "I'm whispering, all right? I'm telling you I never seen the damn woman."

"You know what, Abraham, go ahead and see your Delia. I don't even care, how's that?"

"I'm not seeing no one, there's nothing going on. What do I have to do to make you believe the words coming out of my mouth?"

"I said lower your voice." She turned her face to her pillow.

Alex leaned toward his father and said "Delia" once more, and Abe knew that his son had understood every word that had passed between him and Davy. He needed to be far more careful about what he said around him.

*

Back in December of 1907, a fire had destroyed most of the row houses on Sheepslayer Way in Pittsburgh's Bloomfield neighborhood. Dr. Malkin, newly arrived in Pittsburgh via Ellis Island, bought three burned-out units on the cheap. During the reconstruction phase, he lived under a canvas tarp in one of the shells and hired two Greeks and a Slovenian to make the other two at least look habitable. For immigrant families used to far worse conditions in their native homelands, a roof, four walls, rooms separated by doors and a concrete floor seemed palatial.

By 1909, Malkin was collecting $30 per month per unit—how many people/families living in them was not his concern. When his renters didn't have cash, he took in-kind payment: food, coal, live chickens, lumber, copper, fixtures and sometimes sex, although that was not his preference. He was a businessman first, a lech second.

He set up his ragtag surgery on the second floor of his unit, once the Greeks had finished the planking. To augment the archaic instruments he'd brought with him from the old country, he periodically scavenged discarded medical paraphernalia from the refuse bins of nearby St. Margaret's Hospital. His treasures included an almost new stethoscope and a tarnished speculum.

Sheepslayer Way was then two blocks long, and so narrow, the little sunlight that found its way through the Pittsburgh smog created a sense of perpetual twilight. Children and dogs chased each other around the street's single fire hydrant and through the tiny back yards, where laundry lines provided the demarcation between homes. In the evenings, the women swept the stoops and sat out while men smoked cigars and pipes under the street lamps.

The morning after his fight with Irene, Abe got off the trolley that ran along Penn Avenue, holding Alex on his shoulder. At 4547 Sheepslayer Way, he saw the small plaque with Dr. Malkin's name lettered in both English and Cyrillic. He knocked rapidly. Malkin shouted from a second-floor window, "Come up already, come."

The first floor opened to a small living room with a massive sofa that touched each opposing wall. To the left, through the short hallway, Abe smelled beets and cabbage boiling.

Dr. Malkin's half-sister Masha, a plump woman with thinning orange hair and heavy, loose triceps, emerged from the kitchen, wiping her hands on her brown dress. She took one look at Alex and said, "Oh my goodness, this little thing it is too precious for the words, no? Look at him, he is the sweetest little boychick. Wait, is he hungry, I could feed him a little bit borscht, I'll cool it down special for him." She smiled a gold-toothed smile and extended her arms.

"He don't need none of that," Abe said, although he himself wouldn't have minded a big bowl of borsht with a fat dollop of sour cream. "We're here to see the doctor, he already knows we're here, he said to come right up."

"Such a cute little fellow, I could just eat him up."

Abe thought, if I gave her half a chance, she probably would with those gold teeth of hers. He took the stairs two at a time. A door was open at the end of the short hallway.

Malkin stared down into a microscope, holding a partially eaten chicken leg under the lens. Abe cleared his throat. Malkin jerked the leg away from the lens. "Oh, Miller, you should have knocked, I was looking in here to make it a scientific investigation is all, you know you could learn it a lot from a piece of chicken, but pay this no mind. What is it I can do it for you today? I see you brought him the little one. I wish mine hand to God if only I could fit him under the microscope."

"My boy here has a cough his mother thinks could be something more, but if you ask me there's nothing to it."

"So let us have it a look while I give him the examination, if you please." He stood Alex on a piece of plywood laid over two sawhorses that served as his examination table. "Do you remember me, little mister, it was me what did brought you into this great and cruel world." Malkin listened to Alex's tiny heart and lungs. He placed him on a produce scale he'd gotten from

Horshushky in exchange for a Salvarsan compound the butcher needed for a bout of syphilis. From a paint-stained filing cabinet he took a folder named Little Miller and wrote down Alex's weight and the date, and noticed the regular progressive weight gain with each of the boy's six-month visits. If there were a pattern to his growth, it was beyond Malkin's understanding. On the spur of the moment, he placed the boy's pinky under the microscope lens. "For the closer look, Miller, it does not hurt the boy one bit." All he saw were larger fingerprints.

"All right, Malkin, does he have something or not? We don't have all day."

"It is not to worry, Miller, the boy here—one could even say a dwarf, except his features, they are so regular, it makes me to wonder—he is fine in his condition, his lungs are clean, his heartbeat is regular, it is only a cold, nothing more. But you look it to be in some pain yourself, is it not the case?"

"I have a tooth that's killing me, but first tell me about her."

"Her?"

Alex said, "Delia."

"The little one, he knows her name?"

"Yeah. Talk."

Malkin shook a bottle of vinegar on a plaid handkerchief and wiped it on his stethoscope. "For to kill the germs, you see. So sit, Miller, you look it to me like you're going to have a coronary attack, you're sweating like a steam pipe. Yes, Delia Novak, you have it certainly the good taste in the women. By the way, she is owing it to me some money."

"That ain't my problem. I want to know where she is, goddamn it."

Alex said, "Goddamn it."

Now Malkin looked sideways at Alex. "This boy, there is something I don't understand about him, or how to describe it in the medical terms, this, how do you call it, ability to parrot back the words. Perhaps I could get it from him a urine sample."

Abe grabbed Malkin by his collar. "Tell me where Delia is, damn it."

"All right, please, I will give it to you her address. Wait, I write it down for you in English, if you will let it go of my shirt. Please."

Chapter 5

On December 3, 1909, at approximately 5:30 a.m., the central steam pipe at Fulton Elementary School burst wide open. When Arthur and Benjamin and the other children arrived that morning, to their delight they were sent home for an unexpected long weekend.

In an unrelated event, Alex Miller's arms grew three inches overnight. He was touching his toes without bending at the waist when Irene came into the boy's bedroom that morning to get him dressed.

"See what Alex can do, Momma," said Alex, who had begun to refer to himself in the third person.

"Oh my," said Irene, looking not so much at Alex as the mess of clothes and toys scattered about the room. "Alex is doing his exercises like a big boy."

"Alex is a big boy."

Big, she thought. He's not even three feet tall. She dug through the mess on the floor: an empty can of peanut brittle; a jack-in-the-box whose head Alex had pulled off; a little wooden pony with a curly tail that wiggled when Alex pulled it on its string; filthy socks and underwear, courtesy of the bigger boys; and a red and blue sweater Irene's mother had knitted for Alex and given her two days earlier.

Irene slipped the sweater over Alex's head. The torso came down to his waist, but the sleeves stopped four inches short of his wrists, no matter how much she tugged on them. Could her mother have measured that poorly? And hadn't it fit him when he tried it on the night before?

The front door banged open. Arthur and Benjamin whooped in with cries of No School! No School! Alex scrambled out of the room yelling for his brothers, leaving his mother holding his pants and wondering about the sweater.

"Ma!"

"What are you two doing home?"

"The pipes burst. There's a flood."

"At the school," said Benjamin. "You should see it. They suh...sent us home. For all day. Honest, Ma."

"Yeah, honest," said Arthur. "Can we have something to eat? We're starving."

They were always starving, and always growing out of their clothes, too. Growing out of their clothes—maybe Alex's arms were growing out of his. She laughed to herself at the thought. "First take off those galoshes, you're tracking slush all over the place. Mind your brother and I'll make you some oatmeal."

"But we had it for breakfast."

"Yeah, can we have bacon and eggs and toast and jam?"

Alex said, "Alex wants bacon and eggs."

"Come on, Ma, make it for us, for a treat, there's no school."

Irene looked at her big boys with their arms around Alex. It would make a nice picture, those two big boys, their faces flushed full of life, and her little one, basking in his brothers' attention. So precious. She needed to have pictures taken, before they were no longer so cute. "Well, all right, but you two mind your brother now. I'll call you when it's done."

"Come on, Alex."

Forty minutes later, as Irene stacked Alex's clothes in the cedar chest she used for his dresser, she thought about the sweater again. It was possible some of the stitches could have pulled out, or her mother could have measured the sleeves incorrectly, but her mother was so picky about everything that that seemed unlikely. She came back to the bizarre thought that maybe Alex's arms grew overnight, like Jack's beanstalk. She imagined Alex's arms growing longer and longer, like fleshy runaway vines up the side of the house and into the clouds. No, her mother must have measured wrong.

Something crashed in the living room, followed by a high-pitched shriek. Irene rushed in to find Alex sitting next to a broken clay flowerpot, with dried flowers strewn on the floor. The older boys stood there with their heads down, like dogs about to be beaten.

"Well?"

Arthur said, "What, Ma?"

"Don't you what Ma me. You know what. I told you to mind your brother. What in the name of God Almighty is going on here?"

"See, we were playing muh…monkey in the middle with Alex."

"Benjamin, don't stutter."

"Suh…sometimes I can't help it."

Alex said, "Alex is a monkey." He loped around the room like a chimp, propelling himself with his elongated arms. Arthur and Benjamin tried to control their laughter, lest their mother smack them.

"We'll clean it up, Ma," Arthur volunteered. "But Alex did it."

Alex made more monkey jabber.

"Alex, stop that. You two, you egged him on, I know it."

"But Muh…muh…"

"Just go get the broom and dust pan."

"Then can we go out?"

"Go, for the love of God."

They ran to the kitchen.

"Alex go, too."

She bent down. "Just look at your hands." His knuckles, the size of pencil erasers, were raw and bleeding.

"Alex wants to *go*. Please, Momma? Alex will be good."

The little conniver, she thought. He already knows how to navigate around his mother's heart. Well, maybe she should let him out for a few minutes. It wasn't all that cold. His brothers would watch him, and she could use a minute for herself, maybe read a magazine for ten minutes or figure out how she was going to pay both the butcher bill and the milkman this week.

She washed his knuckles with a soapy dishrag. "All right, Mr. Big Boy." She laid his snowsuit out on the floor. "Can you help Momma put on your snowsuit?"

With his newly elongated arms, it was simple for Alex to reach down and grip the pant legs. However, putting the right leg into the right hole was another matter. He put both feet into one of the snowsuit legs and fell over. He kicked violently, and the more he struggled, the more entrapped he became, as if the snowsuit were a Chinese finger puzzle.

Standing in his red snowsuit, he looked like a small fireplug. The material from the legs bunched up around his ankles, but the arms were still a bit short.

Irene led him out to the snow fort Arthur and Benjamin had built with snow bricks molded from one of her pound cake pans. She went into the kitchen and began to cut stew meat into chunks, rinsed the carrots and the celery, the onions, the potatoes. She monitored Benjamin and Arthur's yells as they cut through the chilly air.

The Miller boys were at war with the Walsh twins, Jackie and Kevin from across Mellon Street. They'd stockpiled a great deal of ordnance—50 snowballs, each the size of a hand grenade. But now the well-provisioned warriors had a new problem—Alex. When the Walsh attack came—imminently, the boys were sure—what were supposed to do with their tiny little brother, who would just be in the way? The Walsh twins were clever, sneaky fighters. Just yesterday, they'd jumped Benjamin, who'd walked home from school by himself because Arthur had to stay for detention. They washed his face with snow and called him a dirty Jew, which sounded tough to them, even though they weren't quite sure what it meant.

Alex picked up a snowball.

"Alex, put that down," said Arthur.

"Why?"

Imitating his father's voice and lack of logic, he said, "Because I said so, that's why."

"Aw, luh…let him have one," said Benjamin.

"Shut up, stutter-mouth." Arthur squatted with his back against the inside front wall of the fort. "Dad said he's gonna take us to the Pirates this year."

"When?"

"I don't know, sometime."

"No, I mean, when did he suh…say that? I didn't hear him say that."

"You didn't hear it, Benjamin, because he didn't say it to you, he said it to muh…muh…me, stupid stutter-mouth. Hey Alex, don't put that snowball in your mouth." Alex dropped his right arm to his side and peered over his left shoulder. He swung his arm like a catapult and tossed the snowball four feet ahead of him.

"Wow," Arthur said.

"Wow," Benjamin said.

This time, the snowball went a foot farther.

Benjamin stood up to retrieve it. Almost immediately, a snowball with a stone inside caught him flush on the cheek. He went down as if shot. Arthur turned toward where the missile had come from, but as he did, Jackie Walsh rushed the fort from the other side, snatched Alex and ran off across the street.

Arthur knelt down beside his brother. "Benjamin, they got Alex. Stop crying and get up…"

"Boys?" Irene's voice rang out from the house.

"Oh shit," said Benjamin, sobbing. "It's muh…Ma."

Irene walked through the slushy snow in her apron and boots, her hair tied behind her head, with two cups of hot cocoa in hand. "Alex," she called, "time to come in."

The brothers stood side by side at attention. Benjamin held his right hand over his cheek, where a red welt the size of a boy's fist was in bloom. He sniffed back the tears as his mother approached.

Arthur said, "Hi Ma."

She pulled Benjamin's hand away from his face. "Jesus, Joseph and Mary, what happened to you?"

With all the stoicism he could muster, he replied, "Nothing, Ma."

"Don't you nothing me—wait a minute, where is Alex?"

Irene gripped her sons by the wrists, and they marched like a drill team across Mellon Street. Benjamin held a chunk of hardened snow to the side of his face, where the bruise was transitioning its way from red to blue to purple.

Irene banged on the Walsh's front door with the fury of Grendel's mother. Her boys cowered beside her.

The door opened tentatively, as if the occupant was expecting a bill collector. Mrs. Walsh, a graying woman with a matching complexion and a sunken jaw line, thanks to several missing molars, scanned the Miller contingent and said, "What's the trouble?"

"My son. Where is he?"

Mrs. Walsh turned toward the living room. "Jackie! Kevin!"

Voices from inside said, "What, Ma?"

Irene was in no mood to wait for an invitation. She swept by Mrs. Walsh and found the boys sitting on a threadbare sofa with Alex propped between them, his snowsuit pulled down to his waist. The twins teased him with a sugar cookie, holding it above his head, just slightly out of his reach. They'd gotten a good fix on the range of his arms.

Irene said, "Stop it."

The twins froze.

With one swift motion she snatched Alex back and pulled up his snowsuit. As she passed by Mrs. Walsh, who hadn't moved from the threshold, she said, "In the future I'll thank you to tell your boys to keep their grubby hands off my son."

"They're just kids. Don't get so high and mighty, Mrs. Miller."

Irene stopped in her tracks. "What?"

"My boys didn't do nothing wrong, no harm to him. They was just playing with the little freak."

Irene's lightning left hook would have done heavyweight champion Jack Johnson proud. The force of the blow knocked Mrs. Walsh back through the threshold and onto her rear end some six feet away, landing at her sons' feet.

With her hand to her cheek, she said, "You hit me."

"Say another word about my son and I'll hit you again."

Irene marched back across the street. Looking over his mother's shoulders at the twins cowering in their doorway, Alex waved bye-bye. Arthur and Arnold followed, heads downcast, faces grinning.

The sun had gained momentum, and the snow in the street had mostly turned to brownish slush, exposing an amalgam of cinders and horse manure. Without looking at the boys, Irene admonished her sons. "Destroy that fort."

"But Ma."

"You want to get it worse than she did? Wait until your father gets home."

Ten minutes later the fort was slush, too.

Inside, Irene pulled off Alex's snowsuit. She tried three different shirts and sweaters on him. All of them were way too short in the sleeves. She bit her lip. It was true. It was incredible. His arms really had grown. What was next?

Much to their surprise, Arthur and Benjamin didn't "get it worse" that night from their father, as Irene had threatened. Their punishment was limited to the two whacks on the rear end with a broom handle from Irene and an afternoon's confinement to their room, where they were forced to copy over their homework ten times. At dinner that evening, Abe asked about the purple bruise on Benjamin's face. Irene told him something about a snowball fight, leaving out the details of the kidnapping, rescue operation and left hook, lest Abe charge next door to extract even more vengeance on Walsh senior, whom Abe had more than once threatened to flatten like a pancake.

After the dinner dishes were cleared, Irene sent Arthur and Benjamin to their room. She gave Alex some measuring cups to play with while she ran warm water into a washtub for his bath. "Abe," she said, "we have to talk."

From the tone of her voice he thought, look out, here it comes. "Yeah?" he said nervously.

Irene said, "It's about Alex."

"What about him?"

"There's something going on with his body."

"What's wrong with his body?" he asked, feigning concern, although what he really felt was relief that this wasn't going to be about Delia.

"He's growing, Abe."

"Growing? Well that's good, right? See, I told you all he needed was a little time." He turned to Alex. "You're gonna be a big boy after all, right Alex?"

"It's not what you think."

"What the hell are you talking about?"

"I'll show you. Alex? Come here, honey. It's time for your bath." She ran hot water into the kitchen sink and tested it until it was lukewarm. She added a handful of soap flakes. As she lathered up his arms, she said, "Take a look at them."

Alex, standing in the tub, splashed soapsuds at his parents. Thanks to the length his arms, he barely had to bend to reach the water.

Abe pressed Alex's arms to his chest, dampening the front of his shirt. Holy God, he thought, what happened here? "Irene?" He released his son's arms. He'd prayed that the boy would grow, but who could ever imagine he'd grow like this? He looked at Alex dangle his arms in the water. How the hell did they get stretched out like that? It had to be painful. He bent closer. "Alex, do your arms hurt you?"

Alex splashed water in his face.

Chapter 6

Three weeks went by. Alex's condition remained stable. He gave no indication that his long arms bothered him in any way. He continued to scoot and crawl around like a wind-up toy, eat like a small horse and throw whatever objects were handy at his brothers and the cat.

However, his arms pained Irene, constantly. Night after night, she had troubling dreams about Alex, in which his nose grew like Pinocchio's, or his head mushroomed and rotted, or his penis elongated grotesquely, in shades of green and blue.

Abe tried his clumsy best to calm her fears. Since Alex didn't express any discomfort, he was of the opinion that perhaps the boy's condition wasn't a problem after all, that it was just a growth spurt—an odd one, to be sure, but then, hadn't Alex been unusual since the day he was born? Maybe his elongated arms were a forerunner, a harbinger of better things to come, an indication that the rest of his body was bound to catch up sooner or later, and that the best strategy was to keep the whole thing on the Q.T., to wait and see what, if anything else, developed.

Besides, Abe had places to go and people to see, namely Delia Novak. The slip of paper Malkin had given him with her address was burning a hole in his pocket. The question was, how was he going to get out of the house? According to the address, she lived across town, closer to where he worked than to Mellon Street, and Irene barely let him out of the house as it was, although he was damned if he knew why she wanted to keep him home. What the hell was there to do at home? Oh, it was all right playing with Alex and the boys. But after they went to bed, what was he supposed to do with Irene, sit there all night and listen to her complain about the price of chicken and the neighbors that didn't take care of their yards, or her mother's reluctance to give her the good china? As if he cared a rat's asshole about china, or wanted to hear her carp about a loose gutter, a drafty window, the state of the furniture—Christ, it never ended. And if it wasn't that, she was moaning about Alex and his arms, and every time he tried to change the subject to something *he* cared about, something that affected *his* life, like the imbeciles at work and his fat lazy boss who hadn't done a day's work in a year, she told him to keep his mouth shut and quit his whining, he was lucky to have a job. Lucky, huh? Try lathing metal pipe ten hours a day in the heat and stink of summer or the aching cold of winter, with the icy wind blowing in off the river, see how lucky you'd feel.

If he wanted to see Delia, and damn it, he sure wanted to, he had to figure out a way to do it during daylight hours. Shields gave him twenty minutes for lunch. He could take an extra fifteen, maybe even half an hour, if he could get Mougianis to cover for him. Hell, he'd done the dumb Greek plenty of favors, he'd covered his ass plenty of times when the man got so drunk during lunch he could hardly turn on his machine, so the man owed him one. He'd take a ride up to Delia's place, just to take a look-see. She probably wouldn't be there anyway, in the middle of the day, she was a waitress, that's what Malkin had said. He'd leave her a note. He'd written it three times over:

> Dear D,
> Heard you was back in town. Want to see you, if it's all right
> with you, for old time sake. What do you say? Get word to
> Malkin or leave word at The Wheel. Just say when.
> Yours Abe.

And so, a little before noon on January 2, 1910, Abe stood on the platform of the Monongahela Incline on East Carson Street, his collar turned against the chilly, sooty air wafting in off the river, his hand cradling the slip of paper with her address, and he felt in the moment and out of it, as if his body was taking him and the rest was just along for the ride. He wondered what would happen if on the off chance she'd be there when he knocked on her door. Would he stand there, hemming and hawing, hat in hand, or would he rush in and take her on the floor?

A cable car squealed to a stop not ten feet away from his face. Twenty riders sprang from the steel and glass cage, faces flushed with exhilaration and relief that they had made the precipitous ride without incident. A little boy in a hat with dangling earflaps begged his mother please let's do it again, why can't we do it again, please I'll be good, Momma, but Momma was having none of it and deflected his entreaties gently at first and then with more vigor, pulling the boy away by the neck.

Abe handed the conductor a nickel and took a seat against a window. Arthur and Benjamin would get a kick out of riding in this contraption, after all, they were crazy for the roller coasters and all the rides at Kennywood Amusement Park. He'd have to take them on this contraption sometime. Even the little one would be thrilled.

The car filled quickly, with a squat mother and father and six children chattering excitedly in some Eastern European dialect Abe couldn't quite get the hang of. The smallest child stared at him. He felt conspicuous in his blue workshop jacket with "Abe" stitched over the breast pocket.

"All righty, folks," the conductor announced as he closed the metal grate and the heavy sliding door, "there's no getting off now, we're about to set off on a wonderful, remarkable, gravity-defying journey reaching stratospheric heights, leaping forth into the wild blue yonder, clinging by the skin of our teeth to the rocky hillside. You, sir," he continued, pointing to the father, "do you realize the gravity—gravity, get it, that's a joke, sir—of our situation, that we are connected to good old terra firma by nothing more than some heavy gauge steel cables, a steam engine and our faith in the Almighty?"

The man blinked. Two of the smaller girls clung to his side.

The conductor, a one-time stage actor of some local notoriety until drink got the better of him, adjusted his blue uniform cap. "Never mind, sir, because the good Lord in His infinite wisdom is looking out for every mother's son and daughter among us. There are no atheists on board, are there?"

The man blinked again.

Abe said, "I don't think they capiche the language too good."

"You don't say. Nevertheless, let me explain the technicalities of our impending journey, for your edification, sir, if not for theirs. We will be traveling on the diagonal some 635 feet up this small mountain and reach our final destination—not in the metaphorical sense, of course—the Grandview Avenue station, elevation approximately 370 feet, moving at the breakneck speed of six miles per hour. But enough physics for now. Folks, please keep your hands inside the windows unless you want to lose them on the way up, and prepare for perhaps the most exciting two to three minutes of your lives."

The passengers let out a collective *ooh* as the cable car fought to gain traction against gravity. Their trepidation turned to shouts of elation as they eked their way up the hillside. Abe was able to make out the Shields Metal Building, where at this time on any other workday he would have been eating lunch and complaining about the boss with the other stiffs, as the men referred to themselves.

The car thumped to a stop at the top of the hill. The relieved travelers applauded, the father shook the operator's hand, and everyone spilled out onto Grandview Avenue. Abe stood cement-footed in the wind, fingering the slip of paper with Delia's address, wondering whether he should turn back now, return to the ordinary life, to the miserable monotony of days with Irene and the boys, or go through with this, what, this irresistible diversion. He'd heard Davy talk about life-changing moments. He wondered if he were having one now.

A woman pushing a stroller bumped into Abe's calf as she hurried by, tossing an excuse me into the wind. It was enough to prod Abe out of his stupor. He put one foot in front of the other in a stiff-legged march, which in seven minutes brought him to 14 Desdemona Way.

*

As Abe was riding up to meet his short-term fate, Irene was wheeling Alex four blocks to St. Philomena's Church, the scene of so many unhappy childhood memories. She stopped at the neatly shoveled and rock-salted front steps. They were all too familiar. Her mother used to make her say a prayer to the Lord on every step before she entered, as if she were a pilgrim paying homage to a holy shrine. She was sure it was just another ploy her mother used to keep her under her Catholic thumb, but on this day, she said fourteen prayers for Alex, pausing on every step.

When she came to the massive wood and wrought iron front doors, she couldn't go through with it. She remembered Father Kiernan's unfeeling condemnation when she'd married out of the faith—she could only imagine his contempt, had he known she was two months pregnant before her marriage. Good Lord, was she that desperate for someone to talk to about Alex's condition, about Abe's infidelities that she would go to a man of God that had proclaimed her godless? Would he really welcome her back, accept her in his good graces as if she were the prodigal daughter? More likely, he would he subject her to a lecture on the wages of sin. She shuddered, not with the cold but with the shame that she'd come so close to opening herself up to the man. "Alex," she said, "let's go see Nana."

Alex stood up in the stroller, spread apart the fingers of his right hand and made the sign of the cross in the air.

Irene dropped to her knees beside him. "Alex? What did you, how do you know how to do that?"

He repeated the motion.

Oh my God, she thought, what does this mean, he can't possibly understand what he's doing, or what a church is, or what it's supposed to stand for; but what if he does, what does that make him, the Second Coming? No, he was simply waving his arms, babies wave their arms all the time, he waves those long arms of his when he wants something, but God, those long arms.

"Alex, baby boy, are you waving to Momma?" She moved her hand back and forth, up and down.

He waved back.

"Let's leave this old church. Let's go see Nana. Do you want to see Nana, Alex?" Without waiting for an answer, she turned the stroller and hurried away from the church as fast as she could wheel through the slush, the wind cold at her back.

Although his mother couldn't see him do it, Alex crossed himself again.

*

It was warm in the lobby of the apartment building, but Abe had the chills. He stared at the register, and there it was, Apartment 6, Novak, just like Malkin's note said it would be, and he thought there still was time to turn around and walk back into his hum-drum life.

"Can I help you, sir?"

Abe wheeled around.

A short, bald black man with white mutton-chop whiskers stood three feet away, leaning on a long push broom.

"What?"

"My name is Baker, but I ain't no baker. That's just a joke. You need some help finding someone, sir?"

"No."

"'Cause the way you was standing there, you looked lost."

Lost. That was a good word for how he was feeling. "No, I ain't lost, I'm looking for number six."

The man propped the broom against the wall. "Miss Delia."

"Yeah. I got a note for her." As if he were a schoolboy eager to show his hall pass, Abe took it out of his pocket.

"You want me to run it up for you? Tell her you was here?"

"Wait, she ain't here right now, is she?"

The man scratched his head. "Well, sir, unless she jumped out the window, and there ain't no earthly reason why she should, or she done disappeared into thin air, which also ain't likely far as I know, she's right there where she was an hour ago, when I brought her up the newspaper. See, I look after this building for the folks what lives here, doing this and that and whatnot, so I know what this one likes and that one likes, and Miss Delia, she likes to read the paper, which, like I said, I took up to her this morning. Now I'll take that note up to her straightaway if you like." He held his hand out.

"No, that's all right."

"You don't want to give it to her now?"

"No. What I mean is, I'll take it myself."

"All right then. Whatever you say, sir."

They stood facing each other for a moment. Abe figured the man wanted a tip. He tried to hand him a nickel. ""No sir, I don't take no tips, except for Christmas time, no sir, the tenants here, they took real good care of Baker this Christmas, just like Baker takes good care of them, yes sir. Now did you want me to ring that bell?"

*

They were wet with snow flurries by the time they reached her mother's house. Irene rang the bell.

Ida came to the door wearing a white sweater over a plaid housedress and a scowl until she saw Alex. "Look who's here, look who's here!" she said, and the wrinkles around her eyes and the corners of her mouth receded as she scooped up her grandson and walked back inside, leaving Irene in the vestibule with a snow shovel and the empty stroller.

In a little-girl-lost voice, Irene called, "Hi, Ma." She trudged after them into the kitchen. She glanced up at the hand-lettered plaque resting on the molding above the entryway that had been there since she was a child. It read, *No matter where I serve my guests, it seems they like my kitchen best.* She threw her wet coat over a chair.

"Look what Grandma has for you, blessed precious, does Alex like Grandma's extra special rice pudding with cinnamon and sugar on top? Is it sweet enough for the world's sweetest little boy?" She fed him pudding with a demitasse spoon.

"Not too much, Ma. He hasn't had his lunch yet."

"What? It's nearly one o'clock. What kind of mother are you?"

"Ma, please, I don't need this today."

"Well, I'm just wondering, one o'clock and no lunch, the poor thing."
She put him on her lap and began to feed him rice pudding.

Irene watched Alex gobble up the pudding, his skinny little tongue
working like an anteater. She was gratified that her mother's attitude had
softened toward him—who couldn't love him?—even if Ida still treated
Irene like a misguided teenager. "Ma, remember when I was a little girl, you
used to feed me rice pudding and tea and crackers when I had a tummy ache?
And ginger ale, too, and you used to tell me stories about far away lands and
how one day a prince charming would come for me and I'd live happily ever
after. Do you remember, Ma?"

Alex rubbed the pudding cup over his nose and mouth.

"Ma?"

"I don't know, I suppose I did. Why are you bringing this up now?"

Irene put her hands on the sides of her cheeks. "I went to see Father
Kiernan this morning."

Ida wiped Alex's mouth with a checkered napkin. "That nincompoop?
What in the world did you want with him?"

"Because, Ma, you always told me that no matter what happened, you
were always supposed to be able to tell a priest your problems and he would
give you good advice, or comfort, or understanding, no matter what you did,
but Ma, I couldn't go through with it."

"Well, at least that was sensible. If I've told you once, I've told you a
hundred times, Kiernan is an idiot. Now Father Delaney, bless his soul, now
there was a priest you could talk to." Ida remembered the day she sobbed her
heart out to Father Delaney after her son, her precious little boy James, had
taken ill and died of a blood infection when he was just four. What kind of
evil God would do that, she asked him, why would God sear her soul like
that, and although she couldn't recall what Delaney had said that soothed
her, she remembered the mellifluous sound of his voice.

"Ma, don't you want to know why I almost went to see a priest?"

Alex made the sign of the cross.

Ida said, "What's he doing?"

"Never mind him for a second."

"Irene, what is wrong with you?"

"Abe is cheating on me, Ma. Some woman named Delia."

Alex said, "Delia."

"I don't know who she is and I don't care. Alex must have overheard something Abe said, that's why he keeps repeating her name."

"So he's cheating on you? What a surprise."

"I was going ask Father Kiernan how I could get the marriage annulled."

"Annulled?" Ida laughed through her nose. "Oh no, annulment is out of the question. Think of the boys, Irene. Think of your upbringing."

"But what am I gonna do, Ma? I can't live like this."

Ida considered telling her daughter, I knew this day would come, I knew you'd come running to me with your pack of troubles, the whole kit and caboodle, I told you this is what you'd get for marrying out of the true faith, and to a Jew, yet. But beneath the streaking tears, this was her daughter after all, her little girl, her only child, looking as frightened as she did during summer thunderstorms, when she would cower against her skirts, and so Ida began in an unaccustomed softer tongue.

"First of all, Irene, settle down, you're upsetting the baby. Here, wipe your face." She handed Alex's napkin to her. "Now, you listen to me. I'm sure you want to do the most sinful things to him. It's only natural. And it would serve him right. Men are the way they are, and there's no changing their swinish nature. Your father, may he rest in peace, was no exception."

Irene sniffed. "Daddy?"

"Yes, your dear Daddy. He had some floozy in Aspinwall. He thought he could hide it from me—they all do—but I knew. A woman always knows. Come here." She put her arm around Irene's shoulders for the briefest of moments. "But now listen to me. You have to stop feeling sorry for yourself. You're not the first woman in this situation and you won't be the last. You need to do what I did." The words of Father Delaney came rushing back to her. "You must perish murderous thoughts from your mind. You must rise above it. You must be better than he is. And sad to say, of course you can't leave him. For lots of reasons. First, it's against the church. And what if you did? You'd be on your own, and who in God's creation is going to marry a woman with three young boys? You might as well have leprosy, that's how close single men will come to you."

"So what do I do?"

"Think about it, Irene. Let him know who's boss. See how he likes cold dinners and colder sheets." She poured tea for her daughter and herself and added a shot of Irish whiskey to each cup. "Here's to better days, daughter." Her double chin shook a little as she took a deep swallow.

*

The door to number six swung open as soon as he knocked.

"Look at you, Mr. Abraham Miller. Look at you with those big brown eyes."

"Hi, Delia."

"What you gonna do, stand in the doorway? Come over here."

Delia's dark bangs clung to her forehead. She wore her New York City hat and a red silky robe that hung down below her ankles, so that Abe couldn't tell if she were wearing those dark stockings with the seams up the backs, but he sure hoped so.

On the far wall of the flat was a glass and mirror breakfront, her mother's, with a variety of porcelain figurines, also her mother's, on the shelves. In the center of the room, over a faux oriental carpet, was a round coffee table with a fringed tablecloth and a photograph of Delia's parents, sitting ramrod straight, three feet apart on a large stuffed sofa. Next to it was another photo, an eight-by-ten of Delia as a little girl in a buckskin dress, sitting on a pinto pony.

Abe said, "Nice place."

Delia imitated his voice. "Nice place? That's all you got to say to me after all this time?"

"You look good, Dee."

She twirled a lock of hair around her finger. "Damn right I do. So what are you doing all the way over there? Come over here." She tightened the sash of her robe so that her breasts rounded against the material. "You nervous or something? You look like you got the heebie-jeebies."

"No, I'm just...you know."

"Relax, Abe, I won't bite. Unless you want me to."

Abe grinned. It was going to be all right. "That's some nightgown."

"You like it?" She spun around. "Criminy Dutch, you men can be so weird sometimes. I thought you'd be all over me by now." She turned her back to Abe. She took a cigarette from a glass box on the table. Before she could put it to her lips, she watched Abe's hands slip over her breasts from behind. She pressed her hands over his, squeezing and massaging. She ground her buttocks against the front of his trousers, up and down, then in tight circles, her grip on his hands never relaxing. Abe thrust himself against her, and she moved her hips in rhythm. She pulled his right hand into her mouth and sucked his fingers. "Now, this is more like the Abe I know. You like that, don't you? Did you miss me?"

Abe grunted like a Neanderthal in heat. The sound excited her. Abe was a real man, muscle and rough whiskers, not like that prissy pants creep Devon, who was like a fancy dessert, and she was a meat and potatoes kind of gal.

"Does your wife do this for you, does she do things for you like I do, does she?"

The chapel bells at Glory Episcopal Church chimed one o'clock. Delia pulled Abe's hands between her thighs and clamped them. "Does she do this for you? Does she?"

Abe mumbled something about never, never.

She pushed back hard against his thrusts. "Well, well, Mr. Man." She turned and ran her hand against the front of his pants. "What do have we here?"

"You know what it is."

She ran her fingernail over his fly. "Did you miss me?"

"Ever since I heard you come back from New York, you were all I could think of. Hell, even before I knew you was back, not a day went by I didn't think of you. But I figured it was over between us, that you were gone for good, and here I was, a married man with three boys."

"You should have left that pill years ago." She stepped away. "So don't ask me to feel sorry for you."

It hurt Abe to think that maybe it was true, his wife was a bitter pill now, and yet there had been a time before the boys were born, it seemed so long ago, when Irene had been playful, provocative and so pretty. But here he was with Delia Novak, and wasn't that the truth. "All I'm saying is, well, compared to my life, you have it free and easy, you come and go as you please to New York and such, you have no responsibilities, you have no one to answer to."

Delia sat in a chair and crossed her legs, exposing most of her thigh. Her stockings gleamed in the lamplight.

"We all have to answer to ourselves." She lit the cigarette. "But let's not fight, handsome." She crossed the room and sat on his lap, grinding into his crotch until she could feel him rise again. "You know, I met this man in New York, a real gentlemen, with fingernails cleaner than mine, but the whole time I thought, he's sweet, he's charming, he says all the right things, but he don't make my knees feel like jelly the way you do. Maybe it's your equipment, or maybe you remind me of my father, God rest his soul. He had a big one, too."

"What?"

"Just kidding. How the hell would I know that?" She winked. "All I know is you get me hot and bothered, but Abe, listen, I didn't come back to Pittsburgh to be the other woman for the rest of my life. You ain't the only Joe in the world. I could find another one, just like that, at The Wheel or that hash house in Oakland where I work. You know damn well I could. So I gotta know, sweetheart, before you get any more of this," she said, pressing into him a little harder, "I gotta know what your intentions are. That's just the way it is. A girl has to protect herself these days."

"It ain't so easy as you think. I could leave Irene tomorrow if it was just her and me, but you have to realize, I got responsibilities to my sons. And the little one, Alex. I could never leave him."

She told him briefly about her encounter with Irene and Malkin at the Home Town Tavern. "Is he as tiny as ever?"

Yes, Abe said, he still was, but now he was awfully smart. He knew all the names of the players on the Pittsburgh Pirates. He could count, forward and backward. And now, it seemed as if he could read. And even though he never seemed to grow any bigger, all of a sudden his arms grew several inches overnight, and one night he said her name out loud, *Delia*.

"He did?"

"Yes." Abe said that he didn't know what it was, but that there was something magical about him, and that he was going to do something truly amazing, and he sure as hell wasn't going to miss it.

*

On her second cup of tea and whiskey, Irene said, "There's something else, Ma. It's about Alex. He's growing."

"Of course he is. All babies grow."

"You don't understand, Ma. About how he's growing."

Ida watched him play on the floor with a wooden spoon and a potholder. "What about it?"

Chapter 7

Although promising research on immunization had begun in the early 1900s, an effective vaccine to combat diphtheria would not be widely available for many years. In the meantime, the disease worked its way through hundreds of thousands of Americans, killing up to 15,000 people in some years, and was particularly lethal to children and the elderly well into the 1920s.

Pittsburgh in 1911 was a particularly fertile nesting ground for "The Dip," as it was commonly referred to with a mixture of dread and gallows humor. The Dip entered the Smokey City on the broad backs of newly arrived workingmen and their families, since at the time there was an unprecedented industrial boom and Pittsburgh needed all the muscle it could get. The word had gone forth to immigrant neighborhoods up and down the East Coast, and to those just off the boat: Come to Pittsburgh, there's work a-plenty. And come they did, with their skills, their strengths and their infectious diseases.

Arthur and Benjamin Miller, who'd been suffering with hacking coughs, were among 35 children at Fulton Elementary School sent home on March 10, 1911, by Rose Thompson, school nurse. The unhappy diagnosis: The Dip. The instructions were to keep them isolated for a minimum of two weeks and hope for the best.

Irene quarantined her sons in their room on the left side of the second floor. She'd never seen them look so miserable. Even Arthur, who insisted he was too big to be hugged and kissed by his mother, begged her to hold his hand.

She settled Arthur on the bottom bunk and Benjamin on the top. It was such a small room for the two of them, with two dressers, a toy chest and a secondhand desk with uneven legs that caused it wobble even though she'd been on Abe to fix it. She was on Abe for any number of things, but nothing ever seemed to get done unless she did it.

Alex's little bed sat in the far corner. She cracked open the single window a few inches. She wanted to leave the door open, too, to let out the mustiness, but she was afraid that somehow The Dip might float down the stairs, seeking out the rest of the family like a hungry, ghostly beast, so she kept it shut tight, even when she was inside, changing their sweaty bedclothes, mopping their fevered brows and trying to cheer them as best she could through their delirium. It was strange, she thought, it was now that she realized how much she loved them. She wished she'd told them more often. She vowed to tell them that she loved them every day if they pulled through.

As worried as she was for the boys, she believed their toughness and shoe leather constitutions could withstand anything The Dip could throw at them. It was Alex for whom she feared the worst. She was certain The Dip could clog and silence his little lungs at its pleasure. Even at three years old—or three quarters, as he and his brothers would say—Alex now weighed just a touch over sixteen pounds, so how could his puny body fight it off? She resolved to have him sleep in her room and move his playthings downstairs to the kitchen, where he'd be away from his brothers, and where she could keep an eye on him.

Even under normal conditions, Alex hated to be separated from Arthur and Benjamin. He pouted at the kitchen window when they marched off to school with their rarely opened books bound in straps slung over their shoulders, while he was left behind in the kitchen with his mother and Tippy the tuxedo cat, who hid from him as much as possible, as if in her walnut-sized brain she sensed there was something odd and vaguely dangerous about the little boy that weighed just two pounds more than she did and threw forks, bits of food and his socks at her head.

Alex listened patiently as Irene explained the dangers of The Dip. When she told him about the new sleeping arrangements, he tossed his breakfast on the floor and refused to get dressed. It wasn't until Irene let him help her load plates of food into his red wagon, which she hauled in to feed his brothers, that he settled down. He added Arthur's ball and jacks and Benjamin's rabbit's foot to the pile of food.

*

During the quarantine, as Irene cooked and emptied chamber pots, Alex sat on the linoleum floor or in his little wooden chair in a corner of the kitchen, with two thin books his grandmother had given him: *A Child's Life of Christ* by WB Conkey, and *The Coloured Picture Bible for Children*. Furiously pressing with Arthur's crayons, he colored the black and white illustrations: orange and purple for Crowning With Thorns, blue and green for The Last Supper, red and yellow and black for The Resurrection. He showed his fledging artwork to Irene.

"Oh my goodness, Jesus has a green and purple face."

"Do you like it, Momma?"

"Wait until I show your grandmother. She'll hit the ceiling."

Alex dropped the crayons on the floor. He plopped the book on his knees and traced his fingers along the letters. To Irene, it looked as if he were reading.

He was. The letters formed words in his mind, and on his lips. He voiced them quietly, matching them to the pictures. He wondered who these men really were; if they lived on Mellon Street, why hadn't he seen them? Some of them seemed nice. He pointed to the figures on the page and asked Irene why, when everyone else was so big, the baby Jesus so little, like he was. Irene told him it was only a story.

"But Momma, does baby Jesus ever get big?"

"Well, yes. He grows up to be a man."

"Will I grow up like baby Jesus?"

She thought about how he'd made the sign of the cross. "I think you just might."

*

After eight days of wheeling in meals and wheeling out chamber pots, applying cold rags and removing sweaty underwear, reading to them from *The Adventures of Robinson Crusoe* and listening to them bang on the door when they wanted more food, Irene was pretty sure her boys had emerged from the depths of The Dip none the worse for wear. Their fevers were long gone, and to counteract the boredom of mandatory confinement, they'd actually begun to read their schoolbooks and write out their arithmetic homework problems. Irene couldn't be sure if Benjamin was doing both his and Arthur's. She wouldn't put it past Arthur to coerce Benjamin into it.

Dr. Malkin stopped in on the ninth day of their illness. The Dip had been very good to him, for healthy physicians were much in demand. Even educated people who normally knew better had requested his services, and for once he could name his price for a house call.

He went into the boys' room, made his way through a jumble of clothes and toys and littered plates and had them strip to the waist. His listened to their hearts and lungs and made them say "ah." He jammed his otoscope into Benjamin's ear, not knowing precisely what he was looking for, but as long as he owned the tool he felt he might as well use it.

Malkin insisted that he examine Alex, too. "Let us be it on the safer side. I must tell it to you, I wonder how is it, Mrs. Irene, that your bigger boys caught it The Dip, but this little one, with his teensy system and the infection running its way around in your house, a mystery to me it is why he wasn't struck down like a sledgehammer to the head. But he has got no sickness, it seems, not even a tiny bit, he looks to be it in the perfect health, which is of course to his good fortune."

"Maybe God looks out for him, Doctor."

"This could be, Mrs., the powers of God the Almighty, that is something which I respect it, but it is beyond my training as medical doctor. Still, it is a curiosity to me, in the medical sense, of course, of how he avoided it this plague." He repeated his request. "May I have it then a moment, if you please, with your Alex, for to give it to him a precautionary examination?"

"I'm not paying extra."

"No, but of course not." He turned to Alex. "Hello there, my little fellow."

Alex stuck out his tongue. His brothers had told him Malkin was a greenhorn, and although he didn't know what it meant, he understood by the way they said it that the doctor was some sort of undesirable.

Malkin pressed his index fingers on either side of Alex's throat, where he believed he would find the thyroid gland, or perhaps it was the pituitary, he sometimes confused the two, but he was virtually certain one or the other or perhaps both were essential for growth. If only he had more time with this little thing, he could do experiments and make a study that could put his name out there in the journals, put him in demand for speaking engagements, medical conferences, fat royalties. If only his family would cooperate and let him have his way, the medical community might come to know and respect the name Sergei Malkin.

He told Alex to say ah, and as he tried to insert a tongue depressor Alex bit down on his finger. His brothers cheered him on.

Malkin stuck his finger in his mouth. "Ouch, he broke it the skin, the little…let us hope it mine hand to God he is not a carrier of The Dip, even though he is not infected as far as I can tell." He wiped his finger with a blotted handkerchief. "Perhaps it is a good idea the little fellow should wear it a muzzle next time I examine him."

Irene said, "Perhaps next time you'll keep your fingers where they belong." She coughed dryly.

Arthur whispered to Benjamin, "Up his ass."

Benjamin laughed and coughed until he was out of breath.

Malkin stowed his stethoscope in his bag. No sense offending the woman, not if he hoped to get Alex into his surgery at some point. "Well, I can see it by their laughter the boys are feeling fine, for laughter it is always a good sign. In fact, some will say it that laughter is the best medicine. Which would put it a doctor like me out of business. Ha ha ha, it is my joke, no?"

Irene and the boys stared silently at him.

"Well, that will be all for today. The fee is one dollar. Please."

No sooner had the boys recovered from The Dip than it hit Irene like a *force majeure*. Her fever reached 103 on the second night of her illness, and in her delirium she wailed for Alex, but Abe had enough sense not let him go near her, despite his son's attempts to crash through the door to her bedroom.

After he got Alex to calm down, Abe went into their bedroom with a bowl of chicken soup from a pot her mother had delivered earlier that afternoon. He assured her that she would be all right, not to worry, that she'd come out of this fine and dandy, that she was a strong woman, and he meant it, but yet, as he looked at her pale, sweating face, he wondered with a mixture of guilt and excitement what his life might be like if she were to die right then and there. He'd be free and clear from her constant nagging, yes, but on the other hand, how would things really change? He'd be saddled with raising three boys alone, and not easy boys at that, the older one a troublemaker already, the younger one a good student, but that stuttering of his. And then,there was Alex. How the hell would he manage all that, would he have to take another wife, and what kind of woman would sign on for this, and what if the new wife was worse than the old one? It made his head hurt, and he hoped he wasn't getting The Dip, too. As for Delia, well, even with Irene gone, he couldn't imagine her becoming mother to his three sons. She simply wasn't the motherly type. She'd cut him off, anyway, complaining she was too tired from waitressing and too tired of him making excuses why he couldn't get out to see her. They were, as she put it, on ice for now.

Irene coughed and cried for her mother, but momentarily forgetting his fear of The Dip, he took her hot hand for a second. He felt if he held it any longer The Dip would seep through her skin and into his, so he let it fall by her side. As much as he felt sorry for her, he was terrified like everyone else of falling to the plague. Before he went downstairs, he washed his hands three times.

At the dinner table, Arthur said, "Dad, Mom is going to die, isn't she?"

Benjamin said, "Sha...shut up, Arthur. You don't na-know anything."

Abe glanced from one boy to the other, his rapidly growing Irish-Jewish hybrids, with Irene's light coloring and reddish hair, their round faces interrupted by his hooked nose. He spooned more mashed potatoes on their plates. "Now, boys, you know your mother is one tough cookie. She's tough on you, ain't she? She'll be fine, you mark my words, once The Dip runs out of steam, all right? You boys beat it, didn't you? Anyway, mothers don't die from The Dip. You stop your worrying now and eat your dinner. More green beans?"

"But Mrs. Cleary on Haw...haw...Hawthorne Street. She's a mother and she died."

"Mrs. Cleary? I don't know no Mrs. Cleary."

"Agnes Cleary is in my class," Arthur continued. "Her mother died last week on account of The Dip and they kept Agnes out of school for the funeral. And her grandmother died, too. She said so."

Abe pointed his fork at Arthur. "Well, that don't mean that's going to happen to your mother, you hear me?"

Benjamin fidgeted in his chair. "Dad, what happens when you duh...die?"

Abe stared blankly at his son. Irene, he thought, she'd be the one to answer a question like this. "What kind of question is that?"

"But what happens?"

"Benjamin, a boy your age don't need to think about such things as dying. You should be thinking about baseball, see? How about those Pirates, huh? 1909 world champs. Last year wasn't so hot, but think can win it again this year? That Chief Wilson, he sure can pitch, can't he, huh?"

"Dad..."

"Look, son, you didn't die from The Dip, did you?"

"But what happens?"

Abe desperately searched for his inner metaphysician. What did Judaism have to say on the subject of Heaven and hell, death and damnation? Damned if he could remember. Not that he ever really knew. Actually, the religion didn't have much to say about the afterlife, not that he knew that. He did remember something about life being like a passing shadow. Then there was all that voodoo—Jew voodoo, his uncle once called it—about the Red Sea and the Burning Bush and Noah's Ark and one drop of oil lasting a week. He sighed. "Look, nothing happens. You're alive one minute and then you're not. You see what I mean?"

"But wuh…what about Heaven?" Benjamin said. "Do we guh…go to Heaven? Ma said when Frisky died, Frisky went to Heaven."

"Well, see? Like I always say, listen to your mother."

Arthur sneered. "Ma said that just to make you stop crying, Benjamin. Frisky was a hamster. Hamsters don't go to Heaven. You only go to Heaven if you're a human being and you're good, but if you're not, you go to Hell."

Alex said, "Go to Hell."

"Now you watch your mouth, buster. You see what you boys are teaching him?"

"But it's true, dad. When you're bad you go down below, the Devil sticks his pitchfork in you to torture you and then you burn in a fire, but you don't really burn up, you just keep burning."

Benjamin was on the edge of tears. "I don't want to burn."

Abe thought about his own flesh rotting in the grave, worms crawling through his eyeballs. He wondered if it was painful, or slimy—just how would it feel? And the cold, and the darkness, and the silence. He shivered. "Yeah, well then, you better be good boys so you don't end up there, so you go up to Heaven and meet up with God."

When he heard the word *God*, Alex remembered a page in his Life of Christ book and said, "And sit at God's right hand." He made the sign of the cross in the air.

"Alex? Arthur, what's he doing?"

Alex said, "There's a picture in the book."

"What book?" Abe said.

Alex held up his *Child's Life of Christ.*

"Where the hell did you get that?"

"Grandma gave it to me."

*

On the third day of her illness, Irene hovered between bad and worse. Around nine in the morning, after Abe had left for work and the older boys were off to school, she thought she might go downstairs and make herself a cup of tea, but she was so wobbly on her feet she tripped over the belt of her bathrobe. She lay on the floor for what seemed like an hour to her, until her head cleared enough for her to get back into bed. She managed a few swallows of tepid water and some oyster crackers, which stuck halfway down her red, raw throat. A plate of eggs and potatoes sat on her night table, the breakfast Abe had left for her, but the thought of eating it made acid rise in her throat. He'd told her that her mother would be watching Alex, but in her fevered state she couldn't be sure if he said her mother was coming or was already here. She noticed a stale smell, then realized it was coming from her and remembered that she hadn't so much as washed her face for what was it, two days or three? Her flannel gown was damp around the neck. She longed for something to read, a mystery, a romance, a cookbook, a Sears catalog, the Bible, even, just something to pass the dizzy monotony of time.

A noise came from downstairs. It sounded like her mother's voice, saying something to Alex. She loved him so much, more than the other boys, she had to admit to herself. Who else did she love? Her bigger boys, yes, in a fundamental way, but they didn't clutch her heart like Alex did. Abe? Maybe at one time there was something close to love, but even that glimmer had faded years ago. Her mother? Did her mother ever love her? Not like she loved her boys. Her mother wasn't capable.

She pulled the blanket up to her chin. It would be warm out soon, wouldn't it, warm enough to turn the soil in the garden plot? She resolved to plant more flowers this year. She would give Alex his own section of dirt. Oh, she couldn't wait to tell him, to see his little features light up. He could wear his Rough Riders cowboy hat to keep the sun off his face. Beans. He could plant beans and it would be like Jack and the Bean Stalk and he could climb up and find the treasure.

But some day, not so far away, she would have to send her fairy tale boy off to school, but then, how could she? Even though he was smart as a whip, she knew all about the mean things boys could and would do to someone so little, and his big brothers wouldn't always be there to protect him.

A fly landed on her water glass. She coughed, and one cough led to another, and it was several seconds before she caught her breath. Her lungs ached so much her eyes teared over.

She heard Alex say, "Don't cry, Momma."

Although her eyes were filmy, she could see that he was sitting on the floor next to the foot of the bed. She wanted to grab him and hug him tight to her chest, but she knew that she couldn't, that he shouldn't even be in the room with her, and how in God's name had he gotten in? Where was her mother, who was supposed to be taking care of him? She picked up the little bell from night table and rang it as hard as she could, hoping desperately her mother would hear. In between rings, she said, "Alex, you have to stay away from Momma, sweetheart."

"Can I read you a story?"

Read me a story? Since when could he read? Had she taught him? In her feverish state of mind, she couldn't remember. He knew his letters, but reading, it didn't seem likely, yet with The Dip swimming in head, she couldn't be sure one way or the other, maybe her mother had taught him, or his brothers, so maybe he really could read. "Yes. Read me a story, Alex."

From *A Child's Life of Christ*, Alex read, "'Very far from our own country lies the land where Jesus Christ was born.' And there's a picture, Momma. Want to see?"

Before she lost awareness, Irene had an image of a bright and sunny garden, with roses and tulips wet with dewdrops, and Alex standing in the center, straight and seven feet tall, in a white robe with a chain of flowers around his neck.

Chapter 8

His long arms easily reached the top of the bed, even though he was a head short of the mattress. Mommy didn't smell like Mommy, he thought, not like her usual vanilla and soap smell. It was a smell he didn't like, and though he knew something was wrong he had to be with her just the same.

He'd worked his way to the front of the bed when Ida lifted him away by the armpits. "Alex, come away from there. Good Lord."

He began to cry, why wouldn't she let him be with Mommy? "Let me go, I want Momma."

"You can't, not now, sweetheart. You don't want to catch The Dip, do you? Plus, can't you see your momma is sleeping?"

As she came down the stairs with Alex in one arm, she traced her hand over the banister, noting with disdain how dusty it was, it probably bred diseases, but then, how much cleaning could she expect from her daughter, who was, after all, flat on her back, and her slob of a husband, he wouldn't lift a finger to do any housework on a bet. No, he left the mess to his mother-in-law.

She put Alex on the kitchen floor with his book and crayons and a sugar cookie. Before too long, Arthur and Benjamin would burst in the door, clamoring for lunch. She tied one of Irene's aprons around her back. It had been a long time since she'd prepared meals for anyone but herself, and her needs were simple. She ate much the same thing every day—a poached egg and toast for breakfast, with tea; a ham and cheese sandwich for lunch, with relish and canned fruit; and a pork roast or a roast chicken for dinner, always with potatoes, or leftovers from the day before, and invariably fish on Fridays. If she felt like it, she'd make a pie or a cake or some soda bread. It was boring and predictable, just the way she liked it.

Hands on hips, she surveyed the mess in the kitchen. If the Lord could create an orderly world, The Light from the Darkness on Day One, The Firmament between Heaven and Earth on Day Two, and so on, then she could surely create order from this kitchen chaos. God wanted us to have order in our lives, she was certain, and she was about to give it to this family. But first she had to check on Alex. She pulled his pants out from the waist and sniffed. Well, she wouldn't have to change him, at least not for the time being. She'd have to ask Irene if he were potty-trained. She hoped to God he was.

She had just finished alphabetizing Irene's spices when the kettle hissed. A cup of tea with a bite of old Bushmills would hit the spot. But maybe she'd hold off until after lunch, when Alex took his nap and the boys went back to school. She rummaged around the icebox for cheese and bread.

"Grandma?"

He held up his book. "What's loaves and fishes?"

*

Half an hour later, as Ida was putting a cold washrag on Irene's forehead, she heard Arthur and Benjamin pounding up the stairs.

"Ma!"

"Shh!" she hissed.

Arthur looked past his grandmother. "She ain't dead, is she?"

"Arthur!"

"But she's just lying there."

"She's sleeping."

Benjamin moved to his mother's side. "Buh...but she's not dead, right?"

"I already told you. Now, you two be quiet and go back downstairs. Your lunch is on the table."

"Yes, ma'am."

They devoured two sandwiches each, six pickles, a bowl of baked beans, four cookies and four glasses of milk. Like a plague of locusts, Ida thought.

Arthur rinsed his plate in the sink. "Grandma?"

"What is it now?"

He placed his plate in the sink. "There's a school fair this afternoon. Me and Benjamin, we saved up allowance for the games and everything so we don't need no money."

"You don't need *any* money."

"No, ma'am."

"And we promised Alex we would tuh...take him."

"Now, just a minute."

"Mom said we could, didn't she, Benjamin?"

Even though their mother had said no such thing, Benjamin knew better than to disagree with his older brother. He nodded.

"Well, I don't know, it's too far for him to walk. You'll have to use the carriage."

"No, see, we'll take him in the wagon. He likes to ride in the wagon, don't you, Alex?" said Arthur, ever the consensus builder.

Alex relished the opportunity to go anywhere with his brothers. "I want to ride in the wagon."

It was hard to resist the notion of having a quiet afternoon, with maybe a chance to take off her shoes and enjoy her regular nap before getting dinner ready. She knew she should check with her daughter first to corroborate the boys' story—they were little schemers with their blank expressions, those two—but then again, what harm could come of going to a school fair, it wasn't as if they were off to play cards or dice in some back alley. She looked at her watch. "You be home by three or there'll be hell to pay. You two understand?"

"Yes, ma'am. Come on, Alex."

*

A persistent cold rain had driven the school fair from the playground to the gym. Benjamin and Arthur carried the wagon with Alex inside, down the steps, with Alex straddling the length of the wagon, his arms balancing on either side. As soon as they put him down, a group of little girls rushed up to them, shrieking, begging to see their baby brother, he's so cute, he's so cute, can we pick him up? He was a bigger attraction than a box of puppies. Alex smiled benignly, as if he were royalty indulging his loyal subjects. He liked the attention, and he liked how the little girls smelled, so much better than his brothers, so he let himself be picked up and hugged, over and over.

A variety of games and booths had been set up throughout the gym. Mothers and grandmothers sold cookies, brownies, turnovers, nuts, jawbreakers, licorice, popcorn, taffy apples, crackerjack and cups of apple cider. There were the obligatory games of chance: a small roulette wheel, a knock-down-the-milk-bottle booth, pin the tail on the donkey for the younger children. The races were to begin at one o'clock—the balloon race, the sack race, the three-legged race and the human wheelbarrow. Arthur and Benjamin had practiced hard for that one. Benjamin had deep scrapes on his fingertips and the heels of his hands.

Mrs. Colter, the science and math teacher, had brought in a cage of guinea pigs, which the children poked at with their fingers and the straws from their drinks. In a glass aquarium next to the guinea pigs was a two-foot green garter snake coiled up in the corner. Arthur tapped on the glass to see if he could get the snake to move until Mrs. Colter pulled his hand away.

The star of the fair was Coco, a capuchin monkey. Attached by a leather strap that stretched from her harness to the wrist of her owner, Carmine Tucci, Coco wasn't just cute. She was a working pet. When she wasn't picking at her anus she snatched hats, balloons and anything else she could get her paws on, including Mrs. Colter's glasses, which she jerked right off her nose and wouldn't give back until Carmine gave her a hunk of banana. Benjamin said that he thought it was mean to keep Coco tied up. Alex watched Coco intently, mimicking her motions with his long arms.

They had what they considered a king's ransom between them—fifty-seven cents. It was the money they'd saved from their infrequent allowances and odd jobs around the neighborhood, and they weren't about to let a fortune like that sit around in their pockets collecting lint. Leaving Alex to his new coterie of big sisters, they jostled each other for a chance to step right up and place their bets on the roulette wheel. After losing half their fortune in five minutes, Benjamin took a nickel and bought five peanut butter cookies while Arthur decided enough with roulette, it was time to knock down the milk bottles. There were valuable prizes to be had, including a genuine scout compass and a bag of marbles. Arthur was about to toss his third baseball when screams came from the general direction where they'd left Alex. Benjamin said, "Oh, no."

They rushed across the gym only to find that things were just fine. Mary Louise Calkins went up to Arthur and said, "Your little brother is so smart. He just recited the alphabet and then he did it backward. Isn't he the berries?"

"I taught him how," Arthur lied, hoping his brother's talent would improve his social status with Mary, the prettiest, most popular girl in his class.

"Say now, what's all the ruckus about over here in these here parts?" It was Principal Darwimple, a.k.a. "Farmer Dar," as he had named himself for the day.

For reasons known only to himself, Principal Frederick Darwimple, a fastidious bachelor in his mid-30s, had abandoned his customary dark three-piece suit, white shirt and bow tie and had dressed for the day as a farmer, or what he imagined was a farmer, with a round straw hat, denim overalls and a plaid shirt. The corncob pipe he clenched between his teeth lent a final touch of pseudo authenticity. The children were much more accepting of his get-up than the grown-ups, where the whispered consensus among parents and faculty was that he looked like a fool.

"Land sakes alive, what do we have here," he said, pointing his pipe toward Alex, who stood in the center of his adoring circle.

"Nothing, sir," Arthur said. "It's just my little brother Alex. He wasn't doing anything."

Principal Darwimple took off his straw hat with an exaggerated swoop intended to produce giggles—it did—and wiped his forehead with his checkered handkerchief. "Tarnation," he said, trying to affect what he believed to be a southern/country accent, even though he'd never been farther south than Wheeling, West Virginia, "if he ain't the gol-dangest little feller I ever laid eyes on. Well, howdy do, buckaroo."

Alex said, "Howdy do."

Over the children's laughter, Darwimple said, "Well now, ain't he just the cat's pajamas. And how old are you, Alex?"

"Three quarters."

"Come again, son."

Benjamin said, "He was born on Leap Year day. That's why he says it like that, sir. He's really three."

"Clever little buckaroo, aren't you, Mr. Alex? Maybe Farmer Dar will be seeing our young cowpoke here at our fine school in a few years. Would you like that, Alex?"

Alex liked Farmer Dar, and he liked the idea of being in school with all the children. "If my momma lets me." The children laughed again.

"Alex, I think you'll find that Fulton Elementary is the finest school in these here parts. Isn't that right, children?"

In a desultory chorus, the children replied, "Yes, Principal Darwimple."

"Well, all righty then."

"Principal...er, Farmer Dar?" It was Mrs. Stanczak, the principal's secretary. "We need you over here."

"Hold your horses, woman, I'm a coming." He turned his back and waved at a group of children and adults standing at the starting line across the gym. "Boys and girls, I have to leave you now. It's time ol' Farmer Dar commenced to getting this here show on the road."

A whistle blared on the other side of the gym. Everyone looked that way except Alex. Faster than you could say monkey see, monkey do, he reached out with his left arm and snatched Darwimple's wallet from his back pocket. Only Benjamin saw it.

The kids ran off to watch the sack race, led by the Walsh brothers. Benjamin held Arthur back by the elbow.

"What?"

"Alex."

"What about him? He's okey dokey here for a minute…" It certainly looked as if Alex were fine, standing in the wagon, brownie icing smeared on his cheek.

"Arthur, Alex…he…he stole."

Arthur put his hand over his brother's mouth. He looked at Alex, who was holding the brownie with two hands. "What are you talking about?"

"He stole Principal Darwimple's wallet." He explained Alex's cobra-quick pilfering.

"Where is it?"

Benjamin looked down. "In the wagon. See?" He pointed to a dark leather wallet lying on top of Alex's blanket.

"We gotta get out of here." He grabbed the front of the wagon. "Hold on, Alex. Benjamin, pick up the back."

*

It was a little after two when the boys got back. They slipped past their sleeping grandmother and up to their room. Arthur sat Alex on the top bunk and ordered Benjamin to jam a sweater into the open space at the bottom of the door so they couldn't be surprised.

He opened Principal Darwimple's wallet. He counted out three one-dollar bills and eighty-seven cents in the change compartment. The miniscule fortune made his head swim. It was more money in his hand than he'd ever held before. He fingered the bills over and over, magic treasures.

"We have to take it buh…back," Benjamin said.

"What?"

"It's stuh…stealing."

"Shut up. Hey, look at this."

Arthur undid the photo compartment. There was a school identification card with the principal's name and address, 1214 Hazlett Street, which was about two miles away from Mellon. There also were two photographs. The first was an older woman in a long dark dress puffed out with petticoats, and standing next to her was a man with a black suit and a white clerical collar. On the back, in blurred handwriting it said, "To our beloved son." The other photo showed a tall, slim man in his 30s, with dark hair slicked back, dressed in tennis whites and holding a racket slung over his shoulder. The inscription on the back read, "To my dear Dar, from you know who." The other item was a laundry claim ticket from Hong's Laundry and Cleaners.

"Arthur, we can't keep it."

Arthur said, "Are you crazy?" He told him he was nothing but a big chicken, cluck cluck cluck, and besides, finders keepers, loser weepers, and that they really didn't steal it at all, Alex stole it, he pick-pocketed it, and what could they do to Alex, he was too little and he didn't know any better, and he didn't even go to school so they couldn't throw him out.

Benjamin countered that it still wasn't right, and that if Arthur wouldn't tell what had happened, he would, at which point Arthur put him in a combination headlock/chokehold until Benjamin turned beet red. He promised his younger brother a multitude of additional, more painful consequences if he didn't keep his stupid mouth shut. "Three dollars and eighty-seven cents, dummy. We could get Pirates tickets, and ice cream and peanuts. You want to give it back? Don't be a stupid baby." He turned to Alex. "Did you like the fair, Alex?"

"Yes."

"How did you know how to take Principal Darwimple's wallet?"

"Just like Coco," Alex said. He made a quick, grabbing motion.

"What's he talking about, Benjamin?"

"He means the monkey."

"Oh yeah, like Coco. Say listen, Alex. Do you think you can do it again, like Coco? It'll be like a game you play. You like games, right?"

"I like to play checkers."

"Yeah, I like checkers, too. But this is a different game. Do you know what that game is called?"

Alex said, "What?"

"It's called Five Fingers."

"Come on, Arthur."

"Just shut your trap. Tomorrow is Saturday. No school. We'll go to East

Liberty and play Five Fingers."

Alex said, "With Farmer Dar?"

Arthur laughed. "No, he won't be there, but it'll be fun, you'll see." Arthur stuck his index finger into Benjamin's chest. "You're coming, too."

Alex began to hop up and down. "I want to play checkers."

"You heard him, Benjamin. Set up the board."

"But all he does is throw the pieces on the floor."

"I said, set it up."

Arthur shoved the money under the felt lining of a box where they kept their school papers. With huge satisfaction he watched Alex's long arms snatch checker pieces. Saturday was going to be a big day.

Chapter 9

Abe smoked in the family's lone armchair, content to read *The Daily Dispatch* until his mother-in-law put dinner on the table, not feeling guilty for not helping since he'd offered and she'd told him he'd only mess things up. Alex climbed on his lap and begged him to read his favorite comic strip, *Pickles Neary*, to him, but unfortunately for both Alex and Abe, Pickle's strip appeared only in the Sunday edition, so Abe had to amuse his son by reading an account of a rooming house fire in Hazelwood that took the lives of seven women. It occurred to him after the second paragraph that perhaps it was a bit inappropriate to read a story about death and disaster to a three-year-old whose mother was seriously ill, which reminded him that he needed to check on her. He left Alex standing on the floor above the newspaper he spread out in front of him.

"Daddy," Alex called, pointing to a column in the newsprint, "what's investigation?"

Abe started to answer, but then he stopped. Had Alex really read that? That children's book was one thing, but the newspaper? That was for adults. Little did Abe know that *The Daily Dispatch* was purposely written to be easily comprehended by the average fourth-grader.

He watched Alex's eyes scan the page. It sure looked as if he was reading. But no, he must just be repeating a word he'd read to him. "Hold on a minute, son. I have to go investigate your mother." He shook his head at his attempt at humor as he climbed the stairs with a tray of food. He wished he were taking it up to Delia after they'd made love.

*

Whether it was the heavy congestion in her throat or the stale air in the room, Irene felt that if she didn't open a window she would suffocate. She swung her legs to the side of the bed and put one foot down on the floor, then the other, and pushed herself to her feet. She opened the curtains and undid the lock on top of the window sash. Down below, in the fading light, she could make out toys scattered in the yard. Irene felt a sliver of hope, for at least she had gotten to her feet on her own without falling, which was more than she had been able to accomplish the day before. She tried to raise the window, and it took all of her strength to lift it three inches. The cool air felt lush on her hands, alive with its dampness.

The door opened. Abe entered with a mug of tea, two slices of buttered toast, a hard-boiled egg on a tray and an admonishment. "Irene, what you doing, woman? You know you're not supposed to be out of bed."

She said in a low, labored voice, "I couldn't breathe hardly."

"You should've asked me, I would've opened it for you."

It would have taken too much energy to explain she was too tired to call him, so she let it go. A low cough stirred from deep in her lungs, and she pressed the back of her hand to her mouth. "You shouldn't stay here too long." She motioned to her night table. "Put the tray over here."

Abe took away the tray of uneaten food he'd left her the night before and set down the fresh one. "Geez, Irene, you gotta try to eat something. You gotta have strength to fight this thing."

You fight it, she thought. You're good at fighting. She grasped the windowsill to keep from falling. "Is my mother here?"

"She's getting dinner ready."

The room was still except for the wheezing of her breath. They stood twelve feet apart, and they thought, this is what we have to say to each other after one year of courtship, ten years of marriage, two boys, two miscarriages and then a strange little miracle child who is here for some purpose we don't understand. "How are my sons?"

"They're fine. Just fine. They went to the school fair today. They took Alex."

"What?"

"They rode him over there in the wagon. He's fine. He said he saw a monkey."

The room began to reel around in her head. She clutched the bedpost to keep from falling. "But he's too little."

"Come on, Irene," Abe said, "nothing happened. His brothers look out for him, you know."

"Please," she begged, "please bring him home."

Abe sighed. "But he is home."

"He is? Oh yes, you said he is." She walked back to the bed. "I better lie down now."

Abe started for the door. "Well, call me if you need anything."

Irene stared at him. "Abe."

"What is it?"

"Could you come over here?" She held out her hand. "Did you ever love me?"

Abe looked out the window. "What kind of question is that?"

"Did you?"

He glanced down at his feet, then back into her eyes. "Didn't I tell you I did? Remember that time in your room when your mother was away, how much I told you that you were the only one for me?"

"Yes. Was that love?"

"And what about the day we were married?"

"You're supposed to say it when you get married."

"Come on, Irene. There've been plenty other times, too."

If she had pressed him, he might have had trouble coming up with another example. But instead, she said, "Say it now. I don't even care if you mean it." She adjusted the pillow behind her head.

He mumbled into his chest, "I love you."

"I wonder."

Abe turned red. "I do."

"Sure you do, don't be upset, I don't want you to get angry. I couldn't take it right now." She took a sip of tepid water. "Bring Alex up to me, will you?"

"But you don't want him to catch The Dip."

She slumped back into bed. "I don't know why, but I don't think he can."

Ida's voice echoed up the stairs. "Soup's on!"

Abe turned toward the door, the call a reprieve. "I'll bring him up after dinner, all right?"

"Please."

He turned to leave.

"Abe?"

"Yeah?"

"Thank you for saying it." Fight it, she thought. Fight it for your sons. She forced a slice of egg and some tea down her throat before she gave herself up to the loopy feeling in her head.

*

Abe and the boys sat around the table, bowls of pea soup in front of them. He watched Alex dip a toy soldier in his applesauce. "Tell me, Arthur, how was the fair?"

Arthur looked at Benjamin, whose eyes stayed glued to his bowl. "Fine."

"That's it? Let's have a little conversation around here."

Alex said, "I saw Coco the monkey."

"You did, son? Do you like him?"

"He smelled like poop."

Arthur and Benjamin started to laugh.

"All right, that's enough, you two." Ida sat down with her soup. "Arthur, put that spoon down. We haven't said grace. Who wants to say it?"

The boys looked at each other.

Abe felt like he was back at his Uncle Jacob's dinner table twenty years earlier, where every meal was preceded by his uncle going on and on with his Hebrew prayers, and he wasn't allowed to touch anything before Jacob finished, no matter how hungry he was, or else he'd get a slap on the back of the hand, which was just another reason why Abe wanted nothing to do with all that religious hooey. He just wanted to sit down and eat his meal. But then, he thought, Ida did cook for us; it wouldn't be so bad just the one time. "Arthur, go ahead."

"What?"

"Say it. You heard me."

"But I don't know how. Why can't Benjamin do it?"

"Me?"

Ida said, "Well, if none of you heathens is willing to say grace, I suppose I'll have to do it. Bow your heads."

"In the name of the Father and of the Son and of the Holy Spirit, Bless us, O Lord, and these thy gifts from thy bounty which we are about to receive."

Abe said, "Amen. Boys?"

They mumbled the word.

Ida said, "Now, was that so hard?"

Arthur said, "Can we eat now?"

Alex banged on his high chair tray until everyone looked up. He extended his arm and made the sign of the cross in the air.

Ida teared up.

Abe slammed his fist on the table. "Look here, Ida. First you give him that Christ book he's been coloring. Fine, it keeps him busy. But now he acts as if he's the Pope of Rome. What the hell have you been teaching him, that's what I'd like to know."

"I didn't teach him a blessed thing. The little angel has chosen the true church all on his own, haven't you, sweetheart?"

Alex burped a splotch of applesauce onto his bib.

"Well, I don't like it, not one bit. Alex, you cut that finger waving out, you hear?" For emphasis, Abe made a cross in the air. "None of that Holy Roller stuff no more, see?"

Alex said, "Peace be with you."

Ida said, "And with you."

Abe said, "Oh geez."

Benjamin, holding his spoon in the air, said, "Can we eat now?"

Abe dipped his spoon into the soup. "What else are we having?"

"Fish. It's Friday, what else would it be? You boys like Fin 'n Haddie?"

*

Shouts and laughter from the dinner table floated up to the bedroom like familiar friends, and Irene longed for the strength to go downstairs to join in the fun, or to tell her boys to mind their manners, anything to be in touch with the living, but now she felt forgotten, an invalid, worthless. It was dark now, broken only by a faint lamplight eking its way up the staircase and into the hallway outside. She wanted to eat, and her stomach made pinging sounds, but when she put a piece of bread into her mouth it seemed to just stay there until she spit it out in a lump.

She touched her cheeks and her forehead, and it felt as if the bones were forcing their way to the surface. She laughed quietly, well, at least I won't have to go on a diet. She ran her hands over her thighs, her stomach, her hips and her breasts. She felt diminished.

As she was drifting off again she heard a voice from far away. She opened her eyes to see that it was Abe, only six feet away, and Alex, standing at the foot of the bed.

"Irene, are you awake? Irene?"

"Momma."

His voice was like cool water. "Yes, Alex. I'm here."

"I brought him up to see you like you asked."

"Thank you. How are you, Alex?"

"Momma, I rode in the wagon and had sugar cookies and I saw Farmer Dar and Coco the Monkey. He's brown and has fur and he got a cap on his head and he can jump, and then Arthur and Benjamin won a race."

"What? Abe, what is he saying?"

Abe sighed and explained again about the fair, and how Alex's brothers took him and looked after him.

"But you shouldn't have let him go, Abe. How could you let him go? He could have been hurt. What's wrong with you?" The bitterness rose in her throat.

"Irene, I told you twice now, he's fine. See?" As if to prove it, Abe lifted Alex and turned him in a circle.

"Bring him to me."

Abe moved two feet closer. "You have to be careful, The Dip could be catching still."

"Alex, your mother loves you very much. Can you hear me, Alex?"

"I hear you, Momma."

"Don't let them hurt him, Abe."

"Who? You mean the boys? They would never hurt him."

"Don't let them—" she began, but her cough overwhelmed her. She waved her hand, move him away from me, Abe, move him away, save him from this invisible monster that has me in its claws, that is eating me from the inside out, tearing at my lungs with its jagged teeth and acid tongue, please keep him safe.

Alex said, "Good night, Momma."

*

Arthur and Benjamin, under orders from their grandmother, had cleared the table, swept the floor and set up the checkerboard. Ida poured hot water from the teakettle over the sink full of dishes.

Alex twisted in Abe's arms like a cat that refused to be held until Abe released him. He monkey-dashed across the floor and plopped down next to his brothers.

Ida rolled her sleeves up to the elbow. Her broad forearms were blotched with liver spots. "How is she, Abe?"

"The same." He set Irene's cold, mostly uneaten dinner on the counter. "She couldn't talk too much. She had one of those coughing fits."

Ida shook soap flakes into the water. "You want to lend us a hand here?

I know you're supposed to be the lord of the manor, but I didn't hire on to be your Irish scrub lady. I'll wash, you dry. Here," she said, offering him an apron, "put it on unless you want to get your shirt soaked. I work fast."

The apron strings reached just halfway around his waist. He caught the gawks from his boys. "You three, stick to your checkers," he said. He thought he heard Alex laugh. "Go ahead, Ida, I'll be fine with this here towel."

Abe dried in silence. He needed Ida at the house to look in on Irene tomorrow afternoon and into the early evening, when he'd be at The Squeaky Wheel for The Wheel's annual Tournament de Darts, a rollicking good time not to be missed, and besides, he'd promised Davy O'Brien he would bring Alex along to watch him defend his crown.

"About tomorrow, Ida. I could really use your help here in the afternoon, at least to look in on Irene."

"It's Saturday. You don't work Saturday. You need to stay home with your wife."

"Dad said we're supposed to watch Alex in the morning, Grandma," Arthur said. "He said we can take him with us to East Liberty. In the wagon."

Benjamin pushed a checker. "Your move, Alex."

Abe glanced at his boys. Benjamin lay on one side of the checkerboard. Alex stood on the other, his arms folded across his chest, staring intently at the red and black squares, as if he were a two-foot, two-inch-tall Napoleon planning an invasion of Russia.

"The boy is with me in the afternoon. See there, Ida," Abe said, trying to affect some jocularity in his voice, "you can take the morning off. Sleep until eleven."

"Don't talk to me as if I work for you." She shoved the last dinner plate into his chest.

"No, it ain't like that, Ida. I appreciate what you're doing for us, for me and the boys, and for Irene, too, you can take my word on it. Let's just see how this goes day by day. Who knows, maybe Irene will be up and around by Sunday, you never know."

"Fine." She untied her apron. "I'm going home now."

"You want me to walk you?"

"I can walk myself."

"Benjamin, Arthur. Get up and walk your grandmother home."

"I said I'd—oh never mind, get your coats on, boys." She pulled her scarf over her head. "Alex, come here, my little sweetheart."

As she kissed him goodbye, she whispered in his ear that Jesus loves the littlest ones the best, and He's given you special gifts, too, because He loves you so much, and Grandma loves you the best, too.

As Ida and the boys walked east toward Graham Street, Delia Novak passed them going the opposite direction, on her way to The Squeaky Wheel to ask John if he could use some extra bar help during the darts tournament the next day. She needed the money. She hoped Abe would be there.

Chapter 10

In the early 1900s, Pittsburgh's East Liberty district featured an assortment of shops and entertainment venues for the rich and poor alike: bistros and beaneries, furriers and secondhand clothing stores, concert halls and penny movie arcades, majestic churches and street corner preachers, as well as a few discreet houses of prostitution, which welcomed all comers.

Of special interest to children was F.W. Woolworth's, one of the nation's first five and ten cents stores. Young shoppers could find stacks of the latest toys, from cap guns and yoyos to dolls and jump ropes. For a few cents, a kid could step right up to the soda fountain and order a cherry or vanilla Coke (which at the time contained a considerable amount of cocaine, which no doubt lead to its popularity among both children and adults alike); or, for a little more, step up to an ice cream sundae or float, a hot dog or a grilled cheese sandwich with real Heinz pickle chips thrown in, no extra charge. It was on the pennies, nickels, dimes and dollars of children and families like the Millers that a grateful F.W. was able to erect his 57-story Woolworth Skyscraper in mid-Manhattan.

Located in Woolworth's basement, between the home goods and damaged merchandise, was the pet section, stocked with goldfish, hamsters, guinea pigs, parakeets and, two weeks prior to Easter, live chicks dyed pink, purple, orange and green. With a little luck from the gods of genetics, a handful of these birds actually lived more than a few days after purchase. Of course, there was no money-back guarantee on livestock.

Arthur and Benjamin were no strangers to the wonders of Woolworth's. It was just a 10-minute walk from home. Irene had taken them there for Christmas blazers, which she purchased two sizes too large so they could wear them for at least two seasons.

As they crossed Ripley Street, Benjamin said, "Are you sure you remember the way, Arthur? We nev…never came here alone."

"Shut up, dummy. I come here plenty of times without you."

"Whu…when?"

"Last week, when I cut school with Gross. Don't you dare tell Dad."

"I wouldn't."

They waited on the corner until a horse-drawn grocery wagon went by. "Alex, you still want to play Five Fingers, don't you?"

Abe rose from the living room couch mid Saturday morning, feeling like a king rather than an indentured servant, since with Irene laid up there was no handwritten list of household chores lording over him. He could take his good old time luxuriating over breakfast, with little to do besides drink coffee and reread last night's newspaper and enjoy the promise of the coming day, with the annual darts tournament only a few hours away. Then there was the prospect of seeing Delia again. She was bound to come to the tournament. He wondered what she'd be wearing.

The pile of laundry in the kitchen could wait until Irene felt better. What did he know about doing laundry, anyway? Maybe Ida would take care of it when she showed up later, although asking her to do it, now that would be tricky, he would have to finesse his way around that one. Maybe he ought to bring her a bottle. If he could afford it. Where the hell did all the money go, anyway? Irene would know, down to the penny.

It was awfully quiet for a Saturday morning. He called for his sons. Usually the boys were up by seven on Saturday mornings, laughing and yelling and carrying on so he couldn't sleep, but there wasn't so much as a peep or a scream or a glass breaking.

He checked their room. Empty. Even Alex was gone. They were up to something; lately, he'd been getting the feeling that Arthur was carrying on behind his back. He went out to the backyard. Nothing. He was about to canvas the neighborhood when he remembered Arthur had told him they were going to East Liberty that morning, with Alex. He let out his breath.

He eyed the half empty bottle of rye whiskey on the end table. How many nightcaps did he have? He couldn't blame it on being upset about Irene, since he truly believed she'd pull through. Was he becoming a rummy, like half the boys at The Wheel? He swore he'd have nothing to drink this day, but then, hell, how could a man go to a tavern and have nothing but water or soda pop? He fingered the two dollars he'd been saving all week.

He had another cup of coffee, sliced some bread and added a hunk of cheddar cheese. He re-opened the newspaper. Halfway through the obituaries, he remembered to check on his wife.

*

It was the fashion for boys in the seventh grade to carry three-inch penknives to school. Their concealed blades were ideal for carving initials into desktops, they were nicely balanced for games of Mumblety-Peg and Stick It, and, just as important, they could inflict a nasty if not lethal wound, settling up a playground dispute.

Arthur's plan was simple. He would sit Alex up on the display case where the knives were kept and ask a sales clerk to show one to him. Once the knife was on the countertop, Benjamin would create the diversion, claiming he was lost and he needed his mommy right away, which was an ideal role for him, since the plan already had him close to tears. When the clerk's attention was diverted, Alex would make the snatch—who would ever suspect him?

Rolling through the Saturday shoppers on Woolworth's first floor, Alex drew his customary crowd. The boys left the wagon on the first landing to the steps to the basement and swung Alex along, each brother holding a long arm.

The heist turned out to be even easier than Arthur had planned. When they arrived at the display case, a tray of penknives sat on the counter, as if it were waiting for them. The sales clerk, a roundish woman in a dark blue shift with a flowered silk scarf tied beneath her double chin, smiled at the boys as she tied price tags on the knives.

A short woman with a crying baby in a stroller asked the clerk if she might see a large carving knife in the case to her left, about six feet away. Naturally, the clerk waited on the woman first, since boys like Arthur were known to moon over knives and tops and cap guns forever, with no money to buy them.

Arthur winked at Alex. The tray would have been out of a normal child's reach, but five seconds later a pearl-plated knife was in Alex's hand, and then his brother's. Arthur lifted Alex from the countertop and signaled for Benjamin. Passing by the woman with the baby, Alex fished her change purse from her handbag like an eagle plucking a trout.

Ten minutes later, Arthur and Benjamin were chomping on chocolate-covered éclairs with vanilla custard filling from Stagnato's Bakery. They'd given Alex a sugar cookie. Benjamin reminded Arthur that their father had said he would kill them if they didn't have Alex home by noon. For once Arthur agreed with him that they should play it safe. He opened the knife, and as they headed home, he whittled a small branch to "break it in." Benjamin shuddered as he watched the chips fly.

*

Abe filled a washbasin with warm water. Halfway up the stairs, he paused to watch Irene stagger from the bathroom and back to bed. He waited a couple of moments until he heard the bedsprings creak.

She was sitting on the edge of the bed, pulling off her nightgown when he entered, and he was struck by how much smaller her breasts looked from just a week ago, how pale they were, gray almost, these breasts he once had taken such pleasure in holding, squeezing, tasting, pressing them to his hairy chest, and now they just hung there. She slipped another gown over her head, and Abe felt relieved that she was covered again.

He cleared his throat, but if she heard him she gave no indication. "How are you feeling?"

She looked at him as if she were mystified as to how he'd gotten into the room. "What?"

Abe spoke slowly. "Are you feeling any better?"

"I don't know. Maybe a little. I got up."

"Here." He set the basin down on the night table, along with a washcloth and a bar of soap. "I thought if you wanted to wash up a little."

Irene turned her head slightly toward the water. "What I want is a cup of tea. Where are the boys?"

He thought twice about telling her they went to East Liberty. "Playing outside."

"Isn't it raining?"

"It stopped."

Irene felt a wave of panic. "Where is Alex? Is he with them?"

"Yes, Alex is fine, you don't need to worry."

"Did you put his scarf on?"

"He's fine, I tell you."

Irene dropped her hand in the washbasin and let it linger, palm up, as if she had slit her wrist and was letting it bleed out. "I'm filthy."

Abe wanted to say, I'm the one that's filthy, a filthy philanderer that's planning on seeing his lover this very afternoon, and all the soap and water in the world ain't about to get me clean. He moved closer. "Here." He dipped the washcloth in the basin. He rubbed the soap against it. "Hold still."

"What are you doing?"

He laughed. "What does it look like? Can't a man touch his own wife?" He swabbed her face.

"Gently," she said.

A bit of color rose in her cheeks as he washed them. Maybe, he thought, it's a little bit of hope rising.

"That feels good, Abe. Do it slower."

He rinsed the cloth and smoothed it over her forehead and on the sides of her neck. He opened the top two buttons of her nightgown and swabbed where her breastbone connected to her shoulder. It seemed sadly erotic to him, the way she closed her eyes and let her head tilt back, as his hand moved close to her breast.

From the first floor, Arthur yelled, "Dad?"

He squeezed water out of the washcloth. "Up here, son. You boys home already?"

"Yeah. We had a good time. Can we have something to eat?"

Before he could answer, Irene said, "My hair is awful. Could you get my brush from the bathroom?"

His boy's clothes covered the bathroom floor. Abe pushed them aside with his boot. He'd have to get on them about cleaning up after themselves, but wasn't that always Irene's job? Maybe he could find a housekeeper to give the place the once over, but then that cost money and would cut into his drinking allowance. Anyway, today wasn't the day to get all worried about that. Today was the tournament at The Wheel.

Soap spatters clung to the mirror of the medicine cabinet like aphids. On the top shelf were Irene's creams and lotions. Abe opened a jar. The cream was dried and cracked. He opened a bottle of perfume, half empty. Had he bought it for her? Wasn't it an anniversary present? He wasn't sure, but the smell was familiar. Nice, but not as provocative as the stuff Delia wore—damn, what was wrong with him, he shouldn't be thinking about her at a time like this.

He thought her heard Irene calling him. "Coming, coming."

By the time he got back to the bedside, her eyes had already closed.

*

Ida arrived before noon. She put out a lunch of baloney sandwiches, peanut butter cookies she'd made that morning and piccalilli. After stuffing themselves, Arthur and Benjamin slipped off to their bedroom. Abe left the house with Alex and a mostly clear conscience, feeling content that he had been attentive to his wife, done what he could, or at least the best he could muster, and anyway, how much could anyone do for her? With a bounce in his step and Alex on his shoulder, the short walk to The Wheel seemed even closer.

Six finalists had been competing in a toss-off to play against reigning champion Davy O'Brien in the tournament finals. Close to thirty dollars had been won and lost on the preliminaries. In addition, there had been three fist fights, one of which culminated when Raymond Kramer jammed a dart two inches into the left shoulder of Red Shipley, who'd accused Raymond of using illegally weighted bronze darts. He'd also accused Kramer's mother of committing unnatural sex acts with large male herbivores.

The crowd had grown to upward of sixty men and a handful of women as one o'clock and the final toss-down approached. Edward "Pecker" Peck, Davy's doubles partner, had emerged from the preliminaries as the man to challenge the incumbent, and although John was giving two-to-one on Davy, or maybe because of it, the brisk betting was divided evenly. There was an unspoken but growing suspicion that Davy's drinking had finally caught up to him, that his hand and eyes were shaky, and indeed, the flow of drink that used to steady his aim seemed to be working the opposite way, as evidenced by some of the errant warm-up tosses Davy had thrown earlier that morning, two of which missed the dartboard entirely.

According to the unwritten rules of the tournament, the final round was one leg instead of the usual three, one game of 301, between the challenger and the champion, who by virtue of his title was permitted to skip the preliminaries. Each player was allowed nine warm-up tosses before the final match. Peck stretched his arms over his head, and with a quick thrust hit a double ring 10, then another double ringer, then a toss that came within a hummingbird's feather of a bull's-eye. He turned to Davy, who had yet to get out of his chair. "Well, will you look at that, Davy, hope to God I didn't blow my wad in the warm-up. You gonna give the crowd here a preview, sir, or do you feel ready already?" He took a huge bite out of a ham and cheese on rye from a tray piled high with them, which John was selling for ten cents each, three for a quarter. Preparing the sandwiches and platters of deviled eggs was John's temporary helper, Delia Novak.

Davy said, "Feeling your oats now, are you, Edward?"

Peck wiped his mouth with the cuff of his flannel shirt. "Like a champion stallion. Any time you're ready, champ."

Davy sipped a shot of Imperial. He stared at the front door. Without looking away, he said, "Five minutes, Edward, give us five minutes here."

"I'll give you six, how's that? You waiting for Jesus himself to walk through that door?"

Davy smiled, but not at Peck's attempt at humor, for at that moment, Abe walked in with Davy's good luck charm riding on his shoulder. He struggled to his feet, flexed his arms over his head, interlaced his fingers and cracked his knuckles so hard the pops echoed across the bar. "There's me boy."

Men who had money on Davy knew he saw Alex as his good luck charm, and shouted, "Here we go, Davy," and "Stick it to him good, lad."

Abe and Alex pushed their way through the glad-handers and well-wishers to Davy's table. Davy opened a rosewood box and took out the special darts he used only for tournament play. Turning to Abe, he said, "May I have the boy?"

Alex said, "I went to Woolworth's."

"Is that right, kiddo?"

"We ate éclairs."

Davy took Alex's right hand and placed it on each dart, one at a time. He then placed Alex's hand on his heart and kissed him three times on the forehead, which made Alex giggle. He turned to the crowd and, looking Peck in the eye, said, "Now that we've had the blessing of the darts, Pecker, let's play."

Delia strutted her way across the floor, evoking a series of catcalls and whistles, carrying the dartboard used only for the Tournament de Darts. She mounted it on the far wall and waved cheerily to the men as they saluted her with a beauty pageant round of applause. Passing by Abe, she gave him only the slightest nod.

Davy toed the line for his warm-up tosses. He braced himself with his left hand on a straight back chair, and while no one was sure if that stance was allowed within the rules, no one was ready to challenge the four-time champion. Davy's first throw grazed the left ear of Fritz Shutzmeir and lodged itself into the wall three feet to the left. Davy said, "Who's the bastard that moved the board on me?"

His supporters laughed uneasily. It was a joke, had to be, wasn't it? Several men rushed to the bar to put money on Peck.

The remainder of Davy's warm-ups, although they hit the board, were only marginally more accurate. The mumbled opinions were divided. Some felt Davy had truly lost his skill and perhaps his vision as well. Others saw his erratic warm-up as a con job, to instill the challenger with a false sense of bravado, since the general belief was that tournament darts was at least as much a mental contest as a physical one.

The cuckoo clock behind the bar, which John had taken in trade from Stanley Kurtz to settle a two-month tab, hooted one o'clock. John climbed up on the bar and announced, "My friends, the betting has officially ended. Let the championship round begin." The men cheered and whistled. "You boys know the rules. One leg of 301. Winner gets ten dollars and possession of The Squeaky Wheel Tournament de Darts silver loving cup." He held the trophy high over his head to a hearty round of applause. "Mr. Peck, are you ready?"

"You're damn straight, John."

"Davy, what say you?"

"I say what I always say, let the best man win." There was polite applause. "As long as it's me."

Abe moved away from Davy's table and back toward the bar, to get closer to Delia. As they bumped and jostled through the crowd, Alex snatched a diamond stickpin from the lapel of Edward Small of Small Brothers Property and Casualty Insurance.

Delia perched on a stepstool behind the bar. Her feathered hat, somewhat worse for wear, sat cocked sideways on her head, and she smoked with a cigarette holder, pinky extended, emulating the way she imagined socialite women smoked. She blew a smoke ring at Abe. "Well, look what we have here." She stretched out her arms.

Abe reached for her tentatively.

Delia said, "Not you, you lug. No, I want to see the little good luck charm." She pulled Alex to her.

The match began slowly. Neither man was able to hone in, though Peck hit a double-ring fourteen to take an early lead. Davy steadied himself with the chair. On his second toss he hit a triple, but the dart fell out before five seconds were up, negating his score, turning his supporters' cheers to groans.

Each time the men had to retrieve their darts, Davy's hobble became more pronounced.

By the third round, Peck was fifty points ahead, his score dropping into the low two hundreds, while Davy had yet to reach two-fifty. Some felt Davy was too drunk to carry the day; others felt he wasn't drunk enough.

Up at the bar, Delia and Alex played Patty Cake Patty Cake. Alex slapped Delia's palms with gusto. "My, my, my, what a strong little man you are, just like your daddy, right?"

Evidently, Alex saw in Delia what his father saw. "Pretty."

"Ooh, I think I got a crush on you, pumpkin. You know what a crush is? You hear how he talks to me, Abe? Why don't you ever tell me I'm pretty, huh?"

"What are you talking about? I tell you all that and more all the time and you know it."

"Alex, did you know that your daddy never buys Delia anything nice?"

"Oh shush, will you, you're mixing up the boy's head."

Delia pulled a paper bag from under the bar and took out something wrapped in brown paper. "Alex, can you guess what this is?"

Alex shook his head.

"It's a present for you from your Aunt Delia. I got it just in case your daddy brought you today. Would you like to open it?"

"Daddy?"

"See how he asks? So polite. He got manners, Abe. I know he didn't get them from you." She bumped his hip with hers. "You, you just take what you want."

Alex opened the bag. "It's a man." He held up a gingerbread man, with white icing for eyes and gumdrop buttons.

"It's the Gingerbread Man. Do you know the Gingerbread Man song, Alex? No? Well, here's how to sing it: Run, run, run, as fast as you can, but you can't catch me I'm the…"

"Gingerbread Man!" Alex shouted.

"Oh, my goodness, you are so smart. Why didn't you tell me how smart he is?" She kissed Alex on the forehead, leaving a faint trace of red lipstick. "He's so yummy I could just eat him up. So anyway, Abe, how's your wife?"

He had an image of Irene, lying flat on her back, looking like death warmed over. And here he was, letting her lie there, and instead of caring for his wife he was gawking at his sometime mistress, her lips full, her cheeks pink. The guilt grabbed at his gut. "Let's talk about something else, all right?"

"I hear she got The Dip, bad."

"You hear?"

She gestured to the crowd. "People talk."

"Well, if she doesn't perk up in a day or two, I'll have to go for Malkin."

"That lowlife? Oopsy, Alex, Auntie Delia said a bad word you should never, ever repeat." She put her hands over his ears. "Well, I hope it doesn't come to that, for her sake. Look, I don't mean your wife no harm or nothing. It's just that, you know."

"What do you mean, you know?"

Her boozy whisper cut through the din in the bar. "Now look, not that I am saying it should happen, but if she was to, you know, not survive, it sure would make things easier for us. Maybe I'm going to hell for saying it, but let's be frank, people all around us are dropping like flies. It's a wonder The Dip didn't get you and your little one."

Abe pulled away from her. "Or you."

She laughed. "Oh no, no Dip will ever get Delia Novak, not this gal."

A roar came from the crowd. Davy had finally tossed a bull's-eye. "Davy, Davy, Davy," came the chant. He'd cut into Peck's lead and his score was down to one hundred ten. The men were saying, it's over now, Davy got his eye back, but in the next round Peck got hot and turned the tide in his favor. Davy tossed another bull's-eye, but for some reason, perhaps a soft spot in the board or a subtle jog in the Earth's orbit, the dart fell to the floor before five seconds, nullifying his score. He knelt down to pick up the errant dart, and as he tried to rise his knees gave way. He collapsed with a dull thud. Hands thrust forward to help him to his feet, but he waved them away, he would have none of it, leave me be, you bastards. He rolled to his side, grasped a table's edge, wheezed to his feet and limped back to the throwing line.

When Abe saw Davy go down, he pulled Alex away from Delia and rushed toward his table.

Years later, the arguments continued as to whether or not what happened that day was within the rules of the tournament, or whether John had the right to make them up as he went along. No one who was actually there, however, disputed the basic facts of what occurred after the fall of Davy.

In the hundred seconds or so that it took Abe to push his way through the crowd, with Alex at his side, Davy had taken another shot of whiskey and another turn for the worse, which may have been an even sharper turn had it not been for the whiskey. He slumped on his chair, and his face was clown-like—red nose, chalky white cheeks. His right hand vibrated independent of the rest of his body, as if it were trying to write a message in the air.

"Davy," Alex said.

The sound of his voice lifted Davy's head off his chest.

"Davy." It was Peck now. "Look my friend, if you can't go on, just say so. No shame in it, no shame at all. You've had a good run, but a forfeit now, there's no shame. You want someone to fetch an ambulance?"

"Ambulance my ass," Davy croaked. He tried to get to his feet but only rose six inches before he fell back.

"John?" Peck said.

The crowd parted as John came out from behind the bar. "Give us some air, back away," he said. He leaned over Davy, who whispered something and closed his eyes. John nodded.

"All right, you bums, listen up. Davy is in no shape to continue here. But, under the rules of The Squeaky Wheel Tournament de Darts, he's allowed to choose someone else to finish out his throws."

Immediately the room broke out into an uproar, and much blood may have been spilled had John not stood on a chair and pulled his revolver from his apron. The noise settled quickly until James Downey, who'd bet half of his weekly salary on Peck, said, "Hold on there, John, I never heard of no rule like that." Other men that had Peck growled in agreement.

"I make the damn rules," John said. "My tavern, my rules." He waved the pistol. "Any further interpretations needed? What say you, Mr. Peck?"

With twenty-four points to go to Davy's fifty-one, Peck acted as if he were in the catbird's seat, and since no one in the bar beside Davy could beat him, with a wave to the men he said, "Go ahead, I got no fight with this. Let the poor man choose."

Davy glanced around the room, but the men looked away.

"Choose." It was James Downey. "Choose, Davy, or finish it yourself, damn it."

Choose, choose, the crowd echoed.

Alex broke free from Abe's grip. He climbed a chair and then onto the table and into Davy's lap. He whispered in his ear, *Davy, I can throw the darts good and straight because Grandma says I am special and I have my long arms from Jesus as a blessing.*

Davy wasn't a religious man per se, but after he heard Alex's words he sat straight up, eyes wide.

Alex repeated *from Jesus.*

"Choose!"

"Come on, Davy," John pleaded.

Davy waved his hand for quiet. He smiled at Alex. "I choose the boy."

Beer sprayed from James Downey's mouth, and soon the rest of the bar joined in the laughter. Even the stoic Peck couldn't conceal a smile. "Thanks for the laugh, Davy, but you can do better than the squirt here."

"I said Alex. Now pull my chair over where I can see."

There was so much shouting that John had to fire a round into the ceiling to get some quiet. Someone yelled for the police. Edgar Timmons, a police sergeant with twenty years on the force and a dollar on Davy, shouted, "Calm down, you bastards, before I arrest every mother's son of you." He turned to Davy. "What in blue blazes are you doing, son? The runt ain't out of diapers yet."

Alex mouthed the word *Jesus.*

Davy said, "Let the boy throw."

Now Alex stood on top of the table, left shoulder facing the dartboard, a dart in his right hand, and if the table were a pitcher's mound, it could be said he was in the stretch position. His Teddy Roosevelt Rough Rider cowboy hat sat low on his forehead. He held the dart loosely, it's size dwarfing his hand. He dipped his right shoulder back toward the floor, and, with his elongated arm, his right hand brushed the tabletop as he rocked into his motion. As he tilted down to his right, balancing on his right leg, his left index finger pointed straight up to Heaven. He twirled it three times. Then he rocked upright, the core of his body a fulcrum, his right arm stretching over his head, gaining speed and momentum as he finally released the dart, which blurred through the air and stuck to the hilt, a double ring "18." Before the men could react he repeated the motion and the next throw netted him a "13," and now his score was down to two, and the men howled. Alex said,

"Watch me, Davy," and with that he went into his motion again, and hit a double ring "1," ending the game, winning the trophy.

Instead of rushing toward the table, the men backed away, as if some alien with powers superior to anything they'd ever know had landed in their midst.

Abe reached for Alex, intending to hoist him up on his shoulders and take a victory lap around the bar, but Alex slipped out of his grip. He picked up a six-inch, wood-handled steak knife from Davy's plate. Men ducked under the tables and hid in corners, not knowing where Alex intended the knife to go. He repeated his motion and hurled the knife. It stuck in the center bull's-eye, its handle vibrating.

Chapter 11

Ida was putting away the few leftovers from lunch when she heard a loud rap on the door. She cracked it open halfway.

"Hello, missus, Dr. Sergei Malkin at your service."

"I know who you are."

"Ah, yes, we have met before at the birth of little Miller. You are Mrs. Ida, the mother of the missus, correct?" The door didn't move. "Perhaps may I come in? I have come by as doctor and friend of the family. I am told Mrs. Miller, she is very ill."

Ida's face soured. "Wipe your feet."

"Yes, of course. I am knowing your son-in-law Abe Miller and the older boys, them I have treated, and the little one Alex. I don't suppose he is at home, I always am enjoying it to see him and to give it to him a quick look-over of his growth progress. He is a very interesting case, with his long arms and the great intelligence of his head." He glanced past her shoulder. "Perhaps the little fellow is around somewhere?"

"He's out with his father. Are you sure you didn't come here to drum up some business? Because as sure as I know Judgment Day is coming, I didn't call for you."

"Please, my presence is, how you would say it, I am making it the courtesy call to the family I am in the service of." He sniffed the air. "But I can see it you are having it your meal."

Ida crossed her arms in front of her chest. "It's soup for dinner."

"Yes, of course, I am simply to mean, I am sorry for it if I am being it an interruption to you. It smells very delicious, by the way, what you are making. It is reminding me of my Grandmother Latushka, may she rest in peace, a wonderful mother to her children, she used to make it a large pot of soup like this for the family every Friday with the remaining parts of the chicken she killed for the dinner. The poor woman, a kinder soul that lived there never was, but sad to say, she was raped and killed by Cossacks at the age of 43. We think. She had it not the official certificate of birth. Such a pity, she died too young, too young." He dabbed at his eyes with a plaid handkerchief. "Often it is said among my family members that I have inherited it some Cossack blood from her, the poor woman." He sighed and bowed his head.

Ida put her hands on her hips. "You want some soup?"

"Oh no, thank you, I shouldn't, after all, it is for your family you have made it."

"You don't want any?"

"Well, of course if it is just for to taste it, then I would have it, since you have offered it to me most generously, then I would not want it to be an insult or make it an offense to you not to take it." He sat down at the table. "Perhaps you have it a napkin?"

"Doctor."

"Yes?"

"My daughter?"

"What? Oh yes, of course, forgive me." He got to his feet. "I was thinking the serving of the soup, it would come now, but I shall go and check in on her condition, certainly, she is upstairs I take it, no?"

"The bedroom on the right."

He bowed. "Yes, thank you, I shall be down in a few moments, but if you wouldn't mind I should like to wash them first my hands before I look in on her, for the sanitation purposes of course with all the sickness going around. May I use it here this dishwater in your sink?"

*

She heard three quick knocks on the door. A watery figure with a dark goatee and close-set eyes entered the room. For a moment Irene thought it was the Devil come to claim her and she began to sob softly, and to apologize to God for her sins and ask for forgiveness, until she recognized from the pince-nez and his black bag it was Malkin.

"Mrs. Miller? Hello, you are awake?"

Irene coughed dryly into the sleeve of her nightgown. "What day is it?"

"So we are awake after all, this, it is a good sign. It is today Saturday. And how are we feeling, Mrs. Miller?"

"Awful."

"Yes, well, that is a symptom of The Dip, no doubt. Would you mind it, I am going to take it your temperature. Open wide, please." He inserted a thermometer under her tongue and felt her forehead, which was hot and wet.

Irene tried to say, "What time is it?" but her voice was a soft croak.

"Please, if you would be so kind as to shush while the thermometer it does it its work for just a few moments." He waited to get a reading, even though the thermometer was normally off by one or two degrees. He took her pulse, although he couldn't rely on the accuracy of his pocket watch, which he had taken in trade for stitching a four-inch slash in flesh between the thumb and index finger of Bernstein the jeweler. With a slight flick of the wrist, he removed the thermometer and gazed at it intently, as if by staring long and hard enough he would be able to ascertain both Irene's body temperature and the progression of her malady.

Even though her forehead had been hot to the touch, the thermometer read 97.8. "Well, it is certain you have it the fever, no doubt from The Dip. I am going to give it to you something to bring that temperature down, which will also give it to you some relief from the symptoms, but you must understand it, The Dip, it has to run its course." He reached in his bag for a bottle of the tonic he concocted for Davy for hip pain. If nothing else, the alcohol would make her sleep.

"Doctor, my throat is on fire."

"A classic symptom, as we in the medical profession have studied it, that is what you have. I should like it to take it a look at your esophagus, if you would be so kind as to open wide again and say 'Ah.'"

Her rank breath hit him full on. He suppressed a gag. Peering over his glasses, he clucked his tongue. "Very red and irritated, like a piece of meat that was dragged on the street, but as I say, the tonic it will give it you some relief from the pain, no? Take two tablespoons every two hours or so until the pain and fever go down." He closed his bag. "God willing."

Irene coughed again. "Am I going to die?"

"We all must die some time, Mrs. Miller. No, please, I am only making it the joke. But you must rest now and you will feel better, all right?"

"All I do is rest. It doesn't help. I want my little boy."

"Yes, I would like it to see him as well. I would like to run certain scientific tests on him to determine it what is the cause of his slow growth. But your mother, as we talked over the soup, she said he is out with his father."

"His father's probably with his whore Delia Novak."

"Such language, it must be it the fever—wait, you said Delia Novak? A curse on the woman, may she get The Dip herself. She is owing it to me two dollars ten cents. You are knowing her as well?"

Irene fought her dizziness and sat up. She grabbed Malkin's wrist. "What do you know of Delia Novak?"

"Please, Mrs. Miller, your fingernails, they are putting their marks in my flesh."

"Momma!" Alex ran into the room. "I have a present. I threw darts."

Malkin halted him by the shoulder. "Not too close, my little one. Your mother, she is very sick."

"But I want to show her."

Irene said, "Alex. Wait."

Malkin unscrewed the bottle of tonic. "Here, you must take it a swallow."

Irene drank, gagged slightly, but almost immediately the burn in her throat began to subside. She took another swallow and felt it all the way down to her stomach. She closed her eyes. She felt as if she were sinking into the mattress.

"You must leave it now the room, little Alex, and let your mother rest."

Alex began to yammer, and Irene thought she heard him say something about a gingerbread man and Delia and a pin and Davy and darts and a knife and John the bartender's gun, but the fever and Malkin's tonic overwhelmed her. She began to snore.

Malkin motioned to Alex. "You see, your mother she is now asleep. We must be very quiet so as not to disturb her. Come come come."

Alex wanted to snuggle in with her, to tell her all about his adventure that morning, to see her smile, to feel her arms around him. He wondered why all she did was sleep. He touched her hand as Malkin pulled him away, "Bye bye, Momma."

Malkin kneeled down next to him. "But now let us have it the quick exam to see how you have grown since I last saw you, my boy. Let us remove your shirt, please."

Alex bared his teeth and growled. He moved away from Malkin and pounded on the door to his brothers' room.

Rather than pursue him, Malkin remembered how hard he could bite. "Perhaps next time, when you are not so upset." He went to the stairs and paused, listening to the shouting coming from the living room. "Oh, the soup."

*

"Your wife is sick to death upstairs and you have me over here so you can go and drink with your pals at that saloon. Which was bad enough, but you took my grandson, too. What kind of a father are you? A saloon is no place for a little boy. You'd know that if you had half the sense you were born with."

Abe draped his coat over a kitchen chair. "You don't know what you're talking about, Ida. They love Alex at The Wheel. You should have seen what he did today. I can't believe it but I seen it with my own eyes."

She shook a finger in his face. "I don't want to know so don't bother me with your malarkey." She grabbed her coat and went to the door. "By the way, that greenhorn doctor of yours is upstairs checking on your wife, in case you give a damn. And shut the flame off under the soup." She slammed the door behind her.

Let her go, Abe thought. She wouldn't appreciate what Alex did, anyway. He spooned some soup into a bowl. That Alex. Entrepreneurship possibilities spun in his head.

*

Arthur propped Alex up on the top bunk. "You want some candy?" He showed him a bag of jellybeans.

"Momma went to sleep again."

"She's just tired, Alex."

"Look." Alex took the diamond stickpin from his pants.

Benjamin said, "Holy moley."

Arthur tried to grab it, but Alex pulled it away. "Where'd you get that?"

"When I went with Daddy."

Benjamin said, "You mean at that buh…bar? But how did you get it?"

"Five fingers."

Arthur said, "Wow."

"I threw darts."

Benjamin said, "Alex, can I see it?"

"I played darts for Davy and won the game."

Arthur said, "Sure, sure."

"I *did*."

Arthur tried to pat Alex on the shoulder. "OK, OK, Alex, I believe you. Just let me see that thing for a minute."

Benjamin said, "It looks like a duh…diamond." When Arthur scowled at him, he offered, "I saw pictures of duh…diamonds in school."

"It's for Momma."

Benjamin shook his head. "But wait. You can't give it to her."

"Why?"

Benjamin said, "Because you…because."

Arthur pushed him away. "He means, because she's sleeping right now. You said she was. Plus, it's not her birthday. If you wait for her birthday, it's a more special present, see? You wrap it in pretty paper and put a ribbon on it. Remember how your birthday presents were all wrapped up in shiny paper, with ribbons and bows? Same thing for Ma. Right, Benjamin?"

Benjamin stammered until Arthur freed his tongue with a punch to the back. "Right."

Alex clutched the pin. "When is her birthday?"

"Pretty soon. April 23rd. Only a few weeks away. Then you can give it to her. And you know what else, Alex? We'll help you wrap it up pretty for Ma. We'll get special paper, even. But we need to hide it somewhere in our room so she won't see it before her birthday, so it will be a big surprise. OK, Alex? You want it to be a surprise, don't you?" Arthur looked around the room, as if he were scanning it for secret hiding places. "Just give me the pin and I'll put in where only you and me and Benjamin will know where it is. Wait, I know." He slid the wooden box where they kept their toy soldiers from under the bed. "We'll put it in here. Ma and Dad would never look in here. Just hand me the pin. No, wait. Alex, you put it in there, you bury it good, OK?"

Alex looked at Benjamin, who nodded. He placed three infantrymen and two cannons on top of the pin and closed the lid.

*

Abe held the five dollars and change he'd won on his bets at the tournament. The money felt warm in his hand—easy money that had come to him, not without a little bit of tension, that was true, but it sure beat working. My God, he thought, how in the world did Alex throw those darts like that? Those arms! God knew what He was doing when He gave them to the boy. It was a goddamn miracle, hell, like Abraham parting the Red Sea, he thought, his mind reeling back to the little he could remember from those Old Testament stories his uncle had told him. Maybe that miracle stuff was true after all.

Even if it wasn't a miracle, it sure was a huge opportunity. In his head he clicked off the bars and taverns in the immediate vicinity: Dee's Café, The Elbow Room, The Brass Rail, Kelly's—no, that joint was way too rowdy for a little boy—The End of the Road, Johnny & Joe's, Taylor's Bar, Kulka's. All were within a five-mile radius, and if the word hadn't spread about Alex's wondrous feat, Abe could walk into any or all of those joints and lay down a challenge to their best dart player. Hell, even if they had heard about Alex, so what? Chances were good they wouldn't believe a story like that, a tiny boy tossing darts with the pinpoint accuracy of Cy Young. He could hardly believe it himself. All he had to do was walk into a joint, lay some cash on the bar and announce, my money here says my little boy can beat any so-called champion dart thrower in the house. If he could shake lose, say, a ten or so from Delia, and God knows she's tight with a buck, why then he could turn his bets into some real money, a nice bit of jack for the two of them. The road ahead offered no shortage of bars and taverns where Alex could whip all comers. The boy was his meal ticket, and good meals at that, steak and potatoes and top-shelf whiskey. Hell, the rich bastards in this country made tons of money without doing a real lick of work. Why couldn't he? All he needed was someone to stake him.

But then, could he really go through with it? Would it be right to use his son like this? The boy seemed to be having a good time, but what if this day was a one-time miracle? How did he know Alex could do it again? And what about Irene? Oh yes, Irene. When she caught wind of it, she'd put the kibosh on it in two seconds. God damn it, he thought, why did things always have to get so complicated? He felt the curtain closing on his dream. But still. This was going to take some thought to make it happen.

"Excuse me, Mr. Miller."

"Malkin. I was just about to come upstairs. How is she?"

"I have given it to her something for the symptoms, yes, but she is quite ill, as you are knowing it. However, with some rest perhaps we shall see it an improvement." He sniffed the air. "Oh, excuse me, but before I had went upstairs to give it to your wife the physical examination, Mrs. Ida, a sweet and gentle woman as there ever is, she had offered it to me some soup. I am wondering now, as I see it is still on the table, as I would not want it should be wasted, if I may have it."

"Yeah, go ahead, help yourself, I don't care. Wait." Abe fingered a bill in his pocket. "What do I owe you?"

Forgetting his charitable offer just minutes before, Malkin said, "For you, just one dollar today. Please."

*

After Alex hid the stickpin, the boys added up the money from Principal Darwimple's wallet and the woman's change purse. Arthur put everything in the purse and told them he'd hide it somewhere in the basement, near the furnace, and that they would spend it a little at a time so nobody would know how much they had, which was a lie, since he had his eye on bigger things, namely a 25-inch pop gun that could shoot cork, peas or gravel.

The brothers shared more candy and sang a few rounds of *Row Row Row Your Boat* so loudly they didn't hear the gurgling sounds coming from their mother's bedroom.

Chapter 12

Irene died the following Monday. Abe swore up and down that her death was due to an overdose of Malkin's tonic, and while it certainly may have been a contributing factor, the Allegheny County Coroner's Office officially listed her death as it had listed the demise of more than 10,000 other Pittsburghers that year: heart and lung failure due to diphtheria.

A surprising number of Mellon Street neighbors turned out for the funeral and burial, surprising because of the nasty late March weather, and because Irene had never been very "social." If a neighborhood woman needed to borrow a cup of sugar or spread a rumor about someone else's husband, Irene Miller would have been far down the list of confidants.

Two inches of fast-melting spring snow had muddied the grounds around the gravesite, and the mourners stepped gingerly between the wet spots, trying to stay on the gray carpet that led to the newly dug grave. They clustered together tightly, perhaps with communal grief, but more likely to trying to find warmth in numbers.

Arthur and Benjamin stood stiff-legged in the slush in their new, poorly fitted black suits and dress shoes that Abe had purchased with his winnings from the wagers he'd made at the darts tournament. Benjamin held Abe's hand and sobbed quietly. Arthur held a handkerchief to his face, pretending to wipe his nose but in reality trying to hide tears.

Abe wore a broad-brimmed hat and his only suit, a navy blue pinstripe, with lapels that were decidedly too sporty for such a solemn occasion. He held Alex in his left arm and stood a bit unsteadily, partly out of grief, partly out of remorse, and partly because he'd been drinking since nine that morning.

Father Kiernan presided over the funeral. Ida had insisted that her daughter be given a Catholic burial and Abe consented, figuring she was brought up that way, let her go out that way. Kiernan instructed the assemblage to close ranks around the coffin, which was covered partially by a tarpaulin canopy. He seemed pleased with the turnout, which was larger than some of his weekday masses.

Despite the tarp, a drippy glaze covered the casket, a mid-priced metal model with a simple silver cross. Father Kiernan cleared his throat and began to speak with his flat, singsong intonation. "O God, by Your mercy, rest is given to the souls of the faithful, please to bless this grave. Appoint Your holy angels to guard it and set free from all the chains of sin and the soul of her whose body is buried here, so that with all Thy saints she may rejoice in Thee forever. Through Christ our Lord, amen."

The crowed said, "Amen."

Mildred Donnelley, standing near the back, whispered, "I hope he's don't go on and on with it."

The wind picked up, and people began to fidget and shiver. Father Kiernan seemed uncomfortable, too, perhaps because he hadn't spoken to Irene in years and the memory of her wild teenage ways and her marriage out of the faith had always disconcerted him. But he pressed on. "Because God has chosen to call our sister from this life to Himself, we commit her body to the earth, for we are dust and into dust we shall return."

As he tried to finish up, Ida kept repeating loudly that it was a terrible thing to outlive your child, that it wasn't natural, and her voice, full of angst and frustration, was so strident, Father Kiernan felt compelled to say, "Ida, please." He gestured to the mourners. "The 23rd psalm."

Standing thirty yards away under a large maple tree were four husky men in dark overalls and boots, smoking cigarettes and leaning on their shovels, seemingly unaffected by the weather or the ceremony. It was just another day, just another hole to dig, just another casket to pry open after the crowd had left, to see what jewelry they could salvage from the fingers and necks of the deceased. After all, who could make better use of the jewelry, the dead or the living?

After the last "amen," the crowd moved as quickly as decorum would allow to the relative warmth of the waiting cars and wagons. On Abe's instructions, Arthur and Benjamin took Ida's arms to help steady her over the bumpy ground. Abe and Alex followed.

The gravediggers moved around the coffin. They knocked the mud from their boots with their shovels. Fanning out around the casket, they maneuvered the burlap straps and began to lower away.

Alex, however, wasn't ready to leave. He twisted out of his father's arms and scrambled back toward the grave as fast as his arms and legs could carry him. Ida cried, "Someone grab him! He's going to throw himself in," but instead, Alex hurled the pick-pocketed diamond stickpin into the grave. Before Abe could retrieve him, as if he knew their intentions, Alex pointed at the gravediggers and shouted, "Leave her alone."

*

Back at Mellon Street an hour later, the mourners arrived in threes and fours, wet, chilly and hungry. Abe had stationed Arthur and Benjamin near the door to take their coats and stack them in the small living room. Hushed, respectful tones soon gave way to louder, more cordial, even slightly jovial exchanges as the well-wishers consumed free liquor and sandwiches, potato salad, deviled eggs and coffee cakes. Abe stood next to the dining room table and accepted heartfelt and not so heartfelt condolences from friends and neighbors, feeling melancholy and slightly numbed from his fourth drink of the day.

A shout came from the living room. "Mom's calling me!" It was Benjamin, pointing frantically to the second floor. "She's calling me now."

Abe jumped up. "Benjamin, calm down, son."

"She's calling me! She wants me right now." He ran up the stairs.

"Arthur, get him," Abe yelled, but Arthur, evidently spooked, stood rooted to the floor.

Upstairs, Abe found Benjamin sitting outside their room. "Mom called me, she said she needed me."

"It's all right, son, it's all right. Come on back downstairs."

"But she wants me here."

Abe put his arm around Benjamin's shoulders. "You're just imagining it, that's all."

Benjamin began to cry. "But she…I want to go to buh…bed."

"All right, Benjamin. You go lie down." Abe sighed. Wouldn't you know it, now it was the quiet son that needed all the attention. He put him to bed and helped him off with his shoes.

Despite Benjamin's hysterics, it was Alex who drew the most sympathy. Women kissed him on the forehead and explained that Momma had gone to a far better place, that she was now up in Heaven with Jesus, looking down on him right this moment, that Heaven is where all the good people go when they pass from this Earth, and even though you don't understand what has happened to your mother, someday you will, and on and on, espousing all the predictable clichés one might say to a lost little boy, a very little boy at that.

More than one of the women commented that they wished they could take the motherless Alex home with them, just look how precious he is.

The only missing member of the extended family was Ida, who had refused to come to Abe's house, preferring to go home by herself, saying that she wanted to go through some of Irene's childhood things. The truth was, she was unwilling to expose herself to the sympathy of strangers. She preferred the company of a bottle.

By one o'clock, the coal and iceman, Mr. Traficante, was halfway in the bag and looking to go all the way. He began to sing Italian folk songs, which thinned the crowd a little. Someone yelled at him to put a lid on it, but he kept on singing, albeit toned down a touch.

During the third chorus of *O Solo Mio*, a crew of a dozen men arrived from The Squeaky Wheel, led by John and Davy O'Brien. They carried platters of food, and John's barman wheeled in a keg of beer. The remaining neighbors decided they could put up with Traficante's singing now that reinforcements had arrived.

More than twenty people stood stuffed around the dining room table, where the food was set up. Cigars were out in full force, generating a low-hanging cloud of smoke. Alex sat in Davy's lap. Soon the conversation moved away from the sadness of Irene's passing into a retelling of Alex's dart-throwing exploits. According to Emil Kozich, who'd lost a dollar on Edward Peck, it was the strangest damn thing he'd ever seen—no wait, it was like a dream, wasn't that right, fellas? Yet and still, he asserted, the whole deal was bogus, John should have made Davy throw himself or forfeit the match. John told him to shut up, it was over and done with, but then even John couldn't help himself, he retold the story and turned to Alex. "Listen, kid, show everyone again how you threw them darts."

Alex looked at Davy, who was sipping Malkin's tonic from a silver flask. His complexion was greenish gray. He said, "Leave the child be, will you. His mother just passed."

"Never mind, I'll show you, " said Edward Peck. He did his best to imitate Alex's herky-jerky catapult motion, but Kozich told him, no, you got it all wrong. He palmed an orange from a fruit basket sent by Plotkin's Grocery and went into Alex's delivery. When he reached the apex the orange flew out of his hand and hit Mrs. Traficante squarely between the eyes, which caused Mr. Traficante to hit Kozich in return, and full-scale mayhem may have broken out between The Wheel crew and the locals had Davy not bellowed out a powerful chorus of *Amazing Grace*. The pushing and shoving gradually subsided, and as Davy crooned, Alex hummed along in a sweet, high-pitched voice.

As Davy sang, all eyes were on him except for Abe's. His gaze was firmly planted on a tall, pretty woman with dark bangs and a feathered hat standing just inside the door.

Delia motioned to Abe. With a furtive glance back at the crowd, which was imploring Davy to sing another, he slipped away to join her.

They stood outside, a couple of steps from the front door. "So," Delia said. "I'm sorry about your wife." She touched his arm. "Really I am. Maybe it ain't the same thing, but I was pretty shook up when I lost my mother, so I guess I know how you feel."

"Thanks."

Mr. and Mrs. Traficante edged by them. Halfway down the walkway, Mrs. Traficante peeked back over her shoulder.

"Anyway, Abe, I hope she didn't suffer too much."

"I don't know. I mean, she was pretty bad off, you know, the fever had her all confused."

"Malkin didn't show his face today, did he?"

"No, and if he does I'll break it for him."

"The son of a bitch."

Abe glanced down at his shoes, still splattered with mud from the cemetery. Irene would have made him take them off on the porch. "She was a good woman, you know."

"Sure."

"She didn't deserve this."

"This? You mean The Dip? Or do you mean, you-and-me this."

"Either. Both." He sniffed and wiped his face with a handkerchief. "Before the boys was born we had some good times, Irene and me. You wouldn't know it, but she was some dancer. Made me look like a cripple next to her."

Delia sighed. "No kidding." She turned her collar up against her neck. "Feels like it could snow some more."

"But then the boys came along and it seemed like our life together was over, at least the part of it where we were young."

"Yeah, well, we were all young once."

"I used to think, I got a good woman that wasn't afraid to marry a Jew, and now I'm a family man and, you know, I never had no family of my own, no brothers and sisters, no parents, grew up under my uncle's roof, so I figured a family would be nice and all. But by the second boy, a lot of things, they just went flat for me."

"And then I came along."

"You. And Alex."

"Yeah, Alex." Her eyes brightened for a second, but then she looked away. "Listen, Abe, I'd love to listen to your life story some more some time, but you got guests and I'm freezing my ass off."

Abe touched her hip. "You gotta go?"

She pressed his hand against her. "Honey, I'm taking a chance being here as it is. What if one of the boys from The Wheel seen me out here yapping it up with you? It don't look right, with your wife still warm in the grave. Don't look like that, I ain't trying to be mean, but she is. So anyway, I'll see you when I see you—how about a couple of Saturdays from now, at The Wheel, all right? I'm working Friday nights and Saturdays there for John now. I just come by today to pay my respects, to say I'm sorry."

Someone inside the house shouted Abe's name. He looked back, then at her. "Well, thanks."

"So anyway." What was she supposed to say now? That she loved him? That she wanted them to have a life together? Did she? She kissed him on the cheek and walked away.

He watched her go. It was all he could do not to follow after her.

Peck's shout hit him in the back of the neck. "Abe? What are you doing out in the cold? Everybody's waiting for you."

*

By five o'clock, the booze and food were gone and so were the visitors. Abe sat in a chair holding a cigar, but he didn't want a cigar. Here one moment, gone the next. How did you figure it? Why was it Irene and not him? No reason at all. No sense trying to figure it out, either. Leave all that to the rabbis and the priests. God's gonna do what He's gonna do, and that's it, and there not a goddamn thing a preacher or a doctor on an Indian chief can do about it. The best thing to do is get drunk. Maybe there was some beer left in that keg. His thoughts drifted to Delia and what she might be doing at the moment.

Alex's scream came from the living room.

Arthur yelled. "Dad, Alex fell off the sofa."

Alex said, "Arthur pushed me."

"Did not."

"Did, too."

Abe sighed. So this was what he was in for. "Come in here, the both of you." Arthur trailed Alex, so Abe knew he'd started it. "Boys, it's been a long day. Don't fight now, your mother wouldn't like it."

That shut them up. He'd have to remember to use that line again. "Do you miss your mother, boys?"

Alex said, "No, Daddy."

"You don't?"

"I can talk to her whenever I want."

Arthur said, "Don't be stupid, she's dead. I told you she was gonna die last week, didn't I?" He began to sob.

The neighbors had washed the dishes, put the food away and taken the trash out, so the downstairs was as clean as if Irene had done it. But without her, the house seemed preternaturally quiet. Every so often, Arthur looked up toward the second floor as if he heard something, too, like Benjamin had. Alex slept on the sofa, a little island of peace, and he looked so beatific Abe wished Irene were there to see him.

The sun was almost gone. "Boys," Abe said, "it's been a long day. It's time we all went to bed." He stretched and wondered what it would be like tomorrow, when the reality of Irene's death began to sink in, both to the boys and to him. He was thankful that Alex was so young. He'd probably be the first to get over it.

Arthur surprised him when he said, "Dad, can we sleep with you tonight?"

Abe had sleeping on the living room sofa, fearful of getting into the bed where Irene had died so miserably. But with his sons along, well, he had to start sometime. "All right. Bring your blankets and pillows and wake Benjamin."

They were all asleep at eight the next morning, until Alex woke up and announced, "Where's Momma?

Chapter 13

Billy Sunday was no stranger to Pittsburgh. From 1888 to 1890 he had manned center field for the soon-to-be defunct Pittsburgh Alleghenys. Although he was a poor to mediocre hitter—during his Pittsburgh years, his batting averages were .230, .240 and .257—the crowds loved his derring-do on the base paths and his hawk-like patrolling of center field. One sports reporter gushed, "The whole town is wild for Sunday."

Twenty-four years later, the town was wild for Sunday again. The former ballplayer now was the Reverend Billy Sunday, and in January of 1914 he set up his evangelical ministry in a tented tabernacle in the Oakland section of town, fittingly enough less than a mile from the city's new baseball stadium, Forbes Field. Over the next few months, Billy would deliver 124 services, drawing nearly 1.6 million townsfolk—way more than the Pirates would draw that year—eager to hear his pitch.

Ida had gotten an earful about the magical Mr. Sunday from her neighbor across the street, Delores Hertzel, who urged her to accompany her to see the man and the miracle. However, Ida wasn't much for the miraculous. "I needed a miracle four years ago, when my poor daughter died, only twenty-seven, with three boys and everything to live for."

Delores wasn't about to take no for an answer. "Perhaps the miracle you've been overlooking is your grandson Alex, and the fact he's alive, that The Dip didn't take him along with your Irene. Perhaps the good Lord has a plan for him. Perhaps his arms are part of the plan, too."

"Perhaps you should keep it to yourself. I'm not interested."

In fact, during the four years following Irene's death, the two things that interested Ida the most were medicating herself with gin or Irish whiskey and caring for her tiny grandson Alex. He lived at Ida's house Monday through Friday, and at Abe's on weekends, an arrangement that Abe had contentiously yet reluctantly agreed to, figuring that even though it broke up his family, what choice did he have? He was in no position to give the boy the attention he demanded, and the older boys were in school all day, at least when Arthur wasn't playing hooky.

Delores finally wore Ida down. On a windy Saturday night toward the end of January, as the full moon intermittently flashed through the clouds of soot that wafted up from the Second Avenue rolling mills, the two women stepped down from the Negley Avenue trolley and into the throng pressing toward Reverend Sunday's makeshift house of worship. Despite her skepticism, Ida felt herself getting swept up in the fervor.

The sidewalks overflowed with some 20,000 or so parched souls, come to look for sustenance from Reverend Billy—men on crutches, women in wheelchairs, the deaf leading the blind, the able-bodied leading the crippled, the daft, the doubters, the poor, the soon-to-be-poor, and everyday hardworking people, all politely pushing and shoving their way in closer, as close as they could come to the reverend, in their heavy coats and boots, sneezing and coughing and smoking and screaming and laughing, thrilled to be in that number marching to salvation.

Although they had arrived early and could get no closer than twenty yards of the man, Delores and Ida could hear Billy loud and clear as he cavorted across the stage. Defying the chilly air as much as the forces of evil, Billy had discarded his white linen suit coat, and beads of sweat poured down his face. He preened and gestured like a fighting rooster, locked in a one-sided conversation with the Devil, as if the Antichrist were sitting cross-legged on a stool in front of him. He went so far as to threaten to punch the Devil in the nose and kick his teeth down his throat, to the roars and laughter of the crowd.

Ida thought she'd never heard such malarkey in her life, and was ready to leave, Delores or no Delores, but during one of Billy's dramatic pauses there was a gap in the crowd in front of her, and she happened to lock eyes with the reverend. In that instant, it was revealed to her via his blue-eyed intensity and toothy smile that she was meant to be there, that she was meant to believe. The rest of the crowd and the world melted away. She thought she heard him say, "Sister, you must be saved by the blood of the lamb." She clutched Delores's arm for balance; with the sudden lightness that came over her, she felt as if she might float away, and in that moment, she was Billy's, hook, line and sermon.

Leaving Alex in the care of Margaret Conroy, her next-door neighbor, she and Delores went back to hear Billy preach every day that week, and every day Ida dropped a dollar and change into the hat that circulated around the room. She wished she could have given more to support such a pious, driven man who'd chosen to bring God's message to the multitudes free of charge. She needn't have worried. The Pittsburgh campaign was very good to Billy. By the end of his eight-week stay, the reverend had pocketed nearly $35,000.

She stopped going to mass completely. All that kneeling and praying, the vagueness of the Latin, the solemnity, the confessions, the rituals, the guilt, the alabaster statues of an agonized Christ, it all seemed so stodgy and dreary and cold compared to the vibrancy of Reverend Sunday and the spark he had kindled in her life. A thought hit her like a line drive from Billy's bat: Reverend Sunday just might be Alex's salvation. She imagined herself and her grandson, hand in hand, his long right arm reaching up toward the heavens, walking the sawdust trail in front of the stage, and perhaps a mere touch from Billy would cure him once and for all, even him out, make him grow like a normal boy.

Almost six now, Alex was the size of a well-proportioned 18-month-old boy, except for his arms, which at rest hung down a touch over two inches below his knees. His brothers called him Stretch, which he hated.

It had taken him weeks to accept living away from the house on Mellon Street, since he insisted over and over that his mother would be coming back and he needed to be there when she did. On the first morning he was scheduled to go to Ida's house, he held onto the frame of his mother's bed so tightly, Abe had had to pry his long arms away.

Alex missed his father, especially in the evenings before bedtime, when Abe would hold him in his lap and let him read the newspaper to him, the comforting smell of cigar smoke on his father's fingers. He hated to be away from his brothers, too, from the joking and teasing and game playing, and the snores and farts at night in their bedroom.

However, he did like his grandmother's cooking, which was a vast improvement on his father's tasteless meat and potatoes, which he cooked on Sunday and reheated the rest of the week. In the hope of stimulating his growth, Ida fed him copious amounts of rich foods: breakfasts of eggs and bacon or sausage, oatmeal with sugar, cinnamon, raisins and cream; farmer's cheese, macaroni and cheese and fat sandwiches and cookies for lunch; and dinners of pork chops with gravy, meatloaf and mashed potatoes with butter and buttered beans, creamed vegetables, chicken and dumplings, liver and onions, all served with glasses of buttermilk or chocolate milk. And for dessert, pies with ice cream, chocolate fudge cake, and more sugar cookies. Alex devoured everything, in portions astonishingly large relative to his size, all to no avail. Ida wondered where it all went—until it was time to empty his chamber pot.

Having his own bedroom was another issue. It was too big, too quiet, too clean. He much preferred to be stuffed in with Arthur and Benjamin, fighting and giggling and pinching each other, than be left alone at night in his mother's childhood bedroom, with its frilly curtains and flowered wallpaper. On those nights, when he felt particularly lonely, Alex would drag his blue blanket into Ida's bedroom and curl up at her feet, next to Jack, the orange Maine Coon cat.

He spent a lot of time reading. He'd tired of his *A Child's Life of Christ* and started on Ida's encyclopedia, beginning with *Volume A-Ar*. Straddling the open book, he often read out loud to Jack, who seemed to regard Alex with a mixture of reverence and horror, alternately nuzzling his legs and hiding from him under a large horsehair chair.

On a sunny Tuesday morning, two weeks after Ida's lightning conversion to Sunday-ism, she burst into the living room carrying a large tin bucket. She tore open the tall cabinet where she kept her liquor. She grabbed a nearly full fifth of Irish whiskey and proclaimed in a strident voice, as if she were the keynote speaker at a Women's Christian Temperance Union meeting, "Whiskey has its place. Its place is in Hell," which was one of Reverend Sunday's most quotable lines regarding proper location of alcoholic beverages.

Alex looked up from the encyclopedia. "Grandma, see the picture. The giant anteater."

Ida paused, but not with wonder at *Mymecophaga Tridactyla*. She stared long and hard at the bottle in her hand. "I must be strong. I must be strong for the Lord, and for you, dear Alex."

"Anteaters, they eat ants. It says an anteater has no teeth but its tongue is two feet long." Alex stuck his tongue out as far as he could. "How long is my tongue, Grandma? I ate an ant once in the backyard. It was brown but it tasted bad."

"You ate what?"

"My tongue. Look. How long is it?"

Ida pulled off a bottle cap. She poured the liquor into the bucket "I'm sending you to Hell."

"Benjamin says 'Hell' is a dirty word."

In five minutes, Ida emptied the entire contents of her liquor cabinet: two quarts of Irish whiskey, a fifth of sloe gin, a pint of rye, a bottle of sherry and a bottle of apricot brandy. She poured the bucket down the drain in the kitchen. The liquor fumes hovering over the sink drifted to her face and made her feel light-headed, either with exhilaration or remorse, she wasn't sure, but now that she had started down the path of righteousness there was no turning back.

She went back to the living room. Alex was still in his pajamas. "Alex, time to get dressed."

"Why?"

"Come on."

Upstairs, as Alex played with toy soldiers, Ida went through his wardrobe. Most of his clothes were hand-me-downs from his brothers' toddler outfits, which Irene had had the foresight to save and which Ida had to tailor to accommodate Alex's unique physique. She pursed her lips. If she were going to take him to a Billy Sunday service, he needed to be dressed properly. It wasn't that the crowds that came to the prayer meetings were particularly well clad. In fact, Ida had been appalled at the slovenliness of the mill workers, coal miners, day laborers and city workers, and especially their children, who looked like so many refugee ragamuffins. She was determined that her grandson needed to be dressed like a little gentleman when he met up with Reverend Sunday, even if it meant taking an advance on her next month's budget.

"Alex, let's get you washed up. It's time to go shopping."

Alex jumped up and down. "Woolworth's, Woolworth's."

Ida picked him up and hugged him tightly. "Not today, my handsome boy. We're going to Kauffman's."

Ida took close to an hour to get ready, for one didn't go downtown to Kaufmann's, Pittsburgh's premiere department store, looking like a housewife in the midst of cleaning the toilet. She tried on three outfits before she decided on a light blue wool suit and white blouse, her Easter outfit, the one she'd decided on for Billy's service that evening. She even powdered her face and put on lipstick for the first time since her daughter's funeral.

With Alex by her side, they barely made it past Kauffmann's cosmetics counter when women shoppers began to glom onto them. At first Ida felt important, as if she were the grandmother of a child movie star, but after a few moments of tolerating the clutches and grabs at her grandson, she reverted to her safer, surlier self and robustly pushed away the curiosity seekers.

They boarded the elevator and rose toward the fifth floor, Children's Wear. As the elevator began to climb, Alex said, "Grandma, the room is moving. Where are we going? Up to the sky? It's too dark."

Elmer Setich, the normally stoic operator, laughed out loud. "Ain't he a cute pup. First time on an elevator, sonny? Say, how old is he, lady?"

Alex said, "I'm almost six."

"Go on with you. You are?"

"But, Grandma, where does this go?"

"Up to our floor. You'll see." She laughed. "Full of questions, night and day."

As the other passengers stared straight ahead, Alex lifted the billfold of Walter Blaney, a saturnine man who was assistant manager, Men's Furnishings. Blaney half turned, as if he noticed a slight movement in his back pocket, but, elevator etiquette being what it was, he remained silent, his eyes tightly focused straight ahead, until he got off on Three.

Two stops later, Alex dropped the emptied billfold on the elevator floor as he and Ida got off. Later that day, Setich turned the wallet into Kaufmann's Lost & Found department, but not before he pocketed thirty-two cents from the change compartment.

Ida and Alex strolled through the toddler's section. Alex ran his fingers over everything he could reach. Two saleswomen tripped over each other trying to wait on them. They showed Ida a variety of shorts, shirts, coats, a checked suit and a tiny sailor's suit, all in two sizes—one for his arms, one for the rest of him—per Ida's instructions. "Oh," said Louise Beverson, the senior sales clerk, "he'll look like a handsome little doll. Blue is his color."

Ida was pleased with the attention. "Alex," she said, "what do you think?"

"I want that." He pointed to an orange cap with a wide brim on top of a manikin.

With three duplicate outfits over her arm, Miss Beverson said, "Will you be taking them with you today?"

"Just the new suit.

"The cap, Grandma."

"And the cap. You can send the others. All right, Alex?"

"Okey dokey." Alex put the cap on his head and turned the narrow brim sideways, so he'd look like a boy he'd seen illustrated in a magazine.

"Isn't he the cutest little monkey? Where did you get those arms, dear?" Alex looked at his grandmother. "Jesus."

It was two o'clock by the time they left Kaufmann's and three by the time they arrived home. Alex had fallen asleep on the trolley. Ida carried him upstairs and placed him down on her bed. She lay down beside him, pulled up the quilt and reached her forearm around his shoulder. She closed her eyes and dreamed of Billy.

*

Even in the early months of 1914 the threat of world war loomed on Europe's doorstep, and Arthur, who'd barely opened a book in four years—he'd repeated seventh grade twice—couldn't get enough of news from "across the pond." He read every article in the daily paper he took home from his after-school job at Plotkin's Grocery Store. Europe's impending conflict had become an obsession with him, and he began to get to school early so he could get to the school library and study the towns and landscapes of France, Germany, Belgium, Bulgaria and Turkey on the world atlas. He knew the locations of the local U.S. army, navy and marine recruiting stations and went by them on Sundays to stare at the recruitment posters in the windows. *Your Country Needs You. Now's the Time to Enlist!* The drumbeat was calling.

Benjamin was interested in the war, too, but had become far more passionate about baseball. Never much of an athlete, he began to blossom physically as he entered his early teens; his limbs lengthened, his foot speed increased dramatically, as did his hand-eye coordination, and he showed a natural propensity for hitting a baseball, no matter how fast the ball was pitched, perhaps due to his keen eyesight, which, had Dr. Malkin the instruments or knowledge to measure properly, would have registered 20/15.

Everything Abe knew about the impending war he got from Arthur's daily updates. Even though Ida took Alex during the week, riding herd on his older sons, working overtime and keeping the house at least semi-habitable meant he barely had time to read the newspaper before he fell asleep at night in his easy chair, a half-smoked cigar resting in the ashtray. Household obligations had cut deeply into his time with Delia Novak, too. Consequently, their relationship, which Delia referred to as "this thing we do," was as stagnant as the air above an open hearth on a humid summer night. As the months went on, Abe realized it had been far easier to have a mistress when he had a wife.

It was close to six o'clock on the Friday before Ida was to take Alex to see Reverend Billy. Abe had gotten home late from work. He carried a large paper sack with four fish and fried potato dinners he'd picked up from The Olde Oyster House in Market Square, in deference to Ida and her Friday preference. Even though he'd "paid through the nose," as he told his boys, he was fairly flush, with steady work and plenty of overtime to be had at Shields Metal now that the steel industry was ramping up production for the inevitable wartime shortfalls of its allies, whomever they would turn out to be.

Arthur stood at the kitchen sink, rinsing breakfast dishes. He was as tall as his father, and almost as broad, with Irene's red hair and light complexion. Benjamin was halfway out the side door, holding an industrial-sized trash barrel with a week's worth of garbage. Will you look at these two, Abe thought, doing what I told them this morning before I left, without me yelling at them, will wonders never cease. He set the sack of food on the counter.

Arthur looked up. "Smells good, Dad."

Abe's stomach gurgled at the aroma of fried potatoes. He took one of the dinners wrapped in newspaper from the sack. "Don't suppose it would hurt to have a little taste before your grandmother and Alex get here, huh? Arthur, get your old man a beer, would you?"

"Yes, sir." Arthur opened the icebox. "Dad, did you hear, the Gerrys might push into France any day now."

"Ain't that jumping the gun a little bit there?"

"Well, I read it just today. They're tight with the Turks and the Austrians. There was a map. We've got to get ready for this thing."

Benjamin closed the door behind him. "He wants to enlist, Dad."

"I would in a minute if I could. I don't see why a 16-year-old can't serve."

Abe fingered a potato. "War is a terrible thing, boys, a terrible thing."

"But you never fought in a war, and now you're too old."

"Yeah, well ask your grandmother sometime about what happened to your grandfather in the Spanish-American War. Poor guy got blown to smithereens when they sunk the *Maine*."

The front door creaked open. "Daddy!" Alex rushed into the kitchen and threw his arms around Abe's legs.

"Wow, look at Alex," Benjamin said. "Where'd you get that hat?"

Ida had dressed him in his new checked suit. "Don't let him get dirty now."

"Come on, Alex." His brothers hoisted him by the arms and headed upstairs.

Abe finished his beer and thought about opening another, but it was Friday, which called for something a little stiffer. He took his bottle of rye from the cupboard above the sink and checked the level to determine if his boys had nipped any. He poured two fingers for Ida and two for himself. "Here's to your health, Ida."

She put her hand over her glass. "None for me, thank you. I've sworn off the stuff."

"You? You're pulling my leg."

"Oh, it's no joke, Abe. Liquor is the Devil's tool."

Abe scratched his head, as if considering that it might be so. "Maybe so. But hell, Ida, that never seemed to bother you before."

"And I'll thank you to want to watch that mouth of yours around me, too. I don't take to cursing now, either."

Maybe the woman is already drunk, he thought. She did seem to have some kind of glow about her, but her smile was too broad, her eyes were too wide open. Something had its hooks into her.

Upstairs, Arthur did twenty-five push-ups with Alex sitting on his back. His side of the room was a neat as a Marine's barracks awaiting inspection.

Alex slid off his back. "Look what I have." He took three one-dollar bills and a faux diamond hatpin from his pockets, the swag from his Kaufmann's heist. He smiled up at Arthur. "See?"

Arthur closed the door. He whispered, "Put that stuff away." He explained to Alex that he didn't want him to steal anymore, he was through with selling stolen stuff at school. He'd been thinking it over, that he couldn't afford to get caught, since he was going to enlist as soon as he could and that he couldn't have a criminal record because the army didn't want criminals.

Besides, it wasn't honorable to do what he'd been doing, no soldier would ever do that, it was against the soldier's code of conduct to commit any sort of crime.

Alex was on the verge of tears. He appealed to Benjamin, his long arm reaching for his brother's waist.

"You know I won't take it, Alex."

Abe called, "Boys, dinner."

Benjamin folded his hand over Alex's. "Just stick it back in your pocket for now."

"Don't tell Dad, either. And Alex, don't steal no more."

"Boys!"

Ida placed bowls of pickles and bread on the table. She sniffed at the paper bag. "Fish?"

Abe said, "Your Friday regular."

"You don't have to do that anymore. I'm no longer with the Romans."

Abe sipped his rye. "What the hell—pardon my French—is going on with you, Ida? No booze, no cursing, and now you're telling me you're not a Catholic, just like that? What's it all about?"

Ida's smile was beatific. "I met a man."

Chapter 14

Three inches of wet snow had turned to sooty slush, but even if it had transformed into quicksand, it wouldn't have deterred the masses that came to clap and cheer and collapse in front of Reverend Billy during his Monday night sermon on the first of February.

Ida and Alex arrived two hours early, so determined was she to find a seat on the aisle, center section, as close to Billy's podium as she could get. She'd packed a dinner of meatloaf sandwiches, green bean casserole and oatmeal cookies, along with a thermos of hot chocolate. She'd considered picking up a pint of Irish whiskey, too, just the thing to navigate a cold, blustery night, but then, she told herself, she was beyond that now. She'd pledged for Reverend Billy. How could she throw over their relationship for a bottle?

Alex insisted on removing his new coat, even though the air inside the makeshift tabernacle was cold enough to vaporize his breath. He watched the workmen sweep the stage and place a bullhorn and microphone on Billy's famous pedestal, from which he'd been known to do leaps and handstands. He wandered up to the men as if he were inspecting their work, and soon became a distraction for them—what's yer name, sonny, you're *how* old, now quit playing with me, my boy. Ida chased after him and tried unsuccessfully to get him to sit still. Finally, to keep him occupied she gave him two cookies and her Bible, randomly opening to Corinthians.

By seven o'clock the makeshift house of prayer was almost full, with both curious first-timers and dedicated regulars. The murmur of anticipation for the evening's service was palpable. Occasionally, groups of people broke out to sing the praises of the Lord, a cappella, a righteous warm-up to the evening's event.

On the side of the aisle opposite Ida two rows back from Billy's pedestal stood a uniformed chauffeur and butler. They held a rope between them that stretched across six seats, and politely but briskly turned away anyone that attempted to occupy the prime real estate. When Alex tugged on their pants or kicked at their ankles to get their attention, they ignored him as if they were guards standing in front of Buckingham Palace.

The very front row was out of bounds, however, even for the holy wealthy, for that row was reserved for Reverend Billy's special cases, which included the infirm, the crippled and members of clergy that came either to "praise Caesar or to bury him," as Billy might joke.

Thirty minutes before the service was to begin, every seat was taken, and then some, with people standing in the back—*God hears you in the back just as good as in the front,* the saying went. Ida and Alex sat next to an older couple, the Santorinis, who had journeyed to the makeshift Mecca from Wheeling, West Virginia, some forty miles south. They were taken by Alex and his sweet voice and smile, and they offered him their hard candies, which he stuffed into his cheeks and pockets.

The Santorinis confided to Ida that, like her, they'd suffered the loss of a child—two, in fact, for their sons had been buried alive in the Monongah Mining Disaster of '07, an explosion that claimed the lives of 362 boys and men and created 250 widows. "And what does the company say to you? Nothing. What do they do for you? Nothing. What is the death of your boys worth to them? Nothing. Not a blessed thing. They're worried about their mine, that's all, about how soon can they get it going again. The almighty dollar, that's their religion. That's who they bow down to. The workingman is like a slave to them, a dime a dozen. Our poor boys, dead and gone." It was their third time to see Reverend Sunday.

"Solace for our suffering. That's why we're here." Ida squeezed Mrs. Santorini's hand. "It's my fourth time, dear, and my Alex's first. Isn't it, sweetheart? Alex? Alex!"

The Bible lay open on the seat, but Alex was nowhere in sight. Ida stared left and right, got down on her hands and knees and groped under their seats. She shouted his name but her voice was swallowed up by singing and organ music.

During a rousing chorus of *Gimme That Old Time Religion,* Alex had worked his way across the aisle and, hidden behind a large woman's legs, gazed intently at the open purse of Mrs. Winston Childs, the wife of a cousin to one of the Fricks. Alex had his eyes on something sparkly, but he thought, Arthur doesn't want me to steal anymore, but I could give it to Grandma. She bought me all new clothes. It would be a present, not stealing.

He scanned the row, taking in the chauffer and butler, who every so often shot a menacing glance at him. Mrs. Childs was on her feet, her white ermine wrap bouncing on her neck as she clapped her hands to the music, along with her best friends and bridge partners, Chappie Morton and Ginny Smith-Walters. When everyone else raised both hands in the air, up to Heaven as Billy implored them, Alex reached into the purse for the bracelet, but simultaneously felt himself being lifted into the air by a man who smelled of pomade and herring.

Meanwhile, Ida went from worshipper to worshipper, tugging arms, tapping shoulders, frantic to find her grandson. When she described him in detail, most people thought she was out of her mind, with or without the Holy Spirit, but one elderly man said he thought he might have seen a very small boy in an orange cap, but which way he went, he couldn't be sure. She doubled back to her seat in the hope that Alex would miraculously turn up on his own, for after all, this was the place for miracles, and the Lord knows she deserved one.

She had sunk to her knees and raised her eyes to the heavens, prepared to tell God she was ready to give up ten years of her life to get Alex back, when there he was, or rather, there was his orange hat. It bobbed up and down above the crowd, coming closer and closer. God has lifted him on high, she thought, above the multitude, until she saw that it wasn't God at all, but a man with a greasy hat, a dark goatee and pince-nez glasses, riding Alex on his shoulders. A few moments later he was in Ida's arms, courtesy of Dr. Sergei Malkin.

Ida hugged Alex tight to her breast. She also twisted his ear so hard his yelp turned heads two rows away. "Don't you ever scare me like that again, you little scamp." She squinted at Malkin. "You. I know you."

"Ah, Mrs. Ida, Dr. Sergei Malkin, at your service." Malkin bowed and bumped his elbow into Mrs. Santorini's ribs. "Excuse me, madam. Such a crowd it is here. Lucky was it that for you and the boy that I happened to be it in the vicinity of which he was standing, no? When he showed it to me where it was you are sitting, I felt it to be it my duty to bring him back to you. It is the second time I am delivering this little one, is it not?"

"What?"

"I am making it a joke with you, you see, for I have delivered him both at birth and now. Well, perhaps it is me only that I find it the humor in it."

"What? I can't understand you with all this noise."

"Yes. Well," he shouted, "I think you should know it that I caught the little one here with his long arms trying to steal it a bracelet."

"What?"

Malkin shouted, "A bracelet I am saying."

"I heard what you said." Ida grabbed Alex again by the ear. "Stealing? Don't you know stealing is a sin, Alex? Thou shalt not steal. Thou shalt not steal. Repeat it after me, Alex. Thou shalt not steal!"

"But I was just looking at it."

Malkin shook his head no.

Ida tweaked his ear even harder. "And thou shalt not lie, either. How could you do this to me, Alex? My grandson stealing, it's a black mark on me. Don't you want me to be saved? Don't you want to be saved, my dear little one?"

Alex thought that if getting saved meant having his grandmother stop pinching him and getting out of this place, he was all for it. "Yes, Grandma."

"Praise the Lord." Ida hugged him. She could see now that she had her work cut out for her, to bring her little one back to the path of righteousness and away from the temptations of stealing and whatever other sins he might have committed. His brothers, they must have put him up to it. Stealing, and a lie on top of it. God forbid Reverend Billy would get wind of a thief in their midst, even such a small, adorable one. She turned to Malkin. "The Christian thing to do would be to thank you. But I'll never forget what that mumbo-jumbo tonic of yours did to my daughter. Probably killed her, that's what."

Malkin bowed his head. "Sorry it is that I am to lose it any patient, particularly the mother of the little one, and I pray it to God she is up in Heaven, but you see, the diphtheria, The Dip, it will take it who it wants until there is a cure, which, by the way, may be with this little boy."

Reverend Sunday shouted, "Can I have an A-men?"

Alex, who hoped his grandmother would hear the repentance in his voice, shouted, "A-men!"

"What are you talking about?"

Malkin explained that it was quite extraordinary that a little one such as Alex could survive The Dip when it took the weak and the old and even the boy's mother, a healthy young woman, and that if Ida would consent to let him study Alex, draw blood and tissue samples and the like, perhaps he could find a cure or an antidote or even develop a vaccination against the dreaded disease. He had felt this way for many years but never had the chance to properly study the boy. "So you see, missus, it is for the scientifical progress of disease prevention for which I am asking it."

Reverend Billy implored the crowd. "Say it with me, ladies. Lips that touch liquor shall never touch mine!"

Women responded heartily. Men frowned.

"I don't have a clue in the world what you're talking about, but whatever it is, it's something you'll have to take up with his father." She turned her attention to Billy, who leaped into the air, his coat tails flaring out behind him. "And anyway, what are you doing here in the first place? You ain't no Christian, that's for sure, not by a long shot."

Malkin reached into his medical bag. "You see?" It was a flyer, promoting his practice—*Dr. Sergei Malkin, Medical Doctor, Dentist and Babies Doctor also.* "There could be it here a lot of new customers for me, God willing, as the preacher he might put it, not that I am in competition with him for the healing."

"Sisters, oh my sisters," Billy said, "who among you are true daughters of Jerusalem?"

*

That week, as part of his penance, Ida had Alex read to her every evening. "Not from the encyclopedia, dear, from the good book."

"But I want to read about Africa. Elephants, Grandma."

"Africa? Where the darkies come from? I don't want to hear about that foolishness. Here." She handed him her copy of the New Testament. Without looking, she flipped open to Luke 24. "Read."

Alex stared at it for a few seconds. The text seemed alien. "'But on the first day of the week, at early dawn, they went to the tomb."

"Tooooomb, dear, not Tom-b, tooomb." She closed her eyes, and she could see the golden desert sand and the palm trees that fluttered in the gentle, restorative breezes of the Holy Land, and camels and goats and holy men dressed in flowing robes, walking to the tomb. If she truly wanted to be a daughter of Jerusalem, as Reverend Sunday had said, she had to find a way to get there.

"They went to the too-oomb, taking spices which they had prepared."

Ten seconds later, she was fast asleep. Alex didn't notice until he stopped reading and asked her what became of Jesus' body.

*

Reverend Sunday moved on from Pittsburgh, but the Holy Spirit was alive and kicking in Ida Murphy, fueled by Alex's recitations of the Ten Commandments and his nightly readings from the good book. The way he pronounced the words was so moving, so sincere—out of the mouth of babes, she thought—that she wondered, perhaps the Holy Spirit had entered him, too.

With a gift like his, so wonderful and rare, the Christian thing to do was share it. She knew Billy Sunday would approve, and so she called on her next-door neighbor, Margaret Conroy.

Despite their friendship, Margaret had never been farther inside Ida's house than the vestibule, and was a bit taken aback when Ida invited her for dinner, ostensibly to thank her for baby-sitting Alex. She arrived at five-thirty in her second-best dress, carrying a loaf of soda bread she'd baked that morning.

After dinner Ida set out tea, and the women made small talk about how the neighborhood was going to hell in a hand-basket, what with the Dagos and Polacks moving in like termites, you couldn't trust them, that was for sure, they were *clannish*, and besides, wasn't it bad enough the Jews already owned half the real estate on the street? "Well, anyway, Margaret," Ida said as she stacked the teacups in soapy water, "you are in for a revelation. Wait until you hear Alex read."

Margaret said, "He can read? I didn't know that. But he hasn't even been to school yet, has he? He's awfully young to know how to read."

"Sometimes I think he's older than Methuselah, the things that come out of his mouth. Alex?"

He came into the room holding a pretzel. "Hello, Mrs. Conroy."

Ida said, "Dear, would you like to read for Mrs. Conroy?"

With nothing better to do, he nodded yes, and took the New Testament from the bookcase.

Margaret hesitated. "I thought you meant a children's book."

Ida beamed. "Just pick a passage. Any passage."

She looked at the tiny boy holding the large volume. Something was out of kilter, but she decided to go along with it. "Well, I've always been partial to Corinthians."

Alex flipped through the pages and began, "Do you not know that you are God's temple and that God's spirit dwells in you? If any one destroys God's temple, God will destroy him. For God's temple is holy, and that temple is you."

Margaret fainted.

By the middle of March, as many as ten people from the neighborhood attended Alex's after-dinner readings, which Ida had moved to a more spacious venue, her living room. The women brought tokens of their appreciation—toys, clothes and sweets for Alex, doilies, knickknacks and candles for Ida. Alex would read a passage, stopping when he was tired or too bored to go on. At that point, the women began to discuss the meaning of the scripture or the meaning of this strange and wondrous little boy so adroit at reciting the word of the Lord.

News of Alex's readings spread faster than crabgrass in summer, and soon Ida had to limit the size of the gatherings, lest her house be overrun by the curious righteous. Order, that was the key. She devised a system based on last names. Letters A through L came Monday and Wednesdays, M through Z Tuesdays and Thursdays. Friday was Alex's day off, when both he and Ida took a needed break.

Running out of gift ideas, the faithful began to leave legal tender of various denominations with Ida: a dime here, a quarter there. At first she declined to accept the cash, but when she considered the wear and tear on her living room and factored in the cost of supplying tea with sugar and lemon and cookies for the after-Alex discussions, she came to expect monetary offerings, and she felt stiffed if someone left without making one. The lion's share of the cash went into her growing Jerusalem fund.

By April, certain spiritually needy individuals began to make discreet inquiries as to the possibility of having private sessions with Alex, and although these consultations would cut into his naptime, Ida felt it was her righteous duty to pursue this new revenue stream. She had seen a newspaper advertisement about a Holland America Line luxury cruise from New York to the Holy Land. True, the trans-Atlantic journey was fraught with peril—who could forget the sinking of the *Titanic* in 1912, when over 1,500 souls went to chilly graves at the bottom of the sea—but then, the road to salvation was paved with perils, and what were her difficulties compared to the Lord's suffering for her sake? And so, the notion of making a pilgrimage to the Holy Land, accompanied by her remarkable grandson, glowed like a hot coal inside her. The child had a gift, no doubt a very special gift, and she was certain it was God's will that she bring Alex to Jerusalem, to walk the paths that Jesus had walked, for after all, he just might be the new Messiah, and wouldn't it be wonderful that she, grandmother and daughter of Jerusalem, had brought him there for the salvation of the world?

To create a more intimate, sanctified setting for their private clients, Ida moved her overstuffed leather chair into her sitting room, stacked three pillows on the seat and placed Alex on top. She dressed him in a white shirt, too broad in the torso but with sleeves long enough to cover his arms, and hung a large silver crucifix around his neck. He insisted on wearing his orange cap, a concession she grudgingly gave in to after he threw a fit. For some reason, the Maine Coon perched on top of the chair during the sessions, Sphinx-like behind Alex. Ida kept the shades drawn and lit a string of votive candles, which created flickering silhouettes of the boy and the cat against the background.

Mrs. Agnes Mullins, from nearby Atkins Avenue, was the first private client. Even though she'd just turned forty-eight, incipient osteoporosis had already shrunk her to less than five feet tall, so that when she knelt before Alex on his cushioned throne, he towered over her, diminutive and iconic.

Agnes looked to Ida, uncertainty welling up in her watery blue eyes, clearly discombobulated at the specter of Alex and the cat looming over her. "Ida," she croaked, "what do I say?"

Ida really hadn't thought about it. She said, "Well, do you have a favorite passage?"

"No, I hadn't planned on one, I'm sorry." Slow moments passed by.

"How about the 23rd psalm? " She had printed it out on white paper for Alex beforehand as a fallback for such an occasion, figuring that, even though it was from the Old Testament, who didn't like the 23rd?

"Oh, that would be fine."

Ida held out her palm.

"Yes, of course, sorry." Agnes put a fifty-cent piece in Ida's hand.

"Alex, go ahead."

Alex looked at the words and decided he wasn't interested. What he really wanted was for this woman to be gone and to have his nap. He yawned.

"Alex," Ida repeated.

He thought about how Reverend Billy preached to the people, and, emulating the minister, stood on the pillows and pointed at Agnes. "Jesus knows what you have done."

Both Agnes and Ida said, "What?"

He repeated, "Jesus knows what you have done." He reached behind him, and thanks to his long arms had no trouble patting the cat on the head, who was staring, unblinking, into cat infinity.

Agnes began to sob. As if on cue, Ida hunkered down beside her. In a small, choked voice, Ida said, "Please, what does Jesus know, Alex?"

Whether or not Alex knew what Jesus knew became pretty much a moot point, since before he could answer, Agnes decided to spill the beans. "It's Tom, isn't it?"

"Mary Agnes?"

"Oh, I have sinned against God and for that I beg forgiveness." She sniffed. Small puddles of tears began to form on the polished hardwood floor. "It's only the one time, I swear it. Oh don't stare at me so, Alex, please. You don't know the misery I have swallowed down all these months, lying awake night after night, and my husband, he won't touch me anymore, won't lie close to me, he won't put his arm around me, I don't know why, I've been a good wife, submissive, caring. But late at night while he sleeps, I can't help it, I have these, these *thoughts*. I know it's wrong, I know it's a mortal sin, but as I lay there one night not so long ago, I saw my neighbor's husband Tom in my mind, with his dark mustache and smile, and I began to…I began to *touch* myself…in that way. Please, I couldn't help it, don't make me say anymore."

Ida put her hand over her mouth. Alex stared at the sobbing, prostrate woman. The cat, evidently feeling that the juiciest part of the confession was over, leaped from the top of the chair and brushed against Agnes, who recoiled from him as if he were The Beast incarnate.

Agnes said, "I know what I've done is a sin. I'm so ashamed, I am impure. I don't know what to do, please tell Jesus to forgive me." She bowed her head again.

Alex leaned forward and rested his chin on his knuckles. Seeing Agnes cry reminded him of his mother, and how she had cried as she lay in bed, in pain from The Dip, and how his mother's tears made him want to cry, too, and crying was sad, and he didn't like to be sad, and he didn't want this old lady to be sad from what he said. "Don't cry."

Agnes wiped her eyes. She managed to look up at him and smile. "Oh thank you, Alex, God bless you. I won't cry anymore, I promise."

The women helped each other to their feet. Before she left, Agnes gave Ida another fifty cents.

As the front door closed, Alex said, "Grandma, can I come down now?"

*

Agnes Mullins felt compelled to tell Betty Koehler about her life-changing encounter with Alex. Betty felt similarly compelled to tell Helen Gault, and on and on it went, and soon the supplicants, as Ida called them, began to stop by her house at all hours in the hope of seeing the messianic little fellow.

Even when Ida turned them away, the seekers left a variety of religious offerings on Ida's front steps, from rosary beads to holy cards and statuettes of the Virgin Mary. There was non-religious tribute as well—bowls of fruit, bags of candy and nuts, toy animals and, for some reason, combs, along with notes and carefully scripted letters regarding sick children, financial difficulties, cheating husbands, the implications of the impending world war on the U.S. economy, as well as unanswerable questions, such as, would the labor movement succeed, what was wrong with the Pirates, would T.R. make another run for the presidency, what is the nature of Divine Grace, is Alex a midget or an angel, or both?

One muggy, rainy afternoon, Alex sat in his usual spot and dangled a paper pinwheel like a scepter at the cat, which swatted back with his paw. A few yards away kneeled Bess Foster, asking Alex what he knew about the condition of her dear sweet mother Rose, who'd passed over to the other side some eight years earlier. "Alex, dear Alex, can you tell me, is my blessed mother in Heaven with the angels? Was she the bright flash in the sky I saw last night?"

The bright flash Bess had observed may have been her mother, or it may have been an explosion at the Number Four blast furnace at the Hazlewood Works, but either way, Alex wasn't interested. He'd flatly refused to read from the New Testament because some of the passages people had requested included long-winded descriptions from the Book of Revelations depicting apocalyptic horsemen and serpents and graves and marching skeletons, all of which he didn't understand but frightened him and made his head hurt.

He'd put his little foot down and was willing to read only from his *A Child's Life of Christ*, a text that included far more pleasant images.

He stared at Bess, then read, "'Brighter than the brightest day is the light from Heaven.'" He closed the little book and yawned, as did the cat.

Tears streamed down Bess's face. "I knew it. I knew it was Mother as soon as I saw the flash. What was she trying to tell me? Is she all right? Is she sitting at the hand of the Lord?" She edged closer to Alex.

"All right, Bess, that's enough," Ida said, drawing Bess back.

"I'll pay, I'll pay more." Bess shook coins from her change purse.

"Mrs. Foster, please," Ida said. "That's enough for one day." Ida had become adept at handling the overzealous, and gently but firmly dragged Bess away, even as she clutched at the carpet with her fingernails. On another day Ida may have left Bess to grovel a little longer, but she'd scheduled Alex for a three o'clock and it was already two-thirty.

After showing Bess the door, Ida collected the coins that for some reason Bess had arranged in a triangle near the base of Alex's chair. Wary of banks, Ida kept the Jerusalem money in a rosewood box in her bedroom, and the last time she counted, they were up to $106.28. It was hardly enough to book passage to the Holy Land, but every day she got a little bit closer, and with her other savings and her husband's life insurance money tucked neatly under her bed, she just might have enough by the beginning the following year, if business kept up the way it had been, praise Jesus.

Alex," she said, "I'm going upstairs to take a short nap. Remember, Mrs. Scully is coming at three o'clock."

"My head hurts."

"There's milk and chocolate cake on the kitchen table. But don't let the cat get your milk."

"I don't want to do this anymore."

"Alex, darling, don't be silly. It's our calling."

"I don't, I don't." Alex tossed his orange cap to the floor and rubbed his temples.

Ida came back into the sitting room. "Alex, please, stop your yelling. Now, you listen to me. You have to do exactly what I say if you want to go to the Holy Land."

"I want to go outside."

"You can go outside later, after Mrs. Scully, all right? I promise. I'll push you on the swings. We'll have ice cream. But first, we must do everything just like I planned it. Remember, sweetheart, it's God's will and you are God's special messenger. You could already be an angel, did you know that? So be a good boy and go have your snack."

Alex sighed. "Yes, Grandma."

"Now, you come upstairs and wake me when the big hand on the kitchen clock is on the nine and the little hand is near the three." She retreated up the stairs.

Alex watched her climb the stairs. "You don't have to say it like that, I already know how to tell time." He swung his pinwheel in wide circles over his head, then in sweeping arcs from the left to the right, easily touching the floor on both sides with his long arms.

His last swing rested for a moment on a burning votive candle. Almost immediately the paper folds ignited, creating a miniature torch. Unaware of the flame, Alex toddled to the kitchen, bearing fire like a miniature Prometheus.

As he reached for the milk with his free hand, the pinwheel fire leaped to the kitchen curtains and quickly embraced the lacquered wood cabinets. Flames from the pinwheel worked their way down the stick, too, and when Alex felt the heat he dropped the stick on the rag rug, which began to smolder as well.

In seconds half the kitchen was in flames. He yelled, "Grandma, Grandma!" He took two steps toward the stairway in the hall, but the smoke and heat terrified him. He turned around and watched the cat leap through a 10-inch rip in the screen door.

Next door, Margaret Conroy was browsing through the latest Sears Roebuck catalogue. She'd become engrossed in the fantasy that her flabby body would look ravishing in one of the lacy corsets featured on pages 27–28. But which one? Why not order two, or three? And who might be the one to ravish her...the butcher? The coal and iceman? The guarantee promised, "Your money back if you're not completely satisfied."

She was up to page 35 when a meaty, smoky smell drifted into her living room. She assumed it was the pork chops she'd left frying in the kitchen, but in fact it may have been Ida's right calf. Margaret went back to her corset fantasy until she was roused into real time by the clanging bells on the hook and ladder wagon from Station #2 as it pulled up next to her house.

Three firemen bashed through Ida's kitchen door and followed the screams coming from the second floor. They hauled what was left of her down the stairs as quickly as possible and loaded her, smoking and comatose, onto a horse-drawn police wagon, which loped off to St. Margaret's Hospital. Lloyd Casey, the deputy chief who'd lost an eye in an oil fire in '03, canvassed the onlookers to see if there might be anyone else in the house, and was about to walk away when someone screamed, "The little boy, Alex! Little Alex Miller!" just as the second floor collapsed into the first.

Chapter 15

Close to four hours passed before the smoldering rubble cooled enough for the firemen to search for the unlikely survivor, Alex Miller. Virtually everything was burned beyond recognition, except for the kitchen sink, the marble mantelpiece from above the fireplace and a scattering of hot coins. Ida's Holy Land folding money and her other important papers had turned to wet, sludgy ashes. The men sifted and shoveled in the fleeting hope of finding the little boy's body—pray to God he died of smoke inhalation, not flames—but all they came up with was an orange cap that had somehow survived the inferno.

A veteran crime reporter from the *Pittsburgh Gazette Times*, Thomas Lowery discovered a tiny boy sitting on the steps of the house across the street, calmly taking in the spectacle. It had to be Alex Miller, given the description from the neighbors. He squatted down in front of him. "Are you Alex Miller?"

The child nodded.

"Can you talk?"

"Where's Grandma?"

Before Lowery called for a doctor, his investigative reporter side got the best of him. He asked Alex how he'd escaped the blaze.

Alex said, "Like the cat. Where's Grandma?"

Gradually the neighbors discovered Alex, too. Everyone said it was a miracle that he was alive. It had to be. How else could you explain that a child, especially one so tiny, could have made it out of that horrendous fire? Perhaps Ida, the poor woman, had been right all along, that God truly did favor the boy and look out for him. Or perhaps Alex had used some God-like powers to keep him from harm. Bess Foster, Alex's most recent client, shouted that Alex *was* God before two of her neighbors led her away.

A minor squabble broke out as to who was going to take short-term custody of the demigod Alex until his next of kin had been notified, which in turn raised the question, who exactly was his next of kin?

Margaret Conroy had the answer.

Alex remained remarkably calm until Mrs. Conroy and her husband

Marshall, who'd slept through the entire fire, brought him to Abe's house, but as soon as the front door closed, he wailed, "Grandma, where is Grandma? I want Grandma, I called her, but it was too hot from the fire to go upstairs and I was afraid, and then I crawled out through the screen door where the cat went, and I sat on the steps but she didn't come out and the firemen came and then the men took her. Where did they take her?" As he babbled, tears rolled down his cheek and onto Abe's chest and singed his father's heart.

Arthur and Benjamin came running down the stairs. Arthur said, "Why is Alex home?"

Benjamin said, "Why is he crying?"

Abe said, "There was a fire at your grandmother's house."

Benjamin, who hadn't stuttered for two years, said, "Wuh...where's Grandma."

Abe thought about what Mrs. Conroy had said when she brought Alex home, how smoke was still rising from charred Ida's body as they carried her out, and sympathy pains shot up the backs of his legs. He explained to his sons that their grandmother was hurt, yes, but that they'd rushed her to St. Margaret's, it's a damn good hospital, boys, and he wondered if he'd sounded convincing, but from the looks on his son's faces he knew they had their doubts.

"But are you sure she's alive?"

Arthur punched Benjamin. "Sure she is, dummy. They don't take you to the hospital if you're dead."

"That's right, Arthur," Abe said, even though he wasn't sure his son was correct. "Boys, listen, they probably won't let me in there tonight. I'll go see your grandmother first thing tomorrow." He wondered what he would see. He thought about a recent incident at the shop when Angus Foley's shirt caught on fire, and how he howled, and how by the time the boys got close enough to rip the shirt from his back Foley's flesh peeled off like strips of burned bacon, and that was nothing compared to what he imagined could have happened to Ida in a house full of flames.

He held Alex tighter. He shivered involuntarily. His precious little boy had almost died. If Irene were still alive, they wouldn't be in this mess and Alex wouldn't have been there at all. God knows what he saw in that burning house. It could have been the kind of thing that could scar him forever.

With his brothers and his father hovering around him, Alex gradually calmed down. Abe tried to feed him meatloaf and peas, but when he turned it down, he made a butter and jelly sandwich for him and a glass of milk. He washed his face and hands and took him upstairs to the master bedroom and held him in his arms until exhaustion got the better of him.

A full moon shone in through the window. Abe stared up at a settling crack in the ceiling. He thanked God for Alex's sleep, and he prayed that the boy would have pleasant dreams, not nightmares, even though he realized that, after all his sins, God owed him no favors. He tried to blot out the image of Ida burning, her hair shriveling in the flames, her arms beating against the fire on her legs. His thoughts drifted to Irene, and how she'd suffered in her last days. It was a life full of suffering, that's what it was.

He stroked his son's hair. As much as he resented Ida, and all that Christian Holy Roller hogwash she'd pumped into the boy's head, she'd done the both of them a tremendous favor by taking him five days a week. What now? What was he going to do with Alex?

He tried to think about something else, to focus on his last time with Delia, a month ago, and tried to envision her lying on her bed, wearing her stockings and a string of black beads and nothing else, but the image wouldn't hold, and as he drifted off, what he saw was his mother-in-law reaching her arms out toward him, moaning his name, her limbs engulfed in flames.

Abe kept Arthur and Benjamin home from school the next morning to take care of Alex. He promised his sons they could visit their grandmother as soon as he learned more about her condition. Alex clung to his leg as he tried to leave, but Benjamin convinced him that they needed to stay home and make get-well cards for Grandma.

Abe stopped by his shop to explain why he needed the day off, so it was almost noon by the time he reached St. Margaret's and found his way along the dimly lit marble hallways to the ward where Ida was being treated. The air was thick with the smell of antiseptic and the moans of the sick. Occasionally he saw patients in wheel chairs, or with tubes coming out of various orifices, and his thighs tingled with sympathy pains.

Several of Ida's friends from the neighborhood, including Margaret Conroy, were conducting a vigil at the entrance to Ida's ward. Abe moved through them, intent on seeing Ida, no matter how grisly she might be, until a nurse emerged from behind the curtains and informed him that Ida could not have visitors, not even family.

Abe returned to the cluster of neighbors. Bess Foster held a cluster of limp daisies. "Are you a relative, sir?"

"I'm her son-in-law."

She looked him up and down. "Oh, my Lord, you're Alex's father."

"Little Alex's father is here!" cried another woman. She ran up to Abe. "But how is Alex? It's a miracle he's even alive, praise God."

"God looks out for your son, Mr. Miller," another voice cried. "Praise Alex. Praise him."

The fervent sanctification of his son, however flattering, made Abe wary—why were these women singing his praises as if he were God come to Earth? What kind of religious voodoo had been going on in Ida's house? But they seemed so genuinely concerned about Alex, maybe this wasn't the time to ask. Instead, he said, "What do you know about Ida? What are they telling you?"

"It's touch and go," Bess said. "Burns over sixty percent of her body."

Sixty percent. Abe's skin crawled. "Well at least she's alive."

She wasn't.

Unbeknownst to her son-in-law and the host of well-wishers, Ida's lungs had given out minutes before Abe arrived at the hospital. Father Kiernan, the priest she detested for years, had been at her bedside during her final moments, offering Last Rites, which she refused, stating just before her last breath that Kiernan wasn't half the man of God Reverend Billy Sunday was, and she didn't regret it in the least telling him so. However, when Father Kiernan came out and told everyone that Ida had died, he added that she'd made final confession and passed in peace. He closed his eyes. Sometimes it took a little lie to keep the faithful faithful.

*

By early spring of 1914, Delia Novak's windfall had dwindled to a pittance. If she wanted to continue to live alone in her apartment and wear decent clothes, she needed to find full-time employment to supplement the money she picked up waitressing at The Wheel. So with reluctance she took a full-time job as a maid in a recently completed mansion around the corner from the Mellon Estate, a mammoth 65-room spread resting on 11 acres. As she told Abe, The Mellon Estate was a damn long way from Mellon Street.

She continued to put in two evenings a week and Saturdays at The Squeaky Wheel, hoping to get her mother's diamond ring out of hock with her tip money. With all the work, there was hardly time to see Abe or anyone else.

So it was close to two weeks after Ida died that Delia finally saw Abe on a slow Thursday night. She sat down at his table opposite Abe and Davy O'Brien. She sipped Abe's beer. "I heard about your mother-in-law. Sorry."

"At least Alex was safe."

Alex. He seemed more upset than when his mother died, but maybe back then he was too young to understand death—as if anyone ever did. He'd perked up a bit lately, thanks to being with his brothers every night, but Abe couldn't keep relying on Mrs. Traficante from across the street to watch him during the day until the boys got home from school. She was too old and her English was broken at best, and Alex had too much energy for her to keep up with him for long. "I got to figure out what to do with the boy."

"He's a cute little bugger. I could take him every once in a while, maybe a Sunday."

"Really?" Abe sipped on his beer. It used to be just the sight of Delia was enough to make him happy and horny, but tonight she looked thin and drained and, he hated to admit it to himself, kind of ordinary. Knowing she worked so much and so hard depressed him. "I appreciate it, but it's the weekdays that are the problem."

She looked up at the bar, where John had set a plate of chicken legs. "Can't you send him to school?"

"Now? He's still too young."

From behind the bar, John called, "Delia. Order's up."

She kissed Abe on the side of the head. She let her hand trail along his shoulder. "You know what? I got another idea. Don't you Jews have religious schools or something?"

Her suggestion awakened uncomfortable memories of his Hebraic past. He recalled the teachers and the rabbis he'd suffered as a boy, always pushing his face down into the *siddur*, smacking the back of his head and shouting, you must look in book, Miller, you must look in book if you want to learn. He hated it so much he skipped it as often as he could, preferring his Uncle Morris's yells and smacks to the rabbi's. However, as much as he'd hated it, he thought maybe Delia had something there. He ought to go down to the local synagogue, the Beth Shalom on Negley Avenue, maybe it was different than the one he had to go to, maybe they had something for a little boy like Alex, like a nursery school or kindergarten during the summer, where he could place Alex. It wasn't as if he knew anyone there, or ever set foot in it, but still, a Jew was a Jew, they couldn't turn him away, they must have something to help out families like his, even if he wasn't a dues-paying member of the tribe, so to speak. It was worth a shot, and even though Alex wasn't one hundred percent Jewish and his head was full of Ida's Christian bunk, still, the rabbis would straighten him out, and besides, what alternative did he have?

Chapter 16

Fifteen minutes after the Sabbath service, most of the worshippers at Beth Shalom Synagogue were downstairs in the function room for the Oneg Shabbat ceremony, enjoying cups of sweet wine and fresh challah and talking of food prices and politics and social justice. As they sang traditional songs in lively, hopeful voices, comfortable in their kinship, a young woman sat by herself in the front row of the sanctuary.

Her prayer book lay open on her lap. She read silently from the Yom Kippur service even though the Jewish New Year was nearly five months away. Over and over, she read a passage that admonished sinners who'd tarnished the beauty of the spirit by committing gross misdeeds. She closed her eyes and prayed that repentance would lead to forgiveness. In her right hand, she clutched an illustration torn from a magazine of a baby in a cradle.

Abe and Alex stood in the entrance to the sanctuary. Abe felt as if he didn't deserve to be there, that despite his origins he was an outsider, that he was trespassing in a holy place. At least he wore a clean white shirt and had on a hat. He listened to the singing floating up from the floor below. He didn't understand the words, but the melody was dimly familiar and somehow encouraging.

Alex tugged on his hand. "Daddy, where is the cross?"

Abe knelt down. "Like I told you on the way here, this is a different kind of church than your grandma's. It's called a shul. It's for the Jewish people."

"Am I a Jewish?"

You are today, son, you sure are. "Yeah, you're Jewish enough."

Alex pointed to a stained-glass window. "What's that, Daddy?"

"That's the Star of David."

"Who's David?"

Before he could answer, Abe noticed a pretty young woman with a white shawl walking up the aisle from the sanctuary. Her eyes were slightly closed, and her lips moved rapidly, as if she were reciting something or something was speaking through her. She came so close to Abe that she almost walked into him.

Abe said, "Miss?"

She stopped a foot short of him. She shrank back. "I'm sorry. I didn't see you."

"No, I should have said something when I seen you—I mean, saw you walking this way."

"That's all right."

"Well, I guess I'm blocking the way. Come on, Alex."

The woman caught Alex's eye the same time he caught hers. Her eyes widened, and her lips began to move again. *Dear God, do not be deaf unto my plea.*

Abe said, "You say something?"

She smiled and extended her hand. "Wait. My name is Hannah Gerson."

"Abraham Miller." He put the emphasis on Abraham. He looked at her hand. Her fingernails were gone and the skin around the cuticles was ripped and raw.

"Well it's so nice to meet you. Are you a new member of the congregation?"

"Well, not exactly. We just come by today for the first time."

"It's all right, you don't have to be a member to come here. God and this synagogue welcome everyone." She knelt down in front of Alex. "And what's your name, my pretty little boy?"

"Alex Miller. I'm a Jewish."

"You are?" She clapped her hands. "Me, too. That's so wonderful. And how old are you, Alex?"

"Six, and one and a half, too."

"What?"

Abe smiled. "He says that because he was born on leap year day."

"Isn't he clever? Such a clever little boy." She moved within inches of Abe's face. "I bet I can guess how old *you* are." She tapped his chest.

"Pardon me?"

"You're thirty-three. Am I right?" As Abe nodded his head, she said, "Oh, don't look so surprised. I can just look at a person and tell things about them. I do it all the time, ask my aunts. It's a talent I have."

Abe put his hand on Alex's shoulder. "Yeah, well, that sure is something. But we really shouldn't be keeping you."

"Don't be silly, you're not keeping me. I love talking to you." She winked. "And to Alex."

Abe looked around the empty sanctuary. "Well anyway, I guess we come by too late. I had wanted to speak to the rabbi or someone else in charge."

"Oh my goodness, this sounds serious."

"Well, it's about my boy here."

Hannah's fingernails went to her mouth. "Oh my God, is something wrong with him?"

"No, it's just that, I mean, if the rabbi isn't here, I could come back another time."

She shook her head. "Oh, but there's no need for that." She took Abe's arm. She glanced around the empty sanctuary and said in a hushed voice, "Whatever you need to tell Rabbi Kaplan, no matter what, I can tell him for you—in strictest confidence, of course. We're very close, the rabbi and me. You might say I'm his closest assistant. He relies on me quite a bit. In fact, not a day goes by we don't speak about things. Important things." She motioned to the last row of seats. "Come, sit down and tell me all about it."

He wondered if he should tell this woman his story, but she seemed so genuinely concerned, and he was already there, and she said she was close to the rabbi. "Well, if you got a minute."

As his father gave her the abridged version of the Alex Miller story, with special emphasis on the death of his mother and grandmother, Alex kept his eyes on Hannah. He watched how her hands fluttered from her chest to Abe's forearm, the way she wiped away a sudden tear with the back of her hand, how she alternately gasped and giggled when Abe told her about the time Alex's brothers had put him on display for money. He watched her feet bounce and twist around her ankles, and how she nodded and finished his father's sentences, and how, every few seconds it seemed, she glanced back at Alex, as if she were worried he might suddenly disappear.

Although he was accustomed to having people stare at him, her look was different than the usual gawker, more intense, and not all pleasant.

After Abe finished, Hannah said, "Dear lord, you've been through so much. I hate to say it, but the synagogue doesn't have anything for Alex right now. But don't leave yet. I have an idea. Maybe I could help you out."

"You could?"

As Hannah outlined her plan, Alex grew restless. He wandered toward the front of the sanctuary. The carpet was smooth and thick, and the wood smelled of fresh polish. He looked up at the oil lamp, the Everlasting Light that burned above the ark. Panic shot through him. He screamed, "Daddy! Fire, fire!"

Abe rushed forward, with Hannah on his heels. He scooped Alex up. "It's all right, son, it's all right."

Tears rand down Hannah's cheeks. She gasped, "Is he all right, Abe, is he O.K.?"

"He's fine, just scared a little is all."

She sniffed. "Maybe I should hold him. Do you want me to hold him?"

"No, I have him."

He mouth turned down. "Oh, all right then. Anyway, I want you and Alex to come by tomorrow night for dinner and to meet my aunts. Once I tell them all about you and Alex and our plans for him, they'll be dying to meet you. Promise me, all right? Please?" She grasped Abe's hands in hers. "Six o'clock. All right?"

Abe looked at her hands squeezing his. This pretty woman, maybe she was a touch on the excitable side, but she seemed very sincere about wanting to help him out. She'd taken to Alex right off, that was for sure. He looked down at his son, who was looking at her. He hated to put him through so many changes, but he had to find something for him, at least until he was ready for school, and Hannah's offer seemed perfect. What was the old expression? Never look a gift horse in the mouth? Sure, it all seemed too good to be true, but even so, he heard himself saying, "Yeah, all right, six o'clock. Thank you."

She kissed Alex on the forehead. "Goodbye, sweetheart. Everything's going to be so wonderful. See you tomorrow."

On the trolley ride home, Abe explained the plan as outlined by Hannah. Since there was no school for him at the synagogue, Hannah—er, Miss Gerson—said she wanted to be his *au pair*, which means she'd be your nanny, Alex, she'd take care of you instead of Mrs. Traficante. She's too old to be running around after you. Just think, Hannah's got a big house with a swing in the backyard and a dog, you like dogs, right, and lots of books to read, and you can bring your soldiers, too. And then when I pick you up after work you'll be with me and Benjamin and Arthur and you can sleep in their room every night, if you like, how does that sound?

"But why can't I go to work with you?"

Abe laughed. "Wouldn't that beat all. But my boss, he wouldn't allow it. A metal shop's not safe for a little boy."

"Is it safe for you, Daddy?"

"Oh, sure. Nothing's going to happen to your old man."

They rode two stops in silence. Alex turned from the window. "Do you like Hannah, Daddy?"

Like her? He liked how she looked, how she smelled, how she smiled, how she seemed to really care about him and Alex, but did he like her? "Yeah, I like her, I mean, she's all right." He opened the window and put his face out next to Alex to catch the breeze. "What about you? Did you like her?"

"Who do you like better, her or Mommy?"

"Well, your mother, of course, son, but she's gone, you know that."

"Her or Delia?"

"What?"

"Benjamin says Delia is your girlfriend. Is Hannah your girlfriend, too?"

"Well, I, no...Hannah is, she's just going to take care of you, that's all. All right?"

Alex turned back to the view. "I guess so."

Chapter 17

Delia Novak leaned on her elbows as she watched the gold and white koi glide around the pond at the far end of the topiary garden, approximately 100 yards from the main house. She fingered the pack of cigarettes in her apron pocket, wondering if she should risk lighting up. She never knew when Marie was watching, acting as if she were the lady of the house instead of just a sniveling bitch of a housekeeper. If Marie caught her smoking again, however, she'd toss her out on her ass, and Delia couldn't afford to get canned.

A gust of wind rattled the leaves on a huge elm tree. Thunder rumbled from a wall of black clouds massed to the west, moving her way. She sprinkled bits of dried bread on the water. The lousy fish had a better life than she did, at least they didn't have to grub for money or ask permission to smoke a lousy cigarette. She felt like grabbing one of them and flipping it onto the lawn to watch it suffocate, so that it would feel the way she did.

Next to her cigarettes was an envelope she'd found in her mailbox that morning, postmarked Chicago, Illinois. What in God's name was her old friend Lotte Henderson doing in Chicago? She had seven more minutes' break time coming to her, and hell, they couldn't fire her for opening a goddamn letter.

The wind kicked up again and rippled through the huge weeping willow that bordered the pond. She opened the letter and began to read:

Dear Dee,

How's tricks, hon? Geez oh man, I wish I was there with you right now to see your face as you read this letter from your old partner in crime, but if I was there, then I wouldn't have to write no letter! Anyways, I'm sorry I have not wrote to you since I got your letter what is it, four or five years ago, when you had wrote to tell me you moved to Pittsburgh, but my life has been crazy since then.

Remember how you always used to say I should join the circus, because I could do all them tricks like bending over backward and putting my head between my knees, and doing the splits and pulling my legs behind her ears, on account of I'm double-jointed? Well, guess what, I did! I joined

Ringling's! Which is why your letter took so long to catch up with me, because I'm always on the road, see.

So anyways, now they call me Miss Lotte Larue, The Elastic Lass, The World's Most Flexible Female. Can you believe it? They even made up a poster of me bending backward over the mouth of a lion, which is just a made up painting, it ain't something I ever really done. I stay as far away from them wild animals as I can. They smell bad and besides, their eyes look so sad it gives me the blues.

Sorry to read about your mother passing away. She was always good as gold to me, even when them other grown-ups in the neighborhood said I would never amount to nothing but a little tramp. She left you a pile of dough, huh? My folks never even left me a pot to piss in, excuse my language.

Anyways, it's been a long time, Dee—they still call you that? Geez oh man, the trouble we used to get into when we was young girls and had them cute little heinies, huh? Golly, did we have the fun.

So how do I like the circus life? Hey, I can't complain. I make good money for a girl—$70 a week, can you believe it, plus three squares a day. Hey, it sure beats sitting behind a sewing machine fifteen hours a day, working for peanuts, which by the way we got plenty of at the circus. Don't mind me, I'm a kidder from way back, you know that.

No, the life here ain't so bad, not really, once you get used to pulling up stakes most every night and taking a train from one burg to another, except when we stay put in a big city for a couple of days, like when we come to Pittsburgh this Labor Day, which is when we'll be there.

Anyway, I been around these United States, the eastern part mainly, but to tell you the truth, a rube is a rube no matter what city you're in, and there ain't a lot you can tell about a place through a train window when you're rolling through it at four in the morning. But like I say, it sure beats the pants off of hanging around in Youngstown and getting put in a family way by some mill-hunky and ending up as fat as a cow, with four brats by the time you turn 30.

Speaking of getting knocked up—hey, I know I'm going on and on but I have so much to tell you—I'm living with a real sweet guy, Mojo the Sword Swallower. He's a Jew, can you believe it, and he treats me real nice. Jews, they make the best husbands, at least that's what I heard, not that he proposed or nothing. So far there's been no fooling around on me—believe me, there are plenty of good-looking skirts hanging around in little circus outfits to tempt a man. How do you think I got Morris! That's Mojo's real name, Morris Josephson. And he's never hit me, not like that bastard Edgar Foster I used to go around with, you remember him. I hope he's six feet under or better yet, he should rot to death with consumption.

Oh, so you probably want to know why this letter come to you from Chicago. That's where I was when I mailed it. Where I am now while you're reading, it could be any of many cities east of the Mississippi.

Anyways, like I was saying, my Morris is a smart guy, and we're saving up so's he can to go to school to become a dentist or a pharmacist, he's not sure which, but something professional. There's good money in that, and we could settle down somewhere nice—not Youngstown—and have a house with curtains on the windows and a white picket fence, and a family. That's what I want. I can't be the Elastic Lass forever.

Geez, Dee, you should see some of the characters we got walking around this place. Half of them can't speak the King's English to save their lives, but that's okey dokey, everyone gets along pretty good most of the time, and we're putting on the greatest show on Earth every day, sometimes twice, and I don't know, getting out there in front of a crowd gets your heart pumping. Plus with all these circus people around, there's always someone to yap with, except for the clowns, which are as miserable and dirty a bunch of goons as you'd ever see in all your born days.

About my act—well, for one thing, I bend over backward and stick my head between my legs and light a cigarette. Then I do a handstand and arch my back so my legs come down to my hair and then I scratch my head with my toes. Then I spell out the alphabet with my hands and legs. I know it sounds dumb, but the rubes, they love it. The men, you should see them, their tongues hang halfway out of their mouths, because I gotta say, all this exercise has the old body in very nice shape and the tight costumes with the spangles and sparkles, well, Mojo says I am an occasion for sin, if you know what I mean.

Anyways, I promised myself I wouldn't write more than a page or two and here I am going on page five like I was Julius Shakespeare or something, but I just want to tell you, Dee, how excited I am that we're coming to Pittsburgh and maybe you and me can get together like old times. Old friends are the best friends, that's the truth. Write me back, o.k.? Just send it in care of the circus at the address here. You let me know how many tickets you want and they will be there waiting for you. And ask for me, we'll go out when my show is over and you can show me the town!

Well, I gotta stop now, Morris will be wanting his supper. Love you, can't wait to see you!

Lotte, the "Elastic Lass" Henderson

PS: Dee, don't forget to write, like I did!

A harsh voice from across the lawn yelled, "Novak! Break's over!"

Delia's cheek was wet with tears. She folded the letter. Her friend was pulling down seventy bucks a week for what, being a freak? Boy oh boy.

Sure, she'd write back to Lotte. She'd tell her a good story, a true story about a tiny little boy that could throw darts and knives with incredible accuracy. They had knife throwers in the circus—hell, people would pay money to see a child throw, wouldn't they? But someone would have to make the introductions, do the negotiations. Seventy dollars a week? If she played her cards right, there would be a place for her in the circus, too.

"Novak!"

In began to rain in fat, cold drops. She ran back to the house with the letter pushed deep in her pocket.

Chapter 18

The yellow brick, two-story, foursquare house was the largest on the block. It had a dining room, foyer, kitchen and pantry, a sitting room, a cold cellar and four bedrooms. The front porch ran the width of the house, and in back, the yard occupied nearly a half-acre, with forsythia and lilac bushes, a vegetable plot and a forty-year-old honey locust tree with a tire swing.

The Gerson sisters, Belle and Lillie, used the kitchen and the dining room and shared the large master bedroom, where they slept together as they had since they were children, born eleven months apart in 1868. Two of the smaller bedrooms were stuffed to the ceilings with their deceased parents' furniture and keepsakes from the old country, covered with sheets and two decades of dust. The second-largest bedroom was Hannah's.

Belle weighed fifty pounds more than "little" sister Lillie. She smoked two packs of Chesterfields every day and drank black coffee from morning until night, except during meals, which were, at Lillie's insistence, always served with wine. Despite her age, her hair was carrot red. She dressed in bilious black housedresses no matter what the weather or the social occasion.

Neither Belle nor Lillie ever married, although Lillie, the petite, pretty sister, once had entertained a proposal from a gentleman ten years her senior, a respected, reserved Jewish mortician named Irwin Kalmenstein, who, to sweeten the pot, pledged that Belle could live with them once they tied the knot. Lillie thought it was a generous offer, but Belle, who called Irwin "Old Gloomy," felt the offer was *too* generous—did he think he was in for a two-for-one deal, and anyway, what kind of man would want to live with his wife's sister? Ultimately, Belle and Lillie agreed that it was better to enjoy life with each other, as they'd always done, rather than outlive and bury a mortician.

Moreover, they didn't need his morgue money. Both had worked as bookkeepers in the payroll department at Union Switch & Signal and, because they lived with their parents, they were able to save most of their salaries. Their frugality, combined with inheriting their parents' moderate savings and paid-off house, allowed them to retire at the ripe young age of fifty-five and live the life they wanted. They had orchestra seats at the

Pittsburgh Symphony, two sets of china, Irish linens, a Polish maid, and two high-holiday seats at the synagogue they rarely attended but annually supported. They treated themselves to annual trips to New York to see the sights and take in a Broadway play or two, always musicals, and vacationed at fancier resorts on Lake Erie or in the Laurel Mountains. They contributed generously to the suffragette movement, since they'd been working women themselves.

They also took in their niece Hannah after her parents had basically disowned her. It wasn't exactly the arrangement they'd planned for in their retirement, but since they were her only relatives, and she their only niece, where else was the poor 20-year-old girl supposed to go, with no job, no friends and virtually no self-esteem?

That had been two years earlier. Hannah had toed the line thus far—no men, no alcohol, no late nights out. True, she'd lost every job the sisters had managed to find for her in six months or less, but they were forgiving, far more than her parents, for they could see the flighty girl was still traumatized by the past and might remain so for some time. It was all she could do to keep up with her shorthand correspondence school courses, but at least she was neat and most of the time cordial and was not a financial burden, as her father, their brother, sent the sisters money every month for Hannah's keep.

Lillie was reheating Friday night's chicken, soup, roast potatoes and green beans for Saturday's lunch, when Hannah banged through the front door. She turned to Belle, who was filling water glasses. "Guess who."

"Belle, Lillie. I'm home. I'm starving."

Lillie said, "She wants lunch? She never eats lunch."

Belle looked up. "Something's gotten into her."

Hannah called from the stairway. "I'm going to wash my hands. I'll be down in a minute. I have wonderful news."

*

Abe and Alex arrived home to an empty house. Benjamin had gone to the Pirates game, not to attend—although he would have loved to watch his heroes Honus Wagner and Babe Adams—but to hawk peanuts and pennants on Bouquet Street outside Forbes Field for Nunzio Fiore of Fiore Importers. Nunzio paid him two cents a bag on the peanuts and ten on the pennants. On the days when attendance was low, Benjamin and his fellow vendors would slip past the sleepy ticket takers to catch the game from the seventh inning to the top of the ninth, at which point they'd have to rush back and try to sell merchandise to the meager post-game crowd. Benjamin relished these brief ballpark interludes, and he imagined himself chasing down fly balls on the vast green lawn and smacking high arcing drives over the right field fence.

Arthur normally worked alongside his brother, but not on this particular afternoon. Instead, he was at Jack Walsh's house, his former enemy and current co-conspirator. The boys, barely sixteen, were in Jack's basement, composing letters to their parents. Their birth certificates lay open on the workbench.

Alex pushed the stepstool up to the icebox. "I'm hungry, Daddy."

Abe looked inside. There wasn't much: a half empty bottle of milk, a jar of pickles, a crumbly hunk of cheddar cheese and a salami that had a green tinge to it. Christ, now he'd have to go food shopping, and the day would be shot, which meant no Delia once again, unless she was working late and he could figure out a way to get the older boys to stay home with Alex. He poured some milk.

Alex dunked an oatmeal cookie. "Am I ever going to be big, Daddy? Like you and Arthur and Davy and John the bartender?"

Abe's eyes got watery. How many time had he had this conversation with him? "Well listen, when I was your age I was little, too."

"Little as me?"

"No, but they used to call me 'shrimp' until I got my growth."

"But when will I get my growth?"

Abe thought that maybe he should go back to that synagogue and ask God to give him the answer, for sure as hell he didn't know. He rubbed Alex's hair. "Why, it could be any time. Anyway, we talked about this before. Why are you asking me now, son?"

"If I got big I wouldn't need to go to Hannah's house."

True, Abe thought, but then, that would take a miracle, and he couldn't wait around for one. What else could he do now, under the circumstances, but take Hannah's offer? Hell, it was only natural the boy was a bit nervous about this new deal, but he'd get over it in a few days. He patted Alex's hand. "Don't worry, son. Hannah's gonna take good care of you." He hoped it was true. He needed a break.

*

"Slow down, Hannah."

"We can't understand a word you're saying when you talk with your mouth full of food."

Hannah kept talking anyway. "You know how you always say we're supposed to do mitzvahs, good things for other people, that good deeds are the best way to please God?"

"Do I always say that, Lillie?"

Her sister shrugged.

Hannah stood and began to pace around the table. Pudgy the dog, a Boston Bull/Cocker Spaniel mix, pranced on her hind legs, doing her best to get some scraps to fall her way. "Well, even if you don't say it, it's true, don't you think? I do. Anyway, this morning, after services, I met this poor man and his darling little boy who stumbled into the synagogue." She went on for five minutes straight, describing in detail how Abe's beautiful and loving wife had taken care of her three boys, especially little Alex, only to sacrifice herself to diphtheria to protect her sons. "And just a month ago, his mother-in-law Mrs. Murphy died in a horrible fire."

Belle said, "Murphy? Are these people Jewish?"

"What? Oh, Abe is Jewish, absolutely. What was I saying?"

Lillie sipped her wine. "The fire, dear."

"Yes, it was horrible." Hannah described the fire in far more detail than Abe or even the newspaper had described it, adding how a courageous fireman had rescued Alex from the flames in the nick of time. She opened the two top buttons of her dress. "Just talking about it makes me warm."

The sisters exchanged a quick glance. Belle said, "So what's the mitzvah?"

For a second Hannah looked perplexed. "Oh. Well, because now Abe has no one to look after Alex while he's at work, and the synagogue can't help him, I said I would take him in. He's so cute." Her eyes flicked back and forth from Belle to Lillie. "It's all right, isn't it? He has nowhere to go."

"You mean bring him here?" Lillie said.

"But he wouldn't be any trouble. I'll watch him every minute. You don't have to do anything."

Belle said, "A little boy running around the place? I don't know."

Lillie put her hand on Belle's shoulder. "Hannah, sweetheart, don't you think you should have asked us first? A boy—how old did you say he is?"

"Oh, he's six, but he's tiny, as tiny as a toddler."

"Why, is there something wrong with him?"

"No, not at all. I think he had a childhood disease, but he's all better now, perfectly healthy, he's just little."

Lillie began to clear the plates. "Well, dear, we're glad you were nice to this man and his little boy, but that's a big responsibility, taking in someone else's child."

Hannah stopped pacing. "You took me in."

The sisters looked at each other. Finally, Belle said, "But that was different."

"How? How was it different?"

Lillie cleared her throat. "Belle, would you hand me the gravy boat?"

"Anyway, they're coming for dinner. I invited them for tomorrow night."

"Tomorrow?" Belle reached for her cigarettes.

Hannah gulped down some water. "And please don't smoke. It's not good for Alex."

*

On Sunday night, Benjamin plowed through a plate of Saturday's leftovers, meatloaf and mashed potatoes, pausing every so often to cock his wrist and swing his knife in an imitation of Pirate shortstop Honus Wagner, the future Hall of Famer who'd recently entered the downward arc of his career. Arthur pecked at his food, which was unusual since he normally out-consumed his father.

Abe didn't notice his oldest son's lack of appetite. He had other things on his mind—getting Alex's suit ironed and overcoming his uneasiness toward Hannah Gerson and her offer. She seemed genuinely interested in caring for Alex, but there was something else, she seemed interested in him, too, judging from how she pressed herself against him. He thought of the old maxim, if it seems too good to be true, it probably ain't, even though he couldn't put his finger on exactly what it was that didn't seem right.

He wrapped a dishtowel around the handle of the iron, which had been heating on the stove. Alex's checkered suit lay stretched on the ironing board. Abe tested the flat surface of the iron with his finger the way he'd seen Irene do it a hundred times. He yelped, "Son of a bitch, that's hot."

Alex said, "Son of a bitch."

Benjamin laughed so hard that mashed potatoes blurted from his mouth. Arthur barely smiled.

"Alex, you watch that mouth of yours when we're at Miss Gerson's house. None of that swearing, you hear me?" Abe pounded the iron on Alex's pants, as if he could beat the wrinkles into submission, wondering how Irene used to get their clothes so smooth.

"But you swore."

"Well, do as I say, not as I do." He flipped the pants over. "Hey Arthur, you ain't said a word all night."

"I was just thinking about something."

Benjamin said, "He's thinking about how many Germans he's going to shoot."

Arthur punched Benjamin in the shoulder. Benjamin kicked him under the table, which earned him an even harder shot to the ribs.

"You two cut it out. Alex, get over here." Abe handed the pants to him.

Alex slipped his short pants over his shoes with a flick of his long arms. He climbed up on a chair next to Arthur. "I want Arthur and Benjamin to come, too."

That's all I need, Abe thought, traipsing into her house with these two animals at each other's throats. "They weren't invited. Go get your coat, Alex."

*

At about 5:30, Lillie knocked four times on Hannah's door. She called her name and tried to enter but the door opened just a few inches. She had to put her shoulder to it to force it open against all the clothes scattered in front of it.

Every dresser drawer was wide open, and every article of clothing Hannah owned lay strewn around the room. Hannah sat on her bed in a camisole and underpants, with her arms wrapped around her sides. Her hair was loose. Her toes clenched and unclenched on the Oriental rug.

Lillie picked up three dresses and draped them over the chair in front of the dressing table. "Your company will be here any minute, dear. Don't you think you ought to get dressed now?"

"I have nothing to wear. I need new clothes."

"Perhaps you do, dear, but for now, let's see if we can make do with what you do have." She held up a white embroidered tea dress. "This is so lovely."

"I hate it. It's ugly. It makes me look ugly."

"What about this one?" She held up a teal blue velvet dress. "You look so wonderful in it. It shows off your beautiful figure."

Hannah rolled her eyes at her. "You don't really think I have a beautiful figure, do you? How can you? They say once you have a baby you lose your figure completely."

Lillie held the dress up to her. "Not you, dearest. At least try it on."

"But what if Abe doesn't like it?"

"He'll love it. You'll look like a princess." She put her cheek next to hers and they both looked in the mirror above her dresser. "Let me pin your hair back."

"Oh, Lillie. I wish you were my mother."

The doorbell rang twice. Hannah shoved her arms into the dress as Lillie buttoned up the back. From downstairs, Belle called, "Hannah, your company is here."

Barefoot, hair flying, Hannah rushed down the stairs. She went to her knees and hugged Alex. She looked back at Belle and Lillie. "Didn't I tell you? Didn't I tell you? Isn't he precious?"

Belle said, "What's wrong with his arms?"

Lillie pinched her sister's behind. "Let's get dinner on the table, Belle. Hannah, why don't you show Mr. Miller and his son the backyard?"

The sisters had put out their second best set of china, crystal wine glasses and a metal cup for Alex. The tablecloth had been their mother's, fine lace from Belgium and similar in pattern to Ida's best tablecloth, which had been vaporized in the fire. Belle sat at one end of the table and Lillie at the other, with Alex seated on three pillows between Abe and Hannah. Lillie served them buttered peas and carrots, candied sweet potatoes, relish and brisket with gravy. Belle poured red table wine for her and her sister and Abe, but none for Hannah, who didn't seem to notice, since she was intent on adjusting Alex's napkin or cutting his meat.

Abe admired his full plate. "Looks good."

Lillie said, "Well, don't be shy."

Alex said, "Wait. Grace." He bowed his head and clasped his hands together.

Hannah touched his shoulder. "Isn't it wonderful, how well-mannered he is? What a darling."

Abe explained how when Alex lived with his grandmother, God rest the poor woman's soul, she had insisted on saying grace before every meal, and now the boy was insistent upon it, and besides, it wasn't such a bad thing, a little prayer never hurt no one.

Lillie agreed, saying that when her parents were alive they always said the blessings over the bread and wine, but now she and her sisters had fallen away from the habit. She giggled, "We're what the rabbi calls 'Holiday Jews,' because we only attend on the high holidays.

Belle said, "And half the time we don't even do that." She looked at Alex's arms, which hadn't moved. "He does this all the time, you say? Well, I don't suppose it would hurt if he said a few words."

"It would be wonderful," Hannah said. "Go ahead, Alex."

Keeping his eyes down, Alex said, "Dear Lord, we thank thee for thy bounty which we are about to receive in the name of the Father, the Son and the Holy Spirit, praise Jesus Christ our savior, amen."

Belle dropped her fork on the floor. "I thought you said you were Jewish."

"Oh," Abe said awkwardly, "we are." He shot a sideways glance at his son. "He just picks up things."

After dinner, Abe and the sisters sat on the back porch while Hannah and Alex went up to her room. Abe took a panatela from his coat pocket. "Mind if I smoke?"

Belle said, "You have another one?"

It took her a few draws to get the cigar going. "So, Mr. Abraham Miller. We've never seen you at the synagogue before. What were you doing there? And your little boy. What about those arms of his?"

Abe blew a smoke ring toward the ceiling. These two old birds, they didn't pull no punches, that was for sure, but he kind of liked them for that. At least they were down to earth, and the food was damn good, he hadn't had an old-fashioned meal like that in a long time. Hannah, well, he still wasn't sure about her, but he liked how she looked in that dress, and she doted on Alex, and with these two women around he was sure his son would receive a hell of a lot of attention, probably more than he could give him. Maybe this would work out all right after all. Feeling expansive, he tapped his cigar. "You want the short or the long version?"

Lillie poured more brandy into his glass. "Take all the time you need."

*

Hannah sat at her dresser and rearranged her dolls and porcelain figurines. As she faced the mirror she explained how her blonde dolly was her favorite growing up, until she was five, but then her aunts gave her a unicorn she named Princess and that was her best friend, but then she stopped playing with dolls when she was eight because it was stupid. Every so often she stopped talking and brushed her hair, first parting in the left, then the right, then middle, then pushing it straight back from her face.

Alex wasn't interested in dolls, and he was tired of watching her move her hair back and forth. He was trying to like Hannah because he believed his daddy liked Hannah, he could see how he looked at her, just like he looked at Delia, and if Daddy liked Hannah, then he was supposed to like her even if he didn't.

As she kept on talking to the mirror, he slipped out of her room and went down the hallway until he came to a dark roll-top desk. He climbed on the chair and pushed it open.

Stacked inside were a number of books and a large black album. Embossed on the cover were the words *Florence Carson Home*. He ran his fingers over the word as he sounded them out. He wondered what kind of story it would be. Was Florence Carson a little girl that came home, or was it about the home where she lived? Maybe there were pictures, too. It was a lot bigger than his *A Child's Life of Christ*, but smaller than the encyclopedia.

He looked up and down the hallway. He could hear Hannah chattering to her dolls.

He opened the cover. Inside was a photograph of a large house and a man in a dark suit and glasses, standing next to a woman on the steps. On the inside of the cover was an inscription that read, *To provide a home and to extend helping hands and Christian kindness to erring and friendless women*. As he pored over the words, he wondered, if Hannah was a Jewish, why does it say Christian?

He heard Hannah's chair scrape against the floor. He wasn't sure why, but he knew he had to put the album back. He closed the desk and hopped down.

"Alex? Where are you, sweetheart?"

He ran toward her, with his arms extended, an innocent lamb. "Hannah, can I have a candy?"

That night, as he tucked Alex in, Abe asked him if he'd enjoyed himself at Hannah's house.

"I like Pudgy. I gave him potatoes under the table."

"Well, don't do that no more, you want to make him sick? Besides, he ain't your dog. What else?"

"Are you going to marry Hannah?"

"Hold on, boy. I didn't say I was going to marry anyone."

"But Hannah said." He stopped and rolled on his side.

"She said what?"

"She told me not to tell."

Abe smoothed his hair. "You like Hannah, don't you?"

"She grabs me all the time."

"That's because she likes you."

"But then she doesn't let me go."

Chapter 19

In 1913, the Pennsylvania General Assembly approved an amendment to the state's constitution to extend women the right to vote. The male electorate summarily rejected it.

Undaunted, the women's suffrage movement continued to grow throughout the state, and on Saturday, May 2, 1914, a large group of prominent suffragettes marched through the streets of Pittsburgh, accompanied by three daring city councilmen evidently not up for re-election. The suffragettes were also joined by a mid-sized contingent of professional women, a troop of Boy Scouts and a mounted police escort. Dr. Sergei Malkin was part of the parade, too, walking along on the periphery, wandering into groups of onlookers to pass out handbills advertising his skills regarding "baby birthing and maternity doctor also."

Marching along with them, albeit a bit self-consciously, was Delia Novak. It wasn't so much that Delia felt the desire to exercise the franchise herself, since she considered all politicians to be crooks, liars and gladhanders, one worse than the next, and none worthy of her support. However, if men like the ignorant slugs she waited on at The Wheel like that pig Horshushky could cast a ballot, why the hell shouldn't she?

As she walked shoulder to shoulder with other women, she began to feel a kind of kinship, even though she could tell from the cut of their clothes that most of these women had never waited a table or cleaned a men's room in their lives. They certainly were friendly, though, and as they proceeded along, past the well-wishers and the hecklers, more than one called her sister, and she liked how it sounded.

After a half-mile or so her feet began to hurt. She'd gone to the side of the street and pulled off her shoe for a quick foot rub when she heard a high, clear voice shout, "Delia!"

It was Alex Miller, waving at her, standing in front of a crowd of onlookers, holding a small American flag in his right hand and a woman's gloved hand in his left. Delia walked over to him, bent down and accepted his hug. "How's my little best boyfriend?"

The woman released his hand. "Alex, who is this?"

"Delia." He took her hand.

"He seems to know you."

Delia said, "Oh yeah, me and my pumpkin here, we go way back, don't we, sugar pie?" She stood and extended her hand to Hannah. Women shaking hands was a new notion to her, new this morning, learned from her new sisters, and she liked the idea. "Delia Novak. Put her there."

The woman looked at Delia's hand as if she didn't know what to do with it. After a moment, she extended her hand and let Delia's encompass it. "Hannah. Hannah Gerson."

"Hello, sister." Delia squeezed Hannah's hand. "Alex, where's your daddy?"

"He had to make overtime."

Hannah rushed to explain that the boy's father, Abraham, was so busy these days, he was a very important person at the metal working shop, a supervisor, indispensable in fact, and that he had asked her to watch Alex this morning, and normally she attended synagogue, the large one on Negley Avenue, but what could she do, Abraham really needed her and so she agreed on short notice to take Alex, not that it was any bother, she loved him so.

Delia laughed to herself. Abe, an important man, a supervisor? In a pig's eye. The crumb, what kind of malarkey was he feeding this girl? "Slow down a minute. What did you say your name was, Hannah? Oh, wait, I know." She looked her up and down. She had to admit the girl was pretty. "You're the nanny, ain't you?"

"His au pair."

"Aha." Delia smiled thinly. Abe hadn't told her how attractive she was, or how young, she couldn't be more than twenty. She was filled out, too, very filled. This girl could be competition, definitely. As she watched her fuss over Alex, straightening his collar, stroking his hair, Delia sensed there was something kind of squirrelly about her, too. "Au pair. Are you French?"

"What? Oh, no, I'm Jewish."

Alex raised his hand. "Delia, I'm a Jewish now, too."

"Yeah, just like your old man. So, Hannah Gerson, are you in favor of the vote for women?"

She twisted her hair. "Me? Well, I don't know exactly. The issue seems so confusing that I thought I should have more information on the subject before I made up my mind, at least that's what my aunts told me. They're in favor of women's suffrage, so when they read about the march in the newspaper, they said they were too old to march but that I should go, and since I had Alex I said to myself, he'll love a parade, I could get him an ice cream, and so here we are, and maybe I'll learn something about the issue, too."

This girl has diarrhea of the mouth, Delia thought, that's for sure. She buttoned her shoe. "Yeah, yeah, so did you?"

"Pardon me?"

She's as thick as John's stew. "Learn anything."

Hannah's lips moved before she spoke. "Well, I guess, I mean, I'm not sure."

"Look, sweetheart, there ain't a lot to learn. You're either in favor or your not."

Alex looked back and forth between the two women. "Delia?"

"Yes, Alex?"

"Are you still Daddy's girlfriend?"

The color faded from Hannah's face. She drew Alex a bit closer. "I didn't know your father had a girlfriend."

Delia chuckled. "I'll bet there's a lot you don't know about old Abe." Volumes, she thought. She was pretty sure this girl had no idea about the Abe she knew: how he smelled when he was lying on top of her, how thick his arms and thighs were, how his eyes rolled back when he was ready to come, how his skin tasted, how soft his touch could be, how hard he was when he was inside her.

"Look, soldiers." The Boy Scouts marched by. Alex raised his right hand in a salute. "Arthur is going to be a soldier. He told me, but I'm not supposed to tell Daddy. Hannah?"

She jumped as if he'd woken her from a dream. "What?"

"I'm hungry."

Delia pointed to Tuttle's Luncheonette. "Come on, I'll buy you a cup of coffee. And a cherry Coke for you, Alex. We'll sit and talk. I want to know all about you. Plus, my feet are killing me."

They were about to enter Tuttle's when a shouting match broke out right in front of them, between a woman carrying a sign that read "Support Women's Suffrage" and a group of hecklers. One of them grabbed the sign away from her and played keep away with his cronies. Others pelted the woman with orange peels.

Delia dropped Alex's hand. She ran headlong into the skirmish and grabbed the sign stealer by the throat, knocking him to the ground. She was about to smash the sign over his head when two policemen grabbed her by the arms.

Alex yelled, "Delia." He shook loose from Hannah's grip and ran into the melee, threw his long arms around a policemen's waist and groped for his revolver.

"What the hell?" the policeman said. He hoisted Alex up by the collar.

Delia said, "Alex, no!" She stopped struggling instantly. "Hold on a minute, let him go, you creep." She grabbed his arm, easing his fingers away from disaster. "Go ahead, sweetheart, go with Hannah. Everything's all right. O.K.? Have your lunch, all right? I'll see you later, all right honey?"

Alex threw a final kick at the policeman and walked back to Hannah. He took Hannah's hand, which was as white as her face.

As the police walked her away, Delia kept her head up, and the little crowd that had gathered applauded. "Yeah," Delia shouted. "You people, go tell the newspaper what you seen here with these goons, beating on women and children. Go ahead, tell them."

Hannah dropped to her knees next to Alex and pulled him tight. "My God, you just scared the life out of me. You could have been injured, do you know that? You're never to run off like that again, understand?"

"But I wanted to help Delia." Alex wondered why she hadn't run after Delia, too. Maybe she didn't like Delia, but he did, better than Hannah. "Where are they taking her?"

"Oh. I don't, uh, well, they're just going to talk to her."

"Delia said I'm supposed to have lunch now. She said she'd come later."

"Well, all right. Maybe we should just go. We'll have lunch at home."

"Does Delia know where you live?"

"What? I don't know. Let's just go for now, all right?"

Alex looked back to where Delia was being led away as Hannah pulled him in the other direction.

Timothy Wagner, a beat cop that had detail duty for the parade, watched two of his fellow officers struggle to cuff a dark-haired woman. He walked over to see if they needed any help with the good-looking broad.

"Hey, Wagner."

He recognized Delia from The Squeaky Wheel. She'd let him slide on a couple of tabs over the last few months when he'd been short on cash due to the demands of his estranged wife and three teenage daughters. He tapped the shoulder of one of the arresting officers. "What'd she do, fellas, rob a bank?"

"Nearly took the head off some slob with one of them signs."

"Sounds like a real dangerous criminal. A menace to society, she is. Give us a moment, will you?"

"You know this skirt?"

"I seen her around."

"Well, all right, she ain't going nowhere with them bracelets."

Wagner took Delia's elbow and walked her to a cobblestone alley lined with a row of trashcans. They stood in the shadows. "What the hell are you doing here, Novak?"

"What's it look like, Wagner, dancing the jig?"

"Nice mouth on you. I never took you for one of them dike broad marchers."

"Yeah? There's a lot about me you don't know. So anyway, how's your wife?"

Wagner frowned. "You ain't making this any easier, Novak. I'm trying to give you a break here."

"Yeah, well you owe me one. Why don't you take these cuffs off me for starters?"

Wagner twirled a key on a chain. "Yeah, sure, I could do that, but what's in it for me?"

Delia smiled. God, men were dumb. "Tell you what. Next time you come by The Wheel when I'm working, I'll take care of you good." She lowered her voice. "Real good."

"Real good?"

"Come by some time and see." She held up her hands. "Come on." The handcuffs clanked against her wrists.

Wagner put his hand on her shoulder. "I got to hold you here a couple of minutes, to make it look good, like I was giving you the business."

"Yes sir, Officer Wagner." She let out her breath. What a goddamn morning. "Got a cigarette?"

Five minutes later, Delia was back at the restaurant, looking around for

Alex and Hannah, but since they were nowhere in sight she decided to head back to her apartment and kick her shoes off for a while. She was due at The Wheel for her off-day job a few hours later. She wondered if Abe would be there. She hoped so. They had a lot to talk about, especially this Hannah character.

*

Abe helped himself to a gumdrop from the pound bag he'd bought for the boys at Rucker's Market on the way from work to pick up Alex from Hannah's house. He was in a pleasant state of mind, at peace for one of the few times since his mother-in-law's death. With Alex being taken care of, his older boys toeing the line, and some extra money in his pocket from the overtime, he felt things were finally going his way. Maybe he could even spend more time with Delia, buy her something pretty.

He whistled as he walked down Black Street to Hannah's house. He knocked on the door, which generated a series of high-pitched arfs from the dog, with two-second pauses in between. After a few moments, he knocked again.

Belle swung the door open. She frowned. "You."

Now, Abe thought, what the hell is wrong with her? They'd been getting along swell for two weeks, they even had him and the older boys to dinner last Friday, and he'd begun to feel the aunts were kind of an unrelated extended family around Alex. He tried to maintain his upbeat mood in spite of the chill he felt from her. "Good Shabbas, Belle."

She put her hands on her broad hips. "So, now he's Mister Jew after denying it for 30 years."

"What?" Abe scratched his head. "Belle, I'm just trying to be pleasant. I don't think God would hold it against me."

She snorted. "Now he's an expert on God. Anyway, Miller, you're late."

"I stopped to get something for the boys." He looked past her shoulder. "Where's Alex?"

"With Hannah, where else would he be? Well, don't just stand there, you're letting the flies in." Her curtness reminded him of how Ida used to treat him when he came to call on Irene; basically, he had to justify his existence every time he came by her house. What the hell had happened since he dropped Alex off this morning to sour Belle on him so bad?

Once inside, Lillie looked at him as if he'd just robbed the rabbi's poor box. On the floor was a ballerina figurine, broken into several pieces. "Lillie, did my boy do that?"

"He was chasing the dog."

Abe took out a roll of bills. "How much is it? I'll pay you for it."

"Put your money away, it was an accident. Besides, you don't have enough."

As the sisters stared daggers at him, he felt as if he were on trial for a crime he wasn't aware he'd committed. But from the tightness of their glares, he realized he wasn't going to get anything out of them by way of explanation. He glanced at the stairs, figuring Alex was with Hannah up in her room. The wall clock chimed. He wanted to be home by three, three-thirty at the latest, to give him enough time to make something up for dinner, clean up Alex, take a quick sponge bath and a shave. Arthur and Benjamin would be home from the ball game by four-thirty at the latest. If they weren't, then he'd have to take Alex to The Wheel. "Well, if it's all the same to you I'll collect my son and be on my way. And thanks for taking him today."

"Don't thank me, thank Hannah."

"Is she upstairs?"

Lillie sat down. "She doesn't want to talk to you."

"Huh? Why?"

"Ask her."

"But you said she doesn't want to…never mind, where are they?" He started for the stairs.

"Other way," said Lillie. "They're on the sun porch."

Crayons were scattered all over the porch next to a coloring book. Outside, Alex dug in the tomato garden with a wooden spoon. Abe watched him for a moment before he turned to Hannah, who sat in a rocking chair with her back to him. "Hannah?"

When she didn't answer, he continued. "I'm sorry I'm late. I already told Belle and Lillie. They give me the business about it, like I got the plague or something."

Without turning around, Hannah said, "You never told me you had a girlfriend."

She knew about Delia? But how could she possibly know? Out in the yard, the dog barked and Alex laughed. Maybe the boy had said something about her, but that was a long shot. But then he remembered how the boy had blurted out Delia's name to Irene one night what seemed like years ago, when he and Irene were on the verge of making love. Still, it seemed so unlikely. "Girlfriend? What girlfriend?"

"Don't play dumb."

"Hannah, come on."

"Delia Novak. Or is there another one you never told me about?"

Christ, the little bugger must have said something. What the hell else had he told her? That he and Delia saw each other at The Squeaky Wheel whenever they could? That every once in a while on a Saturday night, Daddy doesn't come home until very, very late, even later than Arthur stays up, or that one time on a Sunday morning, Miss Delia was at their house, and that he'd wandered into the bathroom and saw her with no clothes on? He remembered how Delia had laughed at that, but inwardly he shuddered. Did he tell her about that, too?

"Hannah, I can explain about her."

"Oh, don't even bother. She and I had a nice conversation about you just this morning. Before she got arrested." Hannah went on to describe how she and Alex had by chance happened to meet Delia at the suffragette parade, and how Delia made a total fool of herself, fighting with policemen, and how Alex was caught up in everything and almost got hurt. But thank God, she was able to force her way through the crowd and pull him away and keep him safe.

"You saved him?Is he hurt?" He began to leave the porch but Hannah grabbed his arm.

"I told you he's fine, I saved him. You can see that."

His son looked all right as he dug in the dirt. "Well, thank you for saving my boy."

"Don't bother." She turned her back on him.

He touched her lightly on the shoulder. "Hey, what's wrong, I thought we was friends."

"Friends."

"Yes. I mean you and me, I thought we was getting to know each other real good, and Alex, hell, excuse my language, he thinks the world of you."

She turned slightly. "He does? He really does?"

"Sure. He talks about you all the time."

Her voice quavered. "Really? Because sometimes I think he's a little cold toward me. No, that's not the right word. Cautious. Or fearful. Why would he be fearful toward me?"

Calling on his rudimentary understanding of child behavior, Abe said, "Well, kids are funny like that sometimes. They change like the weather, you know that. But he likes you plenty, don't worry about that."

She stopped rocking and squeezed a pillow to her chest. She closed her eyes and spoke toward the ceiling, as if she were explaining herself to a higher power. "I love him so much that I would be crushed if anything ever happened to him, my God, like what happened today. You don't know how terrified I was." She stood up, much too close to him, and touched his chest with her index finger. "But I don't want to talk about that any more. I want to know what's going on between you and this Delia Novak, and you'd better tell me the truth because I can tell when a person lies to me, it's one of my special abilities."

If he were to tell her the truth, that Delia still could make him loopy with lust with just a touch in the right place, that there were times he could barely control the lion in heat inside him for her, even though he knew that with Delia, the only future was the immediate future—if he told Hannah all that, this arrangement for Alex would go right out the window, he was sure of it, and then where would they be? Not only that, but he'd begun to think that he could do a lot worse than Hannah Gerson. Maybe the problem was, she needed to get out from under her aunts' thumb. She was young but she wasn't no kid. Plus, the girl had suffered. When she told him that her parents and brother had died of The Dip the same year Irene had, it brought tears to his eyes. Maybe what she needed was a family to take care of. Maybe what he needed was a woman to take care of him and his sons. And it sure as hell wasn't going to be Delia.

He cleared his throat. "Now, Delia and me, we used to go around together a bit, but over the last couple of years or so, things, well, they ain't been the same."

"What do you mean?"

"Well, I'm embarrassed to talk about it."

"Don't treat me like a child, Abraham. I'm not." She threw her arms around the nape of his neck more aggressively than he would have thought. Her lips touched his ear. "I know all about men. I know what they want." Her right hand brushed against the front of his pants.

At first he thought it was an accident, but the way she kept her hand on his pants, he wasn't sure what to think, except the way she moved it, this was no accident. What was he supposed to make of this woman—one minute she acted as if he were the biggest heel that ever lived, and the next she was on him, hot and heavy. As much as he liked how she was stroking him, he knew it wasn't the time or the place. He tried to push her away, but she held firm. "Whatever she can do, I can do better." She reached between his legs and rubbed the back of her hand against his scrotum for a few seconds, then turned her palm up and massaged him.

Breath whistled from Abe's nose. He felt himself getting hard. What if the aunts walked in? He tried to pull away, but she grabbed his wrist with a strength that surprised him, and pulled his hand between her legs. He said, "What are you doing?" even though he knew damn well.

She squeezed her legs tight on his hand. "I know how to make babies. I can show you." The more he tried to pull away, the tighter she held.

"Daddy?" Alex looked up at the two of them locked together, and he thought, Daddy must like Hannah, but he likes Delia, too. Hannah was pretty and smelled good and gave him anything he wanted, but Delia, she said funny things, she called him kiddo and buddy and pumpkin. Hannah called him her baby and he wasn't a baby, and he wished his father would just hurry up and marry one of them. He wanted a mommy.

*

The Saturday afternoon lunch crowd had for the most part gone home to domestic chore-dum and dinner with the wife and kids. It would be a while before the Saturday evening crowd came by, and so at four o'clock The Squeaky Wheel was virtually empty, save for Horshushky the butcher who, as was his custom, was working on his Saturday drunk, which started at noon. The only other regular was Davy O'Brien, who sat at his usual table, puffed on his pipe and read from his *Collected Works of Alfred Lord Tennyson*.

John was perched on a barstool with the newspaper spread out in front of him. He alternately nibbled on a ham sandwich and puffed his cigar. A crack of light slid through the front door, momentarily illuminating Horshushky's beer as Delia entered. She went behind the bar and took an apron from below.

John motioned toward the kitchen. "You want to get the sandwiches ready? I already got the meat sliced."

She rinsed her hands in the sink. "Busy day?"

"Not bad. Should have a decent night if it don't rain." He flipped the page. "Christ, what's the world coming to?"

"What? The war started already?"

"No." He tapped the newspaper. "Listen to this. There was supposed to be some kind of women's march for the vote today, this morning. Damn suffragettes. You heard about this?"

"Oh yeah. I was there."

"You was what?" John burst out laughing. "Quit pulling my leg."

Delia almost told him that she wasn't, but what the hell, let him think it, he was keeping her employed. "So anyway, how you doing?"

Horshushky pounded his mug on the bar.

"Go see what the Polack wants. What a pain in the ass."

Horshushky pushed his hair back behind his ears with the palms of his hands, which were callused and scarred from numerous slips of the knife. Smooth nubs had grown over where the tips of the right thumb and left ring finger used to be.

"What's it gonna be, sir?"

"How's about a smooch?"

"I don't need this today."

Horshushky slipped his hand around her waist. "Come on. What's your Jew boyfriend got that I ain't got?" He flicked his tongue like a lizard. "Something wrong with me?"

"Nothing a week in a bathtub and a new face wouldn't cure." She pushed his hands away. As she went to the kitchen, she tapped John on the shoulder. "Call me when Abe gets here."

Chapter 20

By four o'clock that afternoon, Arthur Miller and Jack Walsh had hitchhiked all the way to Weirton, West Virginia, where they planned to rendezvous with Jack's cousin Robert and enlist Monday morning, bright and early, in Wheeling, 25 miles away. The boys were in high spirits, partly due to the prospect of becoming real men in uniform and partly because, prior to that day, neither had traveled more than five miles from home, much less to another state entirely. Even though Weirton was just a little more than 30 miles from Pittsburgh, as they passed though the countryside colored with red barns, hillsides of green corn and silver water tanks, it was as if they were on a journey to a foreign land.

They sat on a wood bench on Main Street and waited for Robert. According to Jack, his cousin had agreed to put them up until Monday, when all three boys would enlist. Arthur and Jack chewed on sandwiches they'd bought from the general store, and Arthur told Jack that it was the best chicken he'd ever had, that the chicken tasted different in West Virginia, Jack agreed, they sure knew how to make chicken salad down here in Weirton, it was even better than his ma's. He paused.

Arthur rolled the paper wrapper into a ball and dropped it into the waste can in front of the store. He hurried back to the bench, eager to be beside his friend. A few cars drove by. Gas street lamps came on. Arthur took a sweater from his pack and draped it around his shoulders. "Jack? Robert's coming, right?"

Around five o'clock that afternoon, thanks to a Pirates victory, the mood was festive in The Wheel, but Abe was grim as he and Alex wiggled their way into Davy's corner table. Alex jumped onto Davy's lap and said, "What's this?"

"This, my boy, is a recorder. A fine musical instrument, first played in the courts of the great medieval kings of Europe, and Ireland, too, of course, by musicians and jesters alike, to entertain, inform, charm and amuse." He held the recorder to his lips and played several bars of *By the Light of the Silvery Moon.* "Abe, is it all right with you if I instruct squire Alex on how to play this noble instrument, with which someday he may join the hallowed pantheons of recorder virtuosos?"

"I want to see it, Davy," Alex said. He blew until his face turned red. "Nothing comes out."

Four men played cards a few tables to the left, using match sticks for their wagers, since card playing for money in drinking establishments was illegal—although everyone, even the beat cops that periodically stopped in for a quick beer, knew exactly what half and whole matchsticks represented. At the far end of the bar Edward Peck tossed darts with the tottering Horshushky. Peck had long given up asking Alex to throw darts again. Everyone had, for as much as they cajoled him and his father, Alex refused and Abe was adamant—if he don't want to, he don't want to, and that's the end of that.

Davy said, "What's the matter, Abe? You look like you got a toothache."

"It ain't that. It's Arthur." Abe pulled out the note he'd found on the kitchen table when he and Alex came home from the confrontation with Hannah. Arthur apologized for not telling Abe in person, but he'd left to enlist in the army, and said that Abe needn't worry about him, that he could prove he was eighteen, and that it was his patriotic duty to serve. He couldn't wait until he really was eighteen, the big war was coming, and the Germans might win and we can't let that happen, and besides, school wasn't for him, and he and Jack Walsh were going in together, as best friends, so Abe didn't have to worry. They'd look out for each other, he said, and please. tell Benjamin and Alex that he would be home just as soon as could.

"What am I gonna do, Davy? He's only sixteen, a boy. He don't know his ass from a hole in the ground. I don't even know which way he went."

Davy put a hand on Abe's shoulder. "Listen, I wouldn't worry too much. A dollar to a dime says the boy will be banging on your front door about midnight tonight when his stomach starts to rumble and his gumption wears off. Not that I think his intentions are bad, mind you."

"But what if he don't?" Abe shuddered. What if they actually took his son? Abe could see him, stuck in a muddy foxhole with artillery shells coming down on him, or charging across some field into machine gun fire. He could get a bayonet through his stomach, or get blinded by that poison gas they were talking about. Hell, just when things was getting better for rest of the family, he had to go and pull this stunt. Abe had had enough of death already, with Irene's passing and Ida dead in a fire. He looked at Alex. What would another loss do to him?

"Daddy."

"What?"

"Arthur told me he's going to bring me a German flag."

"He told you—wait a second. You knew he was going to take off to join the army?"

"Yes."

"Why didn't you tell me?"

Alex looked at his fingers on the recorder. "He told me not to tell. Benjamin, too."

"But you should have." The dartboard crowd cheered as Peck hit a bull's-eye. Abe looked up to see Delia move toward the bar with a tray of empty glasses. "Alex, you stay here. Davy, watch him for a minute, will you?" He started after her.

Davy nodded and yawned.

After his father left, Alex said, "Davy, is Daddy mad at me?"

Davy's head slumped forward on his chest as he snored.

Alex took the recorder and slipped off the chair. He weaved his way through the tables, pausing to accept pats on the head.

*

Delia had almost reached the kitchen when Abe caught up to her. He said, "I need to talk to you."

Delia stacked glasses on the bar. "I'm working, Romeo." She tried to push past him.

"Come on. What's eating you?"

Delia bumped her rear against the swinging doors, forcing them open. "How's your little girlfriend Hannah?"

Abe was about to try to explain when Horshushky, barely able to stand, threw a meaty arm over Abe's shoulder. With a drunk's heavy strength, he spun him around. "Buy you a drink, Abe?"

"You stink like dead fish, Horshushky."

"Now be nice, my Jewish friend." He pulled him to the bar and signaled for two beers. "A toast to you and Delia Novak, the nicest piece of...the nicest gal in the joint."

Abe let his beer sit and kept his eyes on Delia. "I ain't got time for this, all right? What do you want?"

"What do I want? I want to know what your secret is. How come you can get into her pants when every other slob in this joint can't get the time of day from her? No offense, but you put some kind of Jew spell on her?"

"Christ, you're even dumber than you look." He gulped down his beer and went back to his table.

Davy was asleep. Alex was gone.

*

On one side of The Wheel's bathroom was a long, thigh-high trough made of corrugated tin, which served as a communal urinal. On the other side were four open wood stalls with toilets and a cold-water sink. A fly speckled light bulb hung from the ceiling.

Dr. Malkin had just finished relieving himself when the door opened and Alex wandered in, holding his recorder with both hands. He looked up at Malkin. "Nothing comes out."

Once again an opportunity has been delivered to me, Malkin thought. Although this was not a good room for a proper examination, at least, he thought, he could get the measurements of this boy, since his father had refused to let him come near him since the mother's death, as if it were his fault and not The Dip's.

"Ah, my boy Mr. Alex, I can see it that you are playing it the flute."

"It's a recorder."

"Aha, so it is. But also I can see it you are having no success in the playing, no? Instead of this recorder, how would you like to play it another game, to be it the doctor, like Dr. Sergei, yes? Here, I will give it to you my stethoscope so you can hear it your heart beating." He handed Alex his stethoscope while he looked in his bag for his measuring tape.

Alex put the stethoscope on his chest. "I can't hear it."

"No, no, my boy, you will ruin it with your yanking and pulling. This is a medical instrument, not a toy, you put it the ends of it in your ears. It is not for the pulling, it is for the listening. You have to put the tube part here." He motioned to his ears.

For such a little one, Malkin observed, he certainly has it much strength to stretch the tube out so far, perhaps because of the long arms. He held up the measuring tape. "Alex, my little friend, now if you would be so kind as to hold it your right arm down to your side like this, you see, so that I can make it the accurate measurement of its length. No? But perhaps I will be giving it you this piece candy, for your cooperation, yes? Here."

Alex popped the gumdrop into his mouth and held out his hand.

"More? Now wait it just a minute, young man, I have given it the candy to you, we have made it the deal, you must first allow me to make it the measurement before you can have more."

Alex shook his head no.

A dare, Malkin thought, I shall make it a dare for him, so I shall get my way. "Little Alex, do you know what? I will bet it to you a nickel you cannot do this." He stretched out his arms. "If you can do this you can have it the nickel. But I do not think you can."

"That's easy." As Alex shot his arms out and held them tightly in place, Malkin quickly measured his wingspan and jotted it down on a pad of paper he'd taken from the lobby of the William Penn Hotel that morning, after the suffragette march. As he glanced at the logo, he imagined that he was the hotel's house doctor.

Now he needed to measure the rest of his body. The legs, the feet, everything, he reasoned, they must be measured as well, for to go to the Conference on Childhood Diseases in Philadelphia at the end of August, the child's measurements, they must be on the application, must be specifically recorded at various times in the child's growth, otherwise they might think he was not a scientific doctor. To get to Philadelphia, he would have to take a train with the boy. How this could be done, especially without the father's consent, he didn't know, but he would find a way. When the medical experts saw his work with Alex, they would recognize that Dr. Sergei Malkin, dentist also, was a medical man to be respected for his discovery of a unique childhood condition, and no doubt there would be money in it for him, too, with Alex as his ward, for research, exhibitions and speaking engagements, teaching perhaps, God willing. No more chasing patients at Holy Roller meetings or parades.

But first he needed to get the other measurements, especially the legs and genitalia. Perhaps the growth there was abnormal as well. "All right, so I see it that you can hold them out your arms very well, as you are doing it. But I bet it you cannot do this." Malkin shrugged off his suspenders. His heavy wool pants fell around his ankles. "This time I shall give it to you now two nickels."

As Abe tried to shake Davy awake he felt a hand on his shoulder. "I got a few minutes now," Delia said.

"I need to find Alex."

She looked around the room. "Relax, he ain't going nowhere. First you need to tell me what's going on with this Hannah dame."

"Look, it ain't what you think." Abe explained how he'd met Hannah in the first place—hell, it had been Delia's idea to get help at the synagogue. He told her how Hannah had lived with her two spinster aunts ever since her parents died, and how she was really good to Alex, and how Alex seemed to be taking to her, too, getting along fine with her and the dog and the aunts, who made him all kinds of good old-fashioned Jewish food and bought him clothes and treated him like a little prince, which took a load off Abe's mind, he was damn lucky to have them watch his son. "And that's it."

"So everything is hunky-dory with you and this girl."

"Yeah—wait. What do you mean?"

"I mean she's good-looking. Don't pretend you didn't notice. How do I know you ain't fiddling around with this Hannah? Maybe Delia ain't good enough for you no more."

Abe lowered his voice. "You're plenty good."

"You're damn right I am." She took his chin in her fingers. "You need a shave. But this Hannah stuff, you watch it, you hear? Besides, I got something else I need to talk to you about. It could be big for us, Abe. Very big. But I can't talk here."

"Yeah? Why don't I come by tonight and you can tell me all about it." The thought of spending the night with Delia made him momentarily forget looking for Alex and the mess with Arthur.

"Forget it...I gotta work the mansion tomorrow. I'll come by after Sunday dinner. Now sit. I'll find Alex for you."

Before she could get up, the bathroom slammed open. Edward Peck had Alex on his left hip and Dr. Malkin by the collar. Malkin clutched at his trousers, which were bunched halfway between his ankles and his knees, forcing him to walk in mincing steps, which elicited catcalls and laughter from the drinkers as he struggled by them.

Alex waved at Abe. "Hi, Daddy. Dr. Malkin gave me a nickel to pull my pants down."

"No, wait, please, I did not say it to him exactly like that."

Abe grabbed his son from Peck. "You all right, Alex?"

Peck explained how he'd come into the bathroom moments earlier to "drain the dragon" and found Malkin with his pants down around his ankles, bent over at the waist, his head near Alex's stomach, a tape measure in his hand. "I would have cracked his head open for him right then, Abe, but I figured you'd want to do it yourself."

Malkin waived his arms. "But it was for the scientific research is all."

Alex pointed at Malkin. "He wanted to play a game with me."

Abe handed Alex to Delia. He shook Peck's hand. Then he hit Malkin with a straight left to the nose, sending Malkin's pince-nez flying and ultimately landing in Carl Tosca's beer mug two tables away. "That's one." Abe cocked his right fist, but Peck pulled him away.

"He ain't worth going to jail for, Abe. You see to your boy, we'll escort this piece of dog shit to the door."

Blood dripped from Malkin's nose, and he dabbed it with the back of his soiled cuff. He pointed at Abe. "Nothing I did it to your boy, Miller, except to measure. You will hear it from my attorney of law about this."

"Tell your attorney of law about this, too," Peck said. He and Horshushky took Malkin's arms. They dragged him across the floor, and as they passed the tables, men that were close enough smacked Malkin on the back of the head. Outside, they tossed him to the curb. A moment later, his black bag landed on top of him.

Malkin sat up and leaned his back against a trash barrel. He ran his tongue over his teeth and was relieved that no new ones were missing. He felt his nose and winced. Even without a mirror he could tell it was broken, since it angled slightly to the right.

Two young women in long dresses and felt hats walked by him arm-in-arm. The taller one asked Malkin if he were all right but the other insisted that they move on, he probably was just some drunk they'd thrown out of the bar and that she didn't want some soused-up rummy pawing at her or throwing up on her new patent leather lace-ups, which had cost her almost two dollars.

Riley the beat cop strolled around the corner, on his way to The Wheel for a sandwich and an envelope of cash from John, his fee for allowing The Wheel to host a Saturday night after-hours craps game. He tipped his hat to the two girls. The taller one pointed back at Malkin, who by this time had struggled to his feet. As he approached him, the cop said, "Everything all right, sir?"

Malkin spit out some phlegm and blood. "Yes, yes, officer, it is just an unfortunate fall I was taking over the curb."

Riley looked at Malkin's eye, which was almost swollen shut and had begun to turn colors. "That curb hit you a good one."

"Yes, well, that is true, as you say, but now I must be it on my way to visit a patient that is very ill, perhaps it is she could be dying, no? So I shall be going, officer, if you do not mind it."

Riley rested his club on Malkin's shoulder. "I wouldn't drink no more today if I was you, doc."

"Oh no, I wouldn't touch it the one drop."

Malkin limped away from the bar, his bruised ego hurting even more than his mashed nose, but despite the slings and arrows he had suffered at outraged hands, he had one thing on his mind: He had to find a way to get hold of that boy.

*

The constable tapped Arthur and Jack on the shoulders and told them there was no loitering, that it was time to go home, not knowing that going home for them was not possible, at least for that night.

The boys drifted away down the street in the feeble last light of day. They stopped at a four-story red brick building, The Wayside Hotel, with a sign that advertised clean rooms, $2.50, an amount which would consume nearly one-third of the boy's pooled traveling money.

In the small lobby, a chunky woman with thick glasses sat on a stool behind the counter with a ledger book and a pitcher of water. She read from *The House of a Thousand Candles*, a romance novel ironically set in Pittsburgh. A Pekingese slept on a pillow on top of a desk behind her. She looked up over her reading glasses. "Help you boys?"

Jack said, "That room for two-fifty? Do we get it for the both of us?"

The woman scratched the dog's head. "Fifty cents extra. If you want breakfast, it's another fifty. Hi, Cal." She waved to an old man in a black suit walking though the lobby toward the stairway.

Arthur was all for the offer, but Jack insisted they hold out for his cousin. Finally, they agreed to wait another half hour, until it was completely dark, before they took the room.

They were sitting on a bench outside on the walk, sharing a pack of oyster crackers, when the woman came out with her dog on a pink leash. Her flowered dress came down over her feet, and as she moved it looked as if she were floating. She stopped in front of the boys. "You two still here?"

"Yes, ma'am."

The little dog lifted his leg to urinate on Jack's shoes. "Bad boy, Sparky, bad boy. Lord, the day he listens to me, it will be a miracle, praise Jesus. Won't it, Sparky-poo? But anyhow. Now boys, I ain't trying to pry into your plans for the evening, in the hotel business it don't pay to pry to close, but this here establishment, we ain't got but the one room left for tonight, and I'll bet you a dollar to a donut in a little while from now some traveling salesman will come by needing a place for the night, or some local feller with a snoot full looking for a room to sleep it off, seeing as he can't go home the way he is. So if I was you boys, and I didn't have no other place to go, well, I'd grab me that room afore someone else does. But like I say, that's your business. Come on, Sparky."

A man and a woman walked by them, arm in arm, and entered the hotel.

The boys counted their money for the fifth time that day. Home seemed a long way off.

Chapter 21

The next morning, as Abe slept off four lagers and a shot of Old Overholt, Alex and Benjamin ate apple butter and toast at the kitchen table with the newspaper spread open before them. Benjamin scrutinized the box scores from the previous day's games, while Alex read the front page out loud. He fired off a series of comments—strike breakers battle union, mayor calls for tax increase, arson suspected in South Side fire—maybe it was a fire like at Grandma's house. He shivered at the memory of flames and heat and smoke. He wondered if Grandma were in Heaven with Jesus.

He read the section titled, "From Across the Pond," where armies were massing in France, Russia, England and Germany, and he thought, when my big brother Arthur gets there, he'll beat up the Germans, he said he would. But Benjamin says Arthur doesn't know what he's talking about, and Daddy said yesterday he might get his fool head blown off which means he'd be dead like Mommy and Grandma, and that thought made his head hurt. His missed his brother's sweaty smell and cigarette laughter, and he wished he were right there so they could play checkers or wrestle on the floor. Arthur always let him get him in a headlock before he surrendered. "Benjamin?"

"Yeah?"

"Is Arthur going to get his head blown off like Daddy said?"

"What? No!" Benjamin bit his lip. "I mean, I don't think so. He'll probably come home today or tomorrow when they find out he's only sixteen."

"But what if he doesn't?"

"Well, Arthur's pretty tough. He can beat up almost any kid in his grade, and some older kids, too. So don't worry about it, all right?" He bounced a pinky ball on the floor. "Wanna play catch?"

The boys were on the front walkway when they saw Delia, dressed in her maid's uniform, walking down Mellon Street toward them.

*

Belle grunted as she pulled weeds from around the tomato plants, flipping dandelions and chunks of crabgrass into a corrugated tin bucket. On the opposite side of the yard, Lillie, wearing a floppy sunbonnet and tan gardening gloves, tied pole bean shoots to tall wooden stakes. The dog slept on the bulkhead doors.

The sisters had been working for two hours after a breakfast of herring and eggs and prune Danish. The Liberty Theater was featuring a movie starring Mary Pickford, whom they both adored, and so if they worked diligently enough, they could get the gardening done and still have time for a sponge bath and light lunch before the two o'clock matinee.

"Aunt Belle, Aunt Lillie, good morning." Hannah sprang from the back door, her hair loose, in her nightgown and bare feet.

"Good Lord," Belle said, "put some clothes on."

Lillie put her roll of twine in her apron pocket. "Hannah, dear, it's time to get dressed. It's eleven o'clock already."

"I know what time it is." She squatted down next to the dog and kissed him on the head.

Belle crushed out her cigarette. "Don't you want to come see Mary Pickford with us? She's your favorite."

Hannah hugged the dog to her as if it were her dance partner and twirled like a ballerina across the lawn. "I have to see Papa right away."

Belle looked at Lillie. Lillie looked at Belle. The sisters moved closer to each other and linked arms, as if the sum of their physical presence would lend more weight to their words. "Hannah, what's going on?"

She stopped twirling and set the dog down. "Oh, I'm so sorry." Her dear old aunts, they'd been so good to her for the last few years, they really should be the first to know of her good fortune, even before she told her father. "I have such wonderful news. Magical. Abe and I are getting married! Isn't it glorious, wonderful? Oh, Momma and Papa will be so thrilled. Finally they'll be proud of me."

Lillie said, "Oh my."

"I have to tell them right away, today. There's so much to plan, so much to do. I know they'll want to throw me a big wedding—that's what I want, too, of course. It will be at the synagogue, and we'll invite just everyone, even my cousins from New York, and you two will be my maids of honor. Or is it matrons of honor? I want to wear pink baby roses in my hair…no, yellow…and my gown, heavens, it has to be striking—you must help me pick it out. And the cake! What about the cake?" She was hopping up and down.

"Hannah, please calm down."

"But I am calm! And Alex, oh my God, the dear sweet little thing, he'll be the ring bearer, oh won't it be precious as I walk down the aisle with pink baby rose petals strewn in front of me. Maybe I'll even be barefoot. Oh." She put her hand to her mouth, her teeth to her knuckles. But would her Papa love Abe and Alex the way she did? Abe was a bit rough around the edges, yes, a bit uncultured for their tastes. They would prefer she marry a banker or a doctor, or even a lawyer or a college professor or a business owner, she'd heard that from them since she was eight. But her Abe was so nice and upright, and look at all he's suffered through, and besides, he has Alex, her little boy. Momma and Papa would understand it, they must. "Do you suppose Papa will see me right now? We have so much to discuss."

Lillie said, "You can't go anywhere unless you get dressed."

Hanna shook her nightgown. "But I am dressed."

Belle whispered to her sister, "You take her left arm, I'll take the right."

*

Delia let herself in and went up to the bedroom. Abe's chest was bare, and the sheet was twisted around his waist. She thought about stroking him awake, getting him all hot and bothered with her hands in his crotch, wouldn't he get a thrill out of that, and she would, too, but that kind of stuff would have to wait.

She thumped his shoulder. "Wake up, sleeping beauty."

Abe rolled on his elbows. "Delia?"

"It ain't the Holy Ghost."

He leaned up against the headboard. "But how'd you...my boys, you seen 'em?"

"They're outside playing ball."

Abe rubbed his eyes. He managed a smile. "Delia. I'll be damned. Not that I ain't glad to see you, but what are you doing here? I thought you was working today."

"So did I."

Delia explained how, when she reported to the mansion at seven that morning, the caretaker hustled her into her little office and told her, in no uncertain terms, that she was shit-canned. She handed her an envelope with her week's pay, less the deposit for her maid's outfit, which she would get when she returned it cleaned and pressed. "The nasty broad, I could scratch her eyes out."

"But what happened? You do something wrong?"

"According to them, I did." Apparently, she told him, a society friend of the lady of the house who happened to be downtown shopping recognized Delia as she marched with the suffragettes, and reported it to her employer. If there was one thing the matriarch of the manor wouldn't tolerate, it was anything to do with women's suffrage. The very idea was ridiculous and obscene to her, and a headstrong maid that marched with a bunch of sign-carrying lesbians? That woman had no place in her employ. "Can you believe it, Abe? I should have spit in her face, but I need the money back for this damn uniform."

"Geez, that's tough, kid." Abe scratched under his arm. "You look like you could use some coffee."

Delia took his hand. "Thanks."

Once Abe got the coffee going, Delia sat down at the table. She took off her maid's cap and shook her hair loose. She ran her hand over the letter from her old friend.

"Black, right?"

"Yeah."

He stirred his coffee. "So last night you was telling me something about big plans for the two of us. You wanna tell me?"

"Not here." She reached for a cigarette but let the pack lie on the table. "Abe, would you bring Alex to The Wheel with me?"

"You mean right now?"

"Yeah."

"But it's closed."

"I have a key."

"But what for?"

She put a finger on his lips. "Shush. I'll show you when we get there."

"Boy, you're sure acting cagey." What was the big secret? His birthday was in two weeks. Maybe she was throwing a surprise party for him, with a keg and a big cake and all the boys there—hold on, that wasn't Delia's style. Plus, she just got canned, so how could she pay for it? No, something was up, or she wouldn't be so insistent. "Give me a hint at least."

"I'll give you more than that later on. Let's go."

Half an hour later Delia unlocked the front door. Their footsteps echoed on the linoleum as they walked by tables stacked with chairs. Small pools of light dotted the floor. Beer and cigar odors hung in the air.

Delia spread the newspaper out on the far end of the bar. "Alex, you want to read the comics?" She poured a bottle of sarsaparilla in a beer mug for him and added a straw. "Your daddy and I are gonna talk in the kitchen, all right? You call us if you need anything."

Alex was curious as to why they would leave him, but he was more interested in the serial adventures he followed in the funny pages.

Abe and Delia leaned their backsides against the metal sinks. She said, "You're worried about Arthur, I can tell, but don't be. He's a big boy. He'll be all right. He'll make his way in the world, we all do."

Abe shook his head. "Maybe yes, maybe no. But you didn't bring us here to talk about Arthur."

"That's true. I want to talk about the future."

The future? He wondered if she meant her future, or theirs. He tried to be solicitous. "Hell, I'm sorry you got canned, but I'm sure John will give you more hours."

"I don't want more goddamn hours." She picked up a steak knife and stared at the edge. "Did you ever say to yourself that you wanted something different than what you got now, that you wanted to get the hell out of this town and this life? I have." She stared up at the ceiling, then right into his eyes. Her voice was measured. "There's a big world out there, Abe. I seen it—well, part of it at least, when I was in New York. People there, they ain't all like us, working stiffs and fat women with six kids where a big time is going to a baseball game once a year or watching the fireworks up at Highland Park on the Fourth of July. I'm talking about skyscrapers and museums and plays and big automobiles, and women wearing furs and fancy hats, and restaurants where you can get any kind of food there is, and people from all over the world doing things, really doing things, making fortunes. I seen it, Abe. It's for real."

"What are you saying, you wanna go to New York again?"

She grabbed his arm. "Do you really like busting your ass every day for Shields, working like a slave? The sweat off your back has made him a rich man, and what has he given you, besides a few crumbs every week you call a paycheck? What does he care about the workingman as long as he's making his money? Look, all I'm saying is, don't you ever wish you could go places, see things before you die? I swear, five more years of this here life and we'll all end up like Davy O'Brien, drunks, our bodies broken, just trying get through another lousy day."

Abe let his breath out slowly The last few years had been a blur, with Irene's death and Ida's fire and the constant enigma of Alex, and now Arthur was gone God knows where, and who knows, maybe Benjamin was next, and he couldn't get the touch of Hannah's hands out of his head even though he was standing two feet away from Delia. The one constant in his life was work. At least he had that dull certainty to wake up to every morning, like they say in marriage, for better or for worse, but now here was Delia, her eyes blazing, upsetting his world even more with her wild ideas that he should quit and go gallivanting around the country somewhere. Skyscrapers. What the hell was she saying?

"All that sounds just peachy, Delia, New York and automobiles and all, and gallivanting about here and there, but where's the money gonna come from? My name ain't Rockefeller."

"I already thought of that."

"What? What the hell are you talking about?"

"Listen to me, will ya?" Delia took out the letter. "I have this friend, a very good friend that works in the circus, Ringling's. She goes all over the country, Abe. She sees things, she does things, she's out in the world. Plus, she makes money, Abe, damn good money, way more than you and me combined."

Abe laughed. "Well, good for her. But what's that mean to me?"

"It means this." Delia stuck the steak knife into a butcher's block cutting board.

"What?"

"All you have to do is give me the o.k., and I'll write a letter to my friend about how Alex can throw knives and darts like nothing else."

Abe's eyes narrowed. "Wait a minute. Are you saying you want me to turn my son into a carney freak?"

Delia put her arms over Abe's shoulders. "Not a freak, Abe. An act. An attraction is what they call it in The Greatest Show on Earth. People will go crazy over a little boy, a tiny little boy that can throw knives like he can. All he has to do is toss a few knives and we sit back and collect the dough. Good money, real good money, from what my friend tells me. $75 dollars a week!

You'll be able to buy him things you otherwise could never afford. You grew up poor, just like me. Don't you want better for your sons?"

His throat was dry. Sure, he wanted better for his boys. He'd give them the goddamn world if he could. She made it all sound so easy. "So you got it all figured out." He poured a glass of water from the sink. "What about Benjamin?" As he said it, it hit him that he'd forgotten to mention Arthur.

"What about him? Bring him along. You say he's a smart kid, right? There'll be something for him to do, to learn about everywhere we'd go—the Statue of Liberty, Washington D.C., the Mississippi River… He can write a report for his school work. Hell, he'll probably end up writing a book. Besides, it's only until the end of the fall. If it don't work out, your boys go back to school, Shields takes you back, or you find another place. There's always work for a good metal worker like you. I mean, what's so holy about Shields Metals, anyway?"

She was right about one thing, he knew he could always get a job working with his hands, if not with Shields, with someone else. The words New Orleans came into his head for some reason he couldn't understand.

"I don't know. This is all moving too fast."

She took his glass and took a sip. "You don't have to say yes right now. At least say it's ok for me to write the letter." She kissed him hard on the lips. "It's gonna be an adventure, Abe, for you, for me, for your boys. Life ain't supposed to be all work and no play. You're supposed to have some fun in this life, am I right? There's just one more thing." She held three knives in her palm. "Let's make sure Alex still has it."

*

Belle was able to finally convince Hannah that she needed to at least have something to eat and fix her hair before she went to visit her parents. Lillie buttered a piece of toast for her and asked her when and where Abe had proposed.

Hannah sipped coffee milk and held her cup in midair, in front of her mouth, and stared at it, as if it contained some fundamental truth.

Belle lit a cigarette. "Hannah?"

"What?"

"When did Abe propose to you? Your father will want to know."

She chomped on a piece of toast. "Oh, that. He didn't ask me yet, but I know he will. You know how I can sense things about people, see into their minds. He'll ask me tomorrow, maybe, or Wednesday, but soon, surely by the end of the week. Fate has brought us together. Fate has brought my little boy home to me. He adores me, you know."

"And we adore him, dear," Lillie said. That much was true. The sisters doted on Alex when they could pry him away from Hannah. They had carved out a garden plot for him, and set up a large tin washtub in the yard for a wading pool. Lillie also had him reading passages from the Old Testament in hopes of quashing his Christian leanings. "But, Hannah, wouldn't it be prudent to hold off telling your parents until Abe has actually said the words? Don't you think that's best, dear? I mean, this is such big news, and so sudden. You want everything to go perfectly, don't you?" Lillie could imagine the expressions on her brother's face when she told him during their weekly lunch at the Chinese Pagoda that Hannah had set her sights on marrying a common laborer. Even though he had declared he wanted nothing to do with Hannah since her "transgression," as he called it, he and his wife relied on Belle and Lillie to keep them apprised of every aspect of her life. They had approved of Hannah taking care of the little boy only on the condition that Belle and Lillie monitor the situation, and that perhaps the responsibility would help her mature.

Hannah stood up. In a precise parody of her mother's voice, she said, "Oy, what was I thinking, you are so right, and besides, although this Abraham fella is very sweet on me, just because a fella asks doesn't mean a girl should say yes just like that, no? Better I should play a little hard to get." She brushed crumbs from her dress and switched to her own voice. "Lillie, help me pick out a nice dress for the movie. It's Mary Pickford, after all."

Belle sighed. "Of course, dear."

It could have been the stagnant air or too much sarsaparilla that made Alex's head hurt. More likely, it was because Alex's brain had begun to grow faster than the size of his skull could accommodate.

He began to explore the shelves behind the bar. On the one slightly above his head hung an open padlock. He pulled with both hands and jumped up to see what was inside. It was John's pistol. Alex said, "Bang."

Here was the perfect present for Arthur. He remembered how his brother had admonished him months before for stealing, but maybe that was because he hadn't given him something he really wanted. The gun, though, he could take it to the war, and he could shoot the bad men with it, and every time he shot one he would remember it was thanks to Alex who gave it to him.

With his long arms, the pistol was in easy reach, but it took both hands to lever it out of the drawer. The weight of it sank his arms to the floor. He raised it up on the bar top and stared into the muzzle, his eye touching the barrel opening. It was dark inside and he wondered where the bang sound came from. He held the gun out in front of his face. He could see the bullets in the chambers, but the bullets wouldn't come out, no matter how hard he pulled on them. How did they go out of the gun when the gun went bang? Maybe he had to hit it on the table. He could do that.

"Alex!"

A flash of pain bolted through his forehead from ear to ear as his father screamed his name again.

Abe snatched the pistol away. "Christ, Delia, why the hell isn't this thing locked up?"

"John says if it was locked up and unloaded, what use would it be? He couldn't get to it fast enough." She took the gun and put it back in the drawer, over Alex's objections, who cried that he wanted to give it to Arthur.

At the mention of his son's name, Abe said, "Let's go, Delia, Arthur could be home any minute."

"Just hold on a second, will you?"

She took Alex's hand. They crossed the room to where the dartboard hung on the back wall, three darts stuck in the bull's-eye ring. She hoisted Alex up on a table about eight feet away. "Sweetheart, do you remember when you threw the darts and the knives? Do you?"

Alex rubbed his head again and thought about that day, and how all the men were laughing and yelling, and then after he threw the knives they were quiet for a second and then they started yelling again even louder. And he remembered how his father carried him around the room and everyone wanted to touch him even though he didn't want them to, but they said he was good luck. He looked at Delia. "I did it for Davy."

Delia stroked his hair, and her fingers felt soft, but at the same time the touch made his head hurt a little more, too. "Yes, that was a very good thing to do, Alex, very good to help Davy. It's good to help people, isn't it?"

"Yes."

"So I was wondering, could you do it again, throw the knives just this one time, just to help me and your father?" She placed three knives on the table. "We just want to see if you still can do it, that's all. Just for fun. We're very proud of you, did you know that?" She yanked the darts from the board.

Alex looked at his father as Delia held his hand. He wished his head would stop throbbing. "But you said I never had to do it again."

Abe swallowed hard. "Go ahead, son."

"Alex, you don't have to throw the darts, you can just throw the knives."

He looked at his father, who nodded. He held a knife in his right hand. Something was saying to him not to throw, not to throw, and he thought he heard Benjamin's voice. He couldn't understand why his father and Delia wanted him to throw the knives, he'd only done it to help Davy, Davy was very sick that day. But now Delia and his father stood over him, smiling, telling him he was a good boy, but he already knew he was a good boy, and they were saying Alex you can do it, you did it before. And so to please them, and to quiet the pounding in his head, he went into his tilt-o-world windup, and his long arms catapulted the knife on a trajectory straight and true. When he'd thrown all three into the bull's-eye he asked, as the throbbing in his head subsided, "O.K., did I help you, Daddy?"

Abe watched the knives wobble in the dartboard. He felt a bit wobbly himself. What a wonderful and frightening thing this little boy of his was. He glanced at Delia, who was covering Alex's head with kisses. He folded his arms across his chest. "Go ahead, Delia. Write your letter to this friend of yours. But I ain't saying yes. I ain't promising nothing until I know what the deal is."

Chapter 22

During the week that followed, Abe was greeted every day by what seemed like a new and improved Hannah. In the mornings when he dropped Alex off, she would hand him a brown paper bag with sandwiches, fruit and slices of homemade banana bread and spice cake, which she told him she made especially for him, even though it was Belle that had baked it. She seemed as calm as a happily married newlywed, making smiling inquiries about his work, expressing even-tempered sympathy at Arthur's disappearance, and although she was loving toward Alex, she didn't gush over him as she had been, at least not in front of Abe.

Sometimes at work Abe daydreamed, amid the noise and heat, about her pretty eyes and how much more appealing she was now that, for whatever reason, she'd seemed to have settled down. So, when Friday came and she suggested that they go on a Sunday picnic, just the two of them, he thought, why not? Of course, he'd have to find someone to watch Alex.

*

Earlier that day, Belle and Lillie were saying it was the hottest summer they could remember, which is what they said every summer when the temperature approached ninety, along with ninety percent humidity, which was not unusual for Pittsburgh in late June. They wore loose-fitting housedresses, rolled their stockings below their knees and finished cooking for the day by ten in the morning, before the kitchen became sweltering.

Even Hannah, who usually dressed in sweaters regardless of the temperature, had rolled up her sleeves. She let Alex run around in just his shorts—no shirt, no socks and shoes. She did make him wear his orange hat to protect him against the hazy sun as he tended his garden.

After lunch on Friday, Belle, Lillie and Hannah napped on the shaded back porch. The sisters slept upright, side-by-side on the porch swing, and Hannah lay out on the hammock. Alex pretended to sleep in a chair until he was sure the three of them had drifted off.

He crept off the porch, into the house, climbed the stairs and went straight to the desk in the hallway where he'd found the black album weeks before. He was eager to read the story about Florence Carson. He reread the cover and the inscription on the inside and flipped to the next section. There were two documents pasted on the pages. They had curly designs in the corners and embossed seals on the bottom, accompanied by scribbled signatures he couldn't make out. He read the first one:

> After delivery, Miss Hannah Gerson does of her own free will hereby consent to and place for adoption MALE CHILD, born August 21, 1911, weighing seven pounds six ounces, for placement in such a home as can provide substantial means and moral upbringing as determined by the executive staff of the Florence Carson Home.
>
> Sworn to me on this day, August 24, 1911, Cornelius Bennett, Deputy Director.

He skipped to the second:

> As appropriate adoptive parents have been identified by the executive staff of the Florence Carson Home, hereby with this signature below does Hannah Gerson (birth mother) cede all parental rights in perpetuity regarding MALE CHILD in accordance of the rules and tenants of the Florence Carson Home and the Commonwealth of Pennsylvania in regards to adoption, sworn to me on this day, September 9, 1911.

On the bottom of the next page was a receipt for $300.00, issued from the Florence Carson Home and made out to Mr. Morris Gerson, with his signature at the bottom. Written on top of the receipt, in red crayon, were the words "Blood Money!" He turned the rest of the pages but found nothing else except for a pressed blue flower on the last page.

He wondered about MALE CHILD. He was a male child, too. The papers had Hannah Gerson's name in them. Maybe Hannah could explain about MALE CHILD, but something was telling him that she wasn't the one to ask. *Adoption* and *substantial means* and *Deputy Director* and *in perpetuity* and *adoptive parents*, and especially *blood money!* confused him, too, and his instincts told him this wasn't a happy story, or a funny story, not like Hansel & Gretel or Peter Rabbit or Little Red Riding Hood, or even the ones about Jesus in *A Child's Life of Christ*.

However, he was sure the story was about MALE CHILD, because of the big letters. MALE CHILD was an odd name for a little boy. Everyone he knew was named John or Joseph, names like that. Where did MALE CHILD live, in the Florence Carson Home, and did he have brothers and sisters, and what was he like, and was he a big boy or did he stay little like he was? He hoped MALE CHILD's mommy didn't die like his did.

The dog barked. Alex froze. He heard Belle say, "Quiet, mutt." He held his breath, listening for the porch door to open. After a few moments, all was quiet again.

Maybe he could ask his father, or maybe Benjamin, about the story. But how could he explain it? He turned back to the page with the two documents. He ran his finger over them, and, because they were attached only at the corners, he was able to slip his pinky finger underneath. If he took the papers, Daddy or Benjamin could read them and explain them. But that would be stealing, and he remembered how his grandmother had told him stealing was a sin—"thou shalt not steal, Alex"—and Arthur had told him not to steal anymore, too, that it wasn't honorable. He wouldn't have to steal the papers forever, though; he'd just take them and show them to his father or Benjamin, and then he could put them back, so it wouldn't be the same as stealing.

If he did take the papers, where would he put them? He could fold them up: maybe they would fit in his pocket, or he could put them down the front of his pants. He lifted a corner of one of the certificates. The whole paper came right off.

"Alex! Where are you?"

He ran down the hallway, went into her room and slipped under her bed. He tucked the certificate into a corner of the box spring where the fabric had pulled away.

*

Delia had worked until eleven that Friday night, and she'd been so busy she hadn't had time to grab a sandwich. She ran her fingers along her ribs and calculated that it had been almost twenty-four hours since her last meal, which had been rye toast and a cigarette.

A quick survey of her cupboard and icebox revealed a stick of butter, a pint of souring milk and a heel of rye bread. She emptied her purse on the dresser. At least the tips had been decent the night before, thanks mostly to that pig Horshushky, who was too drunk to count his change.

After a quick trip to Detwiler's Market, she sopped up the remains of her bacon and eggs over easy with a piece of fresh bread. She put her feet up on the windowsill and looked out over the city. Convoys of barges filled with coke and scrap iron slid up and down the river far below. A robin fed bits of worm to two chicks in a nearby tree. "Good momma," she said.

She rubbed her aching knees and feet. She sighed. In a few hours she'd be back at it again. However, she wasn't depressed. Writing to Lotte had put a bounce in her step and hope in her heart that a change was going to come.

She rinsed her plate in the sink. She caught her reflection on the mirror above it. Not bad for an old broad of 29, going on 33. She pressed her fingers against the fledgling crow's feet at the corners of her eyes. Where the hell was her cold cream? She turned on the hot water in the tub.

With a towel wrapped around her wet hair and her bare feet up on a radiator, she read a little of a two-day-old newspaper. They were talking about building a statue to the late George Westinghouse. She shook her head. Building statues to rich bastards while men stood in breadlines in the middle of downtown Pittsburgh. And if he were so high and mighty and wonderful, why had 10,000 Westinghouse workers gone on strike a couple of months ago? The politicians and the rich folk, they were in bed together, and the workingman emptied the bedpan.

Her thoughts drifted to Abe's lukewarm response to her idea for Alex. Oh, well. The kick of being with big Jew had toned down over the last few years. She still admired his strength—no one could ever say he wasn't a real man, not like that New York pansy Devon Jenkins—but it was hard to imagine being with him, or any man, forever.

But the boy. She needed Alex. If Abe still had cold feet when the circus came to town, well, she'd have to work around him. Kids, though, they were temperamental, and Alex was no exception. It hadn't been easy to get him to throw the knives, so what was to prevent him from shutting down altogether when it was his time to do his stuff? She believed that Alex liked her all right, but she needed to get his trust, to be sure she could handle him, so he'd do what she wanted him to do. She kind of liked him, too. The little thing had a smile that grabbed you, you couldn't help but be charmed by him, but then, maybe she was getting soft. Maybe what she really wanted was a child of her own, but that wasn't in the cards, not for a woman like her.

Thank God she had Sundays off, now that she was through with that snooty mansion. Sunday would be the perfect time to take Alex off Abe's hands for the day, give him a break, let Abe spend some time with his older boy or do whatever he wanted. She'd figure out something special for Alex.

She was nodding off at the kitchen table as she thought about Lotte's letter. The girl was pulling down seventy a week, plus room and board. Hell, she could live nice and easy on that, with or without Abe. She yawned.

It was midafternoon when shouts from the street woke her up from a long nap. She stuck her head out the window. Three stories below, men were jumping up and down, yelling and waving their arms. A man in a brown hat caught her eye. He waved a newspaper in the air and yelled, "Hey sister! It's war!"

That night it was bedlam at The Wheel. Germany had declared war on Russia, and the boys argued, prophetically enough, that it was only a matter of days before France, Belgium and England would be in it, too.

It wasn't long before uninformed opinions turned into heated arguments. Fueled by ignorance and alcohol, men became increasingly hostile and at times violent as the evening wore on, passionate regarding which state was right, and which state was more right, who stood to win the war and who had little more than a snowball's chance in hell. The dialogue, such as it was, became particularly vociferous when the issue as to whether the U.S. ought to enter the fray arose, and there was unanimous agreement that America could kick all their asses combined and straighten the whole mess out lickety-split.

At approximately nine o'clock, Albert Bauer waved a handkerchief-sized German flag, at which point he was cold cocked by Horshushky, who, despite being Polish, had decided to align his loyalties to his fellow Slavs, not really knowing if Russians were Slavic or not. It took three men to hold Horshushky from stomping him in the face.

Edward Peck gave two to one odds that the war would be over by November. Neither he nor anyone else would have imagined that the end wouldn't be until November, 1918.

Abe sat at Davy's table and told him that both sides were equally crazy. It wasn't that he was a pacifist. He'd just received a letter from Arthur saying that both he and the Walsh boy had successfully enlisted, and even though the United States was out of it for the time being, he feared that the outbreak of fighting had brought his son one step closer to combat.

Delia was so busy hauling liquor for toasts to the French, the Russians, the Germans and America that she didn't manage to stop by Davy's table until nearly ten o'clock. "Abe, I need to talk to you about tomorrow."

A lump rose in his throat. How could she have known about his so-called date with Hannah? He hadn't told Alex, or had he? He managed to blurt out, "O.K."

"What's the matter with you? You worried that I'm knocked up?"

That's all he needed now, a knocked-up mistress. He tried to keep his voice even. "Are you?"

Delia laughed. "You don't think I'm that stupid, do you?" Before he could answer that one, she told him she'd like to do him a favor and take Alex off his hands and out for the day on Sunday, give him a break from the daddy routine. Maybe she'd take him to the zoo—the kid is always talking about animals and she ain't been to the new zoo yet, but she heard it's a doozy, and Alex will get a kick out of the elephants, he's always going on about them, so what do you say?

Either she had something up her sleeve or he was one lucky bastard. What the hell, his problem was solved. "Yeah, well that's pretty nice of you, thanks."

"So it's settled then, she said, and told him she would pick Alex up at ten and have him home for dinner. She patted his shoulder. "Listen, I got orders. These maniacs are so hopped up on the war, they're making toasts left and right."

A group of men stood with arms linked and sang "American the Beautiful." At a table near the back door, a circle had formed around an older man named Timothy Crimmins, a housepainter who'd fought in the Civil War at eighteen on the side of the Confederacy. A diagonal scar started just above his right eyebrow, ran across the bridge of his nose and ended below his left earlobe. His breath whistled from his nose as a handful of men badgered him—hey old-timer, what was it like back in them olden days when you was fighting in a real war, did you ever bayonet anyone, can you still do the Johnny Reb yell? "Come on, Uncle Tim," Edward Peck said, "give us all the gory details. We can take it."

Crimmins sipped his whiskey. He coughed into a blotchy handkerchief. "Why do you want to know?"

"Hell, I don't know, I may want a taste of it. Maybe I'll join up with the Brits, go over there and shoot me a German or two."

Crimmins closed his eyes. "You do that."

"Come on, Uncle Tim, tell us how you got that scar. Was it a bayonet, or an angry whore with a switchblade?"

Crimmins lit his pipe. He drew on the tobacco until it glowed. He closed his eyes, and the smoke curled around his hat.

Aw, he's probably forgotten about it, one of the men said. He's too drunk to remember, said another, and then one by one they drifted away, all except for Peck. After a few minutes, Crimmins opened his eyes. "You still here?"

"Yeah, Tim. Tell me something."

The old man leaned toward him. "I fought at Gettysburg. For three days." He leaned back and didn't say another word for the rest of the evening.

*

Benjamin and Alex played checkers and ate graham crackers with butter and jelly at the dining room table. Benjamin had stopped at Plotkin's Grocery on his way home from the playground that afternoon and found a newspaper in the trash that had "War in Europe!" in huge letters on the front page.

Alex wanted to know what it meant, now that the war had begun, was Arthur going to fight, did he have a gun, when is he coming home, to which Benjamin replied, "I don't know."

After a few moves, Alex said, "When's Daddy coming home?"

Benjamin did a double jump. "Late, probably. Why do you keep rubbing your head?"

"Sometimes I get a hurt on the inside."

"Well, you're not supposed to rub it. Mom used to say if you rub something, that makes it hurt worse." He made a double jump. "King me."

"I have to tell Daddy something."

"What?"

"You promise not to tell if I tell you?"

"What?"

"It's about Hannah. Benjamin, what's blood money?"

Although he was in the top five of his class and an avid reader, he'd never come across that particular phrase. "I don't know, but it sounds bad, like the money was covered in blood, like in a bank robbery maybe. Where'd you get that?"

Alex explained how he'd explored Hannah's desk and how he found the story of Florence Carson Home, except the story wasn't about Florence or the home but about Male Child, and Hannah was in it, and a deputy. "That's why I want to talk to Daddy, but I wanted to ask you first. What's adoption?"

Chapter 23

The aunts wanted her to wear the belted, sailor-collared tunic she'd worn for her sweet sixteen party, but Hannah wouldn't hear of it, telling them in no uncertain terms that she wasn't a little girl anymore and they damn well knew it. She wanted to get a tight-fitting red hobble skirt, which the aunts flatly refused to buy for her. Finally, they compromised on a white, long-sleeved dress with lace trim and a red sash, and a wide-brimmed hat with a matching ribbon. Hannah made them leave her room as she continued to get ready. She splashed perfume behind her ears and knees, put lipstick in her purse and tied the sash as tightly as she could.

A thunderstorm the previous night had broken the heat and humidity, and for a summer's day in Pittsburgh, the sky was remarkably clear. The rain had washed the soot from the leaf lettuce and tomatoes Lillie had picked that morning to put on the chicken salad sandwiches. She rinsed grapes and red plums and wrapped slices of pound cake in cloth napkins and added hardboiled eggs and a mason jar of iced tea with sugar and lemon.

She wiped her hands on her apron. "You don't think he'll bring liquor, do you?

Belle thought for a moment. "If he does, I'll kill him."

*

Abe watched Alex skip off with Delia, and not without a pang of guilt, since he'd offered no explanation of how he was going to spend the day—she hadn't asked—but then, what was it he felt guilty about? He hadn't lied to her, and he wasn't married to her, either, so spending time with Hannah wasn't cheating, exactly. He wasn't using Delia, either. Hell, she was the one that offered to take the boy for the day.

He stewed over Arthur's letter as he sipped coffee warmed over from Saturday's pot. The boy had somehow gone and done it, lied about his age and enlisted in the service without his consent or advice. The war talk at The Wheel, the enthusiasm for blood, had been unsettling. He hoped the damn thing would be over before America went into it. He stropped his razor harder and harder.

Today would be the first time he'd be alone with Hannah, and he wondered which Hannah would show up—the pleasant, contrite, reassuring one or the hot and wild one. He wouldn't mind a little of both.

He inspected his shirt, one of two white ones he owned. No spots, and not so wrinkled that he'd have to take out the damn iron. Sundays the trolleys ran infrequently, so he needed to give himself plenty of time to get to her house by noon. But he couldn't leave too early. What if he came to the trolley stop and Alex and Delia were still waiting? There would be no explaining that one.

Benjamin stood at the open bathroom door. "Are you gonna be long?"

Abe splashed water on his face. He caught his son's reflection in the mirror and it was as if he were seeing him for the first time in a year. He was stunned at how much his middle boy looked like Irene—the same blue eyes, the reddish hair, only the nose was like his own, and he thought, how long had it been since he and the boys visited Irene's grave? Wasn't that supposed to be what a widower should do on Sundays? He wiped his face with a worn towel. "Almost done."

Benjamin yawned. "Where are you going?"

"I thought I told you."

"Oh yeah, Hannah. Dad, I really gotta go."

"So go."

As Benjamin urinated with his back toward his father, he said, "Did Alex talk to you this morning?"

Abe stopped in the hallway. "Talk to me? What do you mean, talk to me? He talks all the time."

"I mean, he was trying to explain something to me last night, but he really wanted to talk to you. Something about a story with a male child and adoption and blood money. I couldn't figure out what he was saying."

"Wait a minute. He didn't say nothing to me about that, but Delia got here early and I was half asleep when they left."

Benjamin scratched the skinny adolescent hairs emerging from his upper lip. "Something about Hannah and adoption, I think that's what he said."

*

In 1895, Pittsburgh political boss Christopher Lyman Magee donated $100,000 for the establishment of a new Pittsburgh Zoo, free to the public, to be located in the Highland Park section of the city. It may have been because of his love of wild animals, which, if true, was generally unknown at the time. More likely, his beneficence was due to his love for the people, especially the people that were paying customers on the trolleys owned by his company, whose lines not coincidentally terminated next to the zoo's main entrance.

As they rode to the zoo, Alex peppered Delia with his knowledge of all things wild, from aardvarks, which were not part of the collection, to Asian elephants, which were, to zebras, which were as well. Delia took it all in, nodding her head at what seemed to be the appropriate times, thinking, this little thing can talk a mile a minute.

He yanked at Delia's arm as soon as the trolley stopped, pointing to the entrance, adorned with hissing gargoyles. The looming statuaries stopped Alex in his tracks. "What's that, Delia?"

She shrugged her shoulders. "I don't know what you call it, but I wouldn't want to meet one in a dark alley. That's a joke, kiddo."

Hand in hand, they made their way through the swarms of people; working folks mingling with the well-to-do, forgetting for at least one afternoon the gulf that lay between them, both classes marveling equally at a monkey eating a banana or a water buffalo behind thick steel bars relieving itself against a concrete wall. Alex pushed toward the elephants, reminding Delia that she had promised to take him to see them first, and Delia said to herself, whatever he wants.

Twenty yards away, the smell of elephant dung hit her in the face. Delia pulled her scarf over her nose and mouth, but Alex scooted ahead like a water bug, through and around people toward the massive iron bars that kept the captives from the captive audience. Delia watched as he leaned in as close as possible to the biggest elephant, and she thought, that monster could hoist him up and into its mouth before you could blink.

Alex waved his arms and right hand at a huge bull and held out a piece of toast he'd pocketed from breakfast. However, either the elephant didn't see it or wasn't much for toast. It seemed to prefer tossing trunk loads of straw mixed with dung over its back.

A short, stout woman tapped Delia on the elbow. "Excuse me."

Without wavering her eyes from Alex, she said, "Yeah?"

"I'm sorry to bother you, but that little boy there, the one waving at the elephants, is he yours?"

He will be, she thought. "Yeah. What of it?"

"Oh nothing. He's very cute, but well, it's none of my business."

Delia faced the woman. "What?"

"Well, not to pry, but is something wrong with his arms?"

"His arms?"

The woman faltered. "I mean, because they seem very long."

Delia smiled. "Now let me ask you a question. Is there something wrong with your ass?"

"What?"

"Because it seems very fat."

"Well, I didn't mean…"

"You didn't mean what?"

The woman backed away and into the crowd.

To the left of the elephant enclosure was a refreshment stand with popcorn, crackerjack and cotton candy. Delia bought Alex a treat—several, in fact. If the way to a man's heart was through his stomach, the same logic surely would apply to a little boy, even more so. As she approached the stand, she caught a glimpse of what looked like a familiar figure: a burly man with a dark hat, a goatee and pince-nez, wearing a black frock coat, carry a dark satchel. However, before she could call out to him he sped off toward the rhinoceros enclosure, coat tails flapping.

*

Lindenwood Grove was a pleasant three-acre parklet less than a half-mile from the house on Black Street, and since the weather was fine, Abe and Hannah decided to walk there rather than wait for a trolley. Hannah gave Abe a glowing report on Alex, how attentive he was to his garden—the way he named his vegetables was precious—how helpful he was to her and her aunts, picking up after himself and offering to dry the dishes; how delightful it was to see him roll on the floor with the dog; and guess what, the aunts had begun to teach him to say his blessings in Hebrew, and wouldn't it be nice if Abe did that, too, providing he knew them, which she was sure he did.

Abe indulged her semi-manic monologue, concentrating on the descriptions of his son's behavior, and all in all it sounded as if the boy was greatly benefiting from Hannah's tutelage, and blossoming in her family's care, and so he considered himself a lucky son of a bitch that he'd met her that day in the synagogue, for surely his boy was receiving better care than he could ever give him, better even than his mother-in-law and her Jesus hocus-pocus.

They found an empty picnic bench shaded by oak and linden trees. Hannah spread the tablecloth and placed sandwiches, the eggs and the iced tea jug on the table. She poured two glasses and proposed a toast. "Here's to us and Alex, together."

Abe muttered his agreement.

"Can I ask you a question, Abe?"

He was focused on her full lips. "Sure, go ahead."

She gripped his arm and asked, "Do you believe in fate?"

"Fate?"

"Yes. Fate."

Well, he thought, he believed in hard work and standing up for yourself. He believed that you made your own luck, but sometimes, no matter what you did, life came around and kicked you in the ass when you least expected it, like when Irene got The Dip and Ida died in the fire. Who could have called that one? "Yeah, maybe, but I'm not so sure. I think mostly you make your own way in this world, but sometimes things happen and you don't know why they happen, but what you're saying is, maybe some things was meant to happen for some reason." Boy, if the guys at The Wheel could hear him now they'd laugh him out of the place. "Right?"

"I knew you'd understand, I just knew it. Couldn't it be that fate has brought you and me and Alex together?"

It sounded like as good a reason as any. "Yeah, I guess maybe."

"Maybe? It's not maybe. For the longest time I wished for a child and a husband, but I didn't know how to ask God for it. My father once told me we're not supposed to ask God for anything, just praise his name, but I wanted to so much."

Abe took a gulp of iced tea and entertained the idea of adding something stronger. Nearby, a little girl screamed, "Higher, higher," as her mother and father pushed her on the swing.

Hannah put her arm though his. She pointed to the little girl. "Isn't she lovely? And so happy. That could be us, Abe, you and me pushing Alex, couldn't it, Abe? Couldn't it? Alex would be so happy swinging up to the sky. I can see his laughing face right now. I know he wants a mommy. He told me all about his mother."

"He did?" he snapped. "What did he say about Irene?"

Hannah looked lost, as if she were an actress in the middle of her lines and missed a cue. "Wait. What?"

"I said, what did Alex say about his mother?"

"Well he…no, what he said was, he wants a new mommy, that he wants me to be his mommy now, that's what he said."

"He did?" Abe scratched his head. First she brings up Irene and now this, but wait…was *that* what the boy was trying to tell him earlier that morning, something about adoption? He couldn't remember exactly, there was too much commotion, what with Benjamin yelling that the pancakes were ready and Delia showing up early, and then they left. Was Alex telling Hannah he wanted her to adopt him? That made no sense—how did the boy even know what the word meant? Still, he was smart as a whip, so maybe he read something and put two and two together. You never knew with that kid. "You know, Hannah, come to think of it, Benjamin comes to me this morning and says Alex was telling him something about adoption, like in a story he read. I didn't pay it no mind at the time. You think that's what he meant?"

Hannah blanched. She sat down on the bench and put her head between her hands. Her feet began to bounce.

Abe sat next to her. Now what was wrong with her? This girl was up and down more than a yoyo. "Hannah? Christ, you're white as a ghost. You sick or something?"

She waved her hand back and forth, but he couldn't tell if she meant she was all right or not all right. He thought he heard little whimpers coming from her, but with the girl on the swing screaming and laughing, he couldn't be sure.

He fingered the flask in his coat pocket. He'd intended to wait and see how the day went, and if they were in the mood, offer her a nip from his flask. Now that she'd turned so pale and shaky, withdrawn into herself, maybe a little nip of rye might do her some good, perk her up.

He put his arm around her shoulders and felt her cringe. As evenly as he could, he said, "You feeling a little faint? I could give you a little rye in your iced tea, maybe it would make you feel better, perk you up. I mean, if it's not your stomach."

She pressed her head against his shoulder. "What?"

He took the cap off the flask. "A little sip of whiskey, maybe it'll perk you up."

"I'm not allowed."

Abe thought, allowed, who allows her? He took a quick swig.

Seventy yards away, from behind a maple tree, Belle handed Lillie her opera glasses, the ones they'd shared the night before at a performance of *Aida*. "I knew he'd do it. Go ahead, see for yourself."

*

Only with the promise of a hot dog and Coca-Cola was Delia able to extract Alex from the elephant exhibit. She theorized why such a tiny boy was so infatuated with the biggest land animal on the planet. Maybe it was wishful thinking.

She watched him devour his hot dog and half of hers. She could hardly eat anything, particularly meat, since she felt there was something repugnant about biting into flesh after looking into the mournful eyes of so many animals, especially the big cats. A cigarette was what she wanted, but not while the boy was eating.

She sipped stale zoo coffee and listened to Alex recite encyclopedic information regarding Asian elephants, rhinoceri and hippos. Occasionally she broke into his descriptions with a "you-don't-say" or a "my word."

When he wound down a bit, she said, "So you like wild animals, huh?"

"Yes. I like Pudgy, too."

"Who?"

"Pudgy. Hannah's dog."

"Oh, her." Abe hadn't mentioned Hannah's name for weeks, and she hadn't asked. "But Alex, don't you think wild animals are, well, don't you think they're more fun? You know, the elephants and bears, they're more fun to look at, right?"

Alex nodded his head yes and shoved popcorn in his mouth.

"So anyway, honey, wouldn't it be fun if you could see elephants and horses and lions and bears every single day?"

"But I go to Hannah's house every single day. Except Saturday and Sunday."

Delia pursed her lips. Maybe the kid was stuck on this Hannah. Better not try to get in the way of that—what was the expression, you can catch more flies with honey than with vinegar? "Yes, I forgot. So, you like her?"

"Yes." He said it in a way that made her think that maybe he really didn't, that he said it because he was supposed to say it, but she decided not to press the issue.

"You like me, too, right?"

"Yes."

"Good. I like you, too. And guess what? I know a place where you and me and your daddy, and Benjamin, too, we could see wild animals every day, and you could even touch them and maybe even ride them. Would you like to ride a horse? Or a zebra? Would you like that, Alex? Wouldn't that be the berries? Maybe you could even ride a camel!"

"A camel!" Alex bounced up and down.

She put her hand on his shoulder. "Don't jump, honey, you'll spill your drink. Now, this place I'm talking about, it isn't the zoo. Oh no, it's much better, it's much more fun. It's called the circus. Do you think you'd like to go to the circus?"

"Yes yes yes."

"Would you like to go with me?"

"When can we go? Can we go today?"

She wiped his mouth. "Not today, sweetheart, but pretty soon. Just a couple of weeks and you can see all the animals you want."

"Giraffes?"

Delia hadn't the faintest idea. "Sure, giraffes. Absolutely, kiddo."

Alex stopped jumping. He frowned. "But in a couple of weeks Daddy says I have to go to kindergarten."

"Oh, but that was before I told him about the circus." She took his hand. "Now, if you really want to go to the circus, I mean really really *really*, I want you to promise me one thing. Don't tell Hannah or anyone else about it, because it's just for you and me and your daddy."

"And Benjamin."

"Yes, of course, Benjamin, but don't tell him, either, see, he doesn't know yet. It's going to be a surprise. Do you like surprises?"

Alex nodded his head.

"Now pumpkin, do you think you can you keep it a secret about going to the circus? Can you?"

Alex thought about how Arthur had asked him to keep a secret, and when he didn't keep it Daddy got mad at him for telling it, so it must be a bad thing to tell a secret and he didn't want to do a bad thing. "Yes."

"Are you sure? Because if you're sure, repeat this after me: I won't tell anyone we're going to the circus."

Alex repeated it perfectly.

"It's our secret." Delia put her index finger to her lips, and Alex did the same. "Good boy. Now, let's get the sticky stuff off those hands of yours."

They walked hand in hand toward the rest rooms. Off to the left, several yards away and beyond their line of sight, two guards yanked a man by the elbows to the security office.

*

As Hannah watched Abe take a second swallow from his flask, the memory of liquor rose in her mouth. She thought about the summer evening three years earlier, at her parents' 25th anniversary party, when she and the handsome older boy she had a crush on snuck away with a bottle of Cherry Herring liqueur from the cordials table. They went down into the cellar and closed the door to the workroom behind them, and drank from the bottle, and she began to laugh at the silliest things he said. They began to kiss and it felt good for a while, until he began to touch her underneath her dress and pulled her hand inside his open pants front. She was shocked but curious at how his thing felt alive in her hands, and how when she tried to pull away from him he told her no, she couldn't leave him like that, and she wondered, like what? She started to cry out, but he put his hand over her mouth, and then he put a pair of garden shears to her neck and told her that if she ever told her parents about what was going to happen he would sneak into her house late at night with a butcher knife and kill her parents in front of her and then kill himself. She should just relax and enjoy it, he said, and then he forced her legs open and pulled down her underwear and then there was a sharp pain and he was inside her and she felt wet and nauseated as her head spun, and then he grunted and pushed away and held her head down as she vomited into a tin pail.

"Hannah?" Abe shook her shoulder. "You all right? We better go home now, huh? Let your aunts give you some ginger ale, put you to bed."

She opened her eyes. There was Abe, looking so concerned. The contortions in her face dissolved into a smile. "No. Please. I'm all right now. It must have been the eggs. I'm partially allergic to eggs. What was I thinking? But I'm better now. Gosh, I must have given you a terrible scare.

But I'm fine now, really." She stood and twirled around. "See? Right as rain." She took his hand. "Let's go for a walk, down the path to the pond."

"You sure you're all right?"

"I'll bring some bread for the ducks. I love ducks, don't you? We have so much to talk about. Where will we live, where will Alex go to school? Won't it be grand?" She tugged his wrist, and they strolled toward the path that led to the pond.

Belle was all for starting after them, but Lillie said, "She looks all right now. Wait until he gets her home."

*

The Highland Park Zoo chief of security, retired Pittsburgh Police sergeant Joseph Conroy, spilled the contents of Dr. Malkin's medical bag on his desk. Buried amid the stethoscope, speculum, rubber gloves, tongue depressor, screwdriver, bottles of patent medicine, gauze, pinking shears, tack hammer, meat thermometer, blood pressure cuff, flyers and half-eaten salami sandwich was a train schedule with the Pittsburgh to Philadelphia connections circled in red.

Conroy held the schedule up to Malkin's nose. "Going somewhere, my friend?"

"Oh, that, yes, I am planning it a future trip to Philadelphia to see it the Libertine Bell."

"You mean the Liberty Bell."

"Yes, of course, I meant to say it the Liberty Bell. Sorry."

Conroy's assistant muttered, "Greenhorn."

"You can put your things back, except for these." Conroy dumped Malkin's flyers into the trashcan. "Next time you come to the Highland Park Zoo, leave the fliers at home. Folks here want to see the animals, they don't need you to pester them. Capische?"

"I am begging your pardon, what is the word 'capische' meaning?"

"Greenhorn."

*

They walked down a twisting path. The trickle of water they heard in the distance sounded like a gentle brook, but was in fact runoff from a nearby water treatment plant. Abe helped Hannah step around the bigger rocks. They stopped at a small clearing where a low wood sign pointed to Lindenwood Pond.

Abe brushed leaves and twigs from a large flat rock and they sat down, hips touching. "Feeling better now?"

"Yes, very."

Abe was ready for a cigar, and he'd brought two along, but he was concerned that she might get loopy again from the smell of smoke, although the color was back in her cheeks and that vacant look was gone from her eyes.

Two cardinals lighted on a tree branch above them. Abe, eager for a diversion, said, "Hey, look at them redbirds."

"They're a beautiful couple." She nudged a little closer to him. "We're like them, Abe. We're birds of a feather."

"Yeah?" Abe smiled. Here he was, a workingman Jewish boozer with calluses on his palms and three sons by the time he was twenty-eight and a wife dead and buried and a sometimes mistress, and here *she* was, pretty as a picture, ripe as a peach, a young Jewish girl, probably educated, sometimes a little, well, unpredictable, that's for sure, but mostly gentle and loving. "You think so?"

"Oh, of course. We share a religion. We both need someone else to complete us, to make us whole. And we both dearly love Alex. Abe, can't you see, this is what I've been saying, that we belong together?" She threw her arms around his neck and kissed him, gently at first, but with increasing passion, and he found himself pressing back, feeling her breasts against his chest, and he felt as if he were being pulled into her, and though he wasn't sure where this was going, she was so lush, she tasted so sweet he couldn't pull himself away.

As she let his hands explore the small places around her waist and over her thighs, Hannah thought about the desk on the second floor and how as soon as she got home she would destroy all the papers once and forever.

Chapter 24

By three o'clock they had seen all the zoo had to offer three times over. Delia's feet hurt, Alex's head hurt, and so they decided to call it a good day.

Delia pushed her way to a forward-facing seat on the trolley. Alex rested his head against her side. The trolley filled up with parents and children that ranged from excited and happy to tired and cranky, their energies as deflated as their helium balloons.

Alex clutched his stuffed elephant. His head had been bothering him since late in the morning, but the excitement of the zoo had dimmed the pain. Something else was on his mind, too. He tugged on Delia's elbow.

"What, pumpkin?"

"What's adoption?"

Delia thought, the damnedest things come out of this kid's mouth—one minute he's asking her who could win a fight between a lion and a tiger, and now this. "Adoption?" She explained as simply as she could how sometimes children didn't have a mother and father. Alex interrupted her, telling her that he didn't have a mother because she was dead, only a father, and did that mean that if his father died, would he be an adoption, but Delia assured him that wasn't going to happen. She didn't describe the scenario of children born out of wedlock. "Nice people that want to make an adoption become the child's mommy and daddy forever. But why do you want to know?"

Alex wanted to tell her the story of Male Child, but now that he knew what adoption was, it was even harder to understand everything on the paper. Maybe he wasn't supposed to tell anyone about it, maybe it was a secret only for Hannah to know, like going to the circus was his secret, so he answered, "I read it in a book."

She hugged him. "Stick to animals, smart guy."

The trolley, which had been waiting at the stop until it filled up with riders, finally lurched forward. A man in a dark hat and black frock coat banged on the door, and in jumped Malkin. He bumped up against every leg in the aisle as he made his way to the back of the car. He stopped two-thirds of the way. "Oho, it is Miss Novak and the little Alex."

*

By four o'clock that afternoon the sky had become overcast, the air had turned cooler and Abe and Hannah had left the park. They made it back to the aunts' house before the first plops of rain began to fall.

Hannah seemed happy, but spoke little and walked quickly on the way home, pulling Abe along. As soon as they went inside, she dropped his hand and bolted up the stairs. Abe watched her go and thought it was a nice view from where he stood, the way her rear end bounced.

He still wasn't quite sure what to make of her. She'd been acting perfectly normal for weeks, but today, well, one minute she was planning their life together and the next minute she looked as if she were in some kind of trance, and the minute after that she was the warm, willing girlfriend men dreamed of having. It was puzzling, yes, and yet he was feeling pretty full of himself, proud that evidently his looks and personality, if that was the right word, were good enough to just about charm the panties off her. It was amazing that a widower with three boys had not one but two good-looking women after him—well, Delia wasn't exactly after him, it was more like he was after her—but hell, what hen-pecked family man wouldn't trade places with Abe Miller, ladies man?

A finger poked him between the shoulder blades. He turned, and there were Belle and Lillie staring at him, arms akimbo. A cigarette hung from the corner of Belle's mouth, like a tough cop.

Christ, he thought, they looked as if they were ready to take him out and skin him alive with a potato peeler, no questions asked. He was about to ask them what was wrong, since obviously something was, when Belle said, "Got a drink for me, Miller?"

"What?"

Lillie tapped Abe on the front of his coat, pushing his flask against his ribs. "You wanted to get our niece drunk, didn't you?"

"Now hold on." Abe tried to explain how he never intended on letting her have any liquor, it was only when she looked so out of sorts that he was going to give her just a little taste to shake her out of it.

"You give your kids booze when they're sick?"

No, he explained, but Hannah wasn't a kid, in case they hadn't they noticed. He only offered her a nip when she got a little pale, on account of her allergy to eggs.

Belle said, "Eggs?"

Before Abe could answer, something slammed on the second floor and Hannah's voice yelled out, as if she were in physical pain, "Damn it all."

The sisters grabbed each other's hands. Lillie shouted, "Hannah, what happened? Are you all right?

"Yes, I just banged my knee." Then, in a quieter voice, she said, "I'm fine, I'll be down in a second." She went back to searching through the Carson Home album and the rest of the desk, hunting for the missing adoption certificate. Where could it be, where could it have gone, things don't just grow legs and walk away.

She hadn't looked at the papers for two years, not since she held the album open on her knees as she sat on the floor and wept for hours and made her aunts stay away as she held a corkscrew up to her throat like the handsome boy had done with the garden shears. Finally, she wrote Blood Money! on the receipt on the last page, and then took all of her family photographs and tore them to shreds and was about to light them on fire when her aunts grabbed her and convinced her to calm down, none of it was her fault.

No one knew about the album and the papers except her and her parents and her aunts. No one else had been upstairs in the house for years except her and her aunts.

And Alex.

"Hannah?"

She swallowed hard. "In a minute. I'm changing. Give Abe some lemonade."

She dropped her lace dress in a heap at her feet. It felt so good she wanted to run downstairs in her underwear, and if her aunts weren't there and it were just Abe, she would have. She slipped on a yellow sundress.

With the missing certificate and what Abe had said about adoption, now it all made sense. Her little Alex must have taken it. There was no other explanation. She loved him so much, but well, even the best little boy in the world could misbehave, and she made up her mind to give him a good talking to, or maybe a little more, just until he told her what he'd done with it, just until he absolutely understood very well it was wrong to take things that weren't his.

Two minutes later she was downstairs with a smile on her face. She implored her aunts not to be cross with Abe, it wasn't his fault about the flask, other women her age can take a drink, so naturally he would bring one along, and how should he know she didn't imbibe? It was Abe that had the decency *not* to let her drink, and also wasn't it true, even though the aunts said they'd seen them together, that they didn't see *her* drink, did they?

Belle said, "I guess that's true."

Oh, Belle, she went on, if it was anyone's fault it was her own, the eggs made her woozy, and thank goodness Abe had the maturity and wisdom not to try to force alcohol on her, he'd only offered it out of concern for her, he'd actually done an honorable thing with his gesture, and instead of criticizing him they should thank him for being so kind and concerned.

"Well," Lillie said, "when you put it that way."

The entire time Hannah spoke Abe was silent, his mouth slightly open.

"Anyway," Hannah said, turning to him, "thank you for such a wonderful day in the park." She kissed him on the cheek with decibels less intensity that her open-mouthed kisses an hour earlier. "I'll see you tomorrow with Alex, bright and early."

Abe said his goodbyes, feeling happy about his reprieve and not clear at all as to why he'd received it.

After the screen door closed behind him, Hannah said, "Aunt Lillie, can I help with dinner?"

The sisters looked at each other. "Well, you could put some water on to boil and shuck the corn. We're having cold chicken."

Hannah skipped off to the kitchen, humming. Lillie took her sister's arm and walked her to the front porch. "I'm getting too old for this girl. But I have a question."

"I know what you're going to say."

"Go ahead."

"Since when is she allergic to eggs?"

*

Upon learning that Alex was suffering from a headache, Dr. Malkin was quite concerned, primarily for his own future, for if there were something seriously wrong with the boy beyond his limited medical understanding, and the boy was confined by some sort of special treatment, his plans to show off him at the impending conference on childhood diseases, and beyond, could be in jeopardy. He was counting on the little freak to be healthy.

"If I may," he said to Delia, "I would like to touch it this instrument to the boy's head, just to make it here the preliminary examination." He dug his stethoscope from his medical bag and held it up to Alex's forehead.

"Ain't that thing for listening to his heart and lungs?" Delia said.

"Yes, of course, I was merely testing it to hear if there was an abnormal pounding of the blood, you see. This is done as a precaution in some medical circles, and I have learned it myself from my Uncle Dmitri, may he rest in peace, an excellent physician also."

"Well?"

Alex said, "Well?"

"Ah, the boy talks, it is a good sign. But perhaps it would be it the best idea if you could bring him now to my surgery, where I have it the more elaborate medical equipment to conduct the assessment of the boy's headache condition. I am sure his father would want me to have it a thorough look."

"The last time Abe saw you he socked you in the nose."

Malkin winced. "But surely we must let it the bygones be the bygones. I bear him no bad will and have instructed my attorney of law not to proceed in the matter further or in any way."

Alex took his orange cap off and rubbed his head.

Delia watched his face twist in pain. This was all she needed now. A headache in a little boy, that could be a sign of something worse. A sick Alex would ruin her one shot at leaving The Wheel and the stink of the city behind. This Malkin was a damn odd bird, but maybe in his long-winded way he could help the kid get some relief, and she hated to see him suffer. It was worth a shot, anyway. She knew Abe would hit the roof when he found out she let Malkin put his mitts on the kid, but she could deal with him later. She glanced again at the pain on Alex's face. "Your office nearby ?"

"Yes, just several stops from here." A fat man and two children pushed by him. "Ah, a seat two rows back. I shall take it and come when it is time to get off."

*

Traveling in the opposite direction from Alex, Delia and Malkin, Abe stared out the window of his trolley, watching the rain and trying to make sense of the day's events. They go on a picnic. The girl gets sick. Then she gets well and she's all over him like a tigress. He takes her home. She runs upstairs. Her aunts lay into him with both guns blazing. She runs downstairs and explains it all away like she's a city hall lawyer, and by the time he leaves, everything with her is hunky-dory again.

So what was he supposed to do now, get married? She seemed hell-bent on it. But something was off with the girl. Maybe it was her parents' death, that might explain some things, but not everything. He thought about how she had almost passed out when he had said the word "adoption." Strange. The whole situation made his head hurt, which made him think of Alex. The boy had been complaining of headaches off and on. It was time he took him to a real doctor. Probably Hannah or her aunts knew a good one, but if she found out something was wrong with Alex she'd probably go into a fit like she did at the park.

He picked up a newspaper from the empty seat across the aisle. More countries ready to get into the damn war.

The streetcar jolted to a halt. He could see a horse-drawn cart stopped in the middle of a curve in the tracks. The horse was slumped on its forelegs. In the gutter, blood mixed with rainwater. What a goddamn world.

*

Had Dr. Malkin been practicing medicine—or at least his brand of medicine—in the mid-1800s, his specialty may well have been phrenology, also known by the less flattering term, "bump-ology." Malkin was intrigued by the idea that a person's aptitudes, talents and tendencies could be ascertained by feeling the bumps on their head. What's more, becoming a phrenologist seemed to require no special training or expensive equipment, only educated fingers.

In his possession was a tattered, half-century-old copy of *The American Phrenological Journal*, and although he wasn't much for reading, he'd carefully studied the cover illustration that divided the human brain/skull into approximately 35 to 45 distinct sectors. There were specific cranial locations designated for everything from self-esteem to sublimicity.

Delia was having a cup of tea on the first floor with Malkin's second cousin Masha while the doctor examined Alex's head. Alex didn't mind Malkin's probing fingers, and his head felt better when he pressed lightly in certain places.

Every so often, Malkin paused to consult the journal to orient his fingers on Alex's skull. With his eyes closed, he felt Alex's imperfections, as if by touching them he could divine the truth about some condition of his brain.

He worked his way to the left temple. "Aha, I think I have detected the center for se-cre-tive-ness. What secret are you holding, my boy?" He took a cloth measuring tape and wound it around across Alex's forehead.

The circumference was in the normal range for a one and one half year old boy. However, neither Malkin's measurements nor his cursory understanding of phrenology could tell him was this: that while Alex's skull size was normal, his brain was close to the size of an adult's, 25% larger than the space allowed for, and growing, albeit imperceptively, bigger by the day.

Malkin wrote down his measurements in his file entitled, "Little Miller." He had documentation on Alex's height, wingspan, arm length and inseam, and now added this latest measurement. All he needed was a quick look at his genitalia, just to see what proportions they were in relationship to his overall size. The opportunity had eluded him at The Wheel. Here was a second chance, and with no rough men around. "Now, little Alex, if you will, please remove them for me your pants so that I may conclude the examination, and then you will be on your way."

"No."

"No? But I am your doctor. You must do it what the doctor has said. This is required." When Malkin reached for him, he screamed for Delia.

"Quiet, my boy, you shall wake them up the dead."

Delia pounded up the stairs. Malkin and Alex had reached a standoff. "What the hell is going on here?"

Malkin stepped back. "Nothing. Nothing at all. The boy is most uncooperative, but I think he is ready to go now, he was merely calling it out to you to take him."

"What about his head?"

"Yes, I have conducted it the thorough examination, and now as you are leaving, I will give it to him a teaspoon, a child's dose, so to speak, of my special medicine for a children's headache, which may be due to a slight temporary swelling of the brain, such as when a person has it a hangover, which of course could not be the case here. I am sure it will bring it relief from the pain." He uncorked a bottle of his tonic, the same tonic he sold weekly to Davy O'Brien. "Here, take it one spoonful."

Alex made a sour face as the burn traveled down his throat and into his stomach. Within a few minutes, the pain in his head had subsided, thanks to the palliative effect of the alcohol.

Malkin put the bottle in a brown paper bag and handed it to Delia. "Have the boy take it for the pain. That will be seventy-five cents. Please."

Alex took Delia's hand and ten minutes later he was asleep on the trolley, his head on her lap. Forty-five minutes later, as they walked up Mellon Street toward his house, he asked her for another teaspoon.

Chapter 25

Dear Dee,

I can't tell you how excited I was when I got your letter that you wrote back to me. Just seeing your handwriting on the paper brought back so many good memories, and to think we're soon gonna see each other, I get goose bumps.

I gotta say, this little knife thrower of yours, from the way you described it, he sounds almost too good to be true. In the circus they're always looking for the unusual, something that will grab people—how do you think I got my job? Your kid sounds like a natural for the sideshow, if not the big top.

Anyways, I talked you up good to Mr. Markham, the talent man what books the new acts, and it's all set. I explained to him real good yesterday about the knife-throwing midget of yours, but he kept hemming and hawing, so I had to give him what shall I call it, a special favor. Markham is a real pig, what can I say, but you gotta do what you gotta to help out an old friend, right? Plus now he owes me because of what we done, which was definitely against circus rules, Rule 24 in the handbook, do not take strangers or friends into dressing rooms without permission, although I guess I did give him permission, and he ain't no stranger and he ain't no friend.

I didn't talk money with him because I know he won't talk money until he sees the boy throw. Like I told you, I pull down $70 a week, so the dough's plenty good, plus they give you room and board and the food ain't half bad, either, so you can save there, too.

Anyways, here's how we'll play it. You meet me at the main ticket booth around four o'clock. If for some reason I ain't there, just tell them you're here to see me and Mr. Markham. I'll leave word so you'll be all set and they'll give you directions to Markham's wagon. Markham will have knives like the kind the knife-thrower throws—won't he be fit to be tied when your little Alex shows up! Me, too!

We got darts, too, in case the kid wants to toss a few, so you don't need to bring nothing, just show up with him is all. Geez Oh Man, Dee, a knife-throwing midget, it could be a hit! If Markham takes the kid on we'll be together, just like the old days! Can't wait to see you.

Love you to death,

Lotte, the Elastic Lass (hokey, I know it!)

PS

That fellow I was living with, Mojo the Sword Swallower? The lousy mug took off with a gypsy tightrope walker when we had a layover in Toledo on account of a tornado two weeks ago. Men—you can't trust them!

PSPS

We're here just two days over Labor Day, Dee. Don't miss it! Can't wait to see you

Chapter 26

Normally, Alex was awake and running around the house before Abe and Benjamin got out of bed, but on the Monday following his day at the zoo, Abe had to call him three times to get out of bed. He remained lethargic during the trolley ride to Hannah's house, and Abe grew concerned that the boy was coming down with something; he'd been complaining off and on that his head hurt him, so, he needed to find him a good doctor, not that bastard Malkin. Maybe Hannah or the aunts could help him out, he didn't care how much it cost, what the hell was money for, anyway.

After Alex went inside, Abe explained the problem to Hannah. She grasped his hands. "Of course, we'll help, we know very good doctors, children's specialists. My parents know everyone."

"Your parents?"

Hannah blushed. "Oh, I meant, before they died they knew everyone, the best Jewish doctors. Just leave it to us and don't you worry, all right? Here's your lunch." She handed a brown bag to him. Her hand lingered on his. "Yesterday was delightful, Abe."

He shuffled his feet. "Yeah. Well, thanks about that doctor—listen I don't care what it costs, all right? I gotta go." He kissed her on the cheek and walked away.

Later that morning, as Hannah and her aunts were having a talk "just for the grown-ups," Alex drifted up to the second floor. He went into Hannah's room, crawled under the bed and found the adoption document exactly where he'd left it. Listening for Hannah's footsteps, he read the story again, and this time he understood what had happened to MALE CHILD. He wondered why Hannah would make MALE CHILD an adoption, it didn't make sense, even when he thought about what Delia had told him. There was only one way to figure it all out. He needed to show his father and Benjamin the paper, and Delia, too, so they would see he wasn't just making it up. He folded it in quarters and put it in his pants.

He crept to the landing. He could hear Hannah say they really needed to ask her father about a specialist for Alex, didn't they understand, the boy was in pain, he needed the best doctors in the city, that was the most important thing in the world, and then Lillie said that of course she was concerned about Alex, but what about Abe and his drinking, and Morris would be very upset, and then Hannah said how dare you bring that up at a time like this?

Alex couldn't understand the rest because the three of them were yelling at the same time.

Morris. Alex remembered the name Morris from the paper that said Blood Money! Then he heard Hannah scream that she could care less that he was her father, he hates me, he doesn't own me, and Lillie told her that wasn't true, and to calm down.

Father. But Daddy had told him that Hannah's mother and father died from The Dip, just like his mommy. His head began to hurt again. He went halfway down the stairs. Lillie and Belle were at the front door, with their purses over their shoulders. Alex called out to them. "Where are you going?"

Lillie turned around. Her face was red. "Oh hello, Alex."

Alex said, "Why were you yelling?"

"Oh, it was nothing." She turned to her sister. "Belle?"

"We just, we couldn't decide where to go out to lunch."

"Can I go, too?"

"Oh, not today, dear, today it's only for grown-ups."

"But we'll bring you a treat," Belle said, "since you're such a good boy."

Hannah came up behind him and placed her hands on his shoulders. "He's a very good boy. The best. So anyway, have a grand lunch, ladies."

After they left, she told him they'd have their own luncheon, a special one, that he could have anything he wanted for breakfast, a hot dog, a baloney sandwich, pancakes, "or how about an egg in the hole?"

"Egg in the hole."

"Coming up." Hannah squeezed his shoulders again, harder this time. "Ow."

"Oh my goodness, I'm sorry. Did I hurt you?"

She smiled as she apologized, but there was something in the tone of her voice and something about her smile that made Alex think she wasn't sorry at all. He rubbed his shoulder.

Hannah hummed as she fried his egg. She put a glass of chocolate milk on the table. She tried to tuck a napkin on him, but Alex said, "I can do it."

"All right, Mr. big shot."

As he ate, Hannah sat across from him and nibbled at the corners of saltine crackers until they were round. She dabbed up the crumbs with her index finger.

Alex watched her stack the rounded crackers. "Why do you do that?"

"What? Oh, it's nothing, just a game I used to do when I was a little girl. So what would you like to do this afternoon, after your special dessert?"

What he really wanted to do was go home and play with Benjamin, but Benjamin was at work, he had a summer job at the grocery story, delivering packages for Mr. Plotkin, and Daddy was at the shop. He looked at the dog, sleeping in the corner. "Play chase ball with Pudgy."

"Oh, but Pudgy is tired." She munched another cracker. "Alex, do you know the expression, 'let sleeping dogs lie?'"

Alex shook his head.

"It means it's better not to look for trouble. If you know what I mean. I wonder if you do."

What Alex did know was that, from the way she said it, she was trying to get at something that involved him, and whatever it was, it wasn't good.

She cleared his place and started to pace back and forth, staring at the floor. Every so often she'd look up at him. "Alex, do you know the Ten Commandments?"

"Grandma Murphy taught me them. Thou shalt not kill. Thou shalt not steal."

Hannah clapped her hands. "Yes, that's it. You're so smart. Thou shalt not steal. You know what that means, right, sweetheart?"

"Yes." Alex thought about how angry Grandma Murphy was when Dr. Malkin caught him trying to steal the bracelet for her at the Billy Sunday show, and how she made him say "thou shalt not steal" over and over one hundred times until she was satisfied he had learned his lesson.

"Good." She sliced a hunk of cheese from the wedge next to the crackers and held it on her knife. "Now, you would never steal from anyone in this house, would you, Alex? Because, and I'm sure you know this, it would be a very, very wrong to do that, to take something that didn't belong to you. You understand this, don't you?"

"Yes."

"Because it would make the person you stole from very sad." She leaned her elbows on the table and put her face on her knuckles "Or very angry.

You see?"

"Uh-huh." The folded edge of the certificate pressed against his stomach.

"Good." She smiled. "Now of course, there is no good excuse for stealing, but there is a way to make up for it."

Without thinking, he said "What?"

Hannah rubbed her hands together. "Well, if the person that *stole* put whatever it was they stole back where it belonged, then it wouldn't be quite as bad. You see what I mean? And if the person stole something like, let's say, an important paper, if that person put it back by tomorrow, then whoever the paper belonged to, she might be willing to forget all about it. Otherwise."

Alex blurted, "Otherwise?"

"Otherwise, there's such a thing as punishment. You know what punishment is, like when you're a bad boy and your father gives you a spanking."

"But he never did."

"No? But all little boys, when they do something wrong, they have to get a spanking. Otherwise."

There was that word again. He didn't know what it meant. "What's otherwise?"

Hannah pulverized the stack of saltines with her fist, driving them into the table, crumbs flying. She brushed the heel of her hand. "You know, Alex, once I had the sweetest little boy in the world. He's gone now."

Male Child. "Where did he go?"

"Oh, they took him, I mean, he had to go away for a while, but now he's come back to me and I don't want to ever, ever lose him again." She dabbed at the tears collecting at the corners of her eyes.

Did she mean he was Male Child? But he wasn't an adoption, or was he? His head began to hurt again. He wondered if the aunts had a bottle of Dr. Malkin's tonic. He could look in the bathroom on the first floor. "Hannah, I have to go and make pee."

He closed the door behind him. He dragged a stepstool to the medicine cabinet. Among the jars and pills was a bottle of what looked like tonic. It was Hostetter's Bitters, and even on the top shelf he reached it easily with his long arms. He twisted the cap and sniffed.

*

Belle and Lillie felt so elated after their lunch with Morris that instead of taking the trolley home, they splurged on a taxi. Things had gone incredibly well. Their normally dour brother even had a cocktail with them. Usually, he drank only on the high holidays.

Over spring rolls and chow mein, the sisters explained how Hannah had been acting like a mature adult, how taking care of the little boy had matured her—and what an engaging little boy he was, Morris would love him. He might need some medical care, but that was another issue that could talk about another time. They also mentioned that the boy's father, Mr. Miller, was a hardworking, responsible Jewish man and homeowner. In fact, they added, there were even some not so subtle hints that Mr. Miller might be attracted to his daughter.

"Hold on a minute," Morris had said between slurps of egg drop soup. "Hold on a minute. What has she told this Miller about her past?"

Lillie explained that Hannah hadn't really said anything, but that Mr. Miller was such an understanding man that, if and when the whole truth finally came out, they believed his feelings for Hannah would override any concerns there might be.

Morris said that perhaps at some point he ought to meet this Mr. Miller, but not right away, give it another month or so, Hannah is so flighty. "What did you say he did for a living?"

The taxi stopped at their house. Belle paid the driver as Lillie opened a fortune cookie. It read, *There is no wisdom like the wisdom of a child.* "Belle, you do realize this Abe Miller could be doing us all a big favor?"

"You mean by taking Hannah off our hands."

"Yes, but don't say it like that. Maybe she can have a happy life with him. Everyone deserves a happy life. Or at least a normal life, if not a happy one."

"As long as Morris approves."

"We'll keep working on that. Of course, he'll have a lot of explaining to do. It won't be easy."

"That's his problem. He has a lot to atone for."

"Well anyway. From now on, let's be nicer to Mr. Abe Miller. Guide him in the right direction, for Hannah's sake and Alex's sake."

"And our sake."

"I love a late fall wedding, don't you?"

Twenty feet from the door they heard Hannah's screams. Arm in arm, they half walked, half ran to the door. Standing in the foyer, Hannah held Alex in her arms. His head lolled back and his eyes were closed.

"Hannah, what happened? My God."

"I don't know. He was lying on the bathroom floor when I found him. It wasn't my fault. I would never hurt him. Please believe me. Is he going to die? Tell me he's not going to die."

Belle took Alex from her. "He's breathing, Lillie. Help me put him on the sofa. Make some tea, Hannah. Now."

Lillie leaned close to Alex's face. "He smells like he's been drinking." She slapped his cheek. "Alex, wake up."

Belle said, "I know what to do with a drunk." She opened his mouth and put her finger down his throat until he threw up. She held his head until he was done.

A few minutes later, he was sitting up. After fifteen minutes, he was smiling again. Belle fed him sips of tea and bits of fortune cookie from the bag she'd brought home from the restaurant. Hannah stroked his wrist.

Lillie came out of the bathroom with the bottle of Hostetter's Bitters. She sat down next to Hannah and told her it was a good thing she'd found him when she did. She took Alex's hand. "Did you drink this, young man?"

"I wanted to see what it tastes like."

"Now, you listen to me, young man. I don't know what you thought you were doing, but no more of this for you. Do you understand?"

He stared at the bottle. "O.K." He wished he could have another swallow.

By mid-afternoon, Alex had fully recovered. He played chase with the dog, ate three cookies and annoyed the aunts to no end by insisting that they listen to him play an off-key rendition of "Row Row Row Your Boat" on his recorder.

Hannah thought it best that no one report the tonic incident to Abe, since Alex was now fine and there was no earthly reason to worry Abe. After all, she didn't want him to be angry at her for what had happened, even though it wasn't her fault, and of course it would never happen again, and if Alex mentioned it, they would pooh-pooh the whole thing as a "boys will be boys" mistake, done out of natural curiosity, not even worth mentioning.

The aunts readily agreed, for they, too, wished to stay in Abe's good graces, anything, really, to keep him on the straight and narrow path of matrimony to their niece.

So, when Abe arrived at the end of that eventful day he received a warmer than usual greeting—a long "how was your day" hug from Hannah, and a tall glass of chilled lemonade with just a hint of rum from the aunts.

Abe took a big swallow and tipped his glass toward Lillie. "A man could get used to this."

"Hannah makes the tastiest lemonade, doesn't she?" Lillie said, even though it was she that had made it.

Belle said, "Oh, it's a Gerson family recipe, but no one makes it as good as our niece."

Abe held his glass out for a refill. "Where's my boy?"

"He's in the kitchen, finishing a drawing he made especially for you."

Belle took Abe's elbow. "Would you like to stay for dinner? Lamb chops and roast potatoes."

Now that was strange, he thought, usually Belle gives me the bum's rush to clear me the hell out of here. Something was going on with these two birds. Belle kept smiling at him, and he thought maybe this was how the witch in the forest looked when she was trying to fatten up Hansel and Gretel.

Alex ran into the room with the picture he'd colored. It showed stick figures of a man and a woman holding hands.

"Isn't it beautiful, Abe?" Hannah said.

Abe held the picture up. "I say we hang it in the Carnegie Museum. Now, who is it in the picture, Alex?"

"It's Daddy and his girlfriend."

The aunts beamed. Hannah leaned into Abe's shoulder. "See?"

As they walked to the trolley stop, Alex thought about the certificate in his pants. He wanted to show it to his father right then and there, but then he thought, what if Daddy gets mad at me for stealing it? He also thought about what might happen if he didn't put it back like Hannah had said. But he had to know about MALE CHILD.

As soon as they got home, he ran upstairs to tell Benjamin. He found him lying on the floor, flipping a rubber ball at the ceiling and catching it in one hand. Alex jumped on his chest.

"Get off, Stretch."

"Benjamin, look." He took the certificate out of his pants. "Male child."

Benjamin unfolded the certificate. He read it twice. "How'd you get this?"

"From Hannah's house."

"Wow. Wait until Dad sees this."

Chapter 27

Benjamin stood next to his father's easy chair and Alex sat on his lap as Abe read the certificate. He shook his head. "Tell me again how you got this."

Alex recounted the first time he'd seen it in the album called Carson Home, and how he hid it under the bed. He described the other document and the blood money receipt. "Are you mad at me, Daddy, because I stole?"

Abe kissed him on the side of the head. "No, son, I'm not mad. I'm just, well, this Hannah, I can't exactly figure her out." Alex could have told him that *he'd* figured her out, that she was both very nice and very scary.

Abe felt conflicted. He didn't know whether he ought to be upset with Hannah or feel sorry for her because she felt she had to lie to him about her family. Sometimes you had to lie—hell, he'd lied to Irene often enough, but this was different, she was lying about her whole life. Maybe she was living with the aunts because her father had tossed her out after she had the kid out of wedlock—the "male child," as Alex called it—and if he did, well, who really was the bad person—her, or the guy that knocked her up, or her father? "Alex, does Hannah know you took this?"

"She didn't see me, but maybe she knows." Alex told him what Hannah had said about stealing and punishment, and how she smashed a stack of crackers with her fist, and how she'd started crying and said she was sure her little boy had come back to her, and then he thought maybe he was MALE CHILD, but he wasn't MALE CHILD, was he?

"No, you're Alex Miller, plain and simple." He touched Alex's cheek. "You really don't like Hannah, do you?"

"He's scared of her, Dad," Benjamin said. "He told me, but he wouldn't ever tell you."

"But why not, Alex?"

"Because maybe you want to marry her. She says you want to. But I don't want her to be my mommy. I want her." He held up his drawing. "See? You and Delia."

It was getting late, and it was time the boys went to bed. Abe allowed them each a glass of ginger ale and some sugar cookies. He couldn't get rid of the image of Hannah smashing crackers in his boy's face. What would she smash next, his head? He thought about the circus and what Delia had said, but that was weeks away, and besides, he wasn't so sure that her plan was such a good idea. In fact, he was pretty sure it wasn't, it was just that when he was around her, she could make him agree to pretty much any goddamn thing.

Well fine, he'd take Alex to the circus like he'd promised, the kid was dying to go, and he couldn't break his boy's heart, but as for the rest of it, the knife throwing, well, he'd have to see about that.

In the meantime, he needed a plan for Alex. Smashing crackers. There was no way he was going to let Hannah keep watching him. He called Benjamin downstairs. The boy was almost as tall as he was now, and he was only fourteen, or was it fifteen? Christ, all this crazy stuff was making him lose his memory almost as fast as his hair. "Benjamin, listen. I need you to stay home for the rest of the summer and take care of Alex."

"But what about my job?"

"Tell Plotkin you quit."

"He won't like it, Dad. He counts on me."

"I'm counting on you more. Tomorrow is your last day with him. And tomorrow is Alex's last day with Hannah. And Alex? Don't say nothing to Hannah about what we just said, O.K.?"

*

Hannah woke early Tuesday morning. She'd been reassured by the aunts that lunch with her father had gone very well, that there had been no mention of Alex's fainting spell, as they described it, and no castigation of Abe; on the contrary, they had been quite complimentary toward him. Her father had seemed much impressed, and the future was looking up.

Despite the good news, Hannah seemed distracted. Belle noticed her gloom at the breakfast table. "Hannah, is your stomach upset?"

"Something is wrong with Alex. I can feel it."

"But they're not here yet."

"I can feel it. You know how I can sense these things. You know my special abilities."

Lillie said, "I'm sure he's fine, dear. He just had an accident yesterday. He was curious. All little boys are curious." She buttered a piece of toast. "Anyway, Belle and I are going to the grocers this morning. Is there anything special you'd like? How about a pomegranate? You used to love them when you were a little girl."

Hannah brightened a bit. "Do you think Alex would like one?"

"Oh certainly, certainly. Pomegranates are fun to eat."

Hannah frowned. "Unless you choke on the seeds." She glanced at the wall clock. "They'll be here any minute. I have to fix my hair."

*

The boys went upstairs to get washed and dressed. Abe sipped his coffee. He toyed with various ways to break the news to Hannah. Perhaps he could put it to her gently and say that she and her aunts had done far too much for him already, that he felt uneasy about continuing to accept their kindness, that it made him feel as if he were using them. He could say he found a nice summer nursery school for little children right in his neighborhood, conducted by a kindergarten teacher, the same teacher that Alex would have when he started school in the fall, and he thought it was a good idea it to have him around children his own age. He'd bring Alex by from time to time to visit, of course, if it was all right with them.

Such an approach, he felt, would allow him to avoid the bombshell. Such an approach, he knew also, would certainly fail. The aunts would say don't be ridiculous, it's almost the end of the summer, why start him in a nursery school now. Hannah would demand to know why the sudden change of heart, was it something she did, what about them and their future together, all of which would mean he'd have to lie even more, and even though over the years he'd told his share, he wasn't much of a liar.

Conversely, he could take the direct approach and confront her fabrications about family, et cetera, with the manifesto of truth, the adoption certificate. Knowing her, there were two possible reactions to this tactic—depression or unbridled anger.

Then there was the third alternative, the path of least resistance. He simply could say nothing, pick Alex up after work, kiss her goodbye and never come back. If she ever showed up at Mellon Street, at least he could deal with her on his own turf.

No matter which way he decided to go, the best thing would be to hold off until the end of the day. No sense creating a scene early in the morning—and besides, the arrangement was only for one more day.

He read the adoption certificate again. She'd been no more than a kid when she'd had the baby. In many ways she still was.

As they walked to the trolley stop, Alex said, "Do I have to go to Hannah's today?"

"This is the last time, son." He folded the certificate and put it in his pocket. Now matter how things went with Hannah, he'd leave the damn thing on her front porch at the end of the day.

*

The aunts left for the grocery store shortly before Abe dropped off Alex. Hannah had set up a chalkboard in the living room with a series of simple addition and subtraction problems for Alex to solve. He liked to do his numbers, as Hannah had called his elementary computations, but as he computed six plus three, eight plus four, seven minus two, he was aware that she was staring hard at him, not at the chalkboard.

He finished the first row of four. "Are they right, Hannah?"

"Yes, dear. Go on."

He knew he could fill in the answers in the second row without thinking, but he took his time. The last problem was six plus two, and he wrote seven. "Hannah?"

"Yes, very good."

"But you didn't even look."

She stood behind him, so close that he could feel her thighs on his shoulders. "Do you remember what we talked about yesterday, Alex? When we talked about stealing?"

"Yes."

"Everything?"

"Uh-huh."

"I'm going out to the backyard and water the garden, and when I come back, I'm going upstairs to look for something that someone stole, and I hope it's back where it belongs in the desk. Otherwise."

She was halfway out the door when Alex said, "Daddy has the paper. I gave it to him."

The blood drained from her face. She mouthed the words "you little thief."

Why couldn't he have been a good little boy? The good little boy she'd always wanted, a loving and obedient child, not a sneaky little thing that pried where it shouldn't and ruined everything, everything. She clenched her teeth so she wouldn't scream.

But wait. Abe hadn't said anything to her about it when he dropped Alex off. Maybe he hadn't read it. Maybe it wasn't too late. Or maybe it wouldn't matter to him—oh, but it would, of course it would, how could it not? She faced Alex through the screen door. "When did you give it to him, Alex?"

"I'm not supposed to say."

She squeezed his shoulders. "You tell me right now."

"Yesterday."

"Did he look at it?"

"Yes."

"What else?"

"I told him about the blood money paper, too." He twisted away from her. "You're mad at me."

Mad? Was there a better word? Distraught? Devastated? Disgusted? No, mad was correct. She was quite mad. But better not to let him see it. In a calm voice, she said, "Oh, Alex, I can never get mad at you, not really. Just a little disappointed, that's all. You're my baby boy." She glanced at the chalkboard. "Oh goodness, would you look at that, six plus two equals seven? Are you sure that's the correct answer?"

Alex shook his head. "My head hurts. I don't want to do numbers anymore."

"You're right. No more arithmetic today. I have a better idea." She took his hands. "It's such a beautiful day. So sunny and warm. Let's go to the park and have a picnic. Oh, it will be so much fun."

Alex hesitated. "Can the aunts come?"

"Oh no, Alex, not today, just you and me."

"What about punishment?"

"What?"

"You said if a little boy is bad he gets a punishment."

She thought, well, maybe she really should give him a punishment, teach him a lesson, just like her father had tried to teach her—but what was the lesson? She couldn't undo what she had done. Hadn't giving up the child been punishment enough? "No, Alex. I forgive you. You didn't mean to do anything wrong, did you?"

"No."

"Of course not. You were just curious. All little boys are curious, that's what Lillie says, and my boy is no exception. So. You play with Pudgy awhile, all right?"

She took the stairs two at a time to the aunts' bedroom. She opened drawer after drawer until she found a round cookie tin filled with buttons, thread and a wad of money, over one hundred dollars. She put the money in a large quilted sewing bag and dashed back down to the kitchen. In five minutes she'd wrapped four sandwiches, cookies, crackers and apples and filled a thermos with lemonade. She paused to gulp a glass of water. "Alex, are you ready?"

"Can Pudgy come?"

"I told you no."

"But shouldn't we wait until the aunts come home?"

He's a smart little boy, a clever little boy, a devious little boy. "I'll leave them a note. Put your shoes on." She slipped into the bathroom and rummaged through the medicine chest until she found the bottle of Hostetter's Bitters. It was nearly full. She dropped it into the bag. "Alex, are we ready?"

Alex walked into the kitchen, his hands in his pockets. "Why can't we take Pudgy?"

Hannah almost said they don't allow dogs on trains, but that someday, as soon as possible, she would get him another dog, just like Pudgy or maybe a different kind of dog, but what did that matter, they had to go, leave now, before Belle and Lillie came home. "You'll see Pudgy later, all right? We're going to have so much fun together. I have a big surprise for you."

He thought about the surprise Delia had mentioned. "What?"

"I can't tell you now, silly, it's a secret." She took his hand. "Come on, little boy. We're going on an adventure."

"But my head hurts."

"Oh dear, again, really? I'm so sorry, sweetheart." She reached into the bag. "Here, drink this." She poured an ounce of tonic into a glass.

*

In the early 1800s, train travel from Pittsburgh to Philadelphia was quite an odyssey. It could take anywhere from three to four days to get from one end of the state to the other. However, as the century marched on, the railroad tycoons made remarkable advances in moving freight, both human and commercial, and by the 1870s travel time on the same route had been cut to around fourteen hours; by the early 1900s, when the Broadway Limited Line had replaced the Pennsylvania Special, the trip took—conditions cooperating—less than nine hours.

At approximately 11:00 a.m., Hannah got out of her taxi. Over one shoulder was her bag. On the other was Alex, who looked as if he were sleeping. She hailed a porter to take her bag and asked him where they sold the tickets.

When Alex began to stir, Hannah forced another teaspoon of tonic into his mouth, but most of it dribbled down his chin. She looked up at the train schedule on the large board mounted high on the opposite wall. Did she know anyone in Philadelphia, or Altoona? She thought her father may have mentioned that they had cousins in New York City, on the lower East Side, or maybe it was the upper East Side, but the schedule said New York, not New York City, and what was their cousins' names, she couldn't remember. No, it was better not to go to New York. She needed to go somewhere else and make a new start with her little boy, and she had more than a hundred dollars. Altoona sounded nice, she was sure that people there would be friendly and understanding in a small town. Pittsburgh and New York City were much too large.

She sat down on a long wooden bench. She dabbed at Alex's mouth with her cuff. She didn't want to have to keep giving him tonic, but it was the only way she could get him to settle down. Once he realized she was his true mommy forever and ever, things would be different, and he would forget Abe and his girlfriend Delia and his dead mother, she was sure of it.

Announcements kept blaring from loudspeakers, but she couldn't understand what they meant. People bustled by her with their suitcases and cartons, and they all seemed to know where they were going as they disappeared down the stairway or through an alcove, and she attempted to smile at them as if to say, isn't it a lovely day, my boy and I are going away on a vacation, just like you are, we are all travelers together. But no one looked back at her until a large woman in a billowing silk dress asked if the seat next to her was taken. The woman opened a corduroy bag and took out a green apple. "What a cute little boy. Sleeping like an angel."

Hannah smiled at her. This woman was so nice. She wished her own mother had been as nice. "Yes, he's an angel."

"How old is he?"

"Six."

"Six? He's tiny."

"Yes. He's fine, really healthy, but I'm taking him to a specialist to find out why he's so little."

A conductor called out that the eleven o'clock Broadway Limited was leaving on track twelve and that passengers should be on board.

"Is that your train, dear?"

"What? Oh, no, I don't think so." Her feet tapped up and down. "Where are you going, if you don't mind me asking?"

The woman finished her apple. "To Indianapolis. To a funeral. My aunt."

"Oh. I'm sorry."

"She had the cancer. It's better she passed. And you?"

"I'm fine."

"No, I mean, where are you headed?"

"Well, you see, I'm waiting for my husband. He's a very busy man. He owns several metal fabricating plants, for the steel mills, and it's so hard for him to get away from the office, you see, so he sent Alex and I ahead and he'll be joining us later in the week on our vacation."

"I thought you said you were taking him to a specialist."

"Oh, I am, I am, and then Abe will join us. He loves Alex so much, it's hard for him not to be there at the doctor's, but work, you know."

"My husband worked himself to death hauling coal. Keeled over one day with a heart attack, just like that." She snapped her fingers.

Hannah jolted back. "Oh my."

The woman got to her feet. "Well, I think I'll buy myself a couple of magazines for the ride. Where did you say you were going?"

Hannah glanced up at the big board. "Philadelphia. My father says that's where they have the best doctors."

"Well, good luck with that boy of yours. He's a cute one."

The woman had gone three paces when Hannah said, "Wait." She walked up to her, glancing back twice at Alex. "Can I ask you a question?" She clutched the woman's arm.

The woman looked at Hannah's hand. The knuckles were white. "My goodness, what is it, dear?"

Hannah lowered her voice. "How do you buy a ticket? My husband didn't explain."

The woman looked at Alex, then back at Hannah. "You sure your boy is all right?"

"Oh yes, he's just sleeping. He likes to nap."

The woman gently pulled Hannah's hand from her sleeve. She pointed to the ticket counter across the concourse. "Go over there, dear, to the window. They'll help you out. You just tell them where you want to go and they give you a ticket and then you pay for it."

Hannah looked as if she were going to burst into tears. "Of course. Thank you so much, you're so kind."

"I have to go. Trains wait for no one, except the Pope and the President." She squeezed Hannah's hand. "Good luck in Philadelphia."

Hannah watched the woman disappear into the crowd at the far end of the concourse. She began to miss her dearly. Alex slept on the bench with his mouth slightly open. He looked so peaceful, she thought, she wished there were a photographer nearby to take his picture, she could pay, she had money. When she got to Philadelphia, she would arrange for a nice photograph of her and Alex in the park, on a marble bench, in front of a fountain, and he would wear a brand-new suit and she would be dressed in a simple white dress with flowers in her hair, pink baby roses.

Alex moaned in his sleep, something about Arthur fighting the Germans. She looked at his little hands, clenched in fists, as if he were about to fight, too. She had to get the ticket. But the window was across the way and she couldn't leave Alex alone on the bench. She shook him by the shoulders, and when he stirred slightly, she kissed his eyes over and over until he opened them. His breath was like liquor and licorice. She wet her handkerchief with saliva and wiped the corners of his mouth. "Sit up, Alex. Are you awake?"

His cheeks were pale. He sat up and vomited his breakfast into her hands.

She glanced around to see if anyone had noticed as she wiped her hands with her handkerchief. She opened the thermos of lemonade, poured some into the metal cap and held it up to his lips. "Here. This will make you feel better."

Alex pushed her hand away. "I don't want it."

"How is your headache, dear?"

He looked around, blinking, his pupils dilated. "Where are we?"

"We're on our adventure, sweetheart. This is the train station. It's where

all the trains come and go, everywhere—New York, St. Louis, Chicago."
She hugged him. "This is so exciting. But first we have to buy tickets. All
right?" She took his hand and as she pulled him across the concourse, his
legs wobbled.

Joseph Mancuso, a former porter who'd worked his way up to ticket
clerk, eyed Hannah and the little boy that dangled at her arm. "Yes, ma'am?"

"I need a ticket. Well two, actually, one for me and one for my son."

Mancuso leaned over the counter. "He's under two years old, he don't
need one. He can ride on your lap."

She started to tell him that Alex was six, but then she'd have to explain
a lot of things. "Oh. Oh, that's fine, then." She ran her hands over the bills
in her bag. Her father had told her many times to be careful with her money,
to keep it in her purse, don't flash it around for people to see, you never
know who might be a thief, people were out to steal you blind. "How much
is a ticket?"

Mancuso lit a cheroot. His wife had forbid him to smoke in their
apartment, and according to the railroad's rules he was allowed to smoke
only on his break, but it was slow at eleven-thirty in the morning. "That
depends on where you're going, miss. What's your destination?"

"My destination?" It sounded so odd when he put it that way. New York,
Chicago, St. Louis, Philadelphia, Washington, D.C. She bit the insides of
her cheeks.

"Miss?"

"I'm sorry, I…Philadelphia. Yes, that's it, we're going to Philadelphia to
see a specialist for my son."

Mancuso took another look at Alex. "You mean for those arms of his?"

"My husband is a very important plant manager at a steel mill. They
make all kinds of steel. He'll be joining us."

"So you want two tickets to Philadelphia."

"Two? But you said he could ride on my lap."

Another doozy, Mancuso thought. "One for you, one for your husband."

"Wait. I have to see how much money I have."

"Lady, I ain't told you the price yet."

Hannah laid her bag on the ground. "Just wait, please."

As soon as she let go of Alex's hand, he started to run on unsteady legs
in the opposite direction. Mancuso said, "Lady, your boy's running off like

he was in the Kentucky Derby."

"Alex!" She dropped her bag. She reached him in three strides and pulled him back. "You stay with me."

Mancuso waved a finger at him. "Listen to your mother, kid."

Alex screamed, "She's not my mother! She's not my mother." He bit her hand.

Hannah shook him off. "You're hurting me."

Alex rubbed his eyes. "She's not my mother!" He kept yelling despite Hannah's efforts to quiet him. "My name is Alex Miller. I live on Mellon Street with my daddy. She's not my mother." Hannah put her hand over his mouth, but he bit her again. "She took me."

Hannah dumped a handful of bills on the ticket counter. "Please, give me a ticket, please, sir." She took the Hostetter's Bitters from her bag. "Now Alex, stop screaming and I'll give you your medicine, all right?"

Mancuso counted more than forty dollars. He watched Alex scream and spit as Hannah tried to make him drink from a bottle of medicine. Something was fishy here. He pressed a button beneath the countertop. Thirty seconds later, two burly security guards dressed in dark blue uniforms came trotting over.

Hannah sat on the floor with her arms flung around Alex, trying to hold him still. When she saw the guards she got to her knees. "Please. Please don't take my baby away."

One of the guards picked up the bottle of tonic bitters, most of which had spilled on the floor. He looked at Mancuso, who nodded at Hannah and twirled his index finger in small circles next to his temple.

The taller guard said, "Miss, what's going on here?"

"I'm sorry I made a mess. I'm taking my son to see the doctor."

"I'm not her son!" Alex screamed. "My name is Alex Miller. My daddy works for Shields Metals. He lets her watch me when he's at work, but today is the last day."

"Alex, no," she said. She tried to touch him, but he clung to the guard's leg.

The shorter guard patted Alex on the head. "Calm down, sonny. We'll figure this out. Now, miss, what did you say your name was?"

Hannah put her hands over her ears. Why did they have to keep asking her questions? Why couldn't they just give her the ticket and show her where they could get on the train? She'd given them money. All she wanted to do was go to Philadelphia, or was it Indianapolis, but that didn't matter, because what was important was that they were together, she and her baby. But now these big men were there and they didn't understand. She pointed at Mancuso. "He said he would give me a ticket."

Mancuso made the crazy sign again. He'd already pocketed the forty dollars.

"Sure. Sure he did." The guard squatted down next to Alex. "She's your mommy, right?"

"No. She just watches me. My mommy is dead." He pointed at Hannah. "Her name is Hannah Gerson. My name is Alex Miller."

The guard looked at Hannah, who was shivering and hugging herself. "Can you tell me what happened, Alex?"

"She tried to take me away."

Chapter 28

If it had been up to Mayor Willie McGee, he would have issued a proclamation declaring free admission to the circus for every child in the city under 16, thinking that it would be a good investment in his political future. However, his campaign advisors put the kibosh on the noble idea, patiently explaining that, even as powerful as he was, he had no legal basis with which to order a privately owned business to give away their product, and, what's more, if the city had to foot the bill for thousands of admissions, the money would have to come from his re-election fund. Mayor Willie dropped the idea. Ironically, he wasn't elected mayor again until 1922.

The circus arrived in town on a typical Pittsburgh 3-H day—hot, humid and hazy. Despite the overheated, carbon monoxide-clogged air, children and their parents turned out in the thousands to gawk and cheer at the circus' grand parade as it proceeded through the heart of the city. Children of all ages, on bikes and on foot, raced after the horse-drawn calliope wagon, whose enticing pipe organ drew them on like the piper of legend, and they pushed and shoved to see who would be first to touch the gaily painted vehicle. The crowd ooh-ed and awed and waved American flags at the colorfully dressed elephants, which were clad in every color of the rainbow except their natural gray. They thrilled to the enormity of the beasts and elbowed each other for a closer look, marveling at the size of their poop. They gasped at the wild-haired snake charmer, a sinewy Sri Lankan woman festooned with a green python that slithered around her neck. Housewives swooned and fanned themselves at the sight of the poster-handsome ringmaster, who rode atop the United States Bandwagon, a splendid vehicle over seventeen feet long, decorated front to back, top to bottom, in splendid American symbols—gleaming red, white and blue wheels, intricate scrolls of golden flowers and laurel wreaths, buxom gold-winged mermaids, fierce Indian warriors on horseback, fetching tight-bodiced Indian maidens and marching Revolutionary War patriots, all done in bas-relief against a backdrop of the stars and stripes. Carved on the wagon's precipice was a stately bald eagle with a writhing snake in its beak.

Next came a wagon packed with clowns, which the onlookers alternately cheered and jeered. The children either pointed and laughed or hid behind their mothers' skirts. Walking along behind them were jugglers, unicyclists and trapeze artists, waving and throwing kisses and wondering how long it would be until the end of the parade, when they could get their pre-performance meal. Lions, tigers and bears rolled by, asleep in the midday heat, followed by animal trainers, carpenters, gaffers and various roustabouts who would gladly have taken a nap as well. All in all, the procession was close to 100 wagons long. It was a show in and of itself and a spectacular tease for the evening to come.

Alex missed the parade. He spent the morning with Delia and Benjamin at the Millers' house, waiting for Abe to come home from work, where he had managed to convince Shields to give him the afternoon off if he took it without pay.

Unable to contain his excitement, Alex careened from room to room, bouncing off the walls, figuratively and literally. Delia felt antsy, too. Here it was, finally, the day she'd been waiting for week after week, the day that kept her almost sane as she waited on drunken slobs at The Wheel and scraped the mess from their dinner plates into the garbage. Sometimes she would finish their half-eaten sandwiches or chicken legs so she could save her food money to buy decent clothes, maybe not as fine as the outfits she'd worn in New York, but fashionable shoes and a couple of dresses from Kaufmann's with some style to them.

She had on one of her best dresses, a flowery print with a cinched waist, and although she knew she was probably overdressed for the circus, she'd be damned if she'd go out in public looking like a peasant or a frumpy housewife. What's more, she wanted Lotte to see her looking her best, that she hadn't let the day-to-day drudgery of her life as a servant turn her into an unfashionable hag.

Alex grabbed her hand. "When is Daddy coming home? When is Daddy coming home? I want to go to the circus now. Elephants. You said there would be elephants, and giraffes."

It was odd how the tiny little kid was always going on about the biggest of the beasts, she thought. "All right, all right, keep your pants on, we're going as soon as your father gets home and has his lunch. And what about you? Did you eat that cheese sandwich I made you?"

"I don't want a sandwich. I want to go the circus."

The kid was wound tighter than a two-bit watch. He was making her nervous, and she never got nervous. It was going to take some smooth maneuvering to get him to toss the knives. "Now, Alex, do you remember what we talked about? How you are going to show my friend Lotte how you can throw the knives into the bull's-eye? Remember how you promised me?"

"You promised elephants and giraffes first."

"Right. Give me your pinky." They looped their little fingers together. "O.K.?"

"O.K."

She checked her watch. The plan was to get to the circus well before three o'clock, when they were supposed to meet Lotte and this Markham guy, the one that booked the talent, so Alex could see the animals in their cages before the show, and before he threw. It was past noon already. Where the hell was Abe? She decided she couldn't wait any longer. "Alex, let's get this show on the road. Benjamin, you tell your father we just couldn't wait anymore, all right? We'll meet you at the main entrance in a few hours. About four o'clock. Wait there for us."

*

The oak trees were at their late summer fullest, and as he turned off Stratton Avenue and onto the far end of Mellon Street, Abe caught sight of the Browns' little girl, whom he'd known since she was a toddler. She chased after her little brother around a thick tree trunk, and Abe thought, when had that tree gotten so big? It seemed as if the city had just planted them, but that was when Arthur was born, and that was, what, seventeen years ago now? They'd put them in every front yard, a feeble attempt to beautify the neighborhood, but half the saplings had died within a year. Irene had been so proud of their tree until it became infested with some kind of insect and rotted from the inside. Funny, he thought, how so many things reminded him of her.

A Ford Model T was parked in front of the Walsh's house. They'd been the first on the block to have a car of their own. Abe couldn't figure out how Walsh had swung it. Evidently the man was a damned good plumber when he wasn't face down drunk.

It was the same kind of Ford the police had driven him to Penn Station on the day Hannah had run off with Alex. The boys in the shop had been stunned that day when the cops came by to pick him up. Regis Maloney had yelled, "Lock him up and throw away the keys, boys."

The police escorted him down the steps of the station to the main concourse. His heart beat quicker as he saw Alex sitting on a high stool next to a security guard, eating a scoop of chocolate ice cream, half of which was spread over his cheeks. Alex leaped off the stool and into Abe's outstretched arms. One of the policemen said, "Guess you're his old man."

The other officer pointed to Hannah. "You know her?"

Abe looked at the woman balled up in a fetal position on the floor. Hannah looked like a terrified, confused child and nothing like the pretty, alluring woman that had tempted him more than once. He said, "Yes."

"You her husband?"

"No."

"Because she says she's waiting here for her husband to take her to Philadelphia or Indianapolis. You know anything about that?"

"I know she's not married. She is supposed to be taking care of my son, but what the hell she's doing here with him, I don't know."

Alex said, "Daddy, she tried to take me away on a train, but I wouldn't let her."

"What?"

One of the policemen took his hat off. "Actually, Miller, your boy here pretty much summed it up, from all we can gather. We got a witness saw the whole thing, this ticket clerk here." He pointed to Mancuso, who was smoking another cheroot. "She come up to his booth but she was talking kind of crazy to him, didn't even know how to buy a ticket, and when he saw her manhandling the boy, he called the guards."

Smashing crackers. Abe hugged Alex tighter.

The other officer said, "Since she ain't talking to us, at least nothing that makes sense, why don't you tell us her name, where she lives?"

Alex said, "I told you. Her name is Hannah Gerson. She lives on Black Street."

Abe brushed Alex's hair. "He's right."

The policeman laughed. "You're a pip, kiddo. You deserve a reward."

"My daddy's gonna take me to the circus."

Right then, Abe realized he was not going to allow Alex to become some sideshow freak like a fat lady. Yeah, he'd take him to the circus, like he'd promised him, but that was it. If Delia didn't like it, if she put up a stink, so be it. Alex Miller was his son, not hers.

He turned up the walkway to his house. As much as it pained him to remember that day, and how close Hannah had come to taking Alex away, or worse, at least things had turned out all right in the end.

Benjamin stood in the front doorway. "Dad, where were you?"

"Stuck on the trolley. Everyone ready?"

"Delia and Alex left almost an hour ago."

*

A twelve-foot-high painting of an impossibly Reubenesque ballerina in a classic Arabesque pose decorated the outside of the circus wagon where Louis Markham sat and waited. He puffed a fat Cuban cigar and read the local paper, a habit he followed as the circus traveled from town to town. He liked to see how his ads came out, and if the copy were botched or the illustrations were smudged, he'd give the local advertising manager an earful of hell. Every few minutes or so, he checked the time on the gold watch tucked in his vest pocket.

He stood up and brushed ashes from his lap. He was a big man, more than six feet, with a beer barrel belly and bulbous nose pocked with gin blossoms. "Lotte, you sure this dame friend of yours and the eighth wonder of the world are gonna show up?"

"Sure I'm sure." Lotte Henderson had curled her hair and dressed in the snug, glittery leotard she wore in the show, thinking that Delia would get a hoot out of her getup. She paced around the card table she'd set up in the middle of the wagon. On the table were three darts and three recently honed throwing knives, eight inches long, weighing seven ounces. A dartboard was mounted on the far wall of the wagon, and tied around it were three red balloons.

Markham belched. "Because I got better things to do with my time than wait around for just another freak show."

"Oh yeah, like what?"

Markham smiled a gap-toothed, gold-toothed smile. He scratched his crotch. "Come over here to Uncle Lou."

"Aw, cut it out."

"Maybe we got time for a quickie." He rolled his tongue over his lips.

"Leave me alone, Lou. Didn't you get enough last night?"

Markham took off his straw boater and wiped his forehead with a handkerchief. "A big man like me can never get enough."

"Ha, you ain't that big." There was a quick rap on the door. "I told you she'd be here, didn't I?" Lotte flung the door open. At first she saw nothing, but when she looked down, standing there were Bitty Betty Green, who was three feet, seven inches tall, and her husband Bobby Boy Green, who stood four feet one.

"You're blocking the door," said Bobby Boy.

The Legendary Little Greens were one of Louis Markham's proudest discoveries. Not only could they juggle, they could toss miniature Indian clubs back and forth while they rode side by side on Shetland ponies. Their compact, plump bodies were squeezed into their show outfits, matching buckskins accentuated by ersatz emerald and ruby trim. Betty's curls fell out beneath her pink cowgirl hat. Bobby Boy had on his blond wig that tilted slightly to the left. Bandoleers crisscrossed his chest.

Lotte backed away from the Greens. "What are they doing here?"

Markham said, "I want them to check out this kid. I need to know what I'm buying ain't just another midget."

"But darn it, Lou, they could spook him. They spook me and I see them every day."

"Why don't you go contort your ass over an open fire?" Bobby Boy said.

"Easy now, Bobby. Hi there, good-looking." Markham picked up Betty and kissed her on the mouth.

Bobby Boy kicked Lou in the knee. "Watch it, Lou, the next one will be in your nuts."

Lotte waved her arms. "You see, Lou, they're nothing but trouble. Will you get them out of here, please?"

Lou set Betty down next to her husband, who grabbed her by the wrist. "Hey, what are you doing, kissing up to him?"

"Bobby, it wasn't my fault."

"Lou, please."

Markham clipped the end off a fresh cigar. "Calm down, Lotte, you'll live longer."

In a squeaky voice, Bitty Betty said, "Don't get sore, Lotte. Lou asked us. Besides, I just wanted to see the little thing. Me and Bobby Boy, we couldn't have no children of our own."

"Don't blame me, baby, I ain't the one shooting blanks." Before he'd met Betty, Bobby Boy had fathered three children with two different women, one of whom was five feet ten inches tall.

Lou and Bobby Boy broke out a deck of cards. Five more minutes went by with nothing but the slap of cards on the table. Lotte was close to tears when more knocking came to the door. "Who else did you invite, Lou, the bearded lady?"

Standing on the steps were Delia and Alex, who had a helium balloon tied to his wrist. Delia laughed. "Hey, Lotte Henderson. Long time no see."

"Oh my God, Dee! Is it really you?"

"In the flesh."

"Look at you, you look gorgeous, you sure filled out nice."

"So did you, Miss Elastic Lass."

"Oh, stop with that hooey." She grabbed Delia and hugged her. "Gosh, I thought you'd never get here."

"Yeah, I know, sorry. We got lost over on Forbes Street, then he wanted something to eat and I had to show him around a little bit, he's curious, you know how kids are. This one, his mouth runs a mile a minute, he had to see the elephants first. Hey, that's quite the rag you're wearing."

"Oh, this old thing?" Lotte twirled around, then hugged Delia again. "It's so great to see you, Dee. Come on in. And look at this boy. Oh my stars, is he ever precious. What's your name, precious?"

"Alex Miller." He dropped Delia's hand and ran to touch the wall hung with posters of jewel-bedecked elephants, tigers leaping through rings of fire and acrobats riding unicycles on high wires. He bumped into Markham's leg and pulled back.

"Well, this must be the wonder child," Markham said. "Damn, he sure is small, I'll say that for him."

Lotte put herself between Alex and Markham. "Lou, this is my friend Delia Novak, from way back." She giggled at her rhyme. "And this of course is little Alex. The kid I told you all about."

Markham kneeled down near Alex. "How are you doing there, little fellow? Ready to do your stuff for me?" He touched Alex lightly on the cheek and chuckled. "Boy, but ain't he something. I should have brought in the costume gal, she'd have a field day with this one. How old is he?"

"He's six."

"Get the hell out of here, he is? I'll be damned if he ain't almost as little as Tom Thumb," Markham exclaimed, in reference to the famous dwarf P.T. Barnum had showcased a half-century earlier. "Bobby Boy, take a look."

Alex recoiled away from Bobby. Delia said, "What do you think you're doing, buddy?"

"Take it easy, Miss Novak, relax. I just need my diminutive friend here to take a look at your son. Calm down, sonny, he ain't gonna hurt you. I just need to know what I'm buying before I'm buying."

Delia said, "Lotte?'

"It's all right, Dee, just give him a minute, it's gonna be O.K."

Bobby Boy sidled over to Alex. He poked around Alex's legs, his head, took note of his long arms. "I don't know what the hell he is, Lou, but I can tell you this much: with them arms of his, he ain't no midget."

Lou said, "You're sure, Bobby."

"Hey, Lou, you ever heard the expression, 'it takes one to know one?'"

Markham spit a fleck of tobacco. At the time, child labor laws varied from state to state, but there was no federal law in place, at least none that he knew of, regarding the movement of children across state lines. But still, he thought, taking on this kid, or whatever he was, it could be risky, even with his parents around. "Delia? You his mother?"

Delia said, "I'm more like his guardian. His mother died of The Dip."

Alex said, "She's in Heaven with Grandma."

"Oh," Bitty Betty said, "don't he have the cutest little voice? Don't you, sweetheart?" She smiled so broadly her makeup crinkled.

"Put a zipper on it, Betty. I knew I should have left you in the wagon."

"Aw, Bobby, don't be like that."

"Enough," Markham said. "A six-year-old boy this tiny, something ain't kosher here, but I'll be damned if I know what it is. Anyway, let's get the show on the road. The knives and the darts await."

Delia said, "Hold on. I gotta ask you, before he shows you his stuff, what kind of money are we talking about here, Mr. Markham?"

Without looking at Delia, he said, "Geez, Bobby, but don't she got the brass? Listen, lady, I don't make an offer until I see the goods first."

"Oh, we have the goods, don't you worry about that. But I can understand your point, Mr. Markham. Lou, isn't it? Heck, I might be a non-believer myself if I hadn't seen it with my own eyes. So how about this:

If Alex can do what I say he can do, which is hit the bull's-eye with the darts and the knife three times in a row, I get a hundred bucks a week, plus expenses."

"You want to make more money than I do?"

"I don't mind."

Markham laughed. "Listen lady, if he's as good as you say he is, I'll give you forty. That's top dollar for a side show act."

"Eighty-five."

"Sixty. Take it or leave it."

Lotte whispered to Delia, "Don't push him. He's offering you real good money for the sideshow. Plus you get room and board."

Sixty bucks a week for riding around in a train, plus meals and a place to sleep—it wasn't a fortune, but it would do for the time being, with or without Abe. "Sorry I got so loud there, Mr. Markham. Lou. Just sticking up for my boy, you can understand."

"Yeah, yeah. So is it a deal?"

"Deal."

"Fine." Markham clapped his hands. "Now let's see some action here. And listen to me good. If your boy don't come through here, the deal is dead."

Delia helped Alex climb up on the table. He began his windup. As everyone stared at Alex, Delia stared at them. With their heavy makeup and outfits, Betty and Bobby looked like corpulent puppets. Lotte looked like a sad, life-sized kewpie doll. Markham groped Lotte's rear end, pushing under the tight fabric with one hand and scratching his crotch with the other.

The air in the wagon seemed to get thicker. She began to feel queasy. Throwing Alex in with these people, this was what she'd been dreaming about all those weeks? She looked at him standing on the table, as if he were an exhibit, with his arms hanging there. She imagined the hoots and the catcalls that were sure to come from the audiences as he stood in a spotlight—chimp, chimp, chimp!—in some garish, obscene costume, with a frightened look on his face, searching for his father, appealing to her to get him out of the place as she stood off to the side, in the shadows, helpless, ashamed, committed. The hot dog she'd shared with him an hour earlier rose up in her throat.

Markham said, "Well?"

She tapped Alex on the shoulder and whispered, "Miss the bull's-eye."

He started to answer, but Delia put her finger over his lips. She smiled. "I know what I told you before, but now I want you to miss. You don't really want to do this anyway, right? Me neither. So make a bad throw. For me?" She winked.

He winked back.

Bitty Betty said, "What's she saying to him?"

"Shut up," Bobby said.

His first throw went two feet and clattered to the floor. Alex said, "Ah-oh."

Lotte said, "Dee?"

He picked up the second knife and, as if it were too heavy to hold, laid it back on the table near his feet.

Bobby Boy hooted, "Some knife thrower. Lady, you need to stick Tiny there back in diapers."

Markham crushed his cigar with his shoe. He shook Lotte by the collar. "What the hell are you're trying to pull on me here?"

"Hey, Lou, that hurts."

Delia said, "Lay off her, you pig."

Markham released Lotte. He rubbed his fist. "You know what, lady? You wasted enough of my time, and I've had it with that smart mouth of yours. You wouldn't be so good-looking with a busted nose, would you?"

"Drop dead." She stuck out her chin.

Markham took a step toward her, but stopped in his tracks as a knife whizzed through his hat and stuck it to the wall behind him.

Lotte screamed. Bobby Boy and Bitty Betty pushed and shoved their way out of the wagon. Markham patted the top of his bald head, as if he were trying to see if it was still there.

Delia glanced at Alex, who was pointing the third knife toward Markham's face. "Alex, no."

She turned to Markham. "You know what, tough guy? That's what you get for threatening me. And I'll tell you something else. You lay off my friend or his next toss will go through your neck." She hugged Lotte, who was shivering. "Honey, I'm sorry this didn't work out, but I just couldn't go through with it. This ain't no life for a little boy. I should have known it all along. It's no life for you, neither, being jerked around by a shit-heel like him. Stop crying, all right? Your makeup is running down your face."

Lotte looked at Markham, who was still rubbing his head, where a faint red line streaked across the crown. "I don't know what to do, Dee. About all this."

"You'll figure it out. But if I was you, I'd get my ass the hell out of here and save myself. Listen, I gotta go. His old man will be looking for him. Give me a hug."

Markham began to rise to his feet but sagged back, seeing Alex hold the knife in the ready position. Blood trickled down his forehead. "Christ, I'm bleeding. This is your fault, Lotte. Get that kid out of here before I'll call the cops."

Lotte said, "Oh shut up, Lou."

*

"Dad, you're pulling my arm out!"

"Keep up, Benjamin."

Sweat flew from Abe's face as he charged through the crowd milling about at the midway. He elbowed his way to the ticket booth and banged on the counter.

Roseanne Rigby, who'd been a rider in the circus's Wild West show until she broke her coccyx leaping over a barrel, leaned out from the booth. "How many, partner?"

Abe smacked a dollar down. "Where's Lou Markham?"

"Fifth car behind me. Who wants to know?"

Abe shoved open the flimsy wooden gate that led to a line of boxcars. Roseanne leaned out and yelled, "Hey, you ain't allowed back there."

Abe pushed on, dragging Benjamin with him. Goddamn it all. First that crazy Hannah tried to steal his son, and now Delia, damn her, had taken off with Alex, too. Christ, she could have made some kind of deal by now, sold his kid off to the circus. She could be long gone—but if she wasn't, Heaven help her.

He leaped up the stairs to the fifth boxcar and banged the door open. Sitting on the floor was a large bald man in a checked suit. A woman in a gold costume held a cloth blotched with blood to his head. Abe bellowed, "Where's Delia Novak? Where's my son?"

The bald man said, "That little bastard Alex? How the hell do I know?"

In three seconds Abe had his hands around Markham's throat with the intention of bashing his head through the floor. "Where is my son?"

"Abe!" Delia stood in the doorway, holding Alex's left hand. He had cotton candy in his right.

"Daddy!"

Abe dropped Markham's head and rushed to his son. He dropped to his knees to hug him. "Are you all right, Alex?"

"Yes, Daddy."

Abe looked up at Delia. "I should belt you one."

Alex tugged on Abe's shirtfront. "Don't be mad at Delia. We went in there," he said, pointing to the boxcar, "and there was a man and a woman dressed up like cowboys, almost as little as me. There was too, Benjamin, don't laugh. Then I was supposed to throw the knives like I promised, but Delia told me we were going to fool them so then she told me not to throw."

Abe stood and moved next to her. "Is that right?"

"Then the circus man, he was mean to Delia and that lady there, so I threw a knife at *him*. At his hat, I mean. Then we left."

Abe looked at Delia. "Why?"

Delia looked past him, at Lotte and Markham. "What's the difference, Abe? You got your boy back. He ain't hurt or nothing."

"I thought you was going to take him away." Abe had never seen her look lost before. "I guess I should thank you."

She lit a cigarette and waved the smoke away from Alex. "Yeah, well, forget about it. You're here now. You and your boys, you go and enjoy the circus."

Alex said, "You come, too."

Delia kneeled down and kissed his forehead. "Sorry, pumpkin, not today. I gotta spend a little time with my old friend. You go on, have fun. Abe, don't let him eat too much, he's had plenty already." Alex reached for her hand but she backed away. "Go on, go now."

A calliope played *By the Light of the Silvery Moon*. She watched Abe and his boys trail off toward the midway. Alex turned his face once back to her. She waved and went back into the boxcar to retrieve her friend.

Epilogue

A week after his day at the circus, on the morning of his first day of school, Alex got up early, an hour before his father and brother, excited by the prospect of starting at Fulton Elementary. He washed his face, brushed his teeth and plastered down his hair with pomade, as he'd seen Benjamin do. The pain in his head was dull and constant, but he forgot about it with the excitement of the day.

His mind buzzed with the things Benjamin had told him about kindergarten—singing songs, playing games, snack time, coloring. He stood on the stepstool to get to the breadbox on the kitchen counter when he heard the front door swing open. He ran into the foyer, and standing there in full uniform was a soldier.

"Private first class Arthur C. Miller reporting for duty, Mr. Alex." Arthur held his right hand to his temple, waiting to salute.

Alex was so shocked all he could do was salute back.

"At ease, troop." Arthur scooped Alex up in his forearm. "How you doing, Stretch?"

"Arthur, you got real big." He rubbed his hand against Arthur's cheek. "You're a man now."

Tears formed at the corners of his eyes. "It's good to be home, Alex."

Abe's shout from upstairs filled the room. "Is that Arthur? Hold on, son, I'm coming!" His footsteps pounded down the stairs. He practically crushed Alex hugging his older son.

Benjamin joined the three of them, and for a long moment they stood as one. Finally, Arthur said, "Don't you little clowns have to go to school?"

Abe kissed Alex on the forehead. "You be a good boy today, you hear me, Alex? Stick with Benjamin until you have to go to your room. And listen to your teacher, all right? Give me another kiss."

Alex pulled away. "O.K., Dad, I'm not a baby."

*

On the morning of Alex's first day at school, without so much as a goodbye and good luck to anyone, Delia packed a bag, withdrew the remaining $28.50 from her bank account and returned by train to her native

Youngstown, Ohio, to live with her Aunt Tilda, a frugal, religious woman who introduced her to the Reverend Johnston. In turn, the Reverend introduced her to his only son, thirty-year-old Jonah, who'd been a missionary in Guatemala and celibate for three years.

Johnston the younger introduced Delia to the New Testament, and in turn Delia introduced him to the miracle of Old Overholt Rye. Delia joked that she always had a whale of a time with Mr. Jonah, as she called him, even though she found him bland as paint compared to Abe. After eight months of hugging, teasing and eventual bedding, she hinted to Jonah that she might be pregnant—she wasn't—which precipitated an on-the-spot proposal and even hastier marriage, and, although she didn't love him, having a house and a maid and spending money sure beat working for a living.

In three years, she gave him the son and daughter he'd always wanted, and he gave her the freedom of live-in help, which in turn provided her with ample opportunities to begin an on-again, off-again affair with Sanford Goldman, owner of the largest furniture store in Youngstown, who swore up and down he would leave his wife and three daughters for her if she just said the word, which of course she didn't. It wasn't that Goldman was particularly handsome or funny or good in bed, but he did give her great deals on home furnishings. And, as she confided in a long letter to her old friend Lotte Henderson, who'd left the circus and joined a convent in Pittsburgh, for some reason she'd always had a thing for Jewish men.

She also took up painting and found that she had a long-latent talent for watercolor. In a local art show, she exhibited a series of twelve canvases. Each of them had as its central figure a cute little boy with very long arms, wearing an orange hat. When she was approached with a lucrative offer for the series, she told the buyer they weren't for sale.

*

The boys sat around the table at dinner and ate fish sandwiches and fried potatoes as Alex recounted his first day at school. The girls had wanted to play with him, he said, but they were all stupid except for Alice Stanton. Then he had a fight with George because George had called him a baby shrimp and stuck his tongue out, so he threw an eraser at him and hit him in the face, and then George cried, and Mrs. Davidson made him sit in the corner.

Arthur and Benjamin were hysterical, but Abe said, "Alex, don't throw no erasers no more, you hear me?" Despite the admonition, however, Abe thought, damn if he isn't a Miller through and through.

Arthur said, "Then how'd you get the gold star?"

Alex touched the sticker on his forehead. "I forget."

The four of them talked into the evening, with Alex doing most of the narrative, especially regarding his adventure with Hannah and his day at the circus. Abe then laid out the thin family album: He and Irene on their wedding day, Arthur and Benjamin as toddlers, the three brothers posed with their mother. Abe looked at his boys laughing and hugging. He swallowed. At least he had them.

Arthur excused himself. Upstairs in their bedroom, he opened his copy of *The Adventures of Tom Sawyer*. His Honus Wagner baseball card—his good luck charm—was right where he'd left it. He tucked it into his breast pocket.

When he came back to the kitchen, Alex was asleep in his chair and Benjamin was reading. "Dad."

Abe had just lit a cigar. "Yes, son?"

"I have to leave tomorrow."

Abe's face fell. "Already? But you just got home."

Arthur shook his head. "Special training."

Abe pursed his lips. He wondered if he'd ever see him again. "Well, listen. Benjamin is here with Alex. You want to come to The Wheel with me? The boys would love to see you."

"If it's all right, I'd rather be home."

Abe patted his shoulder. "Sure. Sure, son. I won't be long. I just want to stop by and say hi to Delia Novak."

After Abe left, Arthur carried his sleep drunk little brother up to the bedroom. Back downstairs, he and Benjamin shared laughs and one of their father's lagers.

Alex woke up two hours later to the sound of his brothers and father talking and laughing. Not wanting to miss a good time, he pulled on his pants. The cuffs reached only to the middle of his calves. In the brief time he'd been asleep, his legs had grown four inches. They hurt to the touch.

So did his head.

About the Author

Marc Simon has been an English teacher, advertising copywriter, and comedy writer/performer. His short fiction has appeared in several literary magazines, including *The Wilderness House Review* (where he won the annual Chekhov Prize for best story of the year), *Flashquake, Poetica Magazine* and *The Writing Disorder,* among others. *The Leap Year Boy* is his first novel. Marc resides in Naples, Florida.

CPSIA information can be obtained at www.ICGtesting.com
Printed in the USA
LVOW100705160613

338765LV00009B/296/P